THE BLOOD GOSPEL

JAMES ROLLINS
and Rebecca Cantrell

wm

WILLIAM MORROW
An Imprint of HarperCollins*Publishers*

This book is a work of fiction. The characters, incidents, and dialogue are drawn from the authors' imaginations and are not to be construed as real. Any resemblance to actual events or persons, living or dead, is entirely coincidental.

HarperCollins books may be purchased for educational, business, or sales promotional use. For information please write: Special Markets Department, HarperCollins Publishers, 10 East 53rd Street, New York, NY 10022.

FIRST EDITION

Designed by Lisa Stokes

Lead box cover art drawing by Trish Cramblet

Library of Congress Cataloging-in-Publication Data has been applied for.

ISBN 978-0-06-199104-2 (hardcover)
ISBN 978-0-06-224787-2 (international edition)

13 14 15 16 17 OV/RRD 10 9 8 7 6 5 4 3 2 1

THE BLOOD GOSPEL

BY JAMES ROLLINS

Bloodline
The Devil Colony
Altar of Eden
The Doomsday Key
The Last Oracle
The Judas Strain
Black Order
Map of Bones
Sandstorm
Ice Hunt
Amazonia
Deep Fathom
Excavation
Subterranean

BY REBECCA CANTRELL

A Trace of Smoke
A Game of Lies
A City of Broken Glass
A Night of Long Knives

From James:

To Anne Rice

For showing us the beauty in monsters

And the monstrous in the beautiful

From Rebecca:

To my husband and son, for keeping the monsters at bay

And I saw in the right hand of him that sat on the throne a book written within and on the backside, sealed with seven seals.

And I saw a strong angel proclaiming with a loud voice, Who is worthy to open the book, and to loose the seals thereof?

And no man in heaven, nor in earth, neither under the earth, was able to open the book, neither to look thereon . . . Thou art worthy to take the book, and to open the seals thereof: for thou wast slain, and hast redeemed us to God by thy blood. . . .

—REVELATION 5:1–3, 9

I am Lazarus, come from the dead,
Come back to tell you all, I shall tell you all.

—T. S. ELIOT

ACKNOWLEDGMENTS

This book has many fingerprints on it beyond the two authors on the cover. First let me thank my critique group: Sally Barnes, Chris Crowe, Lee Garrett, Jane O'Riva, Denny Grayson, Leonard Little, Scott Smith, Penny Hill, Judy Prey, Dave Murray, Will Murray, Caroline Williams, John Keese, Christian Riley, Amy Rogers, and especially Carolyn McCray, who helped get this story off the ground by asking challenging questions. And, of course, David Sylvian, for being at my right hand at every stage of production and beyond. I must also give a shout-out to Joe Konrath for all his efforts to make this story that much better. Last, of course, a special nod to the four people instrumental to my career: my editor, Lyssa Keusch, and her colleague, Amanda Bergeron; and my agents, Russ Galen and Danny Baror. And as always, I must stress that any and all errors of fact or detail in this book fall squarely on my own shoulders.

Rebecca here. I'd like to thank everyone who worked hard helping to get the book and me out into the world, including my fantastic agents Elizabeth Evans, Mary Alice Kier, and Anna Cottle; and Lyssa Keusch at Harper. This novel, and my other novels, have been much improved by the wonderful Kona Ink writing group of Kathryn Wadsworth, Judith Heath, Karen Hollinger, and David Deardorff. It was a difficult journey, and I couldn't have made it without the support of my steadfast Ironman husband and brilliant son, the family weapons expert. Thanks also to Jim, for inviting me to come play.

THE BLOOD GOSPEL

PROLOGUE

Spring, AD 73
Masada, Israel

The dead continued to sing.

Three hundred feet above Eleazar's head, the chorus of nine hundred Jewish rebels rang out in defiance of the Roman legion at their gates. The defenders had sworn to take their own lives rather than be captured. Those final prayers, chanted to Heaven on high, echoed down to the tunnels below, carved out of the heart of the mountain of Masada.

Abandoning the doomed men to their bitter sunlight, Eleazar tore his gaze from the roof of the limestone passageway. He wished that he could chant beside them, that he could give up his own life in a final battle. But his destiny lay elsewhere.

Another path.

He gathered the precious block into his arms. The sun-warmed stone stretched from his hand to his elbow, the length of a newborn baby. Cradling the stone block against his chest, he forced himself to enter the rough-hewn passage that sliced into the heart of the mountain. Masons sealed the way behind him. No living man could follow.

The seven soldiers who accompanied him forged ahead with torches. Their thoughts must still be with their brothers, the nine hundred above on the sun-scoured plateau. The stronghold had been under siege for months. Ten thousand Roman soldiers, split into enormous camps, surrounded the mesa, ensuring no one could leave or enter. The rebels had vowed, when their chant was complete, to take the lives of their families and then their own, before the Romans overran their walls. They prayed and readied themselves to kill the innocent.

As must I.

Eleazar's task weighed upon him as heavily as the stone in his arms. His thoughts turned to what awaited below. The tomb. He had spent hours praying in that subterranean temple, knees pressed against stone blocks fitted so close together that not even an ant might escape. He had studied its smooth walls and high, arched ceiling. He had admired the careful handiwork of the craftsmen who had labored to make the space sacred.

Even then, he had not dared to look upon the sarcophagus in the temple.

That *unholy* crypt that would hold the most *holy* word of God.

He hugged the stone tighter to his chest.

Please, God, take this burden from me.

This last prayer, like the thousands before it, remained unanswered. The sacrifices of the rebels above must be honored. Their cursed lifeblood must serve a higher purpose.

When he reached the arched doorway to the temple, he could not step through. Others jostled past to their posts. He rested his forehead against the cold wall, praying for solace.

None came.

His gaze swept inside. Torchlight flickered, dancing shadows across the stone bricks that formed an arched roof overhead. Smoke swirled above, seeking escape, but there would be none.

Not for any of them.

At last, his eyes settled on the small girl, on her knees, held down by soldiers. His heart ached at the piteous sight of her, but he would not forsake the task that had been asked of him. He hoped that she would shut her eyes so that he might not have to look into them at the end.

Eyes of water . . .

That was how his long-dead sister had described those innocent eyes, her daughter's eyes, her little Azubah.

Eleazar stared now at his niece's eyes.

A child's eyes still—but it was not a child who glared back at him. She had seen what a child should never see. And soon would see no more.

Forgive me, Azubah.

With one last murmured prayer, he stepped into the torchlit tomb. Guttering flames reflected off the haunted eyes of the seven soldiers who were waiting for him. They had fought the Romans for days, knowing that the battle would end with their own deaths, but not like this. He nodded to them, and to the robed man in their midst. Nine grown men gathered to sacrifice a child.

The men bowed their heads to Eleazar, as if he were holy. In truth, they did not know how unclean he was. Only he and the one he served knew that.

Every man bore bloody wounds, some inflicted by the Romans, others by the small girl they held captive.

The purple robes she'd been forced to wear were too large, making her appear even smaller. Her dirty hands clutched a tattered doll, sewn from leather, tanned the color of the Judean desert, one button eye missing.

How many years ago had he given it to her? He remembered the delight bursting from that tiny face when he knelt and offered it to her. He recalled thinking how much sunlight could be trapped in such a little body, that it could shine so brilliantly, fuel such simple joy at a gift of leather and cloth.

He searched her face now, looking for that sunshine.

But only darkness stared back at him.

She hissed, showing teeth.

"Azubah," he pleaded.

Eyes, once as calm and beautiful as a fawn's, glared at him with feral hatred. She drew in a deep breath and spat hot blood in his face.

He staggered, dazed by the silken feel, the iron smell of the blood. With one shaking hand, he wiped his face. He knelt before her and used a cloth to gently brush blood from her chin, then flung the soiled rag far away.

Then he heard it.

So did she.

Eleazar and Azubah both jerked their heads. In the tomb, they alone heard screams from atop the mountain. They alone knew that the Romans had broken through the stronghold's defenses.

The slaughter above had begun.

The robed one noted their movement and knew what it meant. "We have no more time."

Eleazar looked to the older man in the dusty brown robe, their leader, the one who had demanded that this child be baptized amid such horror. Age etched the leader's bearded face. Solemn, impenetrable eyes closed. His lips moved in silent prayer. His face shone with the surety of a man free of doubt.

Finally, those blessed eyes opened again and found Eleazar's face, as if searching for his soul. It made him recall another stare from another man, many, many years before.

Eleazar turned away in shame.

The soldiers gathered around the open stone sarcophagus in the center of the tomb. It had been carved out of a single block of limestone, large enough to hold three grown men.

But it would soon imprison only one small girl.

Pyres of myrrh and frankincense smoldered at each corner. Through their fragrance Eleazar smelled darker scents: bitter salts and acrid spices gathered according to an ancient Essene text.

All lay in terrible readiness.

Eleazar bowed his head one final time, praying for another way.

Take me, not her.

But the ritual called for them all to play their roles.

A Girl Corrupted of Innocence.

A Knight of Christ.

A Warrior of Man.

The robed leader spoke. His graveled voice did not waver. "What must be done is God's will. To protect her soul. And the souls of others. Take her!"

But not all had come here willingly.

Azubah yanked free of her captors' hands and sprang for the door, swift as a fallow doe.

Eleazar alone possessed the speed to catch her. He grabbed her thin wrist. She struggled against his grip, but he was stronger. Men closed in around them. She pulled the doll to her chest and sank to her knees. She looked so wretchedly small.

Their leader gestured to a nearby soldier. "It must be done."

The soldier stepped forward and snatched Azubah's arm, wrenching her doll away and tossing it aside.

"No!" she cried, her first word, forlorn, still sounding so much like a child, coming from her thin throat.

She tore free again and surged forth with furious strength. She leaped upon the offending soldier, locking her legs around his waist. Teeth and nails tore at his face as she knocked him hard to the stone floor.

Two solders rushed to his aid. They pulled the wild girl off and pinned her down.

"Take her to the sepulcher!" the leader commanded.

The two men holding her hesitated, plainly fearing to move. The child thrashed under them.

Eleazar saw that her panic was not directed toward her captors. Her gaze remained fixed on what had been stolen from her.

He retrieved the tattered figure of her doll and held it in front of her bloody face. It had quieted her many times when she was younger. He strove to block out memories of her playing in the clear sunshine with her laughing sisters and this doll. The toy trembled in his hand.

Her gaze softened into a plea. Her struggles calmed. She disentangled one arm from the men's grasps and reached for the doll.

When her fingers touched it, her body sagged as she succumbed to her fate, accepting that escape was not possible. She sought her only solace, as she had as an innocent child, in the companionship of her doll. She did not want to go into the darkness alone. She lifted the figure to her face and pressed her small nose against its own, her shape a sigil of childlike comfort.

Waving his men away, he lifted the now-quiet girl. He cradled her cold form against his chest, and she nestled against him as she used to. He prayed for the strength to do what was right.

The block of stone gripped in his free hand reminded him of his oath.

To the side, their leader began the prayers binding the sacrifice above to the one below, using ancient incantations, holy words, and tossing pinches of incense into the small pyres. Atop the mountain, the rebels took their lives as the Romans broke their gates.

That tragic payment of blood would settle the debt here.

With the block clutched in his hand, Eleazar carried the girl the few steps to the open sarcophagus. It had already been filled, nearly to the rim, sloshing and shimmering. It was to act as a *mikveh*—a ritual immersion bath for those to be purified.

But rather than blessed water, *wine* filled this bath.

Empty clay jugs littered the floor.

Reaching the crypt, Eleazar peered into its dark depths. Torchlight turned wine to blood.

Azubah buried her face in his chest. He swallowed bitter grief.

"Now," their leader ordered.

He held the girl's small form against his own one last time and felt her release a single sob. He glanced at the dark doorway. He could still save her body, but only if he damned her soul, and his own. This terrible act was the only way to truly save her.

The highest-ranking soldier lifted the girl from Eleazar's arms and held her over the open tomb. She clutched her doll to her chest, terror raw in her eyes as he lowered her to the surface of the wine. And stopped. Her eyes sought out Eleazar's. He stretched a hand toward her, then pulled it back.

"Blessed be the Lord our God who art in Heaven," the leader intoned.

Above them, all chanting stopped. She tilted her head as if she heard it, too. Eleazar pictured blood soaking the sand, seeping toward the mountain's core. It must be done now. Those deaths marked the final dark act to seal this tomb.

"Eleazar," the leader said. "It is time."

Eleazar held out the precious stone block, its holy secret the only force strong enough to drive him forward. The stone block's weight was nothing in his arms. It was his heart that held him trapped for a breath.

"It must be done," the robed one said, softly now.

Eleazar did not trust his voice to answer. He moved toward the girl.

The commander released her into the wine. She writhed in the dark liquid, small fingers grasping the stone sides of her coffin. Red bled over its edges and spilled to the floor. Her eyes beseeched him as he placed the stone block atop her thin chest—and pushed. The stone's weight and the shuddering strength of his arms forced the child deep into the wine bath.

She no longer fought, just held the doll tight against her chest. She lay as quiet as if she were already dead. Her mute lips moved, forming words that disappeared as her small face sank away.

What were those lost words?

He knew that question would haunt his everlasting days.

"Forgive me," he choked out. "And forgive her."

Wine soaked his tunic sleeves, scalding his skin. He held her inert form until the prayers of their leader ceased.

For what seemed an eternity.

Finally, he let go and stood. Azubah remained drowned at the bottom, forever pinned under the weight of the sacred stone, ever its cursed guardian. He prayed that this act would purify her soul, an ageless penance for the corruption inside her.

My little Azubah . . .

He collapsed against the sarcophagus.

"Seal it," the leader ordered.

A limestone slab, lowered with ropes, ground into place. Men slathered the edges of the lid with a slurry of ash and lime to bind stone to stone.

Eleazar flattened his palms against the side of her prison as if his touch could comfort her. But she was beyond comfort now.

He rested his forehead against the unforgiving stone. It was the only way. It served a higher good. But these truths did not ease his pain. Or hers.

"Come," their leader beckoned. "What must be done has been done."

Eleazar drew in a rattling breath of foul air. The soldiers coughed and shuffled to the doorway. He stood alone with her in the dank tomb.

"You cannot stay," the leader called from the doorway. "You must walk a different path."

Eleazar stumbled toward the voice, blinded by tears.

Once they left, the tomb would be hidden, the passage sealed. No living being would remember it. Any who dared trespass would be doomed.

He found their leader's gaze upon him.

"Do you regret your oath?" the man asked. His voice rang with pity, but it also held the hardness of the resolute.

That hardness was the reason why Christ named their leader *Petrus,* meaning "Rock." He was the apostle who would be the foundation of the new Church.

Eleazar met that stony gaze. "No, Peter, I do not."

PART I

Who looks on the earth and it trembles,
who touches the mountains and they smoke!

—Psalm 104:32

1

October 26, 10:33 A.M., Israel Standard Time
Caesarea, Israel

Dr. Erin Granger stroked her softest brush across the ancient skull. As the dust cleared, she studied it with the eyes of a scientist, noting the tiny seams of bone, the open fontanel. Her gaze evaluated the amount of callusing, judging the skull to be that of a newborn, and from the angle of the pelvic bone, a boy.

Only days old when he died.

As she continued to draw the child out of the dirt and stone, she looked on also as a woman, picturing the infant boy lying on his side, knees drawn up against his chest, tiny hands still curled into fists. Had his parents counted his heartbeats, kissed his impossibly tender skin, watched as that tiny heartbeat stopped?

As she had once done with her baby sister.

She closed her eyes, brush poised.

Stop it.

Opening her eyes, she combed back an errant strand of blond hair that had escaped its efficient ponytail before turning her attention back to the bones. She would find out what happened here all those hundreds of years ago. Because, as with her sister, this child's death had been deliberate. Only this boy had succumbed to violence, not negligence.

She continued to work, seeing the tender position of the limbs. Someone had labored to restore the body to its proper order before burying it, but the efforts could not disguise the cracked and missing bones, hinting at a past atrocity. Even two thousand years could not erase the crime.

She put down the wooden brush and took yet another photo. Time had colored the bones the same bleached sepia as the unforgiving ground, but her careful excavation had revealed their shape. Still, it would take hours to work the rest of the bones free.

She shifted from one aching knee to the other. At thirty-two, she was hardly old, but right now she felt that way. She had been in the trench for barely an hour, and already her knees complained. As a child, she had knelt in prayer for much longer, poised on the hard dirt floor of the compound's church. Back then, she could kneel for half a day without complaint, if her father demanded—but after so many years trying to forget her past, perhaps she misremembered it.

Wincing, she stood and stretched, lifting her head clear of the waist-high trench. A cooling sea breeze caressed her hot face, chasing away her memories. To the left, wind ruffled the flaps of the camp's tents and scattered sand across the excavation site.

Flying grit blinded her until she could blink it away. Sand invaded everything here. Each day her hair changed from blond to the grayish red of the Israeli desert. Her socks ground inside her Converse sneakers like sandpaper, her fingernails filled up with grit, even her mouth tasted of sand.

Still, when she looked across the plastic yellow tape that cordoned off her archaeological dig, she allowed a ghost of a smile to shine, happy to have her sneakers planted in ancient history. Her excavation occupied the center of an ancient hippodrome, a chariot course. It faced the ageless Mediterranean Sea. The water shone indigo, beaten by the sun into a surreal, metallic hue. Behind her, a long stretch of ancient stone seats, sectioned into tiers, stood as a two-thousand-year-old testament to a long-dead king, the architect of the city of Caesarea: the infamous King Herod, that monstrous slayer of innocents.

A horse's whinny floated across the track, echoing not from the past, but from a makeshift stable that had been thrown together on the far end of the hippodrome. A local group was preparing an invitational race. Soon this hippodrome would be resurrected, coming to life once again, if only for a few days.

She could hardly wait.

But she and her students had a lot of work to finish before then.

With her hands on her hips, she stared down at the skull of the murdered baby. Perhaps later today she could jacket the tiny skeleton with plaster and begin the laborious process of excavating it from the ground. She longed to get it back to a lab, where it could be analyzed. The bones had more to tell her than she would ever discover in the field.

She dropped to her knees next to the infant. Something bothered her about the femur. It had unusual scallop-shaped dents along its length. As she bent close to see, a chill chased back the heat.

Were those teeth marks?

"Professor?" Nate Highsmith's Texas twang broke the air and her concentration.

She jumped, cracking her elbow against the wooden slats bracing the walls from the relentless sand.

"Sorry." Her graduate student ducked his head.

She had given strict instructions that she was not to be disturbed this morning, and here he was bothering her already. To keep from snapping at him, she picked up her battered canteen and took a long sip of tepid water. It tasted like stainless steel.

"No harm done," she said stiffly.

She shielded her eyes with her free hand and squinted up at him. Standing on the edge of the trench, he was silhouetted against the scathing sun. He wore a straw Stetson pulled low, a pair of battered jeans, and a faded plaid shirt with the sleeves rolled up to expose well-muscled arms. She suspected that he had rolled them up just to impress her. It wouldn't work, of course. For the past several years, fully focused on her work, she acknowledged that the only guys she found fascinating had been dead for several centuries.

She glanced meaningfully over to an unremarkable patch of sand and rock. The team's ground-penetrating radar unit sat abandoned, looking more like a sandblasted lawn mower than a high-tech tool for peering under dirt and rock.

"Why aren't you over there mapping that quadrant?"

"I was, Doc." His drawl got thicker, as it always did when he got excited. He hiked an eyebrow, too.

He's found something.

"What?"

"You wouldn't believe me if I told you." Nate bounced on the balls of his feet, ready to dash off and show her.

She smiled, because he was *right*. Whatever it was, she wouldn't believe it until she saw it herself. That was the mantra she hammered into her students: *It's not real until you can dig it out of the ground and hold it in your hands.*

To protect her work site and out of respect for the child's bones, she gently pulled a tarp over the skeleton. Once she was done, Nate reached down and helped her out of the deep trench. As expected, his hand lingered on hers a second too long.

Trying not to scowl, she retrieved her hand and dusted off the knees of her jeans. Nate took a step back, glancing away, perhaps knowing he had overstepped a line. She didn't scold him. What would be the use? She wasn't oblivious to the advances of men, but she rarely encouraged them, and never out in the field. Here she wore dirt like other women wore makeup and avoided romantic involvement. Though of average height, she'd been told that she carried herself as if she were a foot taller. She had to in this profession, especially as a young woman.

Back home, she'd had her share of relationships, but none of them seemed to stick. In the end, most men found her intimidating—which was off-putting to many, but oddly attractive to others.

Like Nate.

Still, he was a good field man with great potential as a geophysicist. He would grow out of his interest in her, and things would uncomplicate themselves on their own.

"Show me." She turned toward the khaki-colored equipment tent. If nothing else, it would be good to get out of the baking sun.

"Amy's got the information up on the laptop." He headed across the site. "It's a jackpot, Professor. We hit a bona fide *bone* jackpot."

She suppressed a grin at his enthusiasm and hurried to keep pace with his long-legged stride. She admired his passion, but, like life, archaeology didn't hand out jackpots after a single morning's work. Sometimes not even after decades.

She ducked past the tent flap and held it open for Nate, who took off his hat as he stepped inside. Out of the sun's glare, the tent's interior felt several degrees cooler than the site outside.

A humming electric generator serviced a laptop and a dilapidated metal fan. The fan blew straight at Amy, a twenty-three-year-old grad student from Columbia. The dark-haired young woman spent more time inside the tent than out. Drops of water had condensed on a can of Diet Coke on her desk. Slightly overweight and out of shape, Amy hadn't had the years under the harsh sun to harden her to the rigors of archaeological fieldwork, but she still had a keen technological nose. Amy typed on the keyboard with one hand and waved Erin over with the other.

"Professor Granger, you're not going to believe this."

"That's what I keep hearing."

Her third student was also in the tent. Apparently *everyone* had decided to stop working to study Nate's findings. Heinrich hovered over Amy's shoulder. A stolid twenty-four-year-old student from the Freie Universität in Berlin, he was normally hard to distract. For him to have stepped away from his own work meant that the find was big.

Amy's brown eyes did not leave the screen. "The software is still working at enhancing the image, but I thought you'd want to see this right away."

Erin unsnapped the rag clipped to her belt and wiped grit and sweat off her face. "Amy, before I forget, that child's skeleton I've been excavating . . . I saw some unusual marks that I'd like you to photograph."

Amy nodded, but Erin suspected she hadn't heard a word she'd said.

Nate fidgeted with his Stetson.

What had they found?

Erin walked over and stood next to Heinrich. Amy leaned back in her metal folding chair so that Erin had a clear view of the screen.

The laptop displayed time-sliced images of the ground Nate had scanned that morning. Each showed a different layer of quadrant eight, sorted by depth. The pictures resembled square gray mud puddles marred by black lines that formed parabolas, like ripples in the puddle. The black lines represented solid material.

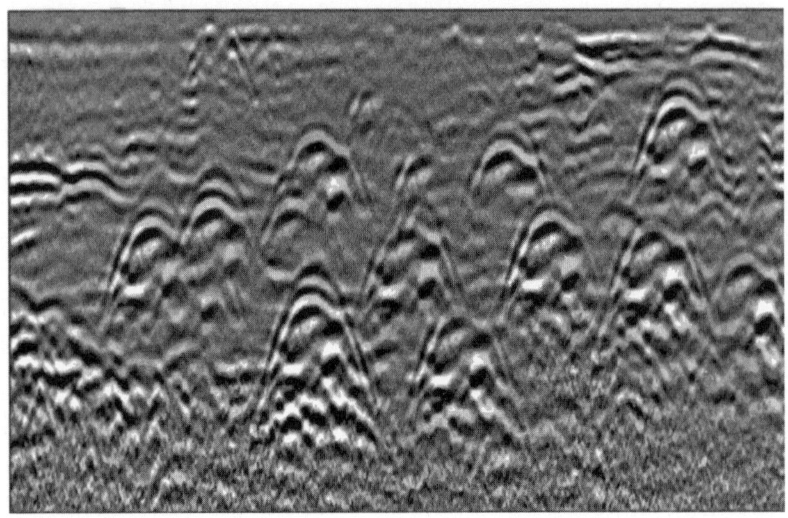

Erin's heart pounded in her throat. She leaned closer in disbelief.

This mud puddle had far too many waves. In ten years of fieldwork she'd never seen anything like it. No one had.

This can't be right.

She traced a curve on the smooth screen, ignoring the way Amy tightened her lips. Amy hated it when someone smudged her laptop screen, but Erin had to prove that it was real—to *touch* it herself.

She spoke through the strain, through the hope. "Nate, how big an area did you scan?"

No hesitation. "Ten square meters."

She glanced sidelong at his serious face. "Only ten meters? You're sure?"

"You trained me on the GPR, remember?" He cocked his head to the side. "Painstakingly."

Amy laughed.

Erin kept going. "And you added gain to these results?"

"Yes, Professor," he sighed. "It's fully gained."

She sensed that she'd bruised his ego by questioning his skills, but she had to be certain. She trusted equipment, but not always the people running it.

"I did everything." Nate leaned forward. "And, before you ask, the signature is exactly the same as the skeleton you were just excavating."

Exactly the same? That made this stratum two thousand years old. She looked back at the tantalizing images. If the data were correct, and she would have to check again, but if they were, each parabola marked a human skull.

"I did a rough count." Nate interrupted her thoughts. "More than five hundred. None larger than four inches in diameter."

Four inches . . .

Not just skulls—skulls of *babies.*

Hundreds of babies.

She silently recited the relevant Bible passage: Matthew 2:16. *Then Herod, when he saw that he was mocked of the wise men, was exceeding wroth, and sent forth, and slew all the children that were in Bethlehem, and in all the coasts thereof, from two years old and under, according to the time which he had diligently inquired of the wise men.*

The Massacre of the Innocents. Allegedly, Herod ordered it done to be certain, absolutely certain, that he had killed the child whom he feared would one day supplant him as the King of the Jews. But he had failed anyway. That baby had escaped to Egypt and grown into the man known as Jesus Christ.

Had her team just discovered tragic proof of Herod's deed?

2

October 26, 1:03 P.M., IST
Masada, Israel

Sweat stung Tommy's eyes. Eyebrows would come in handy about now.

Thanks again, chemo.

He slumped against another camel-colored boulder. All the rocks on the steep trail looked the same, and every one was too hot to sit on. He shifted his windbreaker under his legs to put another layer of protection between his pants and the scorching surface. As usual, he was holding the group up. Also, as usual, he was too weak to go on without a break.

He struggled to catch his breath. The burning air tasted thin and dry. Did it even have enough oxygen? The other climbers seemed to be fine breathing it. They practically sprinted up the switchbacks like he was the grandpa and they were the fourteen-year-olds. He couldn't even hear their voices anymore.

The rocky trail—named the Snake Path—twisted up the sheer cliffs of the infamous mountain of Masada. Its summit was only a handful of yards overhead, sheltering the ruins of the ancient Jewish fortress. From his current perch on the trail, Tommy searched out over the baked tan earth of the Jordan Valley below.

He wiped sweat from his eyes. Being from Orange County, Tommy thought he'd known heat. But this was like crawling into an oven.

His head drooped forward. He wanted to sleep again. He wanted to feel cool hotel sheets against his cheek and take a long nap in air-conditioning. After that, if he felt better, he would play video games.

He jerked awake. This was no time to daydream. But he was so tired, and the desert so quiet. Unlike humans, animals and bugs were smart enough to take cover during the day. A vast empty silence swallowed him. Would death be like this?

"Are you okay, honey?" his mother asked.

He startled. Why hadn't he heard her approach? Did he fall asleep again? He wheezed out, "Fine."

She bit her lip. They all knew he wasn't fine. He yanked his cuff over the new coffee-brown blotch of melanoma that disfigured his left wrist.

"We can wait as long as you need to." She plunked down next to him. "I wonder why they call it the Snake's Path. I haven't seen a single snake."

She spoke to his chin. His parents rarely made eye contact with him anymore. When they did, they cried. It had been like that throughout the last two years of surgeries, chemotherapy, and radiation—and now through his relapse.

Maybe they'd finally look him in the face when he lay in his coffin.

"Too hot for snakes." He hated how out of breath he sounded.

"They'd be snake steaks." She took a long drink from her water bottle. "Sun-broiled and ready to eat. Just like us."

His father trotted up. "Everything all right?"

"I'm just taking a break," his mother lied, covering for him. She wet her handkerchief and handed it to Tommy. "I got tired."

Tommy wanted to correct her, to tell the truth, but he was too exhausted. He wiped the cloth across his face.

His father started talking, like he always did when he was nervous. "We're close now. Just a few more yards, and we'll see the fortress. The actual fortress of Masada. Try to picture it."

Obediently, Tommy closed his eyes. He pictured a swimming pool. Blue and cool and smelling like chlorine.

"Ten thousand Roman soldiers are camped out all around here in tents. Soldiers with swords and shields wait in the sun. They close off any escape route, try to starve out the nine hundred men, women, and children up there on the plateau." His father talked faster, excited. "But the rebels stand firm until the end. Even after. They never give up."

Tommy tugged his hat down on his bald head and squinted up at him. "They offed themselves in the end, Dad."

"No." His father spoke passionately. "The Jews here decided to die as free men, rather than fall to the mercy of the Romans. They didn't kill themselves in surrender. They chose their own fate. Choices like that determine the kind of man you are."

Tommy picked up a hot stone and tossed it down the trail. It bounced, then vanished over the edge. What would his father do if he really chose his own fate? If he offed himself instead of being a slave to the cancer. He didn't think his father would sound so proud of that.

He studied his father's face. People had often said they looked alike: same thick black hair, same easy smile. After chemo stole his hair, no one said that anymore. He wondered if he would have grown up to look like him.

"Ready to go again?" His father hitched his pack higher on his shoulder.

His mother gave his father the evil eye. "We can wait."

"I didn't say we had to go," his father said. "I was just asking—"

"You bet." Tommy stood up to keep his parents from arguing.

Eyes on the trail, he dragged forward. One tan hiking boot in front of the other. Soon he'd be up top, and his parents would get their moment with him at the fort. That was why he had agreed to this trip, to this long climb—because it would give them something to remember. Even if they weren't ready to admit it, they wouldn't have many more memories of him. He wanted to make them good ones.

He counted his steps. That was how you got through tough things. You counted. Once you said "one," then you knew "two" was coming, and "three" right after that. He got to twenty-eight before the path leveled out.

He had reached the summit. Sure, his lungs felt like two flaming paper bags, but he was glad he'd done it.

At the top stood a wooden pavilion—though *pavilion* was a pretentious word for four skinny tree trunks topped by more skinny tree trunks laid sideways to cast patchy shade. But it beat standing in the sun.

Beyond the cliff's edge, desert stretched around him. In its dried-out and desolate way, it was beautiful. Bleached brown dunes rolled as far as he could see. Sand slapped against rocks. Millennia of wind erosion had eaten those rocks away, grain by grain.

No people, no animals. Did the defenders see this view before the Romans arrived?

A killing wasteland.

He turned and scanned the plateau up top, where all that bloodshed had happened two thousand years ago. It was a long flat area, about five football fields long, maybe three times as wide, with a half dozen or so crumbling stone buildings.

This is what I climbed up here for?

His mother looked equally unimpressed. She pushed curly brown hair out of her eyes, her face pink from sunburn or exertion. "It looks more like a prison than a fortress."

"It was a prison," his father said. "A death row prison. Nobody got out alive."

"Nobody ever gets out alive." Tommy regretted his words as soon as they left his mouth, especially when his mother turned away and slid a finger under her sunglasses, clearly wiping a tear. Still, a part of him was glad that she let herself feel something real instead of lying about it all the time.

Their guide bounced up to them, rescuing them from the moment. She was all bare legs, tight khaki shorts, and long black hair, barely winded by the long climb. "Glad you guys made it!" She even had a sexy Israeli accent.

He smiled at her, grateful to have something else to think about. "Thanks."

"Like I told everybody else a minute ago, the name Masada comes from the word *metzuda,* meaning 'fortress,' and you can see why." She waved a long tan arm to encompass the entire plateau. "The casemate walls protecting the fortress are actually two walls, one inside the other. Between them were the main living quarters for Masada's residents. Ahead of us is the Western Palace, the biggest structure on Masada."

Tommy tore his eyes away from her lips to look where she

pointed. The massive building didn't look anything like a palace. It was a wreck. The old stone walls were missing large sections and clad with modern scaffolding. It looked like someone was halfway through building a movie set for the next *Indiana Jones* installment.

There must be a deep history under all that scaffolding, but he didn't feel it. He wanted to. History mattered to his father, and it should to him, too, but since the cancer, he felt outside of time, outside of history. He didn't have room in his head for other people's tragedies, especially not people who had been dead for thousands of years.

"This next building we believe was a private bathhouse," the guide said, indicating a building on the left. "They found three skeletons inside, skulls separated from the bodies."

He perked up. *Finally something interesting.*

"Decapitated?" he asked, moving closer. "So they committed suicide by cutting off their own heads?"

The guide's lips curved in a smile. "Actually, the soldiers drew lots to see who would be responsible for killing the others. Only the last man had to commit suicide."

Tommy scowled at the ruins. So they killed their own children when the going got tough. He felt a surprising flicker of envy. Better to die quickly at the hands of someone who loved you than by the slow and pitiless rot of cancer. Ashamed of this thought, he looked at his parents. His mother smiled at him as she fanned herself with the guidebook, and his father took his picture.

No, he could never ask that of them.

Resigned, he turned his attention back to the bathhouse. "Those skeletons . . . are they still in there?" He stepped forward, ready to peek inside through the metal gate.

The guide blocked him with her ample chest. "Sorry, young man. No one is allowed inside."

He struggled not to stare at her breasts but failed miserably.

Before he could move, his mother spoke. "How're you doing, Tommy?"

Had she seen him checking out the guide? He blushed. "I'm fine."

"Are you thirsty? Do you want some water?" She held out her plastic water bottle.

"No, Mom."

"Let me put some more sunscreen on your face." His mother reached into her purse. Normally, he would have suffered the indignity, but the guide smiled at him, a stunning smile, and he suddenly didn't want to be babied.

"I'm fine, Mom!" he spat out, more harshly than he'd intended.

His mother flinched. The guide walked away.

"Sorry," he said to his mother. "I didn't mean it."

"It's fine," she said. "I'll be over there with your father. Take your time here."

Feeling terrible, he watched her walk away.

He crossed over to the bathhouse, angry at himself. He leaned on the metal gate to see inside—the gate creaked open under his weight. He almost fell through. He stepped back quickly, but before he did so, something in the corner of the room caught his eye.

A soft fluttering, white, like a crumpled piece of paper.

Curiosity piqued inside him. He searched around. No one was looking. Besides, what was the penalty for trespassing? What was the worst that could happen? The cute guide might drag him back out?

He wouldn't mind that at all.

He poked his head inside, staring at the source of the fluttering.

A small white dove limped across the mosaic floor, its left wing dragging across the tiles, scrawling some mysterious message in the dust with the tip of its feathers.

Poor thing . . .

He had to get it out of there. It would die from dehydration or get eaten by something. The guide probably knew a bird rescue place they could bring it to. His mother had volunteered at a place like that back home in California, before his cancer ate up everyone's life.

He slipped through the gap in the gate. Inside, the room was smaller than his father's toolshed, with four plain stone walls and a floor covered by a faded mosaic made of maddeningly tiny tiles. The mosaic showed eight dusty red hearts arranged in a circle like a flower, a row of dark blue and white tiles that looked like waves, and a border of terra-cotta and white triangles that reminded him of teeth. He tried to imagine long-ago craftsmen putting it together like a jigsaw puzzle, but the thought made him tired.

He stepped across the shadowy threshold, grateful to be out of the unforgiving sun. How many people had died in here? A chill raced up his spine as he imagined the scene. He pictured people kneeling—he was certain they would be kneeling. A man in a dirty linen tunic stood above them with his sword raised high. He'd started with the youngest one, and by the time he was done, he barely had the strength to lift his arms, but he did. Finally, he, too, fell to his knees and waited for a quick death from his friend's blade. And then, it was over. Their blood ran over the tiny tiles, stained the grout, and pooled on the floor.

Tommy shook his head to clear the vision and looked around.

No skeletons.

They were probably taken to a museum or maybe buried someplace.

The bird raised its head, halting its journey across the tiles to stare up at Tommy, first with one eye, then the other, sizing him up. Its eyes were a brilliant shade of green, like malachite. He'd never seen a bird with green eyes before.

He knelt down and whispered, his words barely a breath. "Come here, little one. There's nothing to be afraid of."

It stared with each eye again—then took a hop toward him.

Encouraged, he reached out and gently scooped up the wounded creature. As he rose with its warm body cradled between his palms, the ground shifted under him. He struggled to keep his balance. Was he dizzy because of the long climb? Between his toes, a tiny black line skittered across the mosaic, like a living thing.

Snake was his first thought.

Fear beat in his heart.

But the dark line widened, revealing it to be something worse. Not a snake, but a *crack*. A finger of dark orange smoke curled up from one end of the crack, no bigger than if someone had dropped a lit cigarette.

The bird suddenly burst from his palms, spread its wings, and sailed through the smoke as it fled out the door. Apparently it hadn't been that injured. The smoke wafted Tommy's way, beat by the passing wings. It smelled surprisingly sweet with a hint of darker spices, almost like incense.

Tommy crinkled his brow and leaned forward. He held his palm over the smoke. It rose up between his fingertips, cold instead of warm, as if it came from some cool place deep within the earth.

He bent to look at it more closely—when the mosaic cracked under his boots like glass. He jumped back. Tiles slipped into the gap. Blues, tans, and reds. The gap devoured the pattern as it grew wider.

He backpedaled toward the door. Gouts of smoke, now a reddish orange, boiled up through the splintering mosaic.

A grinding groan rose from the mountain's core, and the entire room shook.

Earthquake.

He leaped out the bathhouse door and landed hard on his backside. In front of him, the building gave a final, violent jerk, as if slapped by an angry god—then toppled into the chasm opening beneath it.

The edges crumbled wider, only feet away. He scooted backward. The chasm chased him. He gained his feet to run, but the mountaintop jolted and knocked him back to the ground.

He crawled away on his hands and knees. Stones shredded his palms. Around him, buildings and columns smashed to the ground.

God, please help me!

Dust and smoke hid everything more than a few yards away. As he crawled, he saw a man vanish under a falling section of wall. Two screaming women dropped away as the ground split beneath them.

"TOMMY!"

He crawled toward his mother's voice, finally clearing the pall of smoke.

"Here!" he coughed.

His father rushed forward and yanked him to his feet. His mother grabbed his elbow. They dragged him toward the Snake Path, away from the destruction.

He looked back. The fissure gaped wider, cleaving the summit. Chunks of mountain fell away and rumbled down to the desert. Dark smoke churned into the achingly blue sky, as if to take its horrors to the burning sun.

Together, he and his parents stumbled to the cliff's edge.

But as quickly as it began, the earthquake ceased.

His parents froze, as if afraid any movement might restart the quakes. His father wrapped his arms around them both. Across the summit, pained cries cut the air.

"Tommy?" His mother's voice shook. "You're bleeding."

"I scraped my hands," he said. "It's no big deal."

His father let them go. He'd lost his hat and cut his cheek. His normally deep voice came out too high. "Terrorists, do you think?"

"I didn't hear a bomb," his mother said, stroking Tommy's hair like he was a little boy.

For once, he didn't mind.

The cloud of blackish-red smoke charged toward them, as if to drive them off the cliff.

His father took the suggestion and pointed toward the steep trail. "Let's go. That stuff could be toxic."

"I breathed it," Tommy assured them, standing. "It's okay."

A woman ran out of the smoke clutching her throat. She ran blind, eyelids blistered and bleeding. Just a few steps, then she pitched forward and didn't move.

"Go!" his father yelled, and pushed Tommy ahead of him. "Now!"

Together, they ran, but they could not outpace the smoke.

It overtook them. His mother coughed—a wet, tearing, unnatural sound. Tommy reached for her, not knowing what to do.

His parents stopped running, driven to their knees.

It was over.

"Tommy . . ." his father gasped. "Go . . ."

Disobedient, he sank down beside them.

If I'm going to die anyway, let it be on my own terms.

With my family.

A sense of finality calmed him. "It's okay, Dad." He squeezed his mom's hand, then his dad's. Tears flowed when he thought he had none left. "I love you, so much."

Both of his parents looked at him—square in the eye. Despite the terrible moment at hand, Tommy felt so warm right then.

He hugged them both tightly and still held them as they went limp in his grasp, refusing to let gravity take them as death had. When his strength gave out, he knelt next to their bodies and waited for his own last breath.

But as minutes passed, that last breath refused to come.

He wiped an arm across his tearstained face and stumbled to his feet, refusing to look at his parents' crumpled bodies, their blistered eyes, the blood on their faces. If he didn't look, maybe they weren't really dead. Maybe it was a dream.

He turned in a slow circle facing away from them. The foul smoke had blown away. Bodies littered the ground. As far as he could see, everything was dead still.

It was no dream.

Why am I the only one still alive? I was supposed to die. Not Mom and Dad.

He looked down again at their bodies. His grief was deeper than weeping. Deeper than all the times he'd mourned his own death.

It was wrong. He was the sick one, the defective one. He had known for a long time that his death was coming. But his parents were supposed to carry on memories of him, frozen at the age of fourteen in a thousand snapshots. The grief was supposed to be theirs.

He fell to his knees with a sob, thrusting his hands toward the sun, his palms upraised, both beseeching and cursing God.

But God wasn't done with him yet.

As his arms stretched to the sky, one sleeve fell back, baring his wrist, pale and clear.

He lowered his limbs, staring at his skin in disbelief.

His melanoma had vanished.

3

October 26, 2:15 P.M., IST
Caesarea, Israel

Kneeling in the trench, Erin surveyed the earthquake's damage and sighed in frustration. According to initial reports, the epicenter was miles away, but the quaking rocked the entire Israeli coastline, including here.

Sand poured through the broken boards that shored up the sides of her excavation, slowly reburying her discovery, as if it were never supposed to have been unearthed.

But that wasn't the worst of the earthquake's wrath. Sand could be dug out again, but a cracked plank sat atop the child's skull, the one she had been struggling to gently release from the earth's grip. She didn't permit herself to speculate about what lay under that chunk of wood.

Just please let it be intact . . .

Her three students fidgeted near the trench, keeping to the edge.

Holding her breath, Erin eased up the splintered plank, got it free, and blindly passed it to Nate. She then lifted the tarp that she'd covered the tiny skeleton with earlier.

Shattered fragments marked where the baby's once-intact skull had been. The body had lain undisturbed for two thousand years—until she exposed it to destruction.

Her throat tightened.

She sat in the trench and brushed her fingertips lightly over the bone fragments, counting them. Too many. She bowed her head. Clues to the baby's death had been lost on her watch. She should have finished this excavation before following Nate to the tent to study the new GPR readings.

"Dr. Granger?" Heinrich spoke from the edge of the trench.

She leaned back quickly so he would not think she was praying. The German archaeology student was too bound up with religion. She didn't want him to think that she was, too. "Let's get a plaster cast over the rest of this, Heinrich."

She needed to protect the rest of the skeleton from aftershocks.

Too little, too late, for the tiny skull.

"Right away." Heinrich combed his fingers through his shaggy blond hair before heading toward the equipment tent, which had ridden out the earthquake undamaged. The only modern casualty was Amy's Diet Coke.

Heinrich's sylphlike girlfriend, Julia, trailed behind him. She wasn't supposed to be on the dig site at all, but she was passing through for the weekend, so Erin had allowed it.

"I'll check out the equipment." Amy's anxious voice reminded Erin of how young they all really were. Even at their age, she had not been so young. Had she?

Erin gestured around the hippodrome. It had been in ruins long before their arrival. "The site's been through worse." She injected false cheer into her voice. "Let's get to work putting it to rights."

"We can rebuild it. We have the technology. Better than it was before." Nate hummed the theme music from the *Six Million Dollar Man*.

Amy gave him a flirtatious smile before heading off to the tent.

"Can you fetch me a new board?" Erin asked Nate.

"Sure thing, Doc."

As he left, his tune drifted through her mind. What if they could actually rebuild it? Not just the excavation, but the entire site.

Her gaze traveled across the ruins, picturing what this place must have once looked like. In her mind's eye, she filled in the half that had long since crumbled away. She imagined cheering crowds, the rattle of chariots, the pounding of hooves. But then she remembered what came before the hippodrome was constructed: the Massacre of the Innocents. She imagined the raw panic when soldiers snatched infants from their helpless mothers. Mothers forced to see swords cut short the wailing of their babies.

So many lives lost.

If she was right about her discovery, she began to suspect the real reason *why* Herod had built this hippodrome at this spot. Had it given him some dark amusement to know the trampling of hooves and the spill of the blood further desecrated the graves of those he had slaughtered?

Shrill neighing startled her out of her thoughts. She stood and looked toward the stables, where a groom walked a skittish white stallion. She knew horses. She had spent many happy childhood hours at the compound's stable and knew firsthand how they hated earthquakes. The great, sensitive beasts were restless before a quake struck and unsettled after. She hoped these were being properly taken care of.

Heinrich and Nate returned. Nate had an intact board, while Heinrich carried a box of plaster, a water jug, and a bucket. An art minor, he had careful hands, just what she needed to help put the broken pieces in place.

Nate handed her the board. It brought with it the forest scent of pine, out of place here in this desert. Taking care to avoid the remains of the skeleton, he climbed in next to her. Together she and Nate shouldered the board between its braces and back against the edge of the trench. She hoped it wouldn't fail her like the last one.

While Nate left to check on his equipment, she and Heinrich dug out sand. The board had damaged the skull and the left arm. She remembered the tiny fontanel, the angle of the neck. There had been clues there, she felt certain. Now lost forever.

Intending to preserve what was left, she raised her camera and focused first on the shattered skull. She took several shots from multiple angles. Next, she photographed the broken arm, shattered mid-radius. As she clicked away, her forearm gave a twinge of sympathy. Her own arm had hurt off and on since she was four years old.

Placing her camera down, still staring at that broken limb, she stroked her fingers down her left arm and slipped into a painful past.

Her mother had pushed her toward her father, urging her to show the crayon picture of the angel that she had drawn. Proudly, with the hope of praise, she held it toward his callused hand. He was so tall that she barely reached past his knee. He took the picture, but only glanced at it.

Instead, he sat and pulled her into his lap. She began to tremble. Only four, she knew already that her father's lap was the most dangerous place in the world.

"Which hand did you use to draw the angel?" His booming voice washed over her ears like a flood across the land.

Not knowing enough to lie, she held up her left.

"Deceit and damnation arise from the left," he said. "You are not to use it to write or draw with ever again. Do you understand?"

Terrified, she nodded.

"I will not let evil work through a child of mine." He looked at her again, as if expecting something.

She did not know what he wanted. "Yes, sir."

Then he lifted his knee and snapped her left arm across it like a piece of wood.

Erin gripped the site of the fracture, still feeling that pain. She pressed hard enough to know the bone had healed offset. Her father had not allowed her to visit a doctor. If prayer could not heal a wound, or save a baby's life, then it was not God's will, and they must submit always to God's will.

When she fled her father's tyranny, she spent a year teaching herself to write with her left hand instead of her right, anger and determination cut into every stroke of the pen. She would not let her father shape who she became. And so far, evil did not seem to have invaded her, although her arm ached when it rained.

"So the Bible was correct." Heinrich drew her out of her reverie. He lifted a handful of sand off the baby's legs and deposited it on the ground outside the trench. "The slaughter happened. And it happened here."

"No." She studied scattered bone fragments, trying to decide where to start. "You're overreaching. We have potential evidence that a slaughter occurred here, but I doubt it has anything to do with the birth of Christ. Historical fact and religious stories often get tangled together. Remember, for archaeological purposes, we must always treat the Bible as a . . ." She struggled to find a noninflammatory word, gave up. "A spiritual interpretation of events, written by someone bent on twisting the facts to suit their ideology. Someone with a religious agenda."

"Instead of an academic one?" Heinrich's German accent grew stronger, a sign that he was upset.

"Instead of an objective agenda. Our ultimate goal—as scientists—is to find tangible evidence of past events instead of relying on ancient stories. To question everything."

Heinrich carefully brushed sand off the little femur. "You don't believe in God, then? Or Christ?"

She scrutinized the bone's rough surface. No new damage. "I believe Christ was a man. That he inspired millions. Do I believe that he turned water into wine? I'd need proof."

She thought back to her First Communion, when she had believed in miracles, believed that she truly drank the blood of Christ. It seemed centuries ago.

"But you are here." Heinrich swept his pale arm around the site. "Investigating a Bible fable."

"I'm investigating a historical event," she corrected. "And I'm here in *Caesarea,* not in *Bethlehem* like the Bible says, because I found evidence that drew me to this site. I am here because of facts. Not faith."

By now, Heinrich had cleared the bottom of the skeleton. They both worked faster than usual, wary that an aftershock might strike at any time.

"A story written on a pot from the first century led us here," she said. "Not the Bible."

After months of sifting through potsherds at the Rockefeller Museum in Jerusalem, she had uncovered a misidentified broken jug that alluded to a mass grave of children in Caesarea. It had been enough to receive the grant that had brought them all here.

"So you are trying to . . . debunk the Bible?" He sounded disappointed.

"I am trying to find out what happened here. Which probably had nothing to do with what the Bible said."

"So you don't believe that the Bible is holy?" Heinrich stopped working and stared at her.

"If there is divinity, it's not in the Bible. It's in each man, woman, and child. Not in a church or coming out of the mouth of a priest."

"But—"

"I need to get brushes." She hauled out of the trench, fighting back her anger, not wanting her student to see it.

When she was halfway to the equipment tent, the sound of a helicopter turned her head. She shaded her eyes and scanned the sky.

The chopper came in fast and low, a massive craft, khaki, with the designation *S-92* stenciled on the tail. What was it doing here? She glared at it. The rotors would blow sand right back onto the skeleton.

She spun around to tell Heinrich to cover the bones.

Before she could speak, a lone Arabian stallion, riderless and ghostly white, bolted across the field from the stables. It would not see the trench. She rushed toward Heinrich, knowing she would be too late to beat the horse to him.

Heinrich must have felt the hoofbeats. He stood just as the horse reached the trench, spooking the rushing animal further. It reared and struck his forehead with a hoof. Heinrich disappeared into the trench.

Behind her, the helicopter powered down.

The stallion edged away from the noise, toward the trench.

Erin circled around the horse. "Easy, boy." She kept her voice low and relaxed. "No one's going to hurt you here."

A large brown eye rolled to stare at her. The horse's chest heaved, his quivering flanks coated in sweat, froth spattering his lips. She had to calm him and keep him from falling into the trench where Heinrich lay motionless.

She stepped between the trench and the horse, talking all the while. When she reached up to stroke his curved neck, the stallion shuddered, but he did not bolt. The familiar smell of horse surrounded her. She drew in a deep breath and exhaled. The animal did the same.

Hoping the horse would follow, she stepped to the side, away from Heinrich. She had to move him someplace safer in case he spooked again.

The stallion moved a step on trembling legs.

Nate came running, followed by Amy and Julia.

Erin held up a hand to stop them.

"Nate," she said in a singsong voice. "Keep everyone back until I get the horse away from Heinrich."

Nate skidded to a stop. The others followed suit.

The horse blew out heavily, and his sweat-stained withers twitched.

She threaded her fingers into his gray mane and led him a few steps away from the trench. Then she nodded to Nate.

A cry drew her attention over her shoulder, to a small robed figure flying across the sand. The man, plainly the horse's handler, came rushing forward.

He dropped a lead over the animal's head, jabbering and gesturing to where the helicopter had landed. Erin got it. The animal didn't like helicopters. She didn't much either. She patted the horse on his withers to say good-bye. The handler led him away.

Amy and Julia had already climbed down next to Heinrich. Julia held one hand to his forehead. Blood coated the side of his face. Julia murmured to Heinrich in German. He didn't answer. Erin held her breath. At least he was still breathing.

Erin joined them. Kneeling down, she gently moved Julia's hand aside and felt his head. Plenty of blood, but the skull seemed intact. She stripped off her bandanna and held it against the wound. Far from sterile, but it was all she had. Warm blood wet her palm.

Heinrich opened his gray eyes, groaning. "It takes a sacrifice. In crushed skulls. This site."

She gave him a tight smile. Two skulls crushed on her watch.

"How do you feel?" she asked.

He muttered something in German through bloodless lips. His eyes lost focus, rolling backward. She had to get him to a doctor.

"Dr. Granger?" A voice with an Israeli accent spoke from behind her. "Please stand at once."

She put Julia's trembling hand over the makeshift bandage and stood, hands in the air. In her experience, people used that tone only when they were armed. She turned very slowly, Heinrich's blood already drying on her palms.

Soldiers. A lot of soldiers.

They stood in a semicircle in front of the trench, dressed in desert sand fatigues, sidearms on their belts, automatic weapons strapped around their shoulders. Eight in all, each standing at attention. They wore gray berets, except for the man in front. His was olive green; obviously their leader. The guns weren't pointed at her.

Yet.

She lowered her hands.

"Dr. Erin Granger." It was a statement, not a question. He didn't sound like he ever asked questions.

"Why are you here?" In spite of her fear, she kept her voice even. "Our permits are in order."

He studied her with eyes like two oiled brown marbles. "You must come with us, Dr. Granger."

She had to take care of Heinrich first. "I'm busy. My student is injured and—"

"I'm Lieutenant Perlman. With Aman. I've been ordered to fetch you."

As if to underline his point, the soldiers raised their weapons a fraction of an inch.

Aman was Israeli military intelligence. That couldn't be good. Anger rose in her chest. They had come to fetch her, and their machine had spooked the horse that hurt Heinrich. Erin kept her voice steady, but it still came out cold. "Fetch me to where?"

"I'm not authorized to say."

The lieutenant did not look like he would be backing down anytime soon, but she could make use of him. "Your helicopter frightened a horse, and it wounded my student." She balled her hands into fists at her sides. "Badly."

He looked down at Heinrich, then inclined his head to one of the soldiers. The man pulled a trauma kit from a pack and climbed into the trench. A medic. That was something. She unclenched her hands and wiped her bloody palms on her jeans.

"I want him airlifted to a hospital," she said. "Then, perhaps, we can talk about other things."

The lieutenant looked down at the medic. The man nodded, looking worried.

That couldn't be good.

"Very well," Perlman said.

He gestured, and his men responded quickly. Two soldiers helped lift Heinrich out of the trench; another two hauled over a stretcher. Once loaded, he was carried toward the helicopter. Julia followed them, sticking close to his side.

Erin drew in a deep breath. A helicopter ride to the hospital was the best chance Heinrich had.

She took Lieutenant Perlman's proffered hand, noticing his strength as he pulled her out of the trench.

Without a word, he turned and headed back toward the helicopter. The remaining soldiers stepped in behind her, indicating that she should follow. She stomped after Perlman. She was being kidnapped from her site at gunpoint.

She wouldn't win this fight, but she would get what information she could from them. "Does this have to do with the earthquake?" she called to Perlman.

The lieutenant glanced back, didn't answer, but she read his face. Her mind filled in the blanks. Earthquakes broke things. But they also uncovered them.

All of which raised another question.

There were plenty of other archaeologists in Israel. What reason could they have to drag her out of her own dig? No ancient treasure warranted this kind of urgency. Archaeologists didn't get shuttled around in military helicopters.

Something was very wrong.

"Why me?" she pressed.

Perlman finally responded. "I can only say that it is a delicate situation, and your expertise has been requested."

"By whom?"

"I could not say."

"If I refuse?"

Perlman's gaze bored into her. "You're a guest of our country. If you refuse to come with us, you'll no longer be a guest of our country. And your friend will *not* be taken to the hospital in our helicopter."

"I think the embassy would not condone this treatment," she bluffed.

His lips twisted into an unconvincing smile. "It was a member of the delegation at the U.S. embassy who recommended you."

She fought to conceal her surprise. So far as she knew, no one in the embassy cared anything about her. Either Perlman was lying, or he knew way more than she did. Regardless, the time for talking was past. She had to get Heinrich to a hospital.

So she continued walking toward the helicopter. The soldiers had dropped into formation around her as if she might bolt like the stallion.

Nate and Amy hurried along behind. Nate looked belligerent, Amy worried.

Erin turned and walked backward, calling out instructions. "Nate, you're in charge until I return. You know what needs to be done."

Nate talked over a soldier's shoulder. "But, Professor—"

"Stabilize the skeleton. And have Amy study the left femur before you jacket it."

Nate pointed toward the helicopter. "Are you sure it's safe to go with them?"

She shook her head. "Contact the embassy the second I'm gone. Confirm that they recommended me. If they didn't, call in the cavalry."

The soldiers didn't miss a step, impassive faces staring straight ahead. Either they didn't speak English, or they weren't worried about her threat. Which could be a good thing or a very bad one.

"Don't go," Nate said.

"I don't think I have a choice," she said. "And neither does Heinrich."

She saw him swallow that truth, then nod.

Lieutenant Perlman beckoned from the open cabin door. "Here, Dr. Granger."

The helicopter's whirling blades began to roar louder as she ducked under them.

She climbed inside the chopper and strapped into the only empty seat. Heinrich lay on a stretcher on the other side of the craft with Julia in a seat next to him. Julia flashed her a shaky smile, and Erin gave her a thumbs-up. Did they even do that in Germany?

As the chopper lifted off, Erin turned to the soldier next to her and pulled back in surprise. He was no soldier. He was a priest. He wore black pants, overhung by an ankle-length hooded cassock, along with black leather gloves, dark sunglasses, and the familiar white collar of the Roman Catholic clergy.

She recoiled. The priest leaned away from her as well, one hand reaching to adjust his hood.

She'd had more than enough squabbles with Catholic priests over the years concerning her archaeological work. But at least his presence lent some credibility to her hope that it really was an archaeological site she was being called to, something religious, something

Christian. The downside was that this priest would probably claim the artifacts before she could see them. If so, she would have been pulled from her site and blood spilled for nothing.

That's not going to happen.

2:57 P.M.

The woman seated beside him smelled of lavender, horse, and blood. Scents as out of place in this modern era as Father Rhun Korza himself.

She offered her hand. He had not intentionally touched a woman in a very long time. Even though dried blood streaked her palm, he had no choice but to take it, grateful that he wore gloves. He steeled himself and shook. Her warm hand felt strong and capable, but it trembled in his. So, he frightened her.

Good.

He dropped her hand and shifted away, seeking to put space between them. He had no wish to touch her again. In fact, he wished she would climb back out of the craft and return to her safe study of the past.

For her own sake as much as his own.

Before receiving his summons, he had been dwelling in deep meditation, in seclusion, ready to forsake the greater world for the beauty and isolation of the Cloister, as was his right. But Cardinal Bernard had not let him stay there. He had pulled Rhun from his meditative cell and sent him on this journey into the world to fetch an archaeologist and search for an artifact. Rhun had expected the archaeologist to be a *man*, but Bernard had chosen a *woman*, and a beautiful one at that.

Rhun suspected what that meant.

He gripped the silver cross at his throat. Metal warmed through his glove.

Above his head rotor blades throbbed like a massive mechanical heart, beating fast enough to burst.

His gaze fell on the second woman. She was German, from her whispered words to the man on the stretcher. Blood streaked her white cotton dress. She gripped the hand of the wounded man, never taking her eyes off his face. The iron smell of his blood blanketed the airborne vehicle.

Rhun closed his eyes, fingered the rosary on his belt, and began a silent Our Father. Vibrations shuddered through his prayer.

He would much rather travel on a mule with a naturally beating heart.

But the blades drowned out more dangerous sounds—the heavy drip of blood from the split scalp to the floor, the quick breathing of the woman next to him, and the faraway neighing of a frightened stallion.

As the vehicle banked, the stench of jet fuel rolled in. Its foreignness stung his nostrils, but he preferred it to the scent of blood. It gave him the strength to let himself look at the injured man, at the blood running in threads along the metal floor, then dropping out toward the harsh stone landscape below.

This late in the fall, the sun set early, in less than two hours. He could ill afford a delay to aid a wounded man. Much rested on his shoulders.

Out of the corner of his eye, he studied the woman next to him. She wore threadbare denim jeans and a dusty white shirt. Her intelligent brown eyes traveled once around the cabin, seeming to assess each man. Those eyes skittered past him as if he were not there. Did she fear him as a man, as a priest, or as something else?

He tightened his gloved hands on his knees and meditated. He must purge thoughts of her from his mind. He would need all his holy strength for the task ahead. Perhaps, after it was complete, he could return to the Sanctuary, to the Cloister, and rest undisturbed.

Suddenly the woman brushed him with her elbow. He tensed, but did not jump. His meditation had steadied him. She leaned forward to check on her colleague, her fine eyebrows drawn down in worry. The man would not recover, but Rhun could not tell her so. She would never believe him. What did a simple priest know of wounds and blood?

Far more than she could ever imagine.

3:03 P.M.

Erin's cell phone vibrated in her pocket. She drew it out and held it next to her leg to conceal it from Lieutenant Perlman. She doubted he would want her texting from the helicopter.

Amy wrote her:

"Hey, Prof. Can u talk?"

The lieutenant seemed to be looking the other way.

Erin typed.

"Go."

Amy's answer came back so quickly she must have been typing while Erin was thinking.

"Took a look at that skeleton's femur."

"And?"

"It had gnaw marks."

That confirmed Erin's earlier assessment. She had noted what looked like teeth marks on the bone. She struggled to type as the helicopter jolted.

"Not uncommon . . . Lots of desert predators out here."

Amy's response was slow, her answer long to type out:

"But the bite marks match what I saw on that dig in New Guinea. Same dentition. Same pattern of gnawing."

Erin's heart sped up, knowing the subject of Amy's last dig: the headhunters of New Guinea. That could mean only one thing . . .

But cannibalism? Here?

If true, the story behind this mass grave of children might be even worse than the tale of Herod's massacre. But it still seemed unlikely. The newborn's skeleton had been fairly large, with no obvious signs of malnutrition that might indicate a famine, which might warrant such depraved hunger.

"Evidence?"

she typed back.

"4 incisors. Continuous arch. It was HUMANS who gnawed that baby's bones."

Erin lifted her thumb, momentarily too shocked to type—then Lieutenant Perlman suddenly snatched the phone out of her grip, making her jump. He switched it off.

"No outside contact," he yelled.

She swallowed her anger and crossed her arms, submitting. No point getting further on his bad side.

Yet.

The lieutenant dropped the phone into his shirt pocket. She missed it already.

She was relieved when the helicopter touched down at the pad at Hillel Yaffe Medical Center. Perlman had kept his word. White-suited hospital personnel sprinted toward them. She'd heard that they had a good trauma team, and she was grateful to see such a rapid response. She reached to unbuckle her harness, but Perlman covered her hand.

"No time," he warned.

His men had already climbed out and unfastened the stretcher. Julia stood next to it on the ground, still holding Heinrich's fingers. She lifted her free hand to wave to Erin. Heinrich's chest rose and fell as they wheeled him off. Still breathing. She hoped that would be true the next time she saw him.

As soon as the soldiers were back on board, the chopper lifted fast and hard.

She turned her gaze from the hospital to stare at the spread of desert beyond Caesarea as her thoughts moved from her anxiety about Heinrich to another gnawing worry.

Where are they taking me?

4

October 26, 3:12 P.M., IST
Tel Aviv, Israel

Bathory Darabont stood poised in the shadows, hidden on a second-story landing above the hotel. She stared down to the tiled fountain that dominated the hotel lobby, water splashing from the wall into a half-round basin of monstrous green marble. She guessed the water was two or three feet deep. She stroked the ornate brass railing as she calculated the drop from where she stood.

Twenty-five feet. Probably survivable. Definitely intriguing.

The man next to her rattled on. With his masses of curly dark hair, huge brown eyes, and straight nose, he looked like he had just stepped out of a fresco depicting Alexander the Great. Of course, he knew that he was beautiful and rich, some distant prince of a distant land—and that made him accustomed to getting his own way.

This bored her.

He strove to talk her right out of her designer silk dress and into his bed, and she wasn't necessarily averse to that, but she was more interested in action than in preliminaries.

She pushed back her waist-length red hair with one languid white hand, watching his eyes linger on the black palm tattooed across her throat. An unusual mark, and more dangerous than it looked.

"How about a bet, Farid?"

His brown eyes returned to her silver ones. He really did have the most amazing long dark lashes. "A bet?"

"Let's see who can jump into that fountain." She pointed one long finger down into the atrium. "Winner takes all."

"The stakes?" He flashed her a perfect smile. He looked like he might like games.

She did, too, and held out one slender wrist. "If you win, I give you my bracelet."

The diamond bracelet cost fifty thousand dollars, but she had no intention of losing it. She never lost.

He laughed. "I don't need a bracelet."

"And I give it to you in *your* hotel room."

Farid looked over the railing and fell silent. She liked him better silent.

"If I win . . ." She stepped so close to him that her silk dress brushed his warm leg. "I get your watch—and you give it to me in *my* room."

A Rolex; she suspected it cost about the same as her bracelet. She had no need of it either. But the jump would cut short the flirting and might lead to more inspired and passionate lovemaking than Farid was probably capable of.

"How can I lose?" he said.

She gave him a long and languorous kiss. He responded well. She slipped her phone into his pocket, fingers tracing a metal knife that she found there. Farid was not so defenseless as he appeared. She remembered her mother's words.

Even a white lily casts a black shadow.

When she drew back, Farid slid both hands down her silk-covered back. "How about we skip the jump?"

She laughed. "Not on your life."

Grasping the cold railing with both hands, she vaulted over the side.

She opened into a swan dive, falling, arms out straight and back arched. Her dress fluttered against her thighs. For a moment she thought that she had misjudged the depth and the fall would kill her, and in that moment she felt more relief than fear. She hit the water flat, distributing her weight.

The violent slap stole her breath.

For a second, she floated facedown in the cool blue, breasts and belly stinging, her unsettled blood finally quiet. Then she rolled over, pushing her now transparent bodice out of the water while dipping her head to slick back her hair, laughing brightly.

When she stood up, the entire lobby stared. A few onlookers applauded, as if she were part of a show.

Far above, Farid gaped.

She climbed out of the fountain. Water streamed from her body and spread across the expensive woolen carpet. She bowed to Farid, who returned the gesture with a slight nod, followed by the dramatic unbuckling of his Rolex and the lift of an eyebrow, conceding she had won the bet.

Minutes later, they stood outside her door. She shivered slightly in her damp clothes in the air-conditioned hallway. Farid's bare palm, as soft as silk but as hot as a coal, ran up her back under her thin dress, raising an entirely different shiver. She sighed and glanced darkly toward him, craving the heat of his flesh far more than any companionship he could offer.

She retrieved her key card, the newly won Rolex dangling from her wrist.

As she unlocked the door and pushed it open, her phone buzzed, but it came from Farid's pants. She turned, slipped her hand into his pocket, and tugged it free.

"How did that get there?" he asked, surprised.

"I put it there when I kissed you." She smiled at him. "So it wouldn't get wet. I knew you'd never jump."

A wrinkle of hurt pride blemished his perfect forehead.

Standing in the doorway, she checked her phone. It was a text message, an important one from the name of the sender. She went cold all over, beyond anything a shiver could warm through or a heated touch could soothe.

No more time for play.

"Who is Argentum?" Farid asked, reading over her shoulder.

Oh, Farid . . . a woman likes to keep her secrets.

It was why she traveled under so many false names, like the one she used to book this room.

"It appears I have some pressing business to attend," she said, stepping through the doorway and turning. "I must bid you good-bye here."

A dark disappointment showed in his face, a flicker of anger.

He abruptly shoved her deeper into the room, following close. He grabbed her roughly and shoved her against the wall, kicking the door shut.

"I'll say when we're finished," he said huskily.

She lifted an eyebrow. So there *was* some hidden fire in Farid after all.

Smiling up at him, she tossed her phone to the bed, pulled him even closer, their lips almost touching. She swung him around so he was now the one with his back to the wall. She reached to his pants, which widened his dark smile. But he mistook what she searched for—she removed his hidden knife instead.

She opened it one-handed, and with a quick thrust, she buried it in his eye socket, punching it up and back. She kept hold of his body, pressed against the wall, feeling his body's heat through her thin clothes, knowing that warmth would quickly expire, snuffed out with his life. She savored that waning heat, held him tightly as the death tremors shook through him.

As they ended, she finally let go.

His body sagged to the ground, his life spent.

She left him there, stepped to the bed, and sat down, crossing a long leg. She retrieved her phone and opened the attached image file that had been sent to her.

On the screen, a single photo appeared, of a piece of paper covered with a strange script. The handwriting stemmed from another time, better suited to being scratched on parchment with a sliver of bone. More code than language, it was written in an archaic form of Hebrew.

As part of her training, she had studied ancient languages at Oxford and now read ancient Greek, Latin, and Hebrew as easily as her native Hungarian. She deciphered the message carefully, ensuring she made no mistake. Her breath quickened as she worked.

A quake destroyed Masada.
A great death came with it,
brutal enough to mark Its possible unearthing.

She brought a hand to her white throat, fingertips brushing the mark that blackened her skin, thinking of the night she received it and became forever tainted. Her blood burned still.

She read on.

Go. Search for

כתב דמא

A Knight has been dispatched to retrieve it.
Let nothing stop you.
You must not fail.

She stared at the phrase in Herodian Aramaic. The Belial had waited long for this message.

Her lips shaped impossible words, not daring to speak them aloud.

כתב דמא

The Book of Blood

A surge of unfamiliar fear pulsed through her fingertips.

He whom she served had long suspected the Jewish mountain stronghold might hide the precious book. Along with a handful of other sites. It was one of the reasons she had been sequestered here, deep within the Holy Land. A few hours' distance from dozens of possible ancient landmarks.

But was he correct? Did Masada mark the true resting place for the Book of Blood? Once she and her team revealed their presence, they could not be hidden again. Was this enough of a sign to warrant that risk?

She knew the answer to only the last question.

Yes.

If the book were truly unearthed, it offered a singular opportunity—a chance to end the world and forge a new one in His name. Although she had been trained from a young age, she had never truly expected this day to arrive.

Preparations must be made.

She pressed the second number on her speed dial and pictured the large muscular man who would answer on the first ring.

Her second in command, Tarek.

"Your wish?" His deep voice still bore traces of a Tunisian accent, although he had not spoken with a countryman for a lifetime.

"Wake the others," she ordered. "At long last, the hunt begins."

5

October 26, 3:38 P.M., IST
Airborne above Israel

Erin longed to be on the ground, away from the heat and noise and dust, and from the priest. She was too hot herself, and the priest must have it worse in his long cassock and hood. She tried to remember when Catholic priests stopped wearing hoods. Before she was born. Between his hood and his sunglasses, she saw only his chin, square with a cleft in the middle.

A movie-star chin, but he made her uneasy. As far as she could tell, he had not moved in more than half an hour. The helicopter dropped a few feet, but her stomach stayed up in the air. She swallowed. She wished that she had thought to bring water. The soldiers didn't seem to have any, but they didn't seem to care. The priest didn't either.

Monotonous arid landscape slipped by below. Since the helicopter left the hospital, it had been flying east and north, toward the Sea of Galilee. Every minute of flight changed their possible destination, but Erin had lost interest in trying to guess where she might land.

They closed in on a familiar flat-topped mountain that climbed steeply out of the desert. She made out the white finger of the ramp that the Romans had built to finally breach its walls.

Masada.

It hadn't even been on her list of possible sites. Masada had been thoroughly excavated in the sixties. Nothing new had come out of the site in decades. Tourists had been tramping all over it.

Perhaps the earthquake had uncovered something nearby. A Roman camp? Or the remains of the nine hundred Jewish rebels? Only thirty or so bodies had ever been recovered. They had been reburied with full military honors in 1969.

She craned her neck to get a better view. Unbroken sand stretched in all directions. No sign of activity around the base, but she spotted a large helicopter on the summit. That must be where she was headed. She sat straighter, eager to discover what required her immediate attention.

The priest moved almost imperceptibly, a slight shift of his handsome chin. So he still lived. She had forgotten to take him into account while guessing their destination. Though primarily a Jewish landmark, Masada was also home to the ruins of a Byzantine church, circa AD 500. The earthquake might have exposed Christian relics. But, if the Israelis planned to turn the relics over to the priest, why bring her in the first place? Something didn't add up.

The helicopter descended toward the summit, kicking sand through the open doorway. She squinted against the hot grit and cupped her hands around her eyes. She should have brought protective goggles. And water. And dinner. And a backup phone.

She wished Perlman hadn't taken her cell phone. Surely her students had reported in by now to let her know Heinrich's condition. Otherwise . . . well, she didn't want to think about otherwise. He had been at the site as her grad student. Whatever happened to him was her responsibility.

Erin brought her pinkie finger and thumb to her ear to pantomime the word *phone*.

Perlman fished it out of his pocket. He yelled over the noise. "Keep it off."

"Yes, sir." At this decibel level, he wouldn't hear the sarcasm.

He handed the phone to her, and she stuck it into her back pocket. The second he turned his back, she intended to turn it on and check her messages.

The summit came into view.

She leaned out, searching below, stunned. It took her a thundering moment to understand what she was seeing.

Masada was . . . *gone*.

The walls, the buildings, the cisterns were piles of rocks. The casemate wall that had surrounded the fortress for thousands of years had been completely destroyed. Rubble stood in place of the columbarium and synagogue. The mountain had practically been cleaved in two. She had never seen such devastation up close.

The pilot slowed the engines, and they whined out in a lowering pitch as the skids scraped the top of the mountain and the helicopter settled to a stop.

She strained to see through the cloud of dust surrounding them. Black rectangles had been lined up near the edge of the plateau. They were too regularly shaped to be natural. Two people dropped a new one next to the others.

Body bags. Full ones.

Masada was one of the most popular tourist sites in Israel. It had probably been teeming with tourists when the quake struck. How many more lives had the cursed mountain claimed? Her stomach lurched again, but this time not from the helicopter.

A cool hand fell on her shoulder, and she jumped. The priest. He, too, must have noted the dead. Maybe she had been wrong all along. Maybe he was here to perform Last Rites or look after the dead at the behest of the Church.

She felt sick at the thought of how excited she had been a few minutes before. This was no archaeological site. It was a disaster scene. She wished that she were back in Caesarea.

Lieutenant Perlman jumped out and barked orders in Hebrew. Men spilled from both sides of the chopper and headed toward the body bags. They must have been summoned to collect the bodies. No wonder the officer had been so tight-lipped about it. She didn't envy him his task.

The priest sprang out of the helicopter, graceful as a desert cat. His long cassock swirled in the rotor wash. He pulled his hood closer to his face and turned his head from side to side as if searching.

She fumbled with sweat-slick hands to unclip her safety harness. The floor seemed to lurch when she stood. She steadied herself against the seat back and took a few deep breaths. The Israelis had had a reason to bring her here, and she'd best calm down and find out what it was.

The priest turned and offered her help, gloved palm upturned in an old-fashioned, almost courtly gesture. It was certainly nothing like the way Lieutenant Perlman had hauled her out of the trench before she started this journey.

Grateful for the support, she took his hand. He released it the instant her sneakers touched the limestone.

The wind blew back his hood, revealing a pale face with high cheekbones and thick dark hair. A handsome man, for a priest.

"*Tot ago attero . . . ,*" he murmured as he pulled his black hood back over his head, masking his face again. She translated his Latin words. *So many lost.*

The priest bowed before striding off purposefully, as if he, at least, knew why he was here.

She shielded her eyes and looked at the sun, already low in the sky. The sun set in about an hour. If they did not get the bodies removed by then, jackals would arrive. In spite of the heat, she shivered.

She forced her eyes to look at the ruined site, beyond the body bags, to figures dragging corpses from the rubble. Figures wearing sky-blue biohazard suits.

Biohazard suits for an earthquake?

Before she could ask why such a precaution was necessary, a tall soldier strode forward. He wasn't wearing a biohazard suit. Comforting.

He headed straight for her. Even without the flag sewn on the shoulder patch of his khaki jacket, she would have known that he was American. Everything about him said apple pie: from his wheat-blond hair, shorn into an army standard crew cut, to his square-jawed face and broad shoulders. Clear blue eyes fixed on her, taking her measure in a single tired breath. She liked him. He seemed competent, and not inured to the tragedy he was dealing with. But what was the American military doing on an Israeli mountaintop?

"Dr. Erin Granger?"

So, he did expect her. Should she be relieved or even more worried? "Yes, I'm Dr. Granger."

The soldier looked past her shoulder toward the priest, who headed away through the rubble. One eyebrow rose. "I wasn't apprised of a priest coming here," he said to Lieutenant Perlman.

The Israeli waved to two of his men and pointed to the priest before answering, "The Vatican requested Father Korza's presence.

A Catholic tourist party was here during the quake. It included a cardinal's nephew."

That explained the priest, Erin thought. One tragic mystery solved. The soldier seemed to agree with her assessment and faced her again.

"Thank you for coming, Dr. Granger. We need to hurry." He headed away from the helicopter, aiming toward the worst of the destruction.

She jogged to keep up with his long legs, trying to focus on him and on her footing, not on the body bags. This morning these people had been as alive as she. She talked to keep from thinking. "I was pulled from a dig without a word of explanation. What's going on here?"

"That sounds familiar." His lips slipped into a tired grin. "I was in Afghanistan yesterday, Jerusalem a few hours ago." He halted, wiped his palm on his sand-colored T-shirt, and stuck out his hand. "Let's start over. Sergeant Jordan Stone, Ninth Ranger Battalion. We've been called in by the Israelis to help out here."

His grip was warm and firm without being aggressive, and she immediately noticed a white line on his left hand, where a wedding band should go. Embarrassed that she had focused on that detail, she quickly dropped his hand. "Dr. Erin Granger," she repeated.

He started walking. "Don't mean to be rude, Doc, but if you want any archaeology left to study, we need to hurry. We've been having aftershocks."

She kept pace. "Why the biohazard suits? Was this a chemical or biological attack?"

"Not exactly."

Before she could ask what that meant, the sergeant stopped at the edge of a tumble of limestone that blocked the view forward. He turned fully to her.

"Doc, I need you to brace yourself."

4:03 P.M.

Jordan doubted that Dr. Granger had ever seen anything like this. The path led through a maze of rubble and crushed bodies: some covered, others staring blindly at the unforgiving sun, adults and children. But, short of putting blinders on her like a horse, he saw no way to protect her. She'd have to walk through it to get to the temporary base camp set up at the edge of the chasm that the quake had opened.

He sidestepped a body covered with a blue tarp. He didn't allow himself to be distracted by the dead; he had seen enough corpses in Afghanistan. Later tonight, privately, he might drink too much Jack Daniel's to keep him from thinking too much. Until then, he had to remain in control of both his team and his feelings.

The archaeologist was a bit of a surprise. Not that she was a woman. He had no issues working with women. Some were competent, some weren't; no different from any man. But why had an archaeologist been sent to the site to begin with?

He wiped sweat off his forehead with the back of his wrist. Dusk closed in, but the temperature still crested ninety degrees. He took a deep breath, tasting hot desert air mixed with the copper tang of blood. Then he noticed Dr. Granger was no longer behind him.

He waited for her to struggle over, saw glints of sympathy and compassion in her eyes as she searched the rubble, studying bodies, mourning deaths. She wouldn't soon forget today.

He walked back. "You okay?"

"As long as I keep moving. Stop too long, and you'll be carrying me the rest of the way." She offered him a hollow smile—it seemed to take a gargantuan effort.

He walked, more slowly than before, trying to pick a path that kept them away from the scattered bodies. "Most victims died instantly. Chances are they didn't feel a thing."

It was a lie. And she only had to look at the bodies to know it.

She raised a skeptical eyebrow, but she didn't call him on it, which he appreciated.

She stared at a young woman's body. Blisters covered her face and dried blood crusted around her mouth and eyes. Not your typical earthquake victim. "Not all these bodies were crushed. What happened to the others, Sergeant?"

"Call me Jordan." He hesitated. He bet she'd call him on it if he lied this time. Better to tell her as little as possible than to have her guessing. "We're still testing, but from the initial gas chromatograph readouts, we suspect they were exposed to a derivative of sarin."

She tripped over a stone brick, kept going. He admired her

grit. "Nerve gas? Is that why the American military is involved?"

"The Israelis asked for our help because we're experts in this field. So far, we haven't confirmed the nature of the gas. It most closely resembles sarin. Rapid effects, quick dispersion. By the time the first responders arrived on Masada, the gas was already inert."

A bit of luck there, Jordan thought, or the casualty count would have been much higher. The Israelis had thought the earthquake was their biggest problem. The first responders hadn't donned suits until they found the first bodies.

"Who would do that?" Her voice carried the shocked tone of one unused to confronting everyday evil firsthand. He envied her.

"I wish I had an answer for you."

Even the gas was a mystery. It had none of the markers of a modern, weaponized agent. In breaking down the gas's essential components, his team had found bizarre anomalies. Like cinnamon. Who the hell puts a spice into a nerve agent? His team was still trying to track down several other equally odd and elusive ingredients.

It unsettled him not to know the gas's true origin. That was his job, and he was usually damn good at it. He hated to think he'd found a previously unidentified nerve gas with this kind of killing power, especially in the Middle East. Neither his superiors nor the Israelis would be happy to hear that.

He had to step over a body bag. He reached for Dr. Granger's hand, both to steady her and as a gesture of reassurance. Her grip was more muscular than he expected. She must be lifting more than pencils.

"Was this a terrorist attack?" Her voice remained firm, but he felt the fine tremor in her arm. Best to keep her talking.

"That's what the Israelis initially thought." He released her hand. "But the toxic exposure coincided exactly with the earthquake. We suspect old toxic canisters might be buried underground here, and the tremor cracked them open."

Her brow furrowed. "Masada is a sacred archaeological site. I can't see the Israelis dumping anything like that here."

He shrugged. "That's what my team and I are here to find out."

He had his orders: find the source and safely remove or detonate any remaining canisters.

He and the doctor walked a few steps in silence. He heard a

thump as someone dropped a body bag into a helicopter. They'd better work faster. Night would fall soon, and he didn't want to waste a man on jackal patrol.

He noted that the doctor's eyes had grown glassy and wide, her breathing harder. He needed to keep her talking. "Almost to camp."

"Were there any survivors?"

"One. A boy." He gestured toward the mobile P3 containment lab, the billowing plastic tent where the teenager was being held.

"Was he here alone?" she asked.

"With his parents."

The boy allegedly inhaled several large gulps of the chemical agent and survived. He had described the gas as a burnt reddish orange with a sweet, spicy smell to it. No modern nerve gas fit that description.

Jordan glanced back to her. "His parents didn't make it."

"I see," Erin said quietly.

He stared across the rubble to the containment tent. Through the clear plastic walls, Jordan watched the priest kneel next to the boy. He was glad to see someone with the kid. But what priestly words could the man come up with to comfort him?

Suddenly his own job didn't seem so hard.

"Is that your camp?" She pointed in front of him to a makeshift canvas lean-to pitched at the edge of the fissure.

Camp was a generous description. "Be it ever so humble."

He spared the fissure another glance. It cut through the ground like a giant scar, five yards wide, perhaps a hundred long. Even though a simple earthquake created it, it felt unnatural.

"Is that a mass spectrometer?" the archaeologist asked as they reached the site.

He couldn't help but grin at the surprise on her face. "Didn't think they'd let us grunts work with such ivory-tower toys?"

"No . . . it's just . . . well . . ."

He liked watching her stutter. Everybody assumed that if you wore a uniform you had checked your brain at the recruiter's office. "We just bang on it with rocks, Doc, but it seems to work."

"I'm sorry," she said. "I didn't mean it like that. And please call me Erin. 'Doc' makes me feel like a pediatrician."

"Good enough." He aimed for the tent. "Almost there, Erin."

Two of his men huddled under the meager shelter.

One stood near the computer, sucking hard on a canteen. The other sat in front of the monitor, fiddling with joysticks that guided the team's remote-operated vehicle. The little robot had been lowered by its tether into the crevasse an hour ago.

As he led her into camp, both men turned. Each gave him a brief nod but took a far longer look at the attractive blond doctor.

Jordan introduced her, emphasizing her title.

The freckled young man returned his attention to his joysticks.

Jordan gestured at him. "Dr. Granger, that's our computer jockey, Corporal Sanderson, and the man over there drinking all our water is Specialist Cooper."

The husky black man snapped on a pair of latex gloves. A dozen bloodstained pairs filled the nearby garbage can.

"I'd stay and chat, but I gotta get back to cleanup duty." Cooper looked to Jordan. "Where you hiding the extra batteries? McKay's camera is almost dead, and we have to get everyone photographed before we bag 'em."

Erin winced. She went pale again. Being in-country for so long, Jordan realized how easy it was to forget the sheer horror of what surrounded him every day.

Not much he could do for her right now. Or the bodies outside. "Blue pack, right pocket."

Cooper dug a lithium ion battery from the zipper compartment.

"Damn it!" Sanderson swore, drawing their attention.

"What's wrong?" Jordan asked.

"The rover is stuck again."

Cooper rolled his eyes and left the tent.

The corporal frowned at the image on the color monitor like it was a video game he was about to lose.

Erin leaned over his shoulder and stared at the four monitors, each displaying footage from one of the ROV's cameras. "Is that from inside the crevasse?"

"Yeah, but the robot's jammed up tight."

The screen displayed the reason for Sanderson's frustration. The rover had wedged into a crack. Fallen grit and pebbles obscured two cameras. Sanderson pressed the sticks and the tank treads spun ineffectively, kicking up more debris. "Army piece of crap!"

The *equipment* wasn't the problem. The ROV was state-of-the-art, packed with enough sensing and radar instruments to detect a mouse farting in a warehouse. The problem was that Sanderson hadn't yet mastered the art of manipulating the dual joysticks. Jordan couldn't run them either.

Erin glanced at him, eyes curious. "Is that an ST-20? I've logged hundreds of hours on one. Could I give it a shot?"

Might as well give her something to do. Sanderson didn't look like he'd get the robot out. Plus Jordan respected anyone who was willing to jump in and help. "Sure."

Sanderson lifted his hands in obvious disgust and rolled his chair out of the way. "Be my guest. The only thing I haven't tried doing is crawling down that hole and kicking it."

Erin stood where Sanderson's chair had just been and took both joysticks like she knew what she was doing. She alternated between the front and rear controls, inching the ROV forward and backward much like she was trying to parallel-park.

"I tried that," Sanderson said. "It's not going to—"

The ROV abruptly pulled out of the crack. Jordan saw Erin smother a quick smile of victory, and respected her all the more for trying to spare Sanderson's feelings.

Sanderson stood and put his hands on his hips. "Dude! You're making me look bad in front of my CO."

Then he smiled and pushed his chair behind her like it was a throne. Once she got settled, she looked up at Jordan. "What are we looking for?"

"Our team's been commissioned to find the source of the gas."

"Let me guess," she said with a true smile. "I'm here to assure the Israeli government that you don't destroy any millennia-old artifacts in the process?"

Jordan matched her smile. "Something along those lines."

He didn't take it any further than that, but her presence here was at the request of Israeli intelligence, not the antiquities department. He wasn't sure why yet. And he hated unsolved mysteries.

All eyes were on the monitors as she steered the ROV over a pile of rocks.

"What are you doing in Israel anyway?" Sanderson asked her.

"I have a team digging in Caesarea," she said. "Routine stuff."

Jordan suspected by the tone of her voice that it wasn't routine. Interesting.

The rover slid down a rocky outcropping, then entered what appeared to be a straight passageway.

"Look at the walls." She rotated the rover's cameras. "Sharp-edged chipping."

"So?" Jordan prompted.

"This tunnel is man-made. Dug out by hand and chisel."

"Way down there? At the heart of the mountain?" He stepped closer to her. "Who do you think dug it out? The Jewish rebels who died here?"

"Maybe." She leaned away from him. Personal space issues. He moved back a fraction. "Or the Byzantine monks who lived on the mountain centuries later. Without more evidence, it's impossible to say. I'm guessing this little guy might be the first one down this passage in a very long time."

The ROV climbed over a pile of rubble, halogen headlamps painting the pitch-black crevasse sickly white.

"Damn," Erin said.

"What is it?" Jordan asked.

She turned the rover fully to the right to show a pile of broken stones.

"And?" To Jordan, it didn't look that different from any other pile of rocks.

"Look at the top." She traced the image on the monitor with her finger. "That was a tunnel, but it's collapsed."

"So has a lot of stuff," Sanderson put in. "Why is that a big deal?"

"Look at the sides," she said. "Those are fairly modern drill marks."

Jordan leaned forward excitedly. "Which means?"

"It means that someone cut their way into this tunnel sometime in the last hundred years or so." Erin sighed. "And probably stole anything of value."

"Maybe *they* left the gas." Jordan wasn't sure why he felt relieved that it might be a modern nerve gas and not an ancient one, but he did.

She turned the rover forward again, and it rolled down the path, eventually reaching an open area.

"Stop there," Jordan said. "What's this place?"

"Looks like an underground storage chamber." Erin turned the rover around to get a look at the empty room. No broken canisters yet.

Focusing on his corporal, Jordan asked, "How are the readings?"

Sanderson hunched over a neighboring monitor. He might have trouble piloting the ROV, but the kid knew his instrumentation. "Plenty of secondary breakdown products. No active agent. Still, these are by far the hottest spikes I've seen here. I'd say that chamber is the source of the gas."

A camera angled up to display an arched ceiling.

"That looks like a church," Sanderson said.

Erin shook her head. "More likely a subterranean temple or tomb. The building style is ancient." She touched the screen, as if that would help her feel the stone.

"What is that box?" Jordan asked.

"I think it's a sarcophagus, but I can't be certain until I get closer. The light doesn't go that far."

She sent the ROV forward, but it stopped. She pushed on both joysticks, then let go with an impatient sigh.

"Stuck again?" Jordan asked. They were so close.

"End of the line," she said. "Literally. That's as far as the ROV's tether can reach."

She left the camera pointed at the sarcophagus. "Definitely appears to be a burial container. If so, somebody important must be interred there."

"Important enough to booby-trap the chamber?" That might explain it.

"It's possible, but Egyptians—not Jews—were notorious for engineering elaborate traps." She rubbed her lower lip. "It doesn't make sense."

"Nothing does here." Sanderson snorted. "Like cinnamon-scented nerve gas."

She swiveled her chair around. "What?"

Jordan scowled at Sanderson, then admitted what they'd found. "One of the anomalies about this gas. We've detected traces of cinnamon in it."

"Well, that makes *some* sense with the tomb."

"How so?" It didn't make any sense to Jordan.

"Cinnamon was a rare spice during ancient times," she lectured. "For the rich, it was burned in funeral rites as a scent favored by

God. It's mentioned multiple times in the Bible. Moses was commanded to use it when preparing an anointing oil."

"So the cinnamon is probably a contaminant?" Jordan was grateful for the information. All he knew about cinnamon was that he liked it on French toast.

"The concentration is too high in the gas residue to be just a contaminant," Sanderson piped up.

"What else can you tell me about the ancient uses for cinnamon?" Jordan asked.

"If I'd known there would be a quiz, I'd have studied." Erin offered a soft smile; its warmth caught him off guard. "Let's see, they used it as a digestive aid. Stopping colds. As a mosquito repellent."

"Research it," Jordan ordered. He strode to stand behind Sanderson, as jazzed as if he'd downed a triple espresso.

Sanderson's fingers flew across the keyboard. "On it."

"What?" she asked. "What did I do?"

"Maybe solved part of my problem," Jordan said. "Most mosquito repellents are around two chemical bonds away from nerve gas. The first nerve gas—"

The ground gave a violent shake. Erin's chair rolled backward, threatening to topple. Jordan held it steady as the canvas lean-to swayed, and the metal of the scaffolding creaked in protest.

She tensed as if to jump out of her seat, but he pressed her back in place. "Safer if you ride the aftershock out here," Jordan said.

He didn't add that there was no safe place on the damaged plateau. It wouldn't take much shaking to split the entire mesa in half. The shock died away. "All right, the time for window shopping is over." He turned to Sanderson. "Are you sure there's no active gas in that chamber?"

Sanderson bent over his console, and after a moment straightened. "None, sir. Not a single molecule."

"Good. Fetch Cooper and McKay and alert Perlman. We gear up and head down in five."

The doctor rose as if she expected to go, too. He shook his head. "I'm sorry. You're going to have to stay topside until we secure the chamber."

She scowled. "You pulled me away from my site to come here. I'm not going to—"

"I'm responsible for the four soldiers in my unit. That responsibility isn't one I take lightly, Dr. Granger. There is a probable source of deadly nerve gas down there. I will not have a civilian casualty on my conscience as well."

"Back to 'Dr. Granger,' are we?" Her enunciation was suddenly precise. She reminded him of his mother. "What exactly were your standing orders regarding me, Sergeant Stone?"

"As I told you before, to ensure the integrity of the site." He kept his tone even and polite. He didn't have time to deal with an angry academic who wanted to hurl herself into danger.

"How can I ensure that integrity from up here?"

"You already said the only thing in there was a sarcophagus—"

"I said that's all I could see from up here. But what about what's *inside* the sarcophagus, Sergeant Stone?"

Her tone was a couple degrees frostier than a minute before. He rallied. "I don't much care what's inside it, Doctor. I—"

"You should care. Because it's open."

He stepped back in surprise. "What?"

She tapped the screen with her fingernail, showing a spot on the picture relayed by the ROV. "Right there. That's the lid. On its side next to the sarcophagus. Someone must have broken the seal and lifted it off."

He wished she hadn't seen that. It made his life a lot more complicated.

She lowered her voice. "We have no idea what might be in there. The body of a Jewish king. An intact copy of the Torah. Masada is a treasured historical site to the Jewish people. If anything gets damaged . . ."

He opened his mouth to protest. Instead he took a deep breath and let it out slowly. She was right. The Israelis would have his head if his team made the slightest mistake. Damn it. "There might be intact canisters of gas down there. If so, they could get broken open by an aftershock at any time. And we end up like the people you saw outside."

She blanched, then straightened her back. "I understand the consequences, Sergeant."

He doubted that she did. "Have you rappelled before?"

"Of course," she said. "More times than I can count."

He held her gaze. "I'm assuming you can count higher than one?"

She grinned. "I can count higher than that. Maybe even to a hundred."

He relaxed. At least getting her down there wouldn't be a problem. "As of now, you are under my command. When I say 'jump'—"

She put on a serious face. "I ask how high. I got it."

He touched his earpiece. "Sanderson, get Dr. Granger suited up in a harness. She's going in with us."

6

October 26, 4:42 P.M., IST
Thirty miles from Masada, Israel

Bathory twitched the blackout curtains back into place, concealing the barren desert beyond the airport hangar, wondering if that would be the last she ever saw of the sun.

She took a moment to close her eyes, to center herself. She took a deep breath and pushed back the pain that continually ran through her blood, that dull ache, always there, never forgotten, a reminder of an oath she had taken when she was much younger. The pain marked her as steadfastly as the strangling black palm print tattooed upon her white throat; both had been born at the same time, binding a promise made in blood and sacrifice to serve Him.

Her fingers rose to her throat, to touch the source of pain and promise. It also served one other purpose: *for protection.* It marked her as one of His chosen, elevating her. None could touch her, and all obeyed her.

She forced her arm back down, knowing she must never show a shred of weakness, especially in front of the others.

She turned to face the cavernous dark hangar, lit dimly by pools of light from overhead fixtures in the steel rafters. Her team had already boarded the helicopter, waiting on her.

One of the flight crew clanged shut the rear cargo hatch. Something bumped hard against that closing door, knocking the man back a step, leaving him visibly shaken before he got the latch closed.

She allowed a small smile, reassured. The black mark on her throat was not her only protection.

Hush, she sent forth to that rear hold, *you'll be free soon enough.*

The message was not words, but a casting out of warmth and comfort.

She felt an echo back: *satisfaction, hunger, and a deep well of love.*

Basking in that glow, she adjusted the Kevlar and leather that hugged her form, secured the holstered Sig Sauer in its shoulder harness, and headed across the wide hangar to join her team aboard the helicopter. The chopper's engines were already whining up for liftoff, the noise deafening in the enclosed space.

Ducking under the whirling blades, she climbed into the cabin of the specially designed Eurocopter Panther and slammed the door closed behind her. Inside, it was dark and cool, insulated and whisper-quiet. The medium-size craft would carry ten passengers, along with the additional six hundred pounds of payload secured in the rear hold.

But it was no ordinary chopper. Stealth modifications made it run nearly invisibly, and sound-dampened engines made it run quietly. It had also been painted with Israeli colors, camouflaged to fit the region. Except for the cabin windows—which had been painted black, blinding them to the outside.

As she moved to her lone open seat, eyes tracked her. The nine were all seasoned hunters, well-blooded. She read the raw hunger in their eyes, recognizing the ferocity hidden behind their blank stares.

Ignoring them, she sat next to her second in command, Tarek. In the dim cabin, he was merely a darker shadow, and just as cold. She remembered Farid's heat, the touch of his hot hand on her back. It seemed a distant memory now.

She fitted her headphones in place and radioed the pilot. In the blackened craft, he would be navigating by instruments alone, aided by flight-simulator software.

"What's our status?" she asked.

His answer came back tersely. "I've already radioed the proper Israeli security code for access to the summit. They're expecting a cargo helicopter. We'll be skids down there in twenty-two minutes."

She calculated in her head. *Seven minutes after sundown.*

Perfect.

The engines sped up with a muffled roar from outside. She pictured the hangar doors sweeping open overhead, blazing with sunlight. She felt the craft lurch up toward the sun and pictured their craft racing across the hot sands, a dark mote against a fiery sea.

"How many?" Tarek growled.

She knew what he was asking: *what force could they expect to meet them at Masada?* But she also heard the underlying lust in those two words. It cast a flash of excitement across the cabin, like a match dropped into a pool of gasoline.

She answered him, addressing both what was spoken and unspoken.

"Seventeen."

Tarek's face remained in shadows, but she sensed his hard smile, raising the small hairs on the back of her neck, an instinctive response to the presence of a hidden predator.

According to her intelligence, only a small force of soldiers still guarded the summit of the mountain. With the nine at her side and the advantage of surprise, she estimated it would take no more than a couple of minutes to secure the area.

After that, the book must be found.

Her hand tried to drift to her throat again, but she clutched her fingers in her lap.

She could not fail Him.

But there remained one unknown element as she remembered the warning that came with His note:

A Knight has been dispatched to retrieve it.
Let nothing stop you.

She told Tarek that, too.

"Be prepared. A Knight of Christ may also be present."

Tarek stiffened, his shadow becoming a sculpture of black ice. His voice was a quiet hiss, using the ancient name for such a one like a curse.

"*Sanguinist.*"

7

October 26, 4:44 P.M., IST
Masada, Israel

Erin looked furtively around the empty tent. Jordan had told her to wait inside until he came back. That gave her a few minutes alone. She drew out her cell and checked her messages.

A text from Nate.

"Can't reach the embassy. They're swamped because of the quake. U ok?"

Worried that Perlman might walk by, she texted back quickly.

"I'm fine. It's legit. News on Heinrich?"

The screen stayed dark so long that she feared he was away from his phone.

"Nate?"
"Can you call me?"

The text message blurred, and she blinked. She couldn't call him. Someone would hear. She had no doubt Perlman would destroy her phone if he caught her using it again.

"No,"

she texted back.

"Tell me. Now."

Another pause, then,

"Heinrich didn't make it."

Erin collapsed into Sanderson's chair. Heinrich, gone. He had died in a hospital thousands of miles from home because of her. She'd left him alone in the trench to fetch brushes she didn't need just to spare herself an argument. What would she tell his parents? The smell of blood drifted over from the garbage can full of used gloves. She fought down an urge to retch.

"Doc?" Jordan stuck his blond head around the corner. "We're ready for you if—"

He stepped into the tent. "Erin, are you okay?"

She raised her head to look at him. His voice sounded like it came from far away.

"Erin? Did something happen?" He crossed the tent in two quick steps.

She shook her head. If she told him about Heinrich's death, she would break down right here in a tiny canvas tent in the middle of a field of bodies.

He gave her a concerned look.

Not able to match his gaze, she turned to her phone and texted back a response to Nate. She doubted Jordan would care.

"Understood. I will call when I can."

Once done, she pocketed the phone. "It's just my dig," she said, preparing to believe her lie. "It's been years of planning, and there was earthquake damage."

"We'll get you back soon."

"I know." He'd probably think she was crazy for being upset about some old bones buried in dirt. Still, she felt calmer being able to release even a tiny bit of the anguish about Heinrich. Either that or Jordan had a calming effect on her. How else would she have been able to walk through the death she had seen outside the tent? She took one last deep breath.

"I'm ready," she said, standing up.

"Then step this way. We'll get that harness on you."

She followed him to the edge of the fissure, where he handed her a complicated mess of knots and straps. Military issue, it was nothing like what she was used to. She stared at it blankly.

He turned it around. "Step one leg in here. The other there."

He stood behind her and helped her into the harness. His sure hands moved around her body, straightening straps and fastening clips. The harness was on, and her body temperature had risen by what felt like ten degrees. She quickly fastened the clips across her chest.

A helicopter lifted off. She glanced around the plateau. The teenager had gone, along with most of the crew and the body bags. It looked like only a dozen people worked in the lengthening shadows.

Jordan came around to her front. He reached down and tightened straps around her upper thighs in a way both by-the-book formal and incredibly personal. The webbing cinched against her, pulling her toward him. She looked up into his blue eyes, which were darkening as the sun set.

"If there's anything I need to know before we go down there," he said, "now is the time to tell me."

"Nothing." She wanted to stay up here alone among all the bodies even less than she wanted to go down into the hole. "Bad day."

"Sanderson's got a chair warmed up for you." He studied her face. "With the ROV in place, you could monitor our progress from up here."

Summoning up courage she thought she'd lost, she forced a smile. "And let you have all the fun?"

He gave her one more worried look before returning to his men.

On either side, men tossed ropes over the edge. Blue blankets laid along the fissure's lip cushioned the ropes and lessened friction between the rope lines and sharp, broken stone. They seemed to know what they were doing. She double-checked the ropes anyway.

Sanderson stepped up behind her. He wasn't going down, only

helping the others gear up. He passed her something the length and width of a pen.

"Sarge told me to give you an atropine dart," he said. "Best to stick it in your sock."

"What does it do?"

"If you're exposed to the mystery gas, pop the cap and jab yourself in the thigh."

Fear fluttered in her chest at the idea of that. "I thought there was no active gas down there."

"It's just a precaution, but be careful. Stuff's strong. Don't use it unless you *know* you're exposed. Atropine jacks your heart rate through the roof. Strong enough to blow up your ticker if you're not poisoned. Quick, too."

"Shouldn't we be wearing biocontainment suits?"

"Too bulky to rappel in. And the straps would tear the fabric. Don't worry, at the first sign of symptoms—nausea, bleeding—just use the needle. You should live long enough for us to pull you out."

She scrutinized his freckled face to see if he was joking, trying to scare her.

He squeezed her shoulder. "You'll be fine."

She didn't feel *fine*. Breathing a bit faster, she lifted her pant leg and wedged the dart deep into her sock.

Lieutenant Perlman, along with two other soldiers—a young Israeli and an older American—walked up to the fissure. The American had bushy brown hair and carried a satchel over one shoulder. She read the name stenciled on his fatigues: *McKay*.

On his bag were three prominent letters: *EOD*.

He caught her looking. "Explosive Ordnance Disposal. I blow stuff up."

They must be planning on detonating any intact canisters they found down there. She should be more worried, but the shock of Heinrich's death had left her too numb to panic.

McKay held out a hand. She shook it. He was a large man, a few cheeseburgers away from having a gut, and a decade older than the others. She guessed he was in his early forties. He smiled broadly while shaking her hand.

"Best-looking climbing partner I've had in ages." He winked, and she tried to smile back.

He moved to the edge of the fissure as if stepping up to a curb. She stepped next to him and looked down. Shadows obscured the bottom. The fissure was broad enough to rappel down without worry, but she still shivered. The jagged, ugly thing didn't belong on this mountain.

McKay and Cooper secured their rappelling gear to a pair of ropes.

She stepped to a free line and did the same, pulling it tight twice to check.

Another of Jordan's team—a woman named Tyson—knelt beside the crevasse. She had fed a long hose down into the hole. Next to her camouflaged knee rested a gas chromatograph.

"What's the reading, Tyson?" Jordan called.

"Spikes of nitrogen, oxygen, argon." She kept her eyes on her screen. "A trace of everything you'd expect. No bad gases, Sarge."

"Keep monitoring, Corporal." Jordan faced them. "And everyone keep your atropine at the ready."

"What're we waiting for, Sergeant?" Cooper hung over the abyss. His line looked too thin to support his bulk, but his eyes danced with adrenaline. A born climber.

Jordan circled his arm in the air. "Rangers lead the way!"

With a whoop from Cooper and a tired sigh from McKay, the pair walked backward down the cliff face, as easily as if they were on horizontal ground.

The Israelis clipped on next and dropped over the edge.

Tyson fiddled with her monitoring equipment. She wasn't harnessed up, so she must be staying up here, too.

That left Erin and Jordan. He came forward with a large weapon slung over his back, then secured himself on the rope next to her. Once set, he leaned over and tugged on her line. "Good tie-on."

"You bet."

Jordan flashed a quick grin, leaned back, and took a big step down. He stared up, face serious, words firm. "Anytime now. I'll be right next to you."

She leaned out, felt her hands open and close, letting rope slide through her gloved fingers as she backed up—and next thing she knew she was standing next to Jordan on the cliff face.

4:54** P.M.**—Three minutes before sunset

When his boots hit the ground, Jordan did an automatic inventory of his weapons. He patted the holstered sidearm on his hip, a Colt 1911, then checked the KA-BAR dagger strapped to his ankle. But his primary weapon—a Heckler & Koch MP7—hung on a strap over his right shoulder. The machine pistol fired hardened steel rounds to the beat of 950 per minute, capable of turning Kevlar armor into Swiss cheese.

He quickly checked the weapon's safety, clip, and optics, ensuring he didn't bump it against anything on the way down. He caught Erin staring.

"You need that much firepower down here?" Erin folded her gloves in half and crammed them in her back pocket.

He shrugged. "It's standard carry for my team."

Before he could explain more, Sanderson's voice crackled over the radio in his earpiece. *"Sarge, we've got an Israeli cargo chopper coming in. I'm guessing they've come for the rest of the bodies."*

The evacuation chopper was early, but just as well. Jordan wanted everyone off this bloody mountain as soon as possible. He touched his earpiece. "Got it."

He and Erin joined the rest of the team gathered at a thin seam in the cliff face. The ROV cable trailed down it and vanished into the darkness.

He glanced over at Erin. What the hell had happened to her in the lean-to? At first he'd thought maybe she was scared of heights and worried about the rappel, but she'd handled that without blinking an eye. He suspected she did have more than a hundred climbs behind her. So she must have seen or heard something during the few minutes she was alone that knocked her down. He didn't think she'd told him the whole truth about it. She seemed better now, but he hoped whatever it was wouldn't affect the mission.

Cooper pulled his head out of the two-foot-wide crack the ROV had run through and tossed a glowstick, lighting the way ahead. "That man-made tunnel opens just past this seam."

Hands on his hips, McKay eyed the small opening.

Jordan clapped him on the shoulder. "Tight fit, but you should make it."

McKay shook his head. "Spoken by a skinny guy who can barely bench-press his weight."

Jordan wasn't skinny, and he could certainly bench much more than his weight. But he'd fit through. For McKay in full gear, it would be a tight squeeze.

Cooper smiled an overly broad grin. "You can always strip to your skivvies and rub yourself in grease."

"And give you a free show? Not likely."

Lieutenant Perlman stood with his arms crossed, frowning. The other Israeli soldier shifted from foot to foot.

Jordan saw no reason to delay. The sun was setting, and he wanted to get done here soon. He adjusted his shoulder lamp.

"Let's move."

4:57 P.M.—Sunset

Kneeling, Erin watched the others file into the crack. She drew in a cautious breath. She expected a chemical odor, even though Tyson and Sanderson had given the air a thumbs-up. Instead, it smelled musty, mingled with a staleness that came from places unoccupied for a long time. The familiar and oddly comforting scent of an old tomb.

She patted the dart in her sock and stood to follow Jordan into the narrow opening. Rough stone walls pressed against both shoulders, and she turned sideways, hoping that McKay would make it through without losing too much skin.

The air felt much cooler than on the mountaintop. Underfoot, her sneakers sank in the sand. The glowstick cast an eerie yellow pall along the tunnel. When she reached the stick, she resisted the urge to pick it up and shove it in her pocket. They were littering an archaeological site. She made a note to get it on the way back. She kept one hand running along the top of the crack, making sure that her head wouldn't bump into the fissure's roof as she forged on, anxious to get to the tomb and start exploring.

Ahead McKay let loose with a string of curses as he cleared the seam, mostly involving the tightness of the squeeze. Cooper laughed gleefully.

Erin found herself smiling. She frequently worked with soldiers, often at sites located in areas of conflict. In the past, she had regarded the military as a necessary evil, but she already felt an odd bond with this group, forged by horror and bloodshed above and by tension below.

At last, she and Jordan reached the end of the narrow seam. He stepped out into a man-made tunnel, then helped her to climb free. Out in the passageway, he held up a hand, indicating she should stand pat.

"We wait for the all clear from the team."

He was in charge down here, for now. She stopped and touched the tunnel wall, feeling sharp-edged gouges, picturing chisels and hammers and sweating men. She dropped to a knee and touched the path, pinching up dirt and letting it run through her fingers.

Someone had dug this out thousands of years ago. Who had walked through here? And why?

A few feet away, chunks of rocks closed up the modern tunnel she'd seen on the rover's cameras. The tunnel must have collapsed. She touched the drill marks on the edges. Twentieth century. But when?

She spotted what looked like the elastic straps and the plastic faceplate of a modern-era gas mask crushed under a boulder. She walked toward it, drawing Jordan with her. If this had been an official expedition, she would have known about it. If it was unofficial, how had they concealed that large of an undertaking at such a famous site? There would have to have been a lot going on at the time.

Like a war.

Before they could examine anything further, Jordan's radio buzzed. It was loud enough that she heard Cooper's tinny voice say, "*Chamber is secure, Sarge. You might want to get your asses in here. Some fucked-up shit went down.*"

"Heading over." Jordan waved for her to continue with him. "Stick to my side, Doc."

She followed, making a mental checklist of things to do: use a metal detector to search for tools, scrape soot from the ceiling to judge the type of torches employed by the workers, apply a plaster cast to the wall to discern what tools were used to dig here.

The kinds of things Heinrich had been good at. She stumbled a step, and Jordan caught her arm, his hand warm and reassuring, his eyes concerned. "Doc?"

She shook her head and waved him on.

After another ten yards, they arrived at the entrance to the underground chamber she had just seen through the ROV's cameras. An ancient and well-made doorway.

The doorway was too narrow for two people to enter at once. She hung back and let Jordan duck through first. She estimated the entryway at a hair over six feet tall and reached one hand up to lightly touch the arch, then stepped over the threshold behind him.

Goose bumps rose on her arms. The air was even cooler here. The muted light of three yellow glowsticks that had been tossed randomly inside revealed a well-made limestone floor, tall, soot-streaked ceilings, close-fitted stone blocks on the walls. She would have loved to be able to take pictures of the dust on the floor, maybe see the footprints of the grave robbers who had opened the sarcophagus. But Jordan and his men had already tramped through and overlaid ancient footprints with their own.

The others gathered across the room, huddled on the far side of the sarcophagus, facing the wall. There must be something very interesting there. As soon as she got a better sense of the overall site, she'd let herself join them.

"Please touch nothing," she called, fully expecting them to ignore her.

She entered, stepping past the ROV, and crossed to the stone sarcophagus. As she expected, it was carved from a single stone, the sides finely wrought, each corner perfectly angled, each side perfectly flat. She marveled anew at the workmanship of those ancient craftsmen. Their tools might be considered primitive, but the results certainly weren't. She glanced at the polished top where it lay in one piece on the floor beside the grave it had covered for so long. Odd to see it intact, as grave robbers usually broke the lids of sarcophagi when they pulled them off.

She searched for the pulleys or rope that must have been used, but the plunderers had taken their tools back out with them. Also unusual.

She stepped forward—but a hand stopped her.

"What did I say about sticking close to me?" Jordan asked.

Together, she and Jordan neared the sarcophagus. When she was finally close enough to take some pictures, she dug out the only tool still in her possession: her cell phone. She took multiple shots of the sarcophagus's side and the piles of ashes at the corners, wishing she had her Nikon, but it was back in Caesarea.

She risked a peek inside the coffin. Nothing. Just bare stone, stained deep burgundy. What would make a stain like that? Blood dried brown. Most resins ended up black.

She also took a few pictures of the empty clay jugs around the sarcophagus. They must have carried liquid down here. Usually they were used for wine, but why fill a sarcophagus with wine?

As she straightened, Jordan turned from the far wall. Even in the dim light, she could tell he was upset. "Doc, you want to explain this one?"

She looked over as the men parted to either side.

A macabre sculpture hung on the wall, like a blasphemous crucifixion. She moved past the corner of the sarcophagus. With each step, a growing horror rose in her.

It wasn't a sculpture.

On the wall hung the desiccated corpse of a small girl, maybe eight years old, dressed in a tattered, stained robe. A handful of blackened arrows pinned her in place, a good yard off the floor. They pierced her chest, neck, shoulder, and thigh.

"Crossbow bolts," Jordan said. "Looks like they're made of silver."

Silver?

She stood before the child, struck by one anachronism after another. The girl's burgundy robes looked ancient, both in style and in the degree of decay. The ornamentation and pattern of weave dated from the same period as the fall of Masada. Probably made in Samaria, maybe Judea, but at least two thousand years old.

Long dark hair framed the sunken face. Her eyes closed peacefully, her chin hung to her thin chest, lips parted ever so slightly as if she had died in mid-sigh. Even her tiny eyelashes were intact. Judging by the amount of soft tissue still clinging to her bones, the girl had been dead only a few decades.

Decades. How could that be?

An object lay crumpled under the girl's toes. Erin dropped to a knee next to it.

A doll . . .

Her heart ached. The tiny dried toy was crafted from hardened lumps of leather stitched with scraps of cloth and stained the same burgundy as the robes. The child's slack arm seemed to be reaching for her plaything, forever unable to claim it.

The abandoned doll struck Erin deeply as she remembered

another like it, handmade, too. She had buried it with her baby sister. She swallowed hard, fighting back tears, feeling foolish for it. Heinrich's death continued to throw her off balance, and right now she had to pull herself together in front of the soldiers.

Still on her knees, she glanced up to the child's other hand, half hidden behind her body, and saw a glint from between the curled fingers.

Odd.

She leaned one palm against the wall, feeling hard mortar extruding between the bricks. Though the body was the result of a recent murder, not an ancient one, she still treated the remains with respect. This child was once someone's little girl.

She reached for that hand. The girl's arm trembled, then jerked. The entire mummified body shook against the wall as if the child still lived.

Erin fell back with a gasp.

A hand gripped her shoulder, steadying her.

"Another aftershock," Jordan said.

Fine dust sifted from the stone roof. Behind Erin, a brick thudded to the floor. She held her breath until the quake ceased.

"They're getting worse," Jordan said. "Nothing here for us. Time to go."

She resisted the pull of his arm. This was her site now, and there were still things here for her to explore. She shifted closer to the wall and reached again for the girl's hand.

Jordan noted her attention and dropped beside her. "What is it?"

"Looks like the child grabbed something before she died."

Archaeological protocol dictated that nothing be touched before it had been photographed, but this girl had not been murdered that long ago, so Erin would forgo protocol just this once.

Reaching out, she nudged the girl's fingers open. She had expected them to be brittle but found them eerily pliable. Surprised at the state of the body, she missed catching the object as it fell free. It dropped in the dust.

She didn't need a doctorate in archaeology to recognize this artifact.

Jordan swore under his breath.

She stared dumbfounded at the medal, at the iron cross, at the swastika.

German.

From World War II.

Here was the identity of the grave robbers, the ones who had drilled down here with modern tools. But why was this medal clutched in the mummified fingers of a girl inside an ancient Jewish tomb?

Jordan clenched a fist. "The Nazis must have got here first. Raided and emptied this place out."

His words clarified little. Hitler was obsessed with the occult, but what had he hoped to find in Masada?

She scrutinized the girl's clothes. Why would the Nazis take so much care to dress a child in replicas of the first millennium, only to crossbolt her to the wall?

She pictured the girl ripping the medal off her tormentor's uniform, hiding it, stealing proof of who killed her. Again an upwelling of sympathy for this child—and for the courage of this final act—swept through her. Tears again rose in her eyes.

"Are you okay?" Jordan's face was close enough for her to see a fine scar on his chin.

To hide her tears, she lifted her phone and took several pictures of the medal. The girl had gone to great lengths to secure a clue to the identity of her murderer. Erin would record her proof.

Once she lowered her phone, Jordan reached to the dust, picked up the medal, and flipped it over. "Maybe we can find out who did this. SS officers often carved their names on the reverse side of their medals. Whoever this bastard was, I want his name. And if he's somehow still alive . . ."

At that moment she liked Jordan more than ever. Shoulder to shoulder, they studied the small metal disk. No name covered the reverse side, only a strange symbol.

She took a snapshot of it in Jordan's palm, then read aloud the words along its border. "*Deutsches Ahnenerbe.*"

"That makes sense," Jordan said sourly.

She shot him a quizzical glance. Recent German history was not her specialty. "How so?"

He tilted the medal from side to side. "My grandfather fought in World War Two. Told me stories. It's one of the reasons I joined up. And I'm a bit of a history buff. The *Deutsches Ahnenerbe* were a secret sect of Nazi scientists with an interest in the occult who went around the world seeking lost treasures and proof of an ancient Aryan race. Himmler's band of grave robbers."

And they got here first. She felt a sinking sense of defeat. She was used to studying graves that had already been robbed, but those thefts usually happened in antiquity. It rankled her that this tomb had been despoiled mere decades ago.

He touched the center of the symbol. "That's not their usual symbol. Normally, the *Ahnenerbe* are represented by a sword wrapped in a ribbon. This is something new."

Curious, she touched the central symbol. "Looks like a Norse rune. From Elder Futhark. Maybe an Odal rune."

She drew it in the dust on the floor with a finger.

"The rune represents the letter *O*." She turned to Jordan. "Could that be the medal owner's initial?"

Before she could contemplate it further, McKay barked, "Freeze! Hands in the air!"

Startled, she spun around.

Jordan shouldered his Heckler & Koch machine pistol and twisted toward the tomb's entrance. Again the ground shook, rock dust shivered—and from out of the shadows, a dark shape stepped into the room.

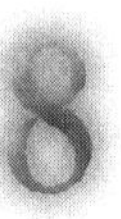

October 26, 5:04 P.M., IST
Masada, Israel

"Hold your fire!" Jordan yelled, lifting up his left arm. "It's the padre."

He lowered the muzzle of his submachine gun and strode over to the clergyman. It was strange enough that the priest had come down here, but he noticed something even more disturbing.

He's not wearing any rappelling gear.

Jordan stepped in front of him as the aftershock faded. "What are you doing down here, Father?"

From under the cowl of his hood, the priest regarded him. Jordan did the same, sizing the other up. Father Korza stood two inches taller than Jordan, but under his long open jacket, he was leaner, muscular, a whip of a man. The hard planes of his face were clearly Slavic, softened only by full lips. He wore his black hair down to his collar—a bit too long for a holy man.

But it was those eyes, studious and dark—*very* dark—that set Jordan's heart to pounding. His fingers involuntarily tightened on his weapon.

He's only a priest, he reminded himself.

Father Korza stared a moment longer at Jordan, then his gaze flicked away, sweeping the room in a single glance.

"Did you hear me, padre? I asked you a question."

The priest's words were whispered, breathless, oddly formal.

"The Church has prior claim to what lies within this crypt."

Father Korza started to step past him. Jordan grabbed his arm—but only caught air. Somehow the priest smoothly shrugged out of his way and stalked toward the open sarcophagus.

Jordan followed, noting the priest's eyes fix to the child staked to the wall, his face unreadable. Reaching the tomb, the man glanced inside the empty sarcophagus and visibly tensed, going statue-still.

Erin approached him from the far wall. She held aloft her cell phone, plainly searching for a signal, hoping to get her photographs uploaded somewhere safe, always thinking like a researcher.

As she reached the sarcophagus, Jordan kept between her and Father Korza. For some reason, he didn't want her near the strange priest.

"This is a restricted area," Jordan warned.

Perlman backed him up, resting a palm on his sidearm. "You should not be here, Father Korza. The Israeli government set strict guidelines on your visit here."

The clergyman ignored them both. He focused on Erin. "Have you found a book? Or a block of stone of such size?" He held out his arms.

Erin shook her head. "We found nothing like that, just the girl. It looks like the Germans cleared this tomb during the war."

His only reaction was a slight narrowing of his eyes.

Who is this guy?

Jordan placed his hand on the butt of his machine pistol, waiting to see what the holy man would do next. Brusque and taciturn, the priest had obvious issues with authority, but so far he'd shown no outward signs of threat.

Peripherally, Jordan watched McKay slip a hand to his own dagger.

"Easy, Corporal," he ordered. "Stand down."

The priest ignored McKay, but he suddenly tensed, freezing in midturn, his ear cocked to the side. He made eye contact with Jordan, but his words were for all of them.

"You must all leave. *Now.*"

The last word bristled with warning.

What is he talking about?

The answer came from Jordan's earpiece: a scream burst forth, full of blood and pain, sharp enough to stab deep into his head.

Sanderson.

From up top.

The scream cut off into a burst of static.

He touched the throat mike. "Sanderson! Respond!"

No reply.

"Corporal, come in!"

The priest moved swiftly to the entrance. Cooper and the young Israeli soldier blocked him from leaving. Weapons were raised all around.

At the threshold to the tomb, the priest lifted his face toward the roof, his whole body going rigid, like a big cat before an attack. His next words were chilling for their calmness.

"Back against the walls." He turned and locked eyes with Jordan. "Do as I say or you will all die."

Jordan raised his weapon. "Are you threatening us, padre?"

"Not I. The ones who *come*."

5:07 P.M.

Erin struggled to comprehend what was happening. The priest's gaze met hers. For a moment a flicker of fear broke through the pale contours of the priest's face, long enough to drive her heart into her throat. She sensed that he worried for their safety, not his own. A terrible sadness haunted his eyes as he looked away, as if he already mourned them.

She swallowed, her mouth suddenly dry.

But Jordan was clearly not giving up so easily. "What's going on? I've got men topside. As does Lieutenant Perlman."

Again that mournful look. "By now, they are dead. As you shall be if you do not—"

A gasp rose from Cooper, who stood by the door. Everyone turned. He opened his mouth, but only blood flowed out. He collapsed to his knees, then his face. The black hilt of a dagger jutted from the base of his skull.

Erin cried his name. The soldiers raised their guns as one. She stepped behind them, out of the line of fire.

Beyond Cooper's body crouched a dark shape, a figure sculpted from shadows. Jordan fired multiple volleys, blasts deafening in the closed space. The shadow shivered back into darkness—

—but not before snagging the young Israeli soldier who was still hovering near the threshold. Erin caught a glint of steel, then he was gone, yanked off his feet and into the black tunnel.

Jordan stopped firing, plainly fearing he'd hit the soldier.

A scream, full of terror and blood, echoed—then silence.

Lieutenant Perlman lurched forward, weapon up. "Margolis!"

The priest's black-clad arm shoved the Israeli back.

Hard.

"Stay here," Father Korza warned, then defied his own words.

With a turn of his wrist, a blade appeared in his fingers as if out of thin air. He bared the edge: a sickle of silver, a hooked dagger, like some prehistoric claw.

With a sweep of his jacket, he dove across the threshold and vanished.

Immediately a savage wailing keened out of the darkness.

The sound sang to fears buried in her bones and bound her in place.

Even the hardened soldiers seemed to sense it. Jordan drew her farther from the entrance. McKay and Perlman flanked them, weapons pointed at the door. Retreating, regrouping, they took cover behind the sarcophagus.

A single piercing scream ripped from the tunnel.

Jordan lifted Erin as effortlessly as if her bones were hollow, her flesh immaterial. She felt that way already, as if she could float away.

He rolled her into the open sarcophagus. "Stay down, stay hidden."

The steel in his voice and iron in his eyes grounded her back in her own skin—not that she wanted to be there. He pressed her lower. "Do you understand?"

"Yes." She wanted to duck away, cover her head, shut out the horror, but when she did, sightlessness scared her more. Her fingers clung to the lip of the box. Like everyone else, she watched the pitch-dark mouth of the tunnel.

To the left, a sharp strike and flash drew her eye. McKay held a flaming flare.

"Toss it!" Jordan pointed to the dark exit.

McKay swung his arm and tossed the flare through the doorway. It tumbled end over end, leaving a trail of fire, and plunged into the well of darkness. Brightness forced back shadows, along with darker shapes. Erin lost count at four.

That left a lone figure in the center, standing in a shredded cassock, lit from the back. He held an arm over his eyes, blinded by the sudden flare. His other hand held up a curved dagger, blade dripping black blood, shimmering with reflected fire.

"Father!" Jordan yelled, raising his weapon. "Get down!"

The warning came too late.

Like rabid dogs, shadowed shapes leaped at the priest. They slammed him down. He landed hard atop the flare, quenching it with his body. Erin winced. Darkness again swallowed the scene—but not before a figure bounded over the priest and leaped headlong into the chamber.

It flew far, hit the stone floor, then shot straight at them, moving impossibly fast. A wolf? No. A man in wrinkled brown leather, arms wide, a butcher's hook held aloft by one muscular arm.

Jordan dropped to one knee and fired up, striking the man square in the chest. The hail of rounds knocked him into the bricked roof. He dropped to the stone floor, hitting hard and going dead-still.

At the door, a mass of shadows rolled into the room. The priest wrestled with two black-suited figures. A third leaped past.

The attacker sped low and fast into Lieutenant Perlman. They hit the wall beside the crucified girl and dropped out of view. The Israeli's rifle barked, blasting upward, rounds sparking off rock. Erin flattened herself in the stone box.

A shadow materialized above her. She caught a flash of teeth—*too many teeth*—and wished that she had a gun or a knife. She crossed both arms in front of her face and waited to feel the teeth in her skin.

Instead, bullets ripped through the torso above, and the bulk dropped atop her. She struggled out from under the body, her jeans wet with blood. Gritting her teeth, she searched the body for a weapon. No gun, but he carried an Egyptian *khopesh* with a long curved blade. She had seen similar swords in hieroglyphs and paintings, but such weapons hadn't been used in battle for seven hundred years.

McKay peered over the edge of the sarcophagus. "You okay?"

Before she could answer, he vanished, hit broadside. She rose up on her knees, clutching the sword.

McKay sailed across the room and slammed into the wall, cracking his head. He fell to the floor, leaving a streak of blood on the wall behind him.

A dark figure leaped atop McKay and lunged at his throat.

5:08 P.M.

Jordan was pinned under an attacker who was stronger than anyone he had ever fought. He'd already lost his gun. The guy was also ridiculously fast.

Jordan twisted and grabbed for his ankle—and the KA-BAR dagger sheathed there. He freed it as bony hands lashed down. One clamped to his throat, the other held his arm pinned against the stone.

Nails dug deep, tearing flesh.

Wrenching his free arm around, he drove the KA-BAR blade deep into the assailant's throat, to the hilt, until he hit bone, then ripped outward.

Blood washed down his arm.

The man went limp. Jordan threw off the deadweight and rolled to a crouch. His attention fixed on Erin, standing in the sarcophagus with a short, curved sword in one hand. She looked ready to climb out to help McKay, who lay on the other side of the room, but McKay was beyond anyone's help now. Like Perlman, who was on the floor nearby, his throat had been torn away.

Jordan shot McKay's attacker full in the chest, knocking him off his teammate's body. Movement turned his head back to Erin.

A shadow loomed behind her.

He leaped toward her, but a hand shoved him aside. It felt like being clipped by a speeding truck. He lost his footing and crashed into the wall.

Dazed, he watched the priest barrel past him, knock Erin down, and tackle her attacker. He struck the bloody man with his shoulder and drove him backward, slamming him into the mummified girl on the wall. Dried bone exploded under their weight.

Korza rebounded back a step.

His opponent remained in place, hanging off the ground, impaled and writhing. The butt end of the crossbow bolts that penetrated his flesh held him aloft. One bolt poked out the man's throat. Fingers scrabbled at it. Blood bubbled out of the wound, as if it were boiling.

Then Korza lashed out, severing the man's throat with an explosive stroke.

Jordan regained his own shaky feet, crouched, searching all around. The priest stood before the wall, shoulders hunched under shredded garments. Dark blood dripped from his blade, from his fingertips. Jordan didn't know how much of it came from the priest's own wounds.

He kept his gun up as he stumbled to Erin. He saw no reason to check on his other teammates. He knew death when he faced it. As far as he could tell, the only ones still alive in this room were the priest, Erin, and him.

He kept a cautious eye on the priest, leery of his allegiances.

With a flare of his long jacket, Korza dropped to a knee, head bowed as if in prayer—but that was not his intent. He snatched something from the floor. It vanished into his black robes as he stood again.

The child's small doll was gone.

Instead of checking on Erin, he'd gone to pick up a doll? Jordan gave up trying to figure the man out.

"Erin?" he said as he reached her side.

She whirled toward him, her sword held high.

"Just me," he said, and shifted his gun to the side, both hands up, palms out.

Her wide eyes came into focus, and she lowered the blade. He pried it out of her fingers and dropped it. Her face white, her eyes lost, she slumped in the corner of the sarcophagus. He lifted her out and sat with his back against the cold stone with her in his lap. He ran his hands over her, searching for wounds. She seemed unharmed.

The priest joined them. Jordan's hand inched toward his pistol, a protective arm encircling Erin. What were his intentions?

"There are no more," Korza whispered as if in prayer. "But we are still not safe."

Jordan glanced over at the battered man.

"They will seal us in," he said with such certainty that Jordan believed him.

"How do you know . . . ?"

"Because it is what I would do." He strode toward the door.

Jordan noted where he headed. The ROV sat on the floor, one camera aimed at them, a green light shining above it. The priest stamped on the lens. Metal and glass shattered under his heel and skittered across stone.

Jordan understood, remembering Sanderson's scream.

They've been watching us.

9

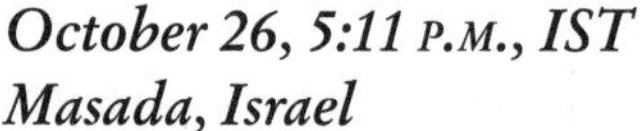

October 26, 5:11 P.M., IST
Masada, Israel

As the last screams echoed across the summit, Bathory crouched before the now-dark monitor, frozen in shock, trapped between the past and the present.

She had witnessed the battle in the tomb, followed by the slaughter of the forces she had sent below. The fighting had been swift, dimly lit, much of it occurring out of camera view.

But she had also spied the few moments before the chaotic fighting.

She had watched a helmeted soldier confront a black-garbed figure, his back to the camera. But she had caught the flash of a white Roman collar as he cast a single glance to encompass the room.

Her pained blood went cold at this fleeting glimpse of the enemy.

Here was that Knight of Christ mentioned in the texted message.

A Sanguinist.

The two men faced off like rams during rutting season. Maybe the soldier would solve her problem for her, but the knight stepped past the soldier and stopped, staring at the far wall—what did he see?

She wished the camera's range extended to the back of the room.

Out of those shadows, a woman in civilian clothes appeared, another surprise. She came waving her phone in the familiar pantomime of someone searching for a signal.

The knight turned to the woman and held out his hands to indicate an object the size and shape of a book.

Bathory's breathing had quickened.

The woman shook her head.

The knight performed a slow circuit of the room. The tomb seemed empty, except for the sarcophagus. No likely hiding places. When the knight's shoulders slumped, she let out her breath.

So they had *not* found the book.

Either it had never been there, or it had been plundered.

Then the knight grew wise to the presence of Bathory's team, requiring a swift response. He should have been defeated, but she had underestimated his skill, also the support by the soldiers. He had taken out half of her forces in seconds.

From his performance, she knew the knight below was not new to the cloth, but someone much older, as well blooded as her own forces.

Then, as that knight crossed to crush the ROV camera, she got a full look at his face: his cleft chin, his broad Slavic cheekbones, his intense dark eyes. The shock of recognition immobilized her and left her hollowed out.

But life was not a vacuum.

Into that void, a molten, fiery hatred flowed, filling her anew, forging her into something else, a weapon of fury and vengeance.

She finally moved, clenching her hand into a fist and gouging her ancient ruby ring down the darkened monitor. Like so much that she possessed, the precious ring had been connected to her family for a long time.

As had the knight.

Rhun Korza.

That name had scarred her as surely as the black palm on her neck—and caused her as much pain. All her life, she had been raised on tales of how Korza's failure had cast her once-proud family into generations of poverty and disgrace. She fingered the edge of her tattoo, a source of constant agony, another debt of blood that she owed that knight.

She flashed to that long-ago ceremony, kneeling before Him to whom she had pledged herself, His hand around her throat, burning in that mark in the shape of His palm and fingers, binding her to Him in servitude.

All because of that knight.

She had seen him in a thousand dreams and had always hoped she might someday find him alive, to make him pay for the deeds that had doomed generations of women in her family to sacrifice, to years of living with torment—enslaved by blood, fated to train, to serve, to wait.

This knowledge came with another truth, a pained realization.

She again felt His strangled hold on her throat, burning away her old life.

Her master must have known that Rhun Korza was the knight sent to Masada to retrieve the book. Yet that secret had been kept from her. He had sent her to face Korza without warning her first.

Why?

Was this to satisfy His own cruel amusements—or was there some greater purpose in all of this?

If she had known that Korza lurked in that tomb, she would never have sent anyone down. She would have waited for the knight to come up with the book, or empty-handed in failure, and shot him off the fissure like a fly off a wall.

The slaughter below told her that Korza was too dangerous to confront in close combat, even if she sent her remaining forces down after him.

But there was another way, a more fitting way.

The anger inside her hardened to a newer purpose.

Before the image went dark, she had spotted the body of one of her team near the tomb's door, carrying a satchel over one shoulder. An identical pack waited near the top of the fissure.

She turned to the two hunters still in attendance.

Tarek had shaved his head like many of the others and riddled his skin with black tattoos, in his case Bible verses written in Latin. Leather, stitched with human sinew, clad his muscular six-foot frame. Steel piercings cut through lips and nostrils. His black eyes had narrowed to slits, furious at the casualties inflicted by those in the tomb. He wanted revenge. Dealt by his own hands.

"The knight is too dangerous," she warned. "Especially when backed into a corner. We are down too many to risk sending more."

Tarek could not argue. They had both witnessed the slaughter on the screen. But there was another option. Not as satisfying, but the end would be the same.

"Blow the fissure." She motioned to the pack on top and pictured the satchel below. "Kill them all."

She intended to entomb the knight and his companions, to rebury the secrets here under tons of rock. And if Korza survived the blast, then a slow death trapped beneath all of that stone would be his fate.

For a moment it seemed that Tarek would disobey her order. Fury ruled him, stoked by all the blood. Then his gaze flicked to her neck. To the tattoo. He knew its significance better than any.

To defy her was to defy *Him*.

Tarek bowed his head once, like bending iron—then turned and folded into the night.

She closed her eyes, centering herself, but a low moan caught her attention, reminding her that she still had work to do.

The freckle-faced corporal named Sanderson knelt in the dust, the lone survivor of the massacre on the summit. He'd been stripped to the waist, his head yanked back by nails dug deep into his scalp by the remaining hunter at her side. This one—Rafik, brother to Tarek—was lean, all bone and malice, a useful tool in trying times.

She shifted closer, the soldier's eyes tracking her.

"I have questions," she said gently.

He only stared, trembling and sweating, doe-eyed with terror, looking so very young. She once had a brother very much like this one, how he had loved roses and chilled wine, but she had been forbidden from any contact with him after taking His mark. She had to cut away all earthly attachments to her past, binding herself only to Him.

Another loss she placed upon Korza's shoulders.

She ran the back of her hand down the corporal's velvety cheek. He was not yet old enough to grow a proper beard. Yet, despite his terror, she read an ember of defiance in his eyes.

She sighed.

As if he had any hope of resisting.

She leaned back and lifted an arm, casting out her desire.

Come.

The pair—she named them Hunor and Magor, after two Hungarian mythic heroes—were never far from her side, forever bonded to her. Without looking, she felt them push out of the darkness behind her, where they had been feeding, and pad forward. She held out a palm and was met by a warm tongue, a furry muzzle, and a low rumble like thunder beyond the horizon.

She dropped her hand, now damp and weeping with blood.

"They're still hungry," she commented, knowing it to be true, feeling an echo of that desire inside her.

The soldier's eyes widened, straining against the unimaginable. Horror at what stood behind her quashed any further defiance.

She leaned very close. She felt his hot breath, almost tasting his anguish. She moved to his ear and whispered.

"Tell me," she said, starting with a simple question, "who was that woman down there?"

Before he could answer, the night exploded behind her. Light, sound, and heat erupted from Masada's summit, shaking the ground, turning darkness to day. Flames blasted out of the chasm, swirling into a cataclysm of smoke and dirt—closing what God had opened only hours ago. She intended to bring this entire mountain down to cover her tracks.

With the detonation, peace again settled over her.

She stared down at the corporal.

She still needed answers.

10

October 26, 5:14 P.M., IST
Masada, Israel

Heat scorched Rhun's back, as hot as the breath of any dragon. He pictured the wall of flames rolling over the top of the sealed dark sarcophagus. But it was the *sound* that hurt the worst. He feared the concussive blast might crack his skull, fountain blood from his ears, and defile this once-sacred space.

Beyond their tomb, stone rained down near the entrance. Unlike the first explosion that had sealed the fissure above, this second one sought to destroy this very chamber.

Thus trapping them.

As fire and fury died down to a rumbling groan, he braced hard against the limestone sides of the tomb. It was fitting that he die in a sarcophagus—trapped as surely as he'd once sealed another behind stone. Indeed, he almost welcomed it. But the woman and soldier had not earned this fate.

He had hurled them both inside the coffin after the first explosion. Knowing this ancient crypt offered the only shelter, he had drawn the stone lid over them, using all of his strength, assisted only slightly by the soldier. If they survived, he did not know how he would explain such strength of limb. The code he lived by demanded that he let them die rather than allow those questions to be asked.

But he could not let them die.

So they crowded together in pitch darkness. He tried to pray, but his senses continued to overwhelm him. He smelled the wine that had once filled this box, the metallic odor of blood that saturated the remains of his clothing, and the burnt paper-and-chalk smell of spent explosives.

None of it masked the simple lavender scent of her hair.

Her heartbeat, swift as a woodlark's, raced against his chest. The warmth of her trembling body spread along his stomach and legs. He had not been this close to a woman since Elisabeta. It was a small mercy that Erin was turned away from him, her face buried in the soldier's chest.

He counted her heartbeats, and in that rhythm, he found the peace to pray—until at last silence finally returned to his mind and to the world beyond their small tomb.

She stirred under him, but he touched her shoulder to tell her to be still. He wanted them to wait longer, to be certain that the room had stopped collapsing before he attempted to shift the tomb's lid. Only then would he know if they were entombed by more rock than even he could lift.

Her breathing slowed, her heart stilled. The soldier, too, calmed.

Finally, Rhun braced his knees against the bottom of the stone box and pushed up with his shoulders. The lid scraped against the sides. He heaved again. The massive weight moved a handsbreadth, then two.

Finally, it tilted and smashed to the floor. They were free, although he feared that they had only traded the small cell for a larger one. But at least the temple held. The men who had dug out this secret chamber had reinforced its walls to hold the tempestuous mountain at bay.

He stood and helped Erin and Jordan out of the sarcophagus. One glowstick had survived the blast and cast a dim glow into the room. He squinted through scorching dust to the tomb's entrance.

It was an entrance no more.

Earth and rock sealed it from floor to ceiling.

The other two coughed, holding cloths to their faces, filtering the fouled air. They would not last long.

The soldier clicked on a flashlight and shone it toward the doorway. He met Rhun's eyes and stepped back from him, his face dark with suspicion and wariness.

The woman cast the beam of a second flashlight around the

ruined chamber. A layer of dust covered everything, transforming the dead bodies to powdered statues, blunting the horror of the slaughter.

But nothing hid the broken pieces of the sarcophagus's heavy stone lid. Her light lingered there. Motes of dust drifting through the beam did not obscure the truth of his impossible act in lifting and pushing that stone free.

The soldier did not seem to notice. He faced the blasted doorway as if it were an unsolvable mystery.

Closer at hand, the woman's light settled on Rhun, as did her soft brown eyes. "Thank you, Father."

He heard an awkward catch in her voice when she said the word *father*. He found it discomfiting, sensing that she had no faith.

"My name is Rhun," he whispered. "Rhun Korza."

He had not shared the intimacy of his full name with another in a long time, but if they were to die here together, he wanted them to know it.

"I'm Erin, and this is Jordan. How—"

The soldier cut her off; cold fury underlay his tone. "Who were they?"

That single question hid another. He recognized it in the man's voice, read it in his face.

What were they?

He considered the hidden question. The Church forbade revealing the truth, its most guarded secret. Much could be lost.

But the man was a warrior, like himself. He had stood his ground, faced darkness, and he had paid in blood for a proper answer.

Rhun would honor that sacrifice. He stared the other full in the eye and offered the truth, naming their attackers. "They are *strigoi*."

His words hung in the air, like the swirling dust, obscuring more than they revealed. Clearly confused, the man cocked his head to the side. The woman, too, studied him, more in curiosity than in anger. Unlike the soldier, she did not seem to blame him for the deaths here.

"What does that mean?" The soldier would not be pacified until he understood, and doubtless not afterward either.

Rhun lifted a stone off one of the dead men and brushed sand from his face. The woman kept her light on his hands as he angled the dusty head toward them. With one gloved hand, he peeled back cold lips, exposing an ancient secret.

Long white fangs glinted in the beam of light.

The soldier's hand moved to the butt of his gun. The woman drew in a sharp breath. Her hand rose to her throat. An animal's instinct to protect itself. But instead of remaining frozen in horror, she lowered her hand and came to kneel beside Rhun. The man stayed put, alert and ready to do battle.

Rhun expected that, but the woman surprised him, when so little else did. Her fingers—trembling at first, then steadying—reached to touch the long, sharp tooth, like Saint Thomas placing his hand in Christ's wound, needing proof. She plainly feared the truth, but she would not shun it.

She faced Rhun, skeptical as only a modern-day scientist could be. And waited.

He said nothing. She had asked for the truth. He had given it to her. But he could not give her the will to believe it.

She waved a hand over the corpse. "These may be caps, put on to lengthen his teeth . . ."

Even now, she refused to believe, sought comforting rationalizations, like so many others before her. But unlike them, she leaned closer, not waiting for confirmation or consolation. She lifted the upper lip higher.

As she probed, he expected her eyes to widen with horror. Instead, her brows knit together in studious interest.

Surprised yet again, he eyed her with equal fascination.

5:21 P.M.

Kneeling by the body, Erin sought to make sense of what lay before her. She needed to understand, to put meaning to all the blood and death.

She desperately ran through a mental list of cultures where people sharpened their teeth. In the Sudan desert, young men whittled their incisors to razor points in a rite of passage. Amid the ancient Maya, filed teeth had been a sign of nobility. In Bali, tooth filing was still a coming-of-age ritual that marked the transition from animal to human. Every continent had similar practices. Every single one.

But this was different.

As much as she wanted it to be true, no tools had sharpened these teeth.

"Doc, talk to me." Jordan hovered over her shoulder, his tense voice loud in the small space. "Tell me what you're thinking."

She fought to keep her tone clinical, both for her sake and for his. If she lost her composure, she might never get it back. "These canine teeth are firmly rooted in the maxilla. Feel how the bony sockets at the base of the fangs are thickened."

Jordan stepped over a pile of rubble to stand between her and the priest. He rested one hand on his gun. "I'll take your word for it."

She flashed him what she hoped was a reassuring smile. It didn't seem to work, because his face stayed stern when he asked, "What does it mean?"

She leaned back on her haunches, eager to put space between herself and the tooth she had just touched. "Such root density is a common trait in predators."

Father Korza stepped away. Jordan's barrel twitched toward him.

"Jordan?" She stood next to him.

"Keep talking." He eyed the priest, as if he expected him to interrupt, but the man stood still. "It's interesting stuff, isn't it, padre?"

She scrutinized the dusty brown face in the rubble. It looked as human as she did. "A lion's jaw exerts six hundred pounds of pressure per square inch. To support such power, the tooth sockets harden and thicken around the fangs, as these have done."

"So what you are saying," Jordan said, clearing his throat, "is that these fangs aren't just a weird fashion statement. That they're *natural*?"

She sighed. "I can't come up with another explanation that fits."

In the dim light of her flashlight, she read the shock on Jordan's face and the fear in his eyes. She felt it, too, and she would not let her feelings overwhelm her. Instead, she turned to the silent priest for answers. "You called them *strigoi*?"

His face had closed into an unreadable mask of shadows and secrets. "Their curse bears many names. *Vrykolakas. Asema. Dhakhanavar.* They are a scourge once known in all corners of the world. Today you call them vampires."

Erin sat back. Did a memory of this horror lie at the root of ritualistic tooth filing, a macabre mimicry of a real terror forgotten in the modern age? Forgotten, but not gone. An icy finger traced up her back.

"And you fight them?" Jordan's skepticism filled the tomb.

"I do." The priest's soft voice sounded calm.

"So what does that make you, padre?" Jordan stepped into a wider stance, as if expecting a fight. "Some kind of Vatican commando?"

"I would not use such words." Father Korza folded gloved hands in front of him. "I am but a priest, a humble servant of God. But to serve the Holy See, I and certain other brethren of the cloth have been trained to fight this plague, yes."

Erin had a thousand questions she wanted to ask, but she had a most pressing one, one that had troubled her since the priest stepped into the tomb and said his first words.

The Church has prior claim to what lies within this crypt.

Suddenly glad to have a soldier between them, Erin watched the bloody figure over Jordan's shoulder. "Earlier, you asked about a book that might be hidden here. Is that why we were attacked? Why we're trapped down here?"

The priest's face closed. He craned his neck toward the brick roof as if seeking guidance from above. "The mountain is still moving."

"What—" A great groaning of stone, accompanied by explosive *booms* of crushed rock, interrupted Jordan's question. The ground shook—at first mildly, then more violently.

Erin stumbled into Jordan's back before finding her footing. "Another aftershock?"

"Or the concussive charges weakened the mountain's infrastructure." Jordan looked at the ceiling. "Either way, it's coming down. And soon."

"We must first find the way out," Father Korza said. "Before we discuss other matters."

Jordan moved toward the collapsed entrance.

"We will gain no passage that way." Father Korza slowly turned in a full circle. "But it is said that those who came to hide the book during the fall of Masada used a path known only to a few. A path they sealed behind them as they left."

Jordan scanned the solid walls. "Where?"

The priest's eyes were vacant. "That secret was lost."

"You're not holding out on us, are you?" Jordan asked.

Father Korza fingered rosary beads on his belt. "The path is beyond the knowledge of the Church. No one knows it."

"Not true." Erin ran both hands along the wall closest to her, digging a nail into the mortar between two stones.

All eyes turned to her.

She smiled. "I know the way out."

5:25 P.M.

Jordan hoped that Erin knew what she was talking about. "Show me."

She hurried to the rear of the chamber, dancing her fingertips along rough stone as if reading a book written in Braille.

He followed, patting the stone with one hand, the other still on his submachine gun. He didn't trust Korza. If the priest had warned them from the start, Jordan's men might still be alive. Jordan wasn't going to turn his back on him anytime soon.

"Feel how clean the masonry is along this wall?" Erin asked. "The blocks fit so perfectly that little mortar was even needed. I suspect they only cemented it as an extra measure to secure the vault against quakes."

"So it's probably the only reason we're still alive," he said. "Let's hear it for overbuilding."

A distracted smile played across her lips. He hoped to see that smile again out in the sunlight, somewhere safe.

At the back wall, she dropped to a knee beside the impaled bodies. Her shoulders tensed, and her eyes fixed on the wall, averted from the dead. But she kept going. He admired that. She placed a palm against the ancient bricks and stroked it downward.

"I noticed this earlier." The ground jolted, and her next words rushed out. "Before the attack. When we were examining the girl." She took his hand and placed it beside hers on the stones. "Feel the ridges of mortar pushing out between the bricks."

He touched the cold unyielding stone.

"This section is unlike the other walls," she rattled on eagerly. "Skilled masons, such as those who built this vault, would skim the excess mortar away, to create a clean look and to protect the mortar from being knocked out if anyone brushed against the wall."

"Are you saying that they got sloppy here?"

"Far from it. Whoever built this section of wall was working from the *other* side. That's why the mortar is bulging out *toward* us here."

"A sealed doorway." He whistled. "Nice going, Doc."

He studied it. The mortared section formed a rough archway. She might be right. He pounded the wall with the flat of his fist. It didn't give. "Feels damned solid to me."

To dig this out would take hours, maybe days. And he suspected they had only minutes. Erin had done a good job, but it wouldn't be enough to save them.

A section of roof near the entrance broke away and fell with a deafening crash. Erin flinched, and he moved toward her protectively. They'd end up buried down here with the corpses of monsters and men.

His men, with Cooper and McKay.

"McKay," he said aloud.

The holy man frowned, but Erin glanced at McKay's twisted body. Her eyes brightened with hope and understanding.

"Do you have enough time?" she asked.

"When I'm *this* motivated? Damned straight."

He headed across the rubble and knelt beside McKay's body.

I'm sorry, buddy.

He gently rolled his lifeless body to the side. He kept his eyes off the ruin of his friend's throat, resting a hand on his shoulder. He held back memories of his friend's barking laugh, his habit of peeling labels off of beer bottles, his hangdog look when confronted by a beautiful woman.

All gone.

But never forgotten, my friend.

He freed the backpack and returned to the wall where Erin waited. He didn't want her to be alone with the priest. He didn't know what the man might do. The holy man was full of secrets, secrets that had cost his men their lives. What would Korza do to keep those secrets if they escaped this prison?

No matter what was planned, the mountain would probably crush them first. Jordan hurriedly unzipped the backpack. As the team's demolitions expert, McKay carried explosives, originally brought along to blow up canisters and neutralize any residual threat. Back when they thought they were dealing with something simple, like terrorists.

He worked fast, fingers inserting blasting caps into blocks of C-4. McKay could have done this faster, but Jordan shied away from that well of pain, unable to face the loss. That would come later. If there was a later.

He shaped and wired charges, doing fast calculations in his head while keeping an eye on Erin as she talked to the priest.

"The girl," she said, waving an arm toward the child on the wall. "You're telling me that she was two thousand years old when she died?"

Korza's voice was so low that Jordan had to strain to hear his answer. "She was *strigoi.* Sealed in here to protect the book. A mission she performed until those silver bolts ended her life."

As he worked, Jordan pictured those grisly events unfolding: *the Nazis opened the sarcophagus, found the little girl still alive in the damn coffin, then staked her to the wall with a hail of silver crossbow bolts.* He remembered the crushed gas mask spotted near the tomb's entrance. The Nazis must have known what they would find here. They had come expecting both the girl *and* that toxic gas.

Erin pressed, clearly seeking some way to understand all of this, to insert it into a scientific equation that made sense. "So the Church used this poor girl. Forced her to be its guard dog for two thousand years?"

"She was no *girl,* and she was asleep, preserved in the holy wine that bathed her." Korza's words fell to a pained whisper. "Still, you are correct. Not all agreed with such a cruel decision. Nor even the choice of this accursed place. It is said the apostle Peter picked this mountain, that tragic time, to bind the blood sacrifice of the Jewish martyrs to this tomb, to use that black pall to protect the treasure."

"Wait," Erin scoffed. "*The* apostle Peter . . . *Saint* Peter? Are you saying he ordered someone to bring the book here during the siege of Masada?"

"No. Peter carried the book here himself." The priest's hands fiddled with his rosary. "Accompanied only by those he trusted best."

Jordan suspected he wasn't supposed to be telling them any of this.

"That can't be," Erin argued. "They crucified Peter during the reign of Nero. Roughly three years *before* Masada fell."

Korza turned away, his voice quiet. "History is not always recorded with precision."

On that cryptic note, Jordan finished his preparations. He stood and lifted the wireless detonator. Erin looked a question at him.

He wished he had more comforting words.

"Either this will work . . . or I'm going to kill us all."

11

October 26, 6:01 P.M., IST
Undisclosed location, Israel

Sitting in his hospital bed, Tommy fingered the IV port sticking out of his chest. He did this numbly, not out of curiosity. He knew why the nurse had inserted it there. He'd had one before. After so many blood draws, they were afraid of collapsing a vein.

His doctor—a thin woman with sharp cheekbones, olive-green scrubs, and a grim expression—had not bothered to tell him her name, which was weird. Usually doctors kept introducing themselves and expected you to remember them. This one acted as if she wanted to be forgotten.

He hiked up the thin flannel blanket and looked around. It seemed like any other hospital room: motorized bed, intravenous lines pumping who knew what into his blood, a table with an olive-green plastic pitcher and cup.

He did miss that there was no television stuck up on the wall, not that he would have understood anything on the Israeli channels. But after his months in the hospital before, he knew there was comfort in the familiar movement on the flickering screen.

With nothing else to do, he got out of bed and pulled his IV pole along with him toward the window, the linoleum tiles cold against his bare feet. The view outside was only moonlit desert, an endless expanse of rocks and shrubs. Beyond the parking lot, not a man-made light could be seen. The Israelis had dragged him out to the middle of nowhere.

Why?

Hospitals were in cities, places with people, lights, and cars. But he had seen none of those things when the helicopter landed in that parking lot, just a cluster of mostly dark buildings.

In the chopper, he had been strapped in the middle seat, between two Israeli commandos. Both had leaned as far away from him as they could, as if they were scared to touch him. He could guess why. Earlier, he had overheard one of the American soldiers mention that he had chemical breakdown elements of that toxic gas still on his clothes and hair. No one dared touch him until he was decontaminated.

Back at Masada, he had been stripped naked inside the contamination tent, his clothes taken. And once he got here, they forced him into a series of chemical showers, seeming to scrub every dead cell off of his skin. Even that dirty water had been collected into sealed tubs.

He bet that was why he was here in the middle of nowhere: to be a guinea pig so they could figure out why he had survived that gas when everyone else died.

After all of that, he was glad he never mentioned anything about the melanoma lesion vanishing from his wrist. One finger absently rubbed that spot, still trying to fathom what that meant. His secret was an easy one to keep. Hardly anyone spoke to him—they spoke *around* him, *about* him, but seldom *to* him.

Only one person looked him in the eye.

Father Korza.

He remembered that dark gaze framed in a gentle face. His words had been kind, asking as much about his mother and father as about the horrors of the day. Tommy wasn't Catholic, but he still appreciated the Father's kindness.

As he thought again of his parents, tears threatened—but he put them in the box. He'd invented the box to deal with his cancer treatments. When things hurt too much, he boxed them up for later. With his declining health and terminal diagnosis, he'd never imagined he would live long enough to ever have to open it.

He stared down at his bare wrist.

Now, it seemed, he would.

12

October 26, 6:03 P.M., IST
Masada, Israel

Erin crouched behind the sarcophagus, her hands clamped over her ears. She flinched as Jordan triggered the C-4 planted against the wall. The blast hit her gut like a blow. Rock dust rolled across the chamber. Sand sifted down from the roof, brushing her exposed skin like the whispery crawl of a thousand spiders.

Then Jordan yanked her up, hard. "Move it!"

She didn't understand his urgency—until the echo of the blast in her ears continued to grow louder. She stared up as the ground jostled under her.

Another aftershock.

The priest took her other arm and pulled her toward the smoking wall. A small hole had been knocked out of it. But it was *too* small.

"Help me!" Jordan called out.

Working together, the three of them yanked out loosened bricks along the edges. Beyond the hole loomed a dark passageway, chiseled out of the rock. Long ago, men had dug it to take them somewhere—and right now *any*where was better than here.

The quaking grew worse. The treacherous ground shifted under her and slammed her into the wall.

"No more time!" Jordan hollered and yanked out one last brick, creating a tight squeeze. "Everybody out!"

Before they could act, a resounding *boom* threw them all to the floor.

Overhead, a crack split the arched roof.

Jordan jumped up, grabbed Erin, and shoved her into the stone opening. Skin ripped off her elbows as she scrambled through. She regained her feet in the passageway and shone her light back at Jordan.

"You next, padre," Jordan called. "You're smaller than me."

With a nod, the priest dove headlong through the narrow hole and rolled into a ready crouch beside Erin. He took a quick look around the passageway. What did he expect to see?

Erin turned back to Jordan. He gave her a quick grin. Behind his back, the entire roof dropped in one large piece, crushing the sarcophagus.

Jordan leaped at the opening. He got one shoulder through the hole, then stuck fast. His face reddened with effort. The tomb continued to collapse behind him, imploding under the mountain's weight. His blue eyes met hers. She read his expression. He wouldn't make it. He motioned his head toward the dark passageway, indicating that she should leave him.

Then Father Korza was there. Impossibly strong fingers snagged Jordan's free arm and yanked with such force that bricks broke away as his body popped free. Jordan fell atop the priest, gasping, his face contorted between agony and relief.

Father Korza lifted and helped him up.

"Thanks, padre." Jordan cradled his arm. "Good thing I don't need that shoulder."

The priest gestured down the dark passageway. It dropped steeply, carved with crude stairs. As the entire mountain shook, it was clear they were not yet out of danger.

"Go!" he said.

Erin wasn't about to argue.

She fled down the tunnel, leaping steps, her tiny flashlight all she had to lead the way. The path zigzagged. The mountain shifted. She lost track of right and left. Up and down. Only forward mattered.

A misstep twisted her right ankle. Before she could fall, the priest scooped her up and hauled her in a fireman's carry. The arm locked around her was iron; his muscular movement as he ran reminded her of the flow of molten rock.

After a precarious flight down a steep section of the passageway, he abruptly stopped and set her down.

She caught her breath and tried her ankle. Sore but not bad. She swept her tiny beam ahead. Light splashed against a wall of limestone that blocked their way.

Jordan groaned as he joined them. "Dead end."

6:33 P.M.

Rhun ran his hands across the flat wall of rock that blocked their way, examining its surface for any clues. A flicker of warmth spread to his hand. Though night had fallen, the stone still held some of the sun's heat.

He closed his eyes, picturing a massive stone, pushed into place to seal the outer entrance to the tunnel. He'd already felt the gaps along the bottom corner.

Next, he laid his ear against the rough surface, listening, concentrating on the world beyond the stone. As he strained, he heard life outside: the soft pad of paws on sand, the faint heartbeat of a jackal—

"Do we go back, padre?" Jordan asked, his voice boomingly loud. "Look for another passage?"

But the American knew there was no other passage.

"We are nearly free," Rhun declared, straightening and turning. "This is the last obstacle."

But time was running short, flowing like sand through an hourglass.

In this case, literally.

Overhead, the mountain continued to shake. Sand now poured down the passageway's steep steps, sifting through fissures and cracks far above and accumulating in this lowest section of the tunnel. It would not take long to completely fill the tiny space.

Jordan joined Rhun and placed a palm on the rock. "So then we push?"

There was no other choice.

Erin joined them, tucking soft blond hair behind her ears.

Rhun threw his weight against the stone next to theirs. He recognized the futility after the first attempt, but he labored with them until their heartbeats betrayed their exhaustion, and he smelled blood on their palms where rock had torn their skin. The shared efforts had not been nearly enough.

All the while Masada shook.

Sand had climbed midway to his calves.

Side by side, the other two rested their backs against the immovable rock.

"How about that grenade on your belt?" The woman pointed. "Could it blow through the stone?"

The soldier sagged. "It's not enough to destroy it. And the blast would deflect right back at us. Even if I hadn't used up the C-4 in McKay's demolition pack, I doubt we could blow that rock without turning us into hamburger."

A strong jolt rocked the mountain. The woman's face whitened. The soldier stared at the rock as if he were vowing to move it by sheer force of will. Desperation etched his features, the raw desire to live another hour, another day.

The soldier slipped an arm around the woman and pulled her close. She softened against him, burying her face in his shoulder. The man gently kissed the top of her head, possibly so softly she never felt it. How effortlessly they had moved into an embrace. The priest stared at the simple comfort of contact, of touch, the solace found only in companionship.

An ache cut into him, a longing to be like them.

But that was not his role. He turned and faced the boulder, determined to serve them.

Sand rained on his brow and lashes. With his face still upturned, he closed his eyes in prayer.

Thy word is a lamp unto my feet, and a light unto my path.

Bits of scripture flowed through his head, both a search for answers and a focus for his mind. He opened himself to God's will, letting go.

As sand slowly climbed his legs, he waited—but no answer came.

So be it.

He would find his end here.

As he touched his cross, a line of scripture suddenly glowed gold before his mind's eye: *And Joseph bought fine linen, and took him down, and wrapped him in the linen, and laid him in a sepulcher which was hewn out of a rock . . .*

Of course.

His eyes flew open, and he studied the immutable stone. He touched its flat surface, picturing an equally flat surface on the other side. He remembered the gaps along the bottom, how he had found that the stone's edges had been *curved*. He imagined that curve extending fully around the stone, forming a circle.

In his mind, he saw it.

A flat *disk* of rock.

His lips moved in a silent prayer of thanks, then he crossed to the others.

The woman stood up to meet him. "What is it?"

She must have noticed something in his face. That alone illustrated Rhun's own desperation, that another could read him so easily. Hope flared in her eyes.

As the soldier joined them, Rhun unclipped the grenade from his belt.

"That won't work," the man said. "I was just explaining—"

"Trust me." Rhun waded through the pool of sand back to the boulder and dug down near the corner, where the rock met the wall. He dug swiftly, but the sand fought him, filling as fast as he could scoop it out.

He couldn't do this alone.

"Help me."

The others flanked him.

"Dig to the floor," he ordered.

They worked together until the sand was clear along the bottom edge, exposing a small curved gap between the stone disk and tunnel floor. Rhun reached down and jammed the grenade deep into that crack, wedging it under the disk's edge.

He then placed a finger in the pin's ring and spoke over his shoulder. "Get back as far up the tunnel as you can reach."

"What about you?" the soldier asked.

With no one digging, sand poured back into the hole, burying his wrist, then his forearm. "I will follow you."

The soldier hesitated, but he finally nodded and pulled the woman with him.

Erin called to him, "How do you know it will work?"

Rhun didn't. He had to trust in God—and in a certain line from the Bible, one concerning boulders sealing tombs.

Mark 15:46.

He whispered it now, both as answer and as prayer.

"And Joseph bought fine linen, and took him down, and wrapped him in the linen, and laid him in a sepulcher which was hewn out of a rock—and rolled a stone unto the door of the sepulcher."

With those words, he yanked the pin on the grenade, pulled his arm free, and fought against the cataract of flowing sand.

He made it in just three steps.

The grenade coughed behind him, a giant, barking wheeze that blew a dusty fireball across his back. His head clipped the edge of a wall as he fell to the floor.

Dazed, vision swimming, he flopped over to his back.

Feet pounded down the steps toward him.

He lay flat, unmoving.

The air tasted of sand and smoke—then a breeze suffused the passageway. A sweet, clean waft of desert air.

"I've got him." The soldier hooked Rhun under the armpits and dragged him across the sand-strewn floor.

The woman ran ahead. "Look! The force of the grenade blast *rolled* the stone two feet to the side. Why didn't I think of that? They'd sealed this place just like Christ's tomb."

"*. . . rolled a stone unto the door of the sepulcher,*" he mumbled, fading in and out.

Of course she recognized what he'd done.

He felt himself dragged past the blackened stone and out into the open air. He looked up. The stars were bright, razor-sharp, eternal. Those stars had watched Masada being built, and now they bore witness to its destruction.

A great crescendo of grating stone and booming rock sounded as the mountain collapsed, utterly.

Then at long last, silence.

Still, Erin and Jordan continued to haul the priest far out into the desert, not taking any chances. But finally they stopped.

A warm hand squeezed Rhun's shoulder. He caught a glimpse of amber eyes. "Thank you, Father, for saving our lives."

Such simple words. Words he rarely heard. As a soldier of God, he often went for days without speaking to another soul. That earlier ache—as he watched the pair embrace on the stairs—returned, only slicing deeper now, almost too painful to bear. He stared into those eyes.

Would I feel this way if she weren't so lovely?

As darkness drowned him, she leaned closer. "Father Korza, what book were you looking for here?"

She and the soldier had fought, killed, and had friends die because of the book. Had they not earned an answer? For that reason alone, he told her.

"It is the Gospel. Written in the blood of its maker."

Behind her, stars framed her face. "What do you mean? Are you talking about some lost apocryphal text?"

He heard the hunger in her voice, the desire for knowledge, but she did not seem to understand. He turned his heavy head to meet her eyes directly. She had to see his sincerity.

"It is *the* Gospel," he repeated as darkness took away the world. "Written by Christ's own hand. In his own blood."

PART II

Jesus did many other miraculous signs in the presence of his disciples, which are not recorded in this book.

—John 20:30

13

October 26, 6:48 P.M., IST
Airborne over Masada, Israel

The Eurocopter spiraled over the smoking caldera that was Masada. The pilot fought thermals rising from the desert as the dark sands slowly released the sun's heat. The blades churned the rock dust, engines whining as they sucked the fouled air.

The helicopter suddenly bumped and banked hard left, coming close to throwing Bathory out the open bay door. She held tight to a railing and stared below. A fire still raged atop the blasted summit. She could feel the heat on her face, as if she were staring into the sun. She closed her eyes, and for a moment imagined a youthful summer day at her country estate along the Drava River in her rural Hungary, sitting in the garden, watching her younger brother, Istvan, play, chasing butterflies with his tiny net.

A groan drew her attention back into the cabin, the interruption piquing her irritation. She turned to the young corporal lying on the floor, whose pale face and pinprick pupils spoke of his deep shock.

Tarek knelt on his shoulders while his brother, Rafik, carved into the man's chest with the point of a dagger, idly, as if bored. Afterward, he absently licked the blade, as if wetting the tip of a pen, ready to continue his writing.

"Don't," she warned.

Tarek glanced hard at her, one corner of his lip curling in anger, showing teeth. Rafik lowered his dagger. His ferret eyes darted between his brother and Bathory, his face lighting with the delight of what might happen.

"I have one last question for him," she said, staring Tarek down.

She met the animal's gaze. To her, that was all Tarek and Rafik were—animals.

Tarek finally backed down and waved his brother away.

She took Rafik's place. She placed a palm on the soldier's cheek. He looked so much like Istvan. It was why she forbade them from marring his face. He stared up at her, piteous, nearly blind with pain, barely in this world.

"I made you a promise," she said, leaning close as if to kiss his lips. "One last question and you'll be free."

His eyes met hers.

"Erin Granger, the archaeologist."

She let that name sink through his stupor. He'd already talked, spilling forth most everything he knew as they escaped the crumbling, fiery summit of Masada. She would have left him there to die with his brothers-in-arm, but she needed to squeeze everything she could out of this man, no matter the cruelty. She had learned long ago the practicality of cruelty.

"You said Dr. Granger worked with some students."

She remembered the woman she'd viewed via the ROV's camera. The archaeologist had been waving her cell phone, clearly attempting to reach the outside world. But for what? Had she been taking pictures? Discovered some clue?

Likely not, but before Bathory left the region, she must be absolutely certain.

The corporal's pupils fixed to her, agonized, knowing what she intended.

"Where are they?" she asked. "Where was Dr. Granger's dig?"

A tear flowed, touching her palm where it rested against his cheek.

For a moment—just a fleeting breath—she hoped he wouldn't say.

But he did. His lips moved. She leaned an ear to hear the single word.

Caesarea.

She straightened, already beginning to plan in her head. Rafik stared intently at her, desire ripe in his eyes. He liked pretty things. His fingers tightened on his dagger.

She ignored him and stroked hair back from the corporal's white forehead.

So like Istvan . . .

She leaned down, kissed his cheek, and slipped her own blade across his throat. Dark blood spurted. A small gasp brushed her ear.

When she straightened, she found his eyes already dull.

Free at last.

"None will touch his body," she warned the others as she stood.

Rafik and Tarek stared at her, not comprehending such a waste.

Ignoring them, she took a seat and leaned her head back. She did not need to explain herself to the likes of them. With her back against the rear cargo hold, she sensed a stirring back there, a heavy shifting. She reached up and placed a palm on the bulkhead.

Calm yourself, she thought, casting out her will, bathed in reassurance. *Everything is fine.*

He settled, but she still felt his agitation, mirroring her own. He must have sensed the distress in her heart a moment ago.

Or maybe it was because his twin was missing.

She stared out the window, down at the desert.

The twin had been sent out to hunt.

She had to be sure.

Sanguinists were hard to kill.

14

October 26, 7:11 P.M., IST
Desert beyond Masada, Israel

Deep in thought, Erin cradled the head of the unconscious priest in her lap. Starlight twinkled above, a sickle moon scraped at the horizon, and a soft evening breeze whispered sand down the faces of dunes.

She studied the man's face, his head resting on her knees.

Is it possible?

The priest claimed that Christ had written a Gospel. Surely he must have been raving. He had a goose egg on the right side of his head, near the temple.

She touched his icy brow. "Jordan!"

The soldier stood a few steps away, scanning the desert, standing guard against any pursuers—or maybe he needed time to think, too. Or mourn.

He turned to her.

"I think he's going into shock," she said. "He's gone so cold and pale."

Jordan came and crouched next to her. Unlike the priest, warmth radiated from his body.

"Guy was already pale," he said. "Probably lives in a library and works out at night."

She took in Jordan's appearance. Even covered in soot and grime, he was an attractive man. She tried not to remember how safe she had felt in his arms back in the tunnel, how natural it was to fold against him, how the musky smell of him had enveloped her as warmly as his body. She could not forget the soft kiss atop her head. She had pretended not to notice, while secretly wanting more. But that moment, born of desperation and the fear of certain death, was over.

The priest's head moved in her lap. She looked down at him again.

Jordan reached out and gently parted the bloody shreds of his shirt, examining the wounds beneath. The white of the priest's well-muscled chest looked like marble against Jordan's tanned skin. A silver pectoral cross, about the size of her palm, hung from a black silk cord and rested over the priest's heart atop a scrap of shirt that had not been shredded.

Inscribed on the cross were the words *Munire digneris me*.

She translated the beginning of the prayer: Deign to fortify me.

"Guy took a beating," Jordan diagnosed.

With his skin bared, the severity of his wounds became clear. Lacerations crisscrossed his flesh, gently weeping.

"How much blood did he lose?" she asked.

"Not too much. Most of his wounds look superficial."

She winced.

"Painful," he admitted. "But not life-threatening."

Still, a shiver shook through her—but not from worry. It was already much colder as the desert quickly lost its heat.

Jordan dug a small first-aid kit from his pocket and went to work on the priest's head. She smelled alcohol as he pulled out a wipe.

He raised a bigger health concern regarding the priest. "I'm more worried about that knock he took when the grenade exploded. He could have a concussion or a fractured skull."

Jordan stripped off his camouflage jacket and spread it over the priest's limp body. "He seemed pretty coherent a minute ago when you two were talking. Still, we need to get him some real medical care soon."

Erin stared down at Father Korza.

Rhun, she reminded herself.

His first name suited him better. It was softer, and hinted at darker mysteries. Atop the shreds of his shirt he wore a Roman clerical collar of white linen, not the plastic worn by most modern priests.

Now that he was unconscious, his face had relaxed from its stern planes. His lips were fuller than she'd first thought, his chiseled features more pronounced. Dark umber hair hung in wavy locks over his brow, down to his round collar. She smoothed them off his face.

Worry burned brighter at the icy feel of his skin.

Would he wake up? Or die like Heinrich?

Jordan coughed. She drew her hand back. Rhun was a priest, and she should not be playing with his hair.

"What about your radio?" she said, rubbing her palms together. She had lost her cell phone. It was now entombed somewhere inside that mountain. Jordan had been fiddling with his handset earlier. "Any luck reaching someone?"

"No." Jordan's face tightened with concern. "Its case got cracked. With time, I might get it working."

Goose bumps ran down Jordan's bare arms from the cold. Still, he tucked his coat more securely around Rhun.

"What's the plan, then?" she asked.

He flashed a quick grin. "I thought you made the plans."

"I thought I was supposed to ask how high and then jump. Weren't those your orders?"

He looked back at the collapsed mountain, and a shadow passed across his face. "Those under my orders didn't fare so well."

She kept her voice low. "I don't see what you could have done differently."

"Maybe if this one," he said, jerking a thumb toward the unconscious priest, "had told us what we were dealing with, we might have stood a better chance."

"He came down to warn us."

Jordan grimaced. "He came down to find that book. He had plenty of time to warn us before we went down, or to warn the men topside that those monsters were coming. But he didn't."

She found herself defending the priest, since the man couldn't do it himself. "Still, he did fight to get us out of there. And he got us into that sarcophagus during the explosion."

"Maybe he just needed our help to get the hell out of there."

"Maybe." She gestured across the wide expanse of sand. "But what do we do next?"

His face was stony. "For now, I think it's best if he's not moved. It's about all we can do for him: keep him warm and quiet. After that explosion, rescue teams must be coming here from all directions. We should stay put. They'll find us soon enough."

He moved aside the coat and felt across Rhun's body.

"What are you doing?"

"Looking for identification. I want to know who this guy really is. He's certainly no ordinary priest."

Erin felt bad at mugging the priest while he was unconscious, but she had to admit that she was just as curious.

Jordan didn't discover any driver's license or passport, but he did draw Rhun's knife from a wrist sheath. He also discovered a leather water flask buttoned in a thigh pocket.

He unscrewed the cap and took a swig.

Thirsty, too, Erin held out her hand, wanting a drink.

Jordan twisted up his face and sniffed at the opening of the flask. "That's not water."

She frowned.

"It's wine."

Wine?

She took the flask and sipped. He was right.

"This guy gets stranger and stranger," Jordan said. "I mean look at this."

He lifted Rhun's knife, the curved blade shaped like a crescent. It shone silver in the moonlight.

And maybe it was silver, like the bolts that had nailed the girl to the wall.

"The weapon's called a *karambit*," Jordan said.

He hooked a finger in a ring at the base of the hilt and demonstrated with fast flicks of his wrist how the weapon could be deployed in several different positions.

She looked away, flashing back to the battle, blood flying from that blade.

"Strange weapon for a priest," he said.

To her, it was the *least* strange part of the night.

But Jordan wasn't done. "Not only because most holy men don't normally carry knives, but because of its origin. The weapon is from Indonesia. The style goes back more than eight hundred years. The ancient Sudanese copied the blade's shape from the claws of a tiger."

She looked at Rhun, remembering his skill.

Like his name, the weapon fit him.

"But here's the oddest detail." He held the knife where she could see it. "From the patina, I'd say this blade is at least a hundred years old."

They both stared at the priest.

"Maybe far older." Jordan's voice dropped to a conspiratorial whisper. "What if he's one of them?"

"One of whom?"

He raised one blond eyebrow.

She understood what he was implying. "A *strigoi*?"

"You saw how he lifted that crypt's lid?" His voice held a challenge.

She accepted it. "He could've been riding a surge of adrenaline. Like women lifting cars off babies. I don't know, but I rode from Caesarea with him. In broad daylight. You met him on Masada's summit while the sun was still up."

"Maybe these *strigoi* can go out in sunlight. Hell, we don't know anything about them." Fury and loss marked his face. "All I know for sure is that I don't trust him. If Korza had warned us in time, more than *three* of us would be standing here."

She put a hand on Jordan's warm forearm, but he shrugged it off and stood.

She stared down at the man in her lap, remembering his last revelation.

It is the Gospel. Written by Christ's own hand. In his own blood.

If this was true, what did it imply?

Questions burned through her: What revelations could be hidden within the pages of this lost Gospel? Why did the *strigoi* want it so badly? And more important, why did the Church hide it here?

Jordan must have read her train of thought.

"And that book," he said. "The one that got so many good men killed. I'm pretty sure there are only *four* Gospels in the Bible. Matthew, Mark, Luke, and John."

Erin shook her head, happy to return to a subject she knew something about. "Actually, there are many more Gospels. The Dead Sea Scrolls alone contain bits of a *dozen* different ones. From various sources. From Mary, Thomas, Peter, even Judas. Only four made it into the Bible. But none of those hint at Christ writing His own book."

"Then maybe the Church purged them. Wiped away any references." He set his chin. "We now know how good the Church is at keeping secrets."

It made a certain sense.

With no references, no hints of its existence, no one would search for it.

She glanced up at Jordan, surprised again at his sharpness, even when he was overwhelmed by emotion.

"Which makes me wonder," he continued. "If I was the Church and I had an ancient document written by Jesus Christ, I'd be waving that thing around for all to see. So why did Saint Peter bury it here? What was he hiding?"

Besides the existence of strigoi? She didn't bother voicing that question. It was only one among so many.

Jordan turned to the priest. He held the blade threateningly. "There's one person who has the answers."

Rhun jerked, sitting straight up. His eyes took in them both.

Had he overheard them?

The priest turned, staring hard into the darkness. His nostrils flared, as if he were testing the air.

He spoke again with that dreadful calmness. "Something is near. Something terrible."

Her heart jolted into her throat, choking her silent.

Jordan voiced her terror. "More *strigoi*?"

"There are worse things than *strigoi*."

15

October 26, 7:43 P.M., IST
Desert beyond Masada, Israel

Rhun held out his hand toward the soldier. "My knife."

Without hesitating, Jordan slapped it into his open palm. Rhun collected the remains of his tattered cassock around himself, knowing he'd need every bit of protection.

"What's coming?" The soldier drew his pistol. Rhun respected that he'd had foresight to scavenge extra ammunition clips from his dead team members back in the tomb.

It would help, but little.

An acrid odor cut through the scents of cooling sand and desert flowers, and Rhun shook his head to clear it. He whispered a quick prayer.

"Rhun?" The woman's brow knit.

"It is a *blasphemare,*" he said.

The soldier checked his weapon. "What the hell is that?"

Rhun wiped his blade along his dirty pants. "A corrupted beast. A creature whose strength and senses are heightened by tainted *strigoi* blood."

The soldier kept his gun up. "What sort of corrupted beast, exactly?"

The howling answer pierced the darkness, echoing all around, followed by the crashing sounds of animals fleeing. Nothing wanted to be near the creature that made that sound.

Rhun gave it a name. "A grimwolf." He pointed his blade to a nest of boulders and offered them one thin chance to survive. "Hide."

The man snapped around, a skilled enough soldier to know when to obey. He grasped the woman's hand and sprinted with her toward the scant cover of the rocks.

Rhun searched the darkness, drawing in his awareness. The howl told him the beast knew it had been discovered. It sought to unnerve them.

And he could not say it had failed.

His fingers tightened on his cold blade, trying to block out the overpowering thump of the wolf's heartbeat. It was too loud for him to nail it down to one specific spot, so he strove to keep it from overwhelming him, to block it out in order to be open for other sounds.

He sensed the creature, a shift of shadows, circling them.

But where . . . ?

A muted thud on the sand behind him.

He could not turn in time.

The beast shed the night, as if throwing off a cloak, its black fur dark as oil. It charged. Rhun dropped, twisting away from its path.

Powerful jaws snapped shut, catching only cloth. The wolf snagged the edge of his ripped cassock and barreled on. Rhun was yanked off his feet, but the cloth ripped, setting him free.

He rolled, sharp desert stones and thorns slicing his bare back. He used the momentum to push into a crouch, finally facing his adversary.

The grimwolf spun, froth flying. Lips rippled back from yellow fangs. It was massive, the size of bears that roamed the Romanian mountains of his boyhood. The beast's red-gold eyes shone with a malignancy that had no place under the sun.

Tall ears flattened to its skull, and a low growl rumbled from its chest. Hooked nails, long enough to puncture a man's heart, scraped the sand. Haunch muscles bunched into iron-hard cords.

Rhun waited. Long ago, when he was fresh to the cross, such a beast nearly ended his life—and then he hadn't been alone. He'd had two others at his side. Grimwolves were nearly impossible to kill, lithe of mind and muscle, with hides as tough as chain mail and a speed that made them more shadow than flesh.

Few blades could harm them. And Rhun had lost his.

He clenched empty fingers. From the corner of his eye, he caught the glint of silver in the sand, where he'd dropped his blade when he was torn off his feet. He could not recover it in time.

As if the wolf knew this, its lips pulled farther back into a savage snarl.

Then it thundered toward him.

He feinted to the right, but the scarlet eyes tracked him. The wolf would not be fooled again. It leaped straight at him.

A harsh shout exploded out of the desert—followed by a shattering blast. In midleap, the wolf's hindquarters buckled. The beast's massive shoulder smashed the sand. Its bulk slid toward him.

Rhun twisted away and scrambled toward his knife.

Beyond the wolf's hackles, he spotted the soldier running toward him, away from the nest of boulders. Muzzle flashes sparked in the darkness as he emptied his clip.

Stupid, brave, impossible man.

Rhun snatched up his knife.

Already the beast had regained its feet, standing between Rhun and the soldier. The wolf's head swiveled, taking them both in. Its blood blackened the sand.

But not nearly enough.

The soldier dropped a smoking clip and slapped in another. Even such a weapon could not deter a grimwolf. Its heart thundering in battle, a grimwolf ignored pain and all but the most grievous wounds.

The scarred muzzle wavered between them. A black-ruby cunning gleamed from its eyes.

Suddenly Rhun knew whom the beast would attack.

With a burst of muscle, it leaped away.

Toward the rocks.

Toward the weakest of them.

7:47 P.M.

The monster barreled toward Erin. With her back to a stack of boulders, she had nowhere to hide. If she ran, it would be upon her in heartbeats. She wedged herself farther into the rocks. Held her breath.

Jordan fired. Bullets stitched across the beast's flank, blasting away spats of fur, but it did not slow. Rhun, too, ran toward her, at incredible speed. Unfortunately, he'd never reach her in time. And he couldn't stop the creature anyway.

The beast skidded on four massive paws, spraying sand into her eyes. Spittle spattered her cheeks. Hot, fetid breath surrounded her.

She pulled out her only weapon—from her sock.

A claw gouged her thigh, dragging her closer, as its jaws opened monstrously wide.

Erin screamed and punched her arm past those teeth, deep into its maw. She drove the atropine dart's needle deep into the monster's blood-rich tongue. Her arm jerked free before the jaws shut.

Startled, the wolf dropped back and spat out the crumpled plastic syringe. Erin remembered Sanderson's warning: *Atropine jacks your heart rate through the roof . . . strong enough to blow up your ticker if you're not poisoned.*

Corrupted or not, a beast was a beast. She hoped. What if the drug had no effect? Her answer came a heartbeat later.

The wolf shoved back another full step, stretching its neck. A howl ripped from its throat. Its eyes bulged. The atropine had spiked its blood pressure. Oil-black blood gushed from its bullet wounds, pumping onto the sand.

She felt a grim satisfaction as it howled, pictured the freckle-faced young corporal who gave her the dart.

That's for Sanderson.

But the beast, too, sought revenge. Fury and pain twisted its features into something beyond monstrous. It bared its teeth—and lunged for her face.

7:48 P.M.

Rhun could not fathom what the woman had done, how she had driven the grimwolf back, made it scream so. But it gave him time to reach the beast. Pain and anger blinded the creature, but it still must have sensed his approach.

With a roar, it twisted away from Erin and sprang for his throat.

But Rhun was no longer there. Still running, he arched back and slid on the soles of his shoes, passing under the slavering jaws. A mere handsbreadth from his nose, teeth gnashed together. He dropped on one shoulder and skidded between the front legs and under the beast. Once there, he lashed up with his silver dagger, jabbing deep into the belly, one of its few weak spots. He dragged the blade's razor edge through muscle and skin, using all his power. He said a silent prayer for the beast, for what was once one of God's creatures. It did not deserve to have been put to such a cruel use.

Gore poured down on him, soaking his arms, his chest, his face.

He rolled free and crouched to wipe his eyes.

To the side, the soldier ran up, firing point-blank at the beast.

Its muzzle reached for the night sky, wailing—a wail that faded until, at last, it crashed to the sand.

The dark ruby glow faded from its eyes, leaving behind a rich gold. The wolf whimpered once, a flicker of its true nature returning—but only at that last moment.

A final spasm, and it lay still.

Rhun raised two fingers and made the sign of the cross over the animal's body. He had set it free from its eternal bondage.

Dominus vobiscum, he said silently. *The Lord be with you.*

The woman climbed out of the rocks, fragrant blood streaming from a cut on her thigh. The soldier held her back. He kept his weapon pointed at the grimwolf's body.

"Is it really dead, Korza?"

The beast's blood steamed off of Rhun's body. He tasted iron on his lips. It heated his throat, bloomed in his chest. It overwhelmed his senses. In his time doing God's work, he had faced countless temptations and had faltered only one dreadful time. Yet, even steadfast determination could not prevent his body from reacting to the blood.

He turned away.

Behind him, the twin heartbeats of the soldier and the woman thundered for his attention.

He refused it.

He reached back, pulled his cassock's hood low over his eyes, and faced the silent desert—hoping they hadn't seen his fangs begin to lengthen.

16

October 26, 7:49 P.M., IST
Airborne to Caesarea, Israel

Dying along with Hunor, Bathory writhed in pain, curled over her stomach, straining against the helicopter's straps. Her fingers clutched hard to her belly, trying to stanch the flow of blood, the tumult of gore through rent flesh.

She felt her blooded bond mate's life escape. She longed to follow it, to gather that spirit to her bosom and comfort it in its journey.

Hunor . . . my sweet one . . .

But he was already gone, his pain fading from inside her. She stared down at her pale palms. She was whole—but not unwounded. Hunor's last whispery howl of release had left her hollowed out as surely as if she, too, had been gutted.

That last cry was answered by another.

Magor mourned loudly in the cargo hold behind the cabin, calling out for his twin, the anguished mewling of one littermate for another. The two pups had been cut from the belly of a dying she-wolf. They were a gift from Him, blood-bonded to her during a dark rite, becoming as much a part of her as the black tattoo on her throat.

She twisted in her seat and placed her palm against the wall that kept her from Magor, wanting to go to him, to pull him close, to hold together what they once shared, as if cupping a feeble flame against a stiff wind.

I'm here, she cast out, bathing him in reassurance, but not hiding her own sorrow.

How could she?

Three were now two.

The words from an old Hungarian lullaby crooned through her, bringing with it the promise of security and peaceful slumber. She gave that to Magor.

Tente, baba, tente.

Magor calmed, his love entwining with her own, merging them together.

Two would survive.

For one purpose.

Vengeance.

Fortified, she collected herself and stared across the cabin.

The helicopter fled through the deep night, leaving the ruin of Masada far behind. Her remaining men sat subdued and silent in the seats across from her. Although spattered with blood, none of them had been wounded.

Tarek muttered Latin prayers, a reminder that long ago he had been a priest. As his lips moved, his cold eyes stared at her, having witnessed her prostration and grief. He knew what that meant.

Only one creature was capable of slaying a grimwolf in his prime.

Korza was still alive.

Tarek's gaze flicked to her shoulder. Only then did she note the fear burning there. She touched her fingers to her upper arm—they came back wet.

With blood.

Lost in Hunor's agony, she must have ripped herself against a bolt sticking out of the neighboring wall, tearing her shirt and skin.

It was a shallow wound.

Still, Tarek jerked back warily from her bloody fingers.

Scarlet tinged with silver.

Even a drop of her blood was poison to him and all others like him, a curse born out of the mark on her throat. Another of His gifts. The curse in her blood both protected her from the fangs of His armies and was the source of that constant pain in her veins, dull but always there, never abating, never forgotten, flaring with every beat of her heart.

She wiped her fingers and bound her wound one-handed, using her teeth to tighten the knot.

Next to Tarek, his brother, Rafik, bowed his head in clear reverence as Tarek resumed his Latin prayers.

Others simply stared at their bloodstained boots. Their bonds with the fallen soldiers went back decades, or longer. She knew that the men blamed her for those deaths, as would He. She dreaded the punishment He would mete out.

She stared out the window, picturing Korza down there.

Alive.

Anger burned hotter than the pain in her blood.

Magor responded, growling through the wall.

Soon, she promised him.

But first she had a duty in Caesarea. She pictured the archaeologist waving her cell phone in the tomb. She had recognized that look on the woman's face: excitement mixed with desperation. The archaeologist knew something.

I'm sure of it.

But what? A clue about the book's whereabouts? If so, had she been able to transmit that information out before the mountain dropped on her?

The only answer lay in Caesarea.

Where again blood would flow.

This time, with no Sanguinist to stop her.

17

October 26, 8:01 P.M., IST
Desert beyond Masada, Israel

"Korza?"

The soldier's harsh and impatient voice broke through Rhun's thoughts as he faced the desert, hidden in the depths of his hooded cassock. He struggled to hear over the wet, beckoning sound of the man's heart.

"Turn around," the soldier said, "or I will shoot you where you stand."

The woman's heart beat faster now, too. "Jordan! You can't just shoot him."

Rhun considered allowing the sergeant to do just that. It would be easier. But when had his path ever been easy?

He faced them, showing them his true nature.

The woman stumbled back.

The soldier kept his gun leveled at Rhun's chest.

He knew what they must see: his face darkened by blood, his body locked in shadows, his teeth the only brightness in the moonlight.

He felt the beast within him sing, a howl struggling to break free. Soaked in blood, he fought against releasing that beast; fought equally against running into the desert to hide his shame. Instead, he simply lifted his arms straight out from his body at shoulder level.

They needed to see that he was weaponless as much as they needed to see the truth.

Transfixed, the woman controlled her initial terror. "Rhun, you are *strigoi,* too."

"Never. I am Sanguinist. Not *strigoi.*"

The soldier scoffed, never letting his weapon waver. "Looks the same from here."

For them to understand, he knew he must debase himself still further. He hated the mere thought of it, but he saw no other way for them to leave the desert alive.

"Please, bring me my wine," he asked.

His fingers trembled with longing as his arm stretched for the flask half buried in sand.

The woman bent to pick it up.

"Throw it to him," the soldier ordered. "Don't get close."

She did as she was told, her amber eyes wide. The flask landed an arm's length away on the sand.

"May I retrieve it?"

"Slowly." The soldier's weapon stayed fixed; plainly he would not flinch from his duty.

Nor would Rhun. Keeping his eyes on the soldier, he knelt. As soon as his fingers touched the flask, he felt calmer, the bloodlust waning. The wine might yet save them all.

Rhun stared up at the others. "May I walk into the desert and drink it? Afterward, I will explain all."

Please, he prayed. *Please leave me this last bit of dignity.*

It was not to be.

"Stay right there," the soldier warned. "On your knees."

"Jordan, why can't—"

The soldier cut her off. "You are still under my command, Dr. Granger."

Emotions flickered across her face, ending with resignation. Clearly, she did not trust Rhun either. It surprised him how much that hurt.

Raising the flask to his lips, he emptied it in one long swallow. As always, the wine stung his throat, flaming all the way down. He fastened both hands to the cross around his neck and bowed his head.

The heat of the consecrated wine, of Christ's blood, burned away the ropes that bound him to this time, to this place. Unmoored and beyond his control, he fell back to his greatest sins, never able to escape until his penance in this world was complete.

Elisabeta swept through her gardens in her crimson gown, laughing, as bright as the morning's sun, the most brilliant rose among all the blooms.

So beautiful, so full of life.

Though he was a priest, sworn to avoid the touch of flesh, nothing forbid him from looking upon the beauty of God shining forth in the pale glimpse of tender flesh at her ankle as she bent to clip a sprig of lavender, or the curve of her soft cheek when she straightened to stare skyward, her gaze ever on the Heavens.

How she loved the sun—whether it be the warmth of a summer afternoon or merely the cold promise of a bright winter's day.

She continued across the garden now, gathering lavender and thyme to make a poultice for her mare, all the while instructing him on the uses of each. In the months since he had known her, he had learned much about medicinal plants. He had even begun to write a book on the subject, hoping to share her gifts as a healer with the world.

She brushed his palm with her soft fingertips as she handed him stalks of lavender. A thrill surged through his body. A priest should not feel such a thing, but he did not move away. He stepped closer, admiring the sunlight on her jet-black hair, the sweep of her long white neck down to her creamy shoulders, and the curves of her soft silk gown.

Elisabeta's maidservant held up the basket for the lavender. The wisp of a girl turned her head to the side to hide the raspberry-colored birthmark that covered half her face.

"Anna, take the basket back to the kitchen and empty it," Elisabeta instructed, dropping in one more sprig of thyme.

Anna retreated across the field, struggling under the heavy load. Rhun would have helped the small girl carry such a burden, but Elisabeta would never allow it, considering it not his place.

Elisabeta watched her maid leave. Once they were alone, she turned to Rhun, her face now even brighter—if that were possible.

"A moment's peace!" she exclaimed gladly. "It is so lonely with my servants constantly around me."

Rhun, who often chose to spend days alone in dark prayer, understood all too well the loneliness of false company.

She smiled at him. "But not you, Father Korza. I never feel lonely in your company."

He could not hold her gaze. Turning away, he knelt and cut a stalk of lavender.

"Don't you ever tire of it, Father Korza? Always wearing a mask?" She adjusted her wide-brimmed hat. She always took great pains to keep sunlight from her fair skin. Women of her station must not look as if they needed to work in the sun.

"I wear a mask?" He kept his face impassive. If she knew all that he hid, she would run away screaming.

"Of course. You wear the mask of priest. But I must wear many masks, too many for one face to bear easily. Lady, mother, and wife. And others still." She turned a heavy gold ring around and around on her finger, a gift from her husband, Ferenc. "But what is under all of those masks, I wonder."

"Everything else, I suppose."

"But how much truth . . . how much of our true nature can we conceal, Father?" Her low voice sent a shiver down his spine. "And from whom?"

He studied the shadow she cast on the field next to him and mumbled as if in prayer, "We conceal what we must."

Her shadow retreated a pace, perhaps because she was unhappy with his answer—a thought that crushed him as surely as if she ground him under that well-turned heel.

The dark shape of a hawk floated across the field. He listened to its quick heartbeat above and the faint heartbeats of mice below. His service to the Church, the verdant field, the bright sun, the blooming flowers . . . all were bounteous gifts, given freely by God to one as lowly as himself.

Should that not be enough?

She smoothed her hands down the front of her dress. "You are wise, Father. An aristocrat who lowers his mask does not survive long in these times."

He stood. "What is it that troubles you so?"

"Perhaps I am simply weary of the intrigues." Her eyes followed the hawk as it fell. "Surely the Church struggles amidst the same cauldron of ambitions, both great and small?"

He touched his pectoral cross with one fingertip. "Bernard shields me from the worst, I think."

"Never trust those who would be your shield. They feed on your ignorance and darkness. It is best to look at things directly and be unafraid."

He offered her some consolation. "Perhaps it is best to trust those who would shield you. If they do it out of love, to protect you."

"Spoken like a man. And a priest. But I have learned to trust very few." She tilted her head thoughtfully. "Except I trust you, Father Korza."

"I am a priest, so you must trust me." He offered her a shy smile.

"I trust no other priests. Including your precious Bernard. But you are different." She placed her hand on his arm, and he savored the touch. "You are simply a friend. A friend where I have so very few."

"I am honored, my lady." He stepped back and bowed, an exaggerated gesture to lighten the mood.

She smiled indulgently. "As you should be, Father."

They both laughed at her tone.

"Here comes Anna, returned again. Tell me once more about the time you had a footrace with your brother and how you both ended up in the stream with fish in your boots."

He told her the story, embellishing it with more details than he had in the last telling to make her laugh.

They had happy times, with much laughter.

Until, one day, she had stopped laughing.

The day that he betrayed her.

The day he betrayed God.

Back in his body, where cold sand pressed against his knees, dry wind chased tears from his cheeks. His silver cross had burned through his glove and left a scarlet welt on his palms. His shoulders bowed under the weight of his sins, his failures. He tightened his grip on the searing metal.

"Rhun?" A woman's voice spoke his name.

He raised his head, half expecting to see Elisabeta. The soldier watched him with suspicion, but the woman's eyes held only pity.

He fixed his eyes on the soldier. He found the man's hard gaze easier to bear.

"Time to start explaining," the soldier said, training his weapon on Rhun's heart—as if that had not been destroyed long ago.

8:08 P.M.

"Jordan, look at his teeth . . . they're normal again."

Amazed, Erin stepped forward, wanting to examine the miraculous transformation, to understand what her mind still refused to believe.

Jordan blocked her with a muscled arm.

She didn't resist.

Despite her curiosity as a scientist, Rhun still scared her.

The priest's voice came out shaky, his Slavic accent thicker, as if he'd returned from a long distance, from a place where his native tongue was still spoken. "Thank you . . . for your patience."

"Don't expect that patience to last," Jordan said, not unfriendly, just certain.

Erin pushed Jordan's arm down, willing to listen, but she didn't step forward. "You said that you were 'Sanguinist,' not *strigoi.* What does that mean?"

Rhun looked out to the dark desert for that answer. "*Strigoi* are wild, feral creatures. Born of murder and bloodshed, they serve no one but themselves."

"And the Sanguinists?"

"All members of the Order of the Sanguines were once *strigoi,*" Rhun admitted, looking her square in the eye. "But now those in my order serve Christ. It is His blessing that allows us to walk under the light of God's brightness, to serve as His warriors."

"So you can walk in daylight?" Jordan asked.

"Yes, but the sun is still painful," the priest admitted, and touched the hood of his cassock.

She remembered her first sight of Rhun, buried in his cassock, most of his skin covered, wearing dark sunglasses. She wondered if the tradition of Catholic monks wearing hooded robes might not trace back to this Order of the Sanguines, an outward reflection of a deeper secret.

"But without the protection of Christ's blessing," Rhun continued, "the touch of the sun will kill a *strigoi.*"

"And what exactly are these *blessings* of Christ?" Erin asked, surprised at the mocking edge to her tone, but unable to stop it.

Rhun stared at her for a long moment, as if he were struggling to find the right words to explain a miracle. When he finally spoke, his words were solemn, weighted by a certainty that had been missing from most of her life.

"I follow Christ's path and have sworn an oath to forsake the drinking of human blood. Such an act is forbidden to us."

Jordan remained ever practical. "Then what do you *feed* on, padre?"

Rhun straightened. Pride radiated from him, beating across the desert air toward her. "I am sworn to partake only of His blood."

His blood . . .

She heard the emphasis in those last words and knew what that meant.

"You're talking about the *blood of Christ*," she said, surprised now by the absence of mockery in her tone. Raised in a devout sect of Roman Catholicism, she even understood the source of that blood. She flashed to her childhood, kneeling on the dirt floor by the altar, the bitter wine poured on her tongue.

She stared at the water skin in Rhun's grasp.

But it did not hold *water*.

Nor did it hold *wine*—despite what she herself had sipped only moments ago.

She knew what filled Rhun's flask. "That's *consecrated* wine," she said, pointing to what he held.

He reverentially stroked the wineskin. "More than consecrated."

She understood that, too. "You mean it's been *transubstantiated*."

She had been taught that word during her earliest catechism and believed it once herself. Transubstantiation was one of the central tenets of Catholicism. That wine consecrated during a Mass became the literal blood of Christ, imbued with His very essence.

Rhun bowed his head in agreement. "True, my blessed vessel holds wine converted into the blood of Christ."

"Impossible," she muttered, but the word lacked conviction.

Jordan also wasn't buying it. "I drank from your flask, padre. It looks like wine, smells like wine, tastes like wine—"

"But it is not," Rhun broke in. "It is the Blood of Christ."

The mocking edge returned to Erin's tone, and it helped to steady her. "So you're claiming transubstantiation results in a *real* change, not a metaphorical one?"

Rhun held out his arms. "Am I myself not proof? It is His blood that sustains my order. The act of transubstantiation was both a pact and a promise between Christ and mankind, but even more so for the *strigoi* whom He sought to save. For a chance to regain our souls, we have sworn off feeding on humans and survive only upon His blessed blood, becoming Knights of Christ, bound by an oath of fealty to serve the Church to the end of our days, when we will be welcomed again to His side. That is our pact with Christ and the Church."

Erin couldn't bring herself to believe any of this. Her father would turn over in his grave at the mere thought of Christ's blood being used in such a way.

Rhun must have read the doubt on her face. "Why do you think the early Christians referred to Communion wine as the 'medicine of immortality'? Because they knew what has long since been forgotten—but the Church has a much *longer* memory."

He turned his wineskin over so that they could see the Vatican seal inscribed on the back: two crossed keys bound with a cord under the triple crown of the triregnum.

His gaze fell upon Erin. "I ask you to believe nothing but what you see with your own eyes and feel with your own heart."

She sat heavily on a boulder and dropped her head into her hands. She had tasted the wine in his flask. As a scientist, she refused to believe it was anything but wine. Still, she had watched the *strigoi* feed on blood, watched him drink his wine.

Both had been strengthened.

She struggled to fit the miraculous into a scientific equation.

It was *impossible* to turn wine into blood, so it must be *belief* that allowed Rhun to drink wine as if it were blood. It must be some sort of placebo effect.

"You okay, Doc?" Jordan asked.

"Transubstantiation is just a legend." She tried to explain it to him. "A myth."

"Like the *strigoi*?" Rhun interjected. "Those who walk in the night and drink the blood of humans? You could accept them, but you cannot accept that blessed wine is the blood of Christ. Have you no faith at all?"

He sounded more upset by that last detail than by all of her arguments.

"Faith did not serve me well." She clenched her hands in front of her. "I saw the Church used as a tool of the powerful against the weak, religion used as an obstacle to the truth."

"Christ is more than the actions of misguided men." Rhun spoke urgently, as if trying to convert her, as priests so often had. "He lives in our hearts. His miracles sustain us all."

Jordan cleared his throat. "That's all well and good, padre. But back to *you*. How did you become one of these Sanguinists?"

"There is little to tell. Centuries ago, I was bitten by a *strigoi,* then forced to drink quantities of its blood." Rhun shuddered. "I was corrupted into one of them, a creature of base desires, a devourer of men."

"Then what happened?" Jordan asked.

Rhun hurried his words, clearly wanting to be done. "I became *strigoi,* but instead of turning to their ways, I was offered another path. I was recruited that very night—before I ever tasted human blood—and ordained into the Order of the Sanguines. There I chose to follow Christ. I have followed Him ever since."

"Followed Him how?" Jordan asked, matching her skepticism. "How does something like you serve the Church?"

"The blessing of Christ's blood allows the Sanguinists many boons. Like walking under the sun. It also allows us to partake of all that is holy and sacred. Though, like the sun, such holiness still burns our flesh."

He peeled off one glove. A red blistering marked his palm in the shape of a cross. Erin remembered him clutching his pectoral crucifix a moment before, and imagined it searing into his skin.

Rhun must have read her distress. "The pain reminds us of Christ's suffering on the cross and serves as a constant remembrance of the oath we took. It is a small price to pay to live under His grace."

She watched him gently tuck his cross back under the shreds of his cassock. Did the crucifix burn over his heart? Is that why Catholic priests had taken to wearing such prominent crosses, another symbol of a hidden secret? Like the hooded cassock, did such accoutrements allow the Sanguinists to hide in plain sight among their human brothers of the cloth?

She had a thousand other questions.

Jordan had only one. "Then, as a warrior of the Church, who do you fight?"

Again Rhun looked to the desert. "We are called up to battle our feral brothers, the *strigoi.* We hunt them down and offer them a chance to join the fold of Christ. If they do not, we kill them."

"And where do we humans fall on your hit list?" Jordan asked.

Rhun's eyes returned to them. "I have sworn *never* to take a human life, unless it is to save another."

Erin found her voice again. "You say your mission is to kill *strigoi.* Yet it sounds like these creatures did not *choose* to become what they are, any more than you did, any more than a dog chooses to become rabid when bitten."

"The *strigoi* are lower than animals," Rhun argued. "They have no souls. They exist only to do evil."

"So your job is to send them back to Hell," Jordan said.

Rhun's gaze wavered. "In truth, soulless as they are, we do not know where they go."

Jordan shifted next to her, lowering his weapon, but he did not relax his stance.

"If *strigoi* are feral," Erin asked, "why do they care about this Gospel of Christ?"

Rhun looked ready to explain, but then froze—which immediately set her heart to pounding. He jerked his head to the side, his gaze on the skies.

"A helicopter comes," he stated bluntly.

Jordan searched around—but only in darting glances, never taking his eyes fully off of Rhun. "I don't see anything."

"I hear it." Rhun cocked his head. "It is one of ours."

Erin spotted a light in the sky heading toward them fast. "There."

"What do you mean by 'one of ours'?" Jordan asked.

"It is from the Church," Rhun explained. "Those who come will not harm you."

As she watched the helicopter's swift approach, Erin felt a nagging worry.

Over the centuries, how many men have died after hearing similar promises?

18

October 26, 8:28 P.M., IST
Caesarea, Israel

Bathory moved silently through the ruins of the hippodrome, shadowed by Magor, who padded quietly behind her. She shared his senses, becoming as much a hunter as the grimwolf. She tasted the salt of the neighboring Mediterranean, a black mirror to her right. She smelled the dust of centuries from the rubble of the ancient stone seats. She caught a distant whiff of horse manure and sweat.

She gave the stables a wide berth, careful to stay downwind so as not to spook the horses. She had left Tarek and the others with the helicopter, glad to put some distance between herself and them. It felt good to be alone, Magor by her side, dark sky above, and her quarry close.

Slowly she and the wolf crossed the sands toward the cluster of tents, aiming for the only one that still glowed with light. She did not need Magor's sharp senses to hear the voices from inside, reaching her across the quiet of the night. She spotted two silhouettes moving, two people. From the timbre of their voices, they were a man and a woman, both young.

The archaeologist's students.

Under the cover of their conversation, she reached the rear of the tent, where a small mesh window had been tied open to the night's breezes. She stood there, spying upon the two, a silent sentinel in the night, with Magor at her hip.

A young man in cowboy boots and jeans paced the length of

the tent while a young woman sat before a laptop and sipped a Diet Coke. On the computer's screen, a silent CNN report of the earthquake played. The woman did not take her eyes from the screen; the palm of her hand held an earbud in place, listening.

She spoke without turning away. "Try the embassy again, Nate."

The young man paced up to the small mesh window, staring out but not really seeing. Bathory remained standing, knowing she was still concealed by the shadows. She loved these moments of the hunt, when the quarry was so close, yet still blind to the blood and horror poised to leap at its throat.

Next to her, Magor stayed as still as the night sky. Once again, she was thankful that Tarek and the others were not here. They did not appreciate the beauty of the hunt—only the slaughter that followed.

Nate turned away, stepped over to the table, and dumped his cell phone beside the laptop. "What's the use? I tried calling them over and over. Still busy. Even tried the local police. Can't get any word on where Dr. Granger was taken."

Amy pointed to the ongoing report on the screen. "What if she was flown to Masada? Reports are saying aftershocks brought the whole mountain down."

"Quit thinking the worst. Dr. Granger could be anywhere. You'd think if the professor had time to send us those weird pics, she could've at least texted us, told us where she was."

"Maybe she wasn't allowed to. That Israeli soldier had her on a short leash. But from that photo of the open sarcophagus, it definitely looked like she was exploring some ransacked tomb."

In the darkness, Bathory smiled, picturing the archaeologist desperately waving her cell phone. So she *had* been transmitting photos, something she had considered important, possibly some clue to the whereabouts of the book.

In the dark, Bathory stroked the bandage on her arm, reminding herself that Hunor had died in pursuit of the secret that those pictures might reveal. Cold anger sharpened her senses, focused her mind, drove back the deep ache in her blood.

"I'm going back to my tent," Nate said. "Going to try to take a nap for a couple hours, then I'll see if I can reach anyone after all this quake hubbub dies down. You should, too. Something tells me it's going to be a long night."

"I don't want to be alone." Amy looked up from her computer at him. "First Heinrich, now no word from the professor . . . I'll never sleep."

Bathory heard the invitation behind her words, but Nate seemed oblivious to it. A pity. It would have made it much easier to steal the laptops and their phones if they were both gone. Such a loss would not be uncommon at this remote camp, dismissed as simple theft.

Instead, she sized the pair up. Nate was tall, well built, handsome enough. She could see why Amy liked having him near.

She herself understood the comfort of a warm male beside you, sharing your bed, picturing poor Farid. Her fingers slipped to her belt and pulled out the Arab's dagger, stolen after she killed him. Even in this small way, Farid was still useful to her.

She stepped back, considering the best way to flush the pair out—or at least separate them. She glanced around the campsite, heard the distant nickering of horses, and smiled.

A quick whisper in Magor's ear, and the wolf loped silently toward the stables.

8:34 P.M.

Racked by guilt, Nate paced the tent.

I shouldn't have let Dr. Granger go off alone.

He owed the professor. She had given him a chance when no one else had. Two years ago, he had been a hard sell as a grad student. At Texas A&M, he'd been raising a younger sister while holding down two jobs. The workload had trashed his GPA, but Dr. Granger took a chance on him. The professor had even helped get his kid sister a full scholarship to Rice, freeing him to travel.

And what did he do to repay her?

He let her step into a helicopter full of armed men all by herself.

As he reached the open flap of the tent, a chorus of frightened whinnies erupted from the stables, echoing eerily across the dark ruins.

He stepped out into the night. Moonlight shone on ancient stone seats and the rectangular trench where his friend Heinrich had received the blow that had killed him.

A cold wind blew sand into his eyes.

Nate blinked away tears. "What's wrong with the horses?"

"I don't care," Amy said, still seated at the laptop. "I hope it's something awful. Especially for that white one."

"The stallion was just frightened. It was an accident." Still he couldn't blame her for being mad at the horse. Heinrich was dead, just like that. Wrong place, wrong time. It could just as easily have been him.

The neighing grew more shrill.

"I'm going to see," he said. "Could be a jackal."

Panic tinged Amy's voice. "Don't leave me here by myself."

He crammed his cowboy hat on his head and rummaged through a wooden crate near the door for Dr. Granger's pistol. She used it for shooting snakes.

"Let the stable people take care of the horses," Amy pressed. "You shouldn't go out there in the dark."

"I'll be fine," he said. "And you're perfectly safe here."

Glad to be doing something besides stewing, he headed out of the tent and across the sand. But the night felt different now. Goose-flesh rose up on his arms that had nothing to do with cold.

Just spooked by Amy, he told himself.

Still, he tightened his grip on the pistol and strode faster—until a shadow rushed by on his right.

He stopped and whirled.

Out of the corner of his eye, he caught a glimpse of something large sweeping past. He didn't get a good look at it, couldn't tell what it was, only that it was bigger than any jackal he'd ever seen, the size of a yearling calf, but moving fast and smooth like a predator. It vanished so quickly he wasn't sure he saw anything.

He looked back at the well-lit tent. It seemed far away now, a single lamp in the darkness.

Behind him, a horse screamed.

8:36 P.M.

Under the cover of the stallion's cry, Bathory poked the tip of Farid's dagger through the tent's fabric and dragged the blade down. Its finely honed edge sliced through the taut material with barely a whisper.

All the while she kept an eye on Amy, who remained seated at the laptop, her focus fully on the tent's door, her back to the new door opening up behind her.

Bathory pushed sideways through the sliced fabric, slipping silently into the tent. Once inside, she stood behind the frightened young woman, who remained oblivious to her presence. One earbud was still seated in Amy's ear, the other dangled loosely. Bathory heard the tiny buzz of the CNN report playing on the laptop's screen.

She was struck by how unconsciously most people moved through their lives, unmindful of the true nature of the world around them, safely ensconced in their cocoon of modernity, where news came 24/7, filtered and diluted, where jolts of caffeine were needed to nudge them blearily through their ordinary lives.

But that was not living.

Deep in her heart, Magor's hunt stirred inside her, a distant haze of blood, adrenaline, and predatory glee.

That was the *true* face of the world.

That was living.

Bathory stepped forward, and with a single savage slash under the woman's chin, she snuffed out that feeble flicker of the young woman's wasted life. She tipped the body off the camp stool before the spray of blood doused the laptop.

Amy twitched on the floor, too stunned to know she was dead. She managed to squirm a few feet toward the tent's door before finally slumping in defeat, crimson pooling under her.

Bathory worked quickly. She closed the laptop, slipped it into her backpack, along with the pair of cell phones on the table.

To the side, the tent flap twitched.

She turned to see Nate stepping inside. He took in the scene with a glance, his pistol jerking up to point at her. "What the hell . . . ?"

Bathory straightened, smiling warmly.

But she was not greeting the young man.

Behind Nate's shoulder, shadows shifted to reveal a pair of red eyes, shining with bloodlust.

The night's hunt was not yet over.

She cast her will to her bond mate, a desire summarized by one word.

Fetch.

19

October 26, 8:37 P.M., IST
Desert beyond Masada, Israel

Jordan scanned the sand and rocks one more time, seeking a place to hide, but there was no true cover, especially from the air.

Overhead, the chopper closed in, its blades cutting through the night. He studied it, recognizing the sleek silver nose and smooth lines. He'd only seen pictures of the EC145 online, advertised as the most luxurious helicopter that eight million dollars could buy. It was basically a Mercedes-Benz with rotors.

Whoever was backing Korza had money.

The priest moved to the side to meet the helicopter.

If Jordan remembered correctly, the aircraft could seat up to eight, including a pilot and a copilot. So he faced a potential of eight opponents with no defensible ground. Recognizing that hard truth, he holstered his pistol. He couldn't fight and win, so he'd have to hope Korza wasn't lying and they wouldn't be harmed.

He turned to Erin. "Can you stand?" he asked quietly. He wanted her on her feet in case they had to move fast.

"I can try."

When she stood, she winced and shifted her weight to her right leg. A wet patch of blood darkened the left leg of her pants.

"What happened?" he asked, kicking himself for failing to note her injury earlier.

She glanced down, looking as surprised as he was. "The wolf. Scratched me. It's nothing."

"Let me see."

She raised an eyebrow. "I'm not about to take my pants off here."

He freed his dagger from its ankle sheath. "I can cut your pant leg just above the wound. It'll ruin your pants, but not your dignity."

He smiled.

She returned the smile as she sat back down on the boulder. "That sounds like a better plan."

Jordan sliced through the seams with his dagger, careful to keep the blade away from the soft skin underneath. He tore the fabric, then threaded the pant leg down over her sneaker. It was an intimate gesture. He focused on getting it off without hurting her, and keeping his hands from lingering on her bare leg, which looked fantastic in the moonlight. Not that he noticed.

He turned his attention to her injury. The wound ran down her thigh—not deep but long. He stared suspiciously at it and called over to Korza, yelling to be heard as the helicopter reached them.

"Padre! Erin got scratched by that grimwolf. Anything we need to know about that kind of wound?"

The priest glanced at Erin's bare leg, then back out at the desert, clearly uncomfortable. It was the most priestlike thing Jordan had seen him do in a while. "Clean it properly, and you need have no concerns."

Erin wiped at her thigh with the scrap of her pant leg.

Before he had time to dig out his first-aid kit, the sleek helicopter landed. Rotor wash pushed sheets of sand in their faces. Jordan cupped his hand over the wound on Erin's leg to protect it.

Crouched at her side, he stared back over his shoulder.

Three figures, all dressed in black, jumped out of the chopper's cabin, exiting before the skids had even settled to the ground. Hoods obscured their faces, and they moved impossibly fast, like Korza did in battle. Jordan wanted to run, but he forced himself to stand still when they swept up and surrounded them.

The trio conversed with Korza, whispering in a language that sounded like Latin. Jordan noted the Roman collars of the priesthood.

More Sanguinists.

Erin stood up, and Jordan stood by her.

One of the priests came forward. Cold hands slid across Jordan's body, taking away his guns. The man didn't notice Jordan's knife, or he didn't care. Either way, Jordan felt grateful that he left it.

Another figure retreated a few paces into the desert with Korza.

The third crossed to the grimwolf's body. He splashed liquid across the dead bulk, as if baptizing the beast in death. But it was not holy water. A match flared, got tossed, and the body ignited in a huge swirl of flames.

The smell of charred fur smoked out across the dark sands.

The first priest stayed to guard Jordan and Erin. Not that she seemed capable of putting up much of a fight. The spunk seemed to have drained right out of her. Her shoulders sagged, and she swayed on her good leg. Jordan moved toward her, but the guard raised a palm in warning. Jordan ignored the silent command and slid an arm around Erin.

Out in the desert, Korza and his companion argued fiercely, likely about the fate of the two surviving humans. Jordan kept a close watch on that outcome. Would they abandon Erin and him here in the middle of nowhere, or worse yet, send them to the same fiery end as the grimwolf?

Whatever their specific words, Korza seemed to win the argument.

Jordan didn't know if that was good or bad.

As if sensing Jordan's attention, Korza turned and locked gazes with him. He pointed to the helicopter and gestured for him and Erin to board.

Jordan still didn't know if that was good or bad. He knew the skill with which military black-ops teams could make a man disappear. Were he and Erin about to suffer the same fate?

He ran over various scenarios in his head and figured their best chance of surviving lay in getting into that helicopter. He'd fight if he had to, but this battle wasn't one he could win.

Yet.

He helped Erin limp toward the open cabin door, the two ducking under the swirling blades.

He waited for the others to board, gave one last look toward the open desert, and weighed the option of running. But Erin had only one good leg.

Korza remained at his shoulder, as if silently reminding him of the impossibility of escape. He had retrieved Jordan's jacket from the sand and handed it to him. That simple gesture went a long way toward making Jordan feel less anxious.

"After you," the priest said politely.

Jordan draped his coat around Erin's shoulders and helped her into the chopper. She paused, crouched in the hatch.

The inside of the helicopter's cabin was as opulent as he expected. Soothing blue light fell on polished dark wood. The smell of expensive leather filled his nostrils. Smooth lines shouted luxury. It was far from the utilitarian crafts he usually flew in. He wished he were in one of them now.

"There are only two open seats left," she said.

Jordan peeked around and saw she was right. "So, Korza, which one of us is riding in cargo?"

"I apologize. They had expected to retrieve only me, and perhaps the boy. It will be tight quarters, but the flight is not long."

Erin glanced back, looking to Jordan for guidance.

"We can double-buckle," Jordan said, and pointed to one of the large luxurious seats in back.

She nodded, squeezed past the others' knees, and took the seat, scooting over to make room for him.

He followed her and pulled the harness out to its farthest length before he squeezed next to her. "My mom had a lot of kids," he explained, snapping them in together. "She used to buckle two of us in with the same seat belt. Didn't yours?"

Her voice was dull with shock. "My mother wasn't allowed to drive a car. None of the women were."

He remembered her earlier statement. *I saw the Church used as a tool of the powerful against the weak*. For now, he filed that all away to ask about later.

Korza climbed in last. The priest was smaller than Jordan, and it would have been less snug if he'd buckled Erin in with Korza, but Jordan sure as hell wasn't going to let that happen.

The priest took the last open seat, directly across from theirs. Hidden within a hooded cassock, Korza's neighbor leaned to whisper in his ear. Jordan didn't understand the words, but he could tell the speaker was a woman. That surprised him. Was she human? Or did the Church recruit female *strigoi* to the fold of the Sanguinists?

After that, no one spoke.

The others sat still as statues, which Jordan found more disturbing than if they had been racing at double speed.

As the helicopter roared and rose from the desert in a flurry of sand, he tried to think about anything besides Erin's warm body tucked against his. At first, she had struggled to keep as much space between them as possible, but she soon gave up on that, trapped together by the harness. As the helicopter droned onward through the night, she eventually relaxed into sleep, too exhausted to resist.

Her head came to rest against his shoulder, and he shifted to the side so that it wouldn't fall forward. It had been far too long since a beautiful woman had fallen asleep on him. Her blond hair had escaped its rubber band and spilled to her shoulders. This close, he noted the lighter strands woven through the richer honey, likely bleached white by her time digging under the sun.

He wanted to trace a finger along one of those strands, as if following a thread in a larger tapestry, trying to understand the warp and weft that made up this woman at his side. Erin had been through a lot in the past few hours. He intended to get her out of this mess and home safely. He had to. He'd failed everyone else under his command.

Better shut down that alley.

Instead, he turned his attention to the wound on her tanned thigh. Though it was not deep, the puckered edges were a nasty red and dusted with sand. Moving slowly so as not to wake her, he pulled out his tiny first-aid kit.

Freeing an antiseptic wipe, he gently cleaned the wound, keeping his touch soft, moving slowly. Still, she moaned in her sleep.

Every Sanguinist looked in her direction.

With a chill, Jordan moved his free hand toward his dagger and rested his palm there.

"Do not fear us," Korza whispered, his face hidden again inside his hood. "You are quite safe."

Jordan didn't bother to answer.

And he didn't move his hand.

9:02 P.M.

Erin's head jolted forward, snapping her awake. Deafened by the roar of the helicopter, she found herself looking into an amazing pair of eyes, light blue with a darker ring around the edge of the iris.

The eyes smiled at her. She smiled back before she realized that they belonged to Jordan.

She had fallen asleep on his shoulder and woken up smiling at him.

A married man.

In a helicopter full of priests.

With her face burning, she straightened in her seat and shifted in the harness to create an inch of space between them. She could almost hear her mother's disappointed sigh and feel the back of her father's hand.

She turned to the window, the only safe place to look while her cheeks lost their embarrassed blush. Beyond the window, the lights of a city blazed ahead, drowning out the stars. A golden dome shone brightly amid the urban sprawl.

"Looks like we're coming into Jerusalem," she said.

"How can you tell?" he asked, probably trying to rescue her from her embarrassment.

She accepted his offer. "That dark mountain to the east is the Mount of Olives. An important historical site to all three major religions: Judaism, Islam, and Christianity. And it's said that's where Jesus supposedly ascended to Heaven."

A few of the Sanguinists stirred at the word *supposedly,* clearly offended, but she kept going.

"The Book of Zechariah says that during the Apocalypse it will split in two."

"Great, let's hope that doesn't happen anytime soon. I've had enough mountains splitting in two for one day." Jordan pointed toward that glowing golden dome she'd noted earlier. "What's that one?"

"That's the Dome of the Rock. It sits atop the Temple Mount." She shifted to give Jordan a better view out the window. "Around it you can see the wall of the Old City. It's like a ribbon of light, see? To the north is the Muslim quarter. South and west is the Jewish quarter with the famous Western Wall."

"The Wailing Wall?"

"That's right."

He leaned forward, and his body slid along hers.

She glanced across at the priests, their expressions invisible behind their hoods. Except for Rhun, whose face reflected the city's shine as the helicopter banked into a turn. His impassive dark eyes watched her.

A blush rose again on her face, and she turned back to the view. What must Rhun think of her? What must he think of the view? She tried to picture the sight through the prism of eyes that had been open for centuries. Had Rhun been on the Temple Mount when Mahmud II restored it in 1817? She shivered at the thought—fearful, but also with a touch of awe.

"Are you cold?" Jordan reached over and adjusted his jacket across her other shoulder.

"I'm f-fine," she stuttered breathlessly. She was actually too warm. Her proximity to Jordan did unpredictable things to her body temperature. For the past decade, she had kept too busy to allow herself to be attracted to a man. It was just her luck that she was now strapped to one who was both damnably attractive—and married.

"Thank you for the jacket."

"We will land soon." Rhun's quiet voice claimed their attention.

"Where?" Jordan leaned a tiny bit away from her, and she missed the warmth of his body against hers. She glanced down at the strip of white skin on his ring finger.

Evidence. Always take into consideration the evidence before reacting.

Now if only she could convince her body to do the same.

"We must blindfold you both," Rhun warned, his expression never changing.

Jordan sat straighter. The harness tugged against her shoulder. "What? So we're your prisoners now?"

"Guests," Rhun answered.

"I don't blindfold my guests." Jordan folded his arms. "Seems downright inhospitable."

"Nevertheless . . ." Rhun unclipped his harness.

The priest next to him passed over two strips of black cloth.

Jordan's leg went rock-hard next to hers. His feet pressed solidly against the floor. He seemed ready to take on the Sanguinists with nothing but his fists and his indignation.

She touched his hand. "This isn't the time, Jordan."

He looked at her, as if suddenly remembering that she was there. He studied her for a long moment before nodding.

Rhun stood, balancing nimbly in the moving aircraft. He tied on Jordan's blindfold first, then wrapped black cloth over her eyes. His cold fingers tied the knot behind Erin's head, working gently with her hair. After he finished, he left his palm flat against the back of her head for a second longer than necessary, as if to comfort her.

She then heard him retreat and the *snap* as he buckled back into his seat.

A hand found hers and gripped it tightly. Jordan's palm burned warmly in hers as he, too, sought to reassure her. His message here was plain.

Whatever was to come, they were in this together.

20

October 26, 9:13 P.M., IST
Jerusalem, Israel

Rhun helped the soldier and the woman out of the aircraft, passing under the whirling blades. He herded them off the helipad atop a building, down a series of stairs, and out onto a narrow street. All the while, the soldier kept a firm clasp on the woman's hand.

Despite their brave faces, Rhun heard the frightened flutter of their hearts, smelled the salt of their fear, and noted the sheen of their skin. He did his best to shelter them from the others, to leave enough space for both. He refused to entrust them to any of his brethren—not that he feared that anyone would harm them. He simply felt protective of them, responsible for them.

He watched them lean closer together on the streets.

Erin and Jordan.

At some point, they went from being an archaeologist and a soldier in his mind's eye to being simply Erin and Jordan. He didn't like that growing familiarity. It created bonds when there should be none. He had learned that hard truth centuries ago.

Never again.

He turned away.

Out on the street and moving again, Rhun breathed the nighttime scents of the old city—soot, cold rock, and fouling garbage from the bazaar. The other Sanguinists surrounded the trio. Rhun hoped that their presence would keep the blindfolded humans hidden from curious eyes.

So far, nothing had stirred on the dark avenue, the shops remained shuttered, the lights dark. He listened for nearby heartbeats in the cramped alleyways and cross streets that made up the maze of this quarter of the city. He found nothing amiss, but he still pressed them to move faster. He worried that they could be seen at any time.

After a few minutes, the group reached a rough-hewn stone wall where a robed man waited, tapping his leather shoe on the sidewalk, both impatient and nervous. The figure was as short as he was round. His face had a reddish cast, as did his bald pate.

Like a vulture.

Rhun knew the man—Father Ambrose—and cared little to find him here, guarding the gateway.

Ambrose stepped forward both to greet them, and to block them. His eyes ignored Rhun and the other Sanguinists and fixed a steely gaze upon Erin and Jordan. His words were terse enough to be considered rude.

"You may share nothing concerning what you see beyond this gate. Not with your family, not with your superiors in the military."

Still blindfolded, Jordan dug in his heels and stopped, pulling Erin to a halt beside him. "I'm not taking orders from someone I can't see."

Rhun understood the man's consternation and whipped off the two blindfolds before Ambrose could protest. The pair had already seen and been told too much. Adding the knowledge of this location seemed trivial in comparison. Besides, they must get indoors.

Jordan held out his hand to Ambrose. "Sergeant Stone, Ninth Ranger Battalion, and this is Dr. Granger."

"Father Ambrose, assistant to His Eminence, Cardinal Bernard." He wiped his palm on his fine cassock after shaking Jordan's hand. "You have been summoned to meet with His Eminence. But I must once again stress that everything from this moment forward must be held in strictest confidence."

"Or what?" Jordan loomed over Ambrose, and Rhun liked him all the more for it.

Ambrose stepped back. "Or we shall know of it."

"Enough," Rhun declared, and brushed roughly past Ambrose.

He stepped forward and placed a hand against the limestone blocks of the wall, moving his fingers stone by stone in the sequence of the cross. The limestone felt rough and warm under his hands.

"Take and drink you all of this," he whispered, and pushed the centermost stone inward, revealing a tiny basin carved in a block, like the vessel that holds holy water at the entrance to a church.

Only this basin was not meant to hold *water.*

Rhun slipped free his curved blade and poked the center of his palm, in the spot where the nails had been driven into the palms of Christ. He squeezed his fist and let a few drops of blood splatter into the stone cup, its inner surface long darkened by the passage of countless Sanguinists who had entered this place before him.

"For this is the Chalice of My Blood, of the new and everlasting Testament."

Erin gasped behind him as cracks appeared in the wall, revealing the outline of a gate so narrow that a man must turn sideways to pass.

"Mysterium fidei," Rhun finished, and shoved the door open with his shoulder—then stepped back.

The other Sanguinists glided through ahead of him, followed by Ambrose. Erin and Jordan remained on the street with Rhun.

The woman remained fixed in place, staring up and down the city wall. "I've studied all the gates into the Old City, sealed and open," she said. "There is no record of this one."

"It has gone by many names over the centuries," Rhun said, anxious to get them all off the street before they were discovered. "I assure you that you will find safe shelter inside. This gateway has been sanctified. The *strigoi* cannot cross its threshold."

"They're not the only ones who worry me." Jordan stepped into a wider stance. "If Erin won't go in, I won't either."

The woman finally stepped forward, placing her hand on the rough stone lintel. He heard her heart skip faster at the touch. From the hungry shine in her eyes, the sharper beat was not born of fear, but of a raw, aching desire.

"Here is living history." Erin glanced back to Jordan. "How can I *not* go inside?"

***9:19* P.M.**

Jordan followed Erin across that dark threshold, squeezing sideways to enter. He wasn't happy about it, but he suspected the choice of entering or not was not ultimately theirs anyway. He remembered Father Ambrose's words: *You have been summoned to meet with His Eminence.*

It was clearly less an invitation than a demand.

Korza entered last and drew the gate shut behind him. A suffocating and complete blackness closed over the group. Breathing harder as he stood in the darkness, Jordan reached out and found Erin's hand again.

She squeezed his fingers in return, tightly, gratefully.

A familiar rasping sound preceded a tiny *pop* of flame, flickering brilliantly in the darkness. A Zippo lighter shone in the fingers of a cowled Sanguinist ahead of Jordan. The sight of the familiar, modern-day object cheered him, made everything feel a bit more real.

The Sanguinist picked up a candle from a small wooden stand by the door and handed it to Erin. She held the wick up to the lighter's golden flame. In turn, Jordan received and lit his own candle. The smell of smoke and beeswax pushed back the dry dust of the air, but the fragile light did not reach far.

Without a word and apparently needing no light of their own, the other Sanguinists turned and headed down the steep tunnel. Jordan was not thrilled to be going underground again, but Erin set off after them, and he followed.

Even with the candle, Jordan could barely see where he was going. He swept the flame low in front of him. Smooth stone surrounded him. He hung back, wanting to keep everyone where he could see them, not that there was a hell of a lot he could do if things went bad.

Korza seemed to understand his hesitancy and squeezed past him.

Erin, already a few paces ahead, sheltered her candle's flame with one cupped hand. Her head swiveled around so fast he thought it might come right off. To her, this must be like slipping out of present time and into history.

To Jordan, it was simply a minefield, where any misstep could kill them both.

He tried his best to keep track of their path. The passageway seemed to be angling downward, heading to the northeast, but he couldn't be sure. And without knowledge of the city's layout, he had no idea where they might be going. With no other recourse, he fell back on his military training and counted his steps, trying his best to keep track of the crisscrossing passageways, building a three-dimensional map in his head. At the very least, it might help them find their way back.

At last, the tunnel evened out and stopped in front of a thick wooden door with heavy iron hinges. At least this door didn't require the blood of a Sanguinist to open—only a large ornate key, which was wielded by Father Ambrose.

"Is this where we meet the Cardinal?" Erin asked.

Father Ambrose glanced up and down her body, his lips pursed with distaste, settling on her wounded leg, on her torn pants. "It would be unseemly to greet His Eminence in your present condition."

Jordan rolled his eyes. So far, the only thing this new priest had going for him was that he was *human*. When they'd shaken hands outside, Jordan had felt the heat of real blood in his veins.

Still, Jordan looked down at his own filthy blood-soaked clothes. Erin looked little better, and Korza was a disaster.

"We had a bad night," Jordan admitted.

A laugh burst out of Erin's throat, sounding slightly hysterical at the edges, but she stifled it quickly.

"I cannot imagine," Ambrose said, ignoring her.

The priest turned back to the door and unlocked it with an iron key as long as his hand. He pulled the door open, bathing them in the light from the hallway beyond.

The group filed past Ambrose. Jordan went last, stepping into a long stone passageway softened by a Persian carpet runner on the floor and tapestries on the walls. Electric lights shone from wall sconces. Rows of wooden doors, all closed, dotted both sides of the hall.

Jordan blew out his candle but kept hold of it, in case he needed to light his way to freedom again.

Father Ambrose relocked the door and pocketed the key, then gestured to the right. "That is your room, Dr. Granger. On the left is yours, Sergeant Stone. You may clean up inside."

Jordan took Erin's elbow. "We'd prefer to stick together."

Father Ambrose's voice went frosty. "While you bathe?"

A blush rose on Erin's cheeks.

Jordan liked watching it.

"It is safe here," Korza assured them. "You have my promise on that."

Erin caught Jordan's eye, passing on a silent message. She wanted to talk, once they were alone—which meant cooperating until the priests left.

He would go along with that.

At least for now.

9:24 P.M.

Rhun watched the pair disappear inside their respective rooms before he followed Ambrose. The man led the way up a rising passageway and to another door that had to be unlocked. The Church had many locks, and many secrets to hide behind them, but this doorway merely led to a winding stone staircase hewn out of the rock more than a thousand years ago.

Very familiar with it, Rhun moved to enter on his own, but Ambrose blocked the way with an arm.

"Wait," the man warned. The thin mask of civility that he had presented for the newcomers fell away, revealing his raw disgust. "I will not present you to His Eminence with the cursed blood of a grimwolf upon you. Even I can smell that foul stench."

Rhun glowered, letting Ambrose see his anger. "Bernard has seen me far worse."

Ambrose could not face that fury for more than a breath. His arm fell, and he shrank back, his thick heartbeat tripping over itself in fear. Rhun felt a flicker of guilt—but only a flicker. He knew Ambrose. The priest was driven by human desires, possessive of his rank, full of pride, and protective of his role as Cardinal Bernard's assistant. But Rhun also knew how loyal the man was. He guarded Bernard's position in the Church hierarchy as devotedly as any watchdog—and in his own bitter manner, he served the Cardinal well, making sure no one insulted or slighted his superior.

But Rhun did not have time for such civilities. He swept past Ambrose and swiftly climbed the stairs, leaving the priest far behind. On his own, he threaded through dark passageways until he reached the mahogany door of Cardinal Bernard's study.

"Rhun?" Bernard called from inside, his Italian accent rolling on the hard *R,* softening it with a warmth of friendship that spanned centuries. "Enter, my son."

Rhun stepped into a chamber lit by a single white candle in an ornate gold candlestick. He needed little light to see the jeweled globe next to the massive desk, the ancient wooden crucifix attached to the wall, and the rows of leather-bound volumes lining one side. He breathed in the familiar smells of old parchment, leather, and beeswax. This room had not changed in a century.

Bernard rose to meet him. He wore full cardinal attire, the crimson cloth shining in the candlelight. He greeted Rhun with a warm embrace, not flinching from the stench of grimwolf blood. A Sanguinist himself, Bernard had fought many battles in the past and did not shy away from the vulgar aftermath of combat.

Bernard led him to a chair and drew it back for him. "Sit, Rhun."

Not protesting, he settled to the seat, truly feeling his wounds for the first time.

Bernard returned to his own chair and slid a golden chalice of consecrated wine across the desktop. "You have suffered much these past few hours. Drink and we will talk."

Rhun reached for the cup's stem. The scent of wine drifted up: bitter, with a hint of oak. He craved it, but he hesitated to drink it. He did not want the pain of penance to distract him during this conversation. But his wounds also throbbed, reminding him that they, too, could distract him.

Resigned, he took the cup and drained it—then bowed his head so that Bernard would not see his expression, and waited. Would another vision of Elisabeta haunt him again tonight, reminding him of his sin? But that was not to be—for he had committed a greater sin, one that damned him for eternity.

Rhun's knees pressed against cold, damp earth as he prayed at the gravestone of his younger sister. A moonless night cloaked him in darkness, blacker than the sober seminary robe he wore. Even the stars of Heaven hid behind clouds.

Would no light ever shine again in his heart?

He stared at the dates carved into the gravestone.

1527 ✝ 1554

Less than a month before childbirth, death had claimed his sister and her infant son. Without the absolution of baptism, the infant could not be buried with his mother. She lay here on consecrated ground; her child could not.

Rhun would visit his tiny unmarked grave later.

Every night since her burial, he had left the quiet of the monastery after everyone slept and had come to pray for her, for her child, and to allay the sorrow in his own heart.

Soft footsteps sounded behind him.

Still on his knees, he turned.

A shadow-cloaked figure stepped close. Rhun could not make out its features in the darkness, but the stranger was not a priest.

"The pious one," the newcomer whispered, his accent foreign, the voice unfamiliar.

Rhun's heart quickened; his fingers sought his cross, but he forced his hands to remain clasped, tightening his fingers.

What did he have to fear from this stranger who showed no threat?

Rhun bowed his head respectfully to the man. "You are in the Lord's cemetery late, my friend."

"I come to pay my respects to the dead," he answered, and waved long pale fingers toward the grave. "As do you."

Icy wind blew through the field of stone crosses and carved angels, rustling the last leaves of autumn and bringing with it the odor of death and decay.

"Then I leave you to your peace," Rhun said, turning back to his sister's resting place.

Oddly, the man knelt next to Rhun. He wore fine breeches and a studded leather tunic. Mud besmirched costly boots. In spite of his coarse accent, his finery betrayed his origin as a nobleman.

Growing irritated, Rhun turned to him, noting the long dark hair that fell back from a pale brow. The stranger's full lips curved up in amusement, although Rhun could not fathom why.

Enough . . . it is late.

Rhun gathered his rough-spun robes together to stand.

Before he could rise, the man wrapped an arm around his shoulder and pulled him to the wet ground, as if he were taking a lover. Rhun opened his mouth to yell, but the stranger pressed one cold hand on his face. Rhun tried to push the man away, but the other caught both of his wrists in one hand and held them as easily as if he were a small child.

Rhun struggled against him, but the man held him fast, leaning down. He used his rough cheek to tilt Rhun's head to the side, exposing his neck.

Rhun suddenly understood, his heart galloping. He had heard legends of such monsters, but he had never believed them.

Until now.

Sharp fangs punctured his throat, taking away his innocence, leaving only pain. He screamed, but no sound escaped him. Slowly, the pain turned into something else, something darker: bliss.

Rhun's blood pulsed out of him and into the stranger's hungry mouth, those cold lips growing warmer with his hot blood.

He continued to struggle, but weakly now—for, in truth, he did not want the man to stop. His hand rose on its own and pulled that face tighter to his throat. He knew it was sinful to give in to such bliss, but he no longer cared. Sin had no meaning; only the aching desire for the probe of tongue into wound, the gnaw of sharp teeth into tender flesh, mattered now.

There was no room in him for holiness, only an ecstasy that promised release.

The man drew back at last.

Rhun lay there, spent, dying.

Strong fingers stroked his hair. "It is not yet time to sleep, pious one."

A sliced wrist was pressed against Rhun's opened lips. Hot silken blood burst on his tongue, filled his mouth. He swallowed, drew in more. A deep moan rose in his throat, drowned itself in the blood.

Soon his entire existence glowed with one word, one wish.

More . . .

Then that precious font was ripped from him, leaving an unfathomable well of hunger inside him, demanding to be filled with blood—any blood.

Above him, the stranger was struggling with four priests.

A blade flashed silver in the moonlight.

"No," Rhun screamed.

Rough hands pulled him to his feet and dragged him stumbling back to the silent monastery, where the gift of eternity soon became his curse.

Rhun shed his penance with a shudder. Even now, he missed

that man who had killed him, who destroyed his old life. In quiet moments, he still longed for that first taste of his blood. It was a sin he had repented many times, but it never went away.

Across the desk, Bernard watched him, his face as full of sorrow as it had been the night that Rhun was brought before him, covered in blood, weeping and trying to escape the monks and flee into the night. Bernard had saved him then, shown him how he could serve God in his new form, kept him from ever feeding on innocent human blood.

Rhun shook his head to clear it of the past.

He faced Bernard, both friend and mentor, remembering the events at Masada and in the desert. Here was the man who had set much of it in motion, a man who kept too many secrets.

"You have gone too far," Rhun said hoarsely, still feeling his torn throat, the wash of hot blood from the stranger's wrist.

"Have I?" The Cardinal ran a robust hand through his white hair. "How so?"

Rhun knew the man was testing him. He gripped his pectoral cross, using the pain to control his anger. "You sent that archaeologist into danger. You sent me to face the enemy alone—*strigoi* of the Belial sect."

His friend leaned back and steepled his fingers. His eyebrows knitted with concern. "You believe your attackers were *Belial*? Why?"

Rhun related his experiences on and under the mountain, then explained. "The *strigoi* who came were not mere scavengers drawn to the tragedy. They came with plain purpose. And used concussive charges."

"Employing the weapons of man." Bernard lowered his hands. He sat straighter, his warm brown eyes pained. "I did not know that they would come for it."

The Belial were a sect of the *strigoi* who were in league with humans, combining the worst of both worlds—merging human cunning to feral ferocity, uniting modern weaponry with ancient evil. They were a scourge whose numbers had swollen over the past century, posing an ever greater threat to their order and to the Church. Even after decades of fighting them, hunting them down, much was still unknown about the Belial, such as who truly ruled them: *was it man or monster?*

Rhun's anger calmed. "The Belial must have caught wind of the strange deaths surrounding the earthquake and guessed what it meant as well as we did."

The Cardinal remained statue still. "Then they seek the Gospel—like we do—and are desperate enough to reveal themselves for it."

"But the book was gone, the crypt empty," Rhun said. "They did not find it either."

"No matter." The familiar face looked softer in the candlelight, relieved and reassured. "If the prophecies are correct, they cannot open it. Only the *three* may bring it back to this world."

Rhun's chair creaked when he leaned forward, an old fury kindling back to life. He knew all too well what Bernard meant by evoking the *three* mentioned in the prophecies surrounding the Gospel, the three figures who were destined to find and open the book.

The Woman of Learning.

The Warrior of Man.

The Knight of Christ.

Even now he saw the glimmer of hope in Bernard's eyes, knew what the Cardinal suspected.

He pictured Erin's face, bright with curiosity—*a Woman of astounding Learning.*

And Jordan's heroic attack on the grimwolf—*a Warrior of Man.*

He gripped his own cross—*marking him as a Knight of Christ.*

He forced his fingers to let go of the silver, hoping his friend could do the same with his foolish hope. "Bernard, you place too much trust in those old prophecies. Such conviction in the past cost much misery and bloodshed."

The Cardinal sighed. "I do not need to be reminded of my past mistakes. I carry that burden as heavily as you do, my son. I attempted to force God's hand in Hungary all those centuries ago. It was hubris of the highest order. I thought the portents pointed to Elisabeta, that she was meant to join you. But I was mistaken. I admitted it then, and I do not recant that foolishness now." He reached over and placed a cold palm atop Rhun's hand. "But do you not *see* what happened today? You stumbled out of that rubble with a Woman of Learning to your left and a Warrior of Man to your right. It must *mean* something."

Rather than dimming, the glimmer in his friend's eyes grew brighter.

Rhun drew his hand away. "But *you* put the woman there."

That realization stabbed Rhun with misgiving. Was his friend *still* trying to force the hand of prophecy? Even after the tragic consequences of his past attempt? When another woman suffered as a consequence of his *mistake*?

Bernard dismissed this all with a wave of his fingers. "Yes, I used my influence to send a woman of learning to Masada. But, Rhun, it was not *I* who knocked down the mountain of Masada. It was not *I* who saved the woman *and* the warrior and led them out of the tomb, the last resting place of the Book. Against all commandments, *you* saved them both."

"I could not leave them there to die." Rhun looked down at his shredded garments, smelled again the blood on his skin.

"Don't you see? The prophecy is a living force now." Bernard lifted the silver cross that hung around his neck and kissed it, his lips reddening from the heat of silver and holiness. "We each have our role to play. We must each humbly bow to our own destinies. And whether I'm right or wrong, you know we must keep the Gospel from the hands of the Belial at all costs."

"Why?" Bitterness tinged Rhun's next words. "A moment ago, you were certain that the Belial could not open it. Yet now you seem to doubt that part of the prophecy."

"I do not presume to understand God's will, merely to interpret it as best I can."

Rhun thought of Elisabeta's silvery-gray eyes and Erin's amber ones.

Never again will I fall so low.

"And if I refuse this destiny?" Rhun asked.

"Now who presumes to know God's heart better than He?"

The words stung, as they were meant to.

Rhun bowed his head and prayed for guidance. Could this truly be a challenge that God had placed before him? A chance for absolution? What greater task could God ask of him than to protect His son's final Gospel? Rhun still did not trust Bernard's deeper motives, but perhaps the Cardinal was correct to see the hand of God in today's actions.

He considered all that had come to pass.

The final resting place of the book had been sundered open, heralded by quakes, bloodshed, and the survival of one boy, an innocent child spared.

But with the lavender scent of Erin's hair fresh in his nostrils, Rhun resisted that path. He would surely fail her—as he had failed another long ago.

"Even if I were to consent to aid in your search for the Gospel—" Rhun stopped at the smile on Bernard's face. "Even so, we cannot force the two here to go after it, not with the Belial in play."

"That is true. We can force no one. The two must enter the search of their own free will. And to do so, they must give up their worldly attachments. Do you think that they are ready for such a sacrifice?"

Rhun pictured the pair that Bernard believed to be the Woman and the Warrior. When he first met the two, he considered them, much as the Cardinal had done, to be little more than what was revealed by their roles: an archaeologist and a soldier.

But now he knew that was no longer true.

Such labels were pale reflections of the two who had bled and fought at his side.

There were truer ways to describe them, and one was by their given names.

Erin and Jordan.

The Cardinal's last question plagued him. *Do you think they are ready . . . ?*

Rhun hoped, for their sakes, that the answer was no.

21

October 26, 9:33* P.M.*, IST
Jerusalem, Israel

Hallelujah for small miracles.

Jordan discovered several gifts waiting for him on the bed of his small, monastic cell. A set of clean clothes had been folded atop the pillow—and on the blanket rested his weapons, returned to him.

He crossed quickly and examined his Heckler & Koch machine pistol and his Colt 1911. They were loaded—which both relieved him and disturbed him. His hosts either trusted him or were plainly not worried about any threat he might pose.

But that trust was a one-way street.

Standing in place, he gave the small room a once-over. It had been dug out from solid rock. The space contained a single bed that had been jammed against one wall to make room for a wide washstand topped with a copper basin full of steaming water.

He did a fast and thorough search for surveillance equipment. Considering the spartan accommodations, there weren't many places to hide a listening device. He searched the mattress, felt along the edges of the raw wood bed frame, and examined the washstand.

Nothing.

He even stepped to the crucifix on the wall, took it down, and checked behind it, feeling vaguely blasphemous for doing so.

But still nothing.

So, they apparently weren't listening in—at least not with modern technology. He eyeballed the door. How sharp was the hearing of a Sanguinist?

Considering his level of paranoia, he wondered how wise it had been to come here after all. Should he and Erin have waited in the desert and taken their chances with the jackals? Or maybe another grimwolf?

That didn't sound any better.

And at least by coming here, they were still alive. Others had not been so lucky. He pictured his teammates' broken bodies, buried now under tons of stone.

He thought of the calls and visits he would have to make once this ordeal was all over: to the parents, to the widows, to the children.

He sank to the bed in defeat and grief.

What in the hell could he tell them?

***9:52** P.M.*

Cramped was a generous description for Erin's room.

She kept hitting her elbow on the wall as she tried to scrub herself clean at the washbasin. She had stripped down to a bra and panties, and once clean, she faced the clothes that had been laid out for her.

It was no problem to slip into the white cotton shirt she found on her bed—but what to do about that long black skirt? It was just like the ones she'd worn as a girl, the ones that always tripped her up, kept her from climbing trees, made it almost impossible to ride horses. In her former world, women wore skirts, while men enjoyed the freedom of pants.

She had worn a skirt or dress throughout her childhood and balked at returning to one. But with her jeans cut to shreds and covered in blood, sweat, and sand, she'd have to wear the dress—unless she wanted to run around in front of Jordan and the priests in her underwear.

That settled it.

She transferred the contents of her jeans to her skirt pocket: the Nazi medallion from the tomb, her wallet, and a faded scrap cut from a quilt many years before, no bigger than a playing card.

Her fingertips lingered over the last item, drawing both strength and anger from it. She always carried the scrap with her, along with the anger and guilt it represented. She pictured the baby's quilt from which it had been cut, how she'd stolen it before it was buried with her infant sister. She shut down that memory before it overwhelmed her and stuffed it away, shoving the piece of cloth deep into the skirt's pocket.

That done, she wiggled into the garment, hating how it felt against her legs. The sandals she left by the bed. Her sneakers were staying with her.

Once dressed, she returned to the door, found it unlocked, and peeked out into the hallway. She found it empty and stepped out of the room. As she turned to shut her door—something scraped across stone, sounding like nails clawing out of a grave.

Spooked, already on edge, she bolted across the hall. She didn't want to be caught outside of her room, especially by whatever made that scraping noise. She pictured the slavering jaws of the grimwolf.

Without knocking, she burst through Jordan's door.

She found him wearing only a towel and a surprised expression. In his right hand he jerked up a pistol—but then lowered it immediately.

"Oh, God, I'm sorry." She blushed. "I shouldn't have . . . I didn't mean to . . ."

"It's all right," he said, smiling at her fluster, which only drew more heat to her cheeks. "I'm glad you came over. I wanted to talk to you alone anyway. Away from the others."

She nodded. That was why she had headed over here, too, but she had expected that conversation to be one during which they were both *clothed*.

She stepped against the door, trying not to look at Jordan's muscular chest, at the thin line of hair that split his washboard abs, or at the length of his tan legs.

She wanted to turn away, but her eyes caught on an unusual tattoo that spanned his left shoulder and ran partway down his arm and across a corner of his chest and back. It looked like the branching roots of a tree, all rising from a single dark spot on his upper chest. There was a certain flowery beauty to it, especially etched on such a masculine physique.

He must have noted the object of her attention. He drew a finger down one of those branching lines. "I got this when I was eighteen."

"What is it?"

"It's called a Lichtenberg figure. It's a fractal pattern that forms after something gets struck by a lightning bolt. In this case that something was *me*."

"What?" She stepped toward him, both intrigued by and glad for the distraction.

"I was playing football in the rain. Got hit near the goalpost after catching a touchdown."

She stared up at his blue eyes, half smiling, trying to judge if he was making fun of her.

He lifted three fingers. "Scout's honor."

Of course he was a Boy Scout.

"I was pronounced dead for three minutes."

"You were?"

He nodded. "Uh-huh."

"What was it like being dead?"

"I didn't have that whole dark-tunnel, bright-light thing, but I came back different."

"Different how?" He seemed pretty grounded, but was he going to tell her that he'd seen God or been touched by an angel?

"It's like my number was up." He flattened his palm over his heart. "And everything after that moment was a bonus."

She stared at the design on his chest. That's how close he'd gotten to death. He went through and came out the other side, like the Sanguinists.

He grinned and traced down one of the lines. "These patterns are sometimes called lightning flowers. They're caused by the rupture of small capillaries under the skin due to the passage of electric current following the discharge of a lightning strike. I got hit here." He touched the center of the branching on his chest. "The pattern spread outward. It was bright red for a while, but it faded and left a little scar."

"But then?"

"I had the original pattern tattooed to remind me that this life is a bonus." He laughed. "Drove my parents crazy."

She lifted a finger, wanting to examine the design, to touch it—like she did all things she found incredible, then realized what she was about to do and stopped, leaving her finger hovering over the black mark on his chest.

He reached up and drew her hand closer. "It's raised up a bit where the original scar was."

She wanted to resist but couldn't. As her fingertip touched his skin, a jolt shook her, as if some of the lightning's energy were still trapped in his scar—but she knew it was something more than electrical discharge.

He must have felt it, too. His skin tightened where she made contact, the thick muscle hardening underneath her finger. His breath drew in deeper.

He still held her hand. She looked up into those blue eyes, those lips—the upper lip with a divot at the top like a bow.

His eyes darkened, and he leaned down toward her, as if wanting to assert that he was alive now.

She held her breath and let him, wanting the same after the long day of horrors.

His kiss started gentle and featherlight, lips barely brushing hers.

Heat flashed through her, as electric as it was warm.

She rose up on her toes and deepened the kiss, needing to explore it further, to explore *him* further. She wrapped her hands around his bare shoulders and pulled him closer, wanting more of him, more connection, more warmth. She dissolved into the kiss, letting it fill her and blot out the horrible events in the tomb.

Then she flashed on the pale ring of skin around his tanned finger.

It was a kind of tattoo that marked him as readily as the lightning scar.

He was a married man.

She leaned back, bumping into the washstand. "I'm sorry."

His voice was hoarse. "I'm not."

She turned her head away, angry at herself, at him. She needed to catch her breath and get her head on straight. "I think we need to step back from this."

Jordan took a careful step backward. "Far enough?"

That wasn't exactly what she meant, but it would do. "Maybe another step."

Jordan gave her a quick, embarrassed smile, then retreated another step and sat down on the bed.

She sat on the other end, her arms crossed over her chest, needing to change the subject. Her voice came out too high. "How's your other shoulder?"

He had hurt it while being yanked through the hole as they escaped the collapsing tomb.

Jordan swiveled his arm around and winced. "Hurts, but I don't think it's serious. Less serious than being pancaked in the mountain."

"Being pancaked in the mountain might have been easier."

"Who says the easy path is the right one?"

She blushed, still feeling the heat, the pressure, of his kiss. She looked down at her hands. She spoke after the silence stretched for too long, glancing toward the door. "What do you think they want with us?"

He followed her gaze. "Don't know. Maybe to debrief us. Swear us to secrecy. Maybe give us a million dollars."

"Why a million dollars?"

He shrugged. "Why not? I'm just saying . . . let's be optimistic."

She looked at the dirty toes of her sneakers. That was hard to do, to be optimistic, especially with Jordan sitting half naked next to her. The heat of his bare skin reached across the distance between them. How long had it been since she'd been in a room with a naked man? Let alone one who looked as good as Jordan, or who could kiss half as well?

Silence again stretched out between them. Jordan's gaze went far away; likely he was thinking of his wife, of the brief betrayal of this moment.

She searched for another topic of conversation. "Do you still have your first-aid kit?" she blurted out too loudly, startling him out of his reverie, causing him to flinch.

"Sorry," he mumbled. "Guess I'm still a bit on edge."

"I don't bite."

"Everybody else does here," he said with a grin.

She smiled back, feeling the tension break between them.

He dug his first-aid kit out of the pocket of his discarded pants, still on the bed. "Let's start with your leg."

"I'd better do it."

Right now she'd rather bleed to death than let him mess with her thigh. Once he got started there, who knew where it would lead?

"Maybe you'd better get dressed while I deal with this cut?" she suggested.

He smiled sheepishly and handed her the kit. She turned her back to him as he pulled on clean black pants. She kept her eyes focused on her leg. The wolf scratch wasn't as bad as it seemed in the desert. She washed her wound carefully, then slathered it with antibacterial ointment and taped on a gauze bandage.

Jordan stood uncomfortably close, but at least he was wearing pants now. "That dressing looks pretty good. Do you have any medical training?"

"In a manner of speaking. I grew up in a compound where outsiders were forbidden from touching us—not even to take care of us when we were sick."

It was rare for her to share this part of her life with anyone. Shame surrounded her past, shame for being so gullible, for not fighting back sooner. A therapist once told her that was a common emotion for survivors of chronic abuse, and she would probably never fully escape it. So far, the therapist had been right.

Still, bits of her history had somehow spilled out to Jordan.

"That's nuts," he said.

She hid a small grin. "That's a succinct way of summarizing it. But it made sense at the time, as isolated as we were kept."

"I grew up in Iowa in a cornfield. With a passel of brothers and sisters, we were all about scrapes, skinned knees, the occasional broken bone."

A twinge in her left arm reminded her that she'd suffered the latter, too. But she doubted that Jordan's brothers' and sisters' breaks were inflicted on purpose, as lessons. She kept silent. She didn't know Jordan nearly well enough to talk about that.

To the side, Jordan dried off his chest.

She fixed her eyes on the old wooden door, the stone floor, anything but him.

He finally picked up a clean shirt and tugged into it. "How did you get out of that place?"

She busied herself packing up the first-aid kit. "After they tried to force me into an arranged marriage when I was seventeen, I stole a horse and rode into town. I never went back."

"So you lost contact with your family?" Jordan lowered his eyebrows sympathetically, in the way that only someone with a normal loving family would.

"I did. Mother's dead now. Father, too. No siblings. So, I'm all there is."

She didn't know how to end the conversation and was afraid she would suddenly start babbling about her father and her sister, who had died when she was only two days old—and then who knew what else she'd spill?

She stood and crossed to the door. Maybe waiting in her room was a better idea.

Jordan followed, touched her shoulder. "I'm sorry. I don't mean to pry."

A voice—Rhun's—called from the hallway, its tone urgent with worry. "Sergeant, Erin is not in—"

The door opened on its own, and Rhun stopped short, staring inside, surprise etched on his face.

Jordan spoke from behind Erin. "Doesn't anyone knock around here?"

Rhun quickly collected himself but remained in the hallway. The ruined garments from the desert still hung off his body in tatters, but he had washed most of the blood from his skin. His dark eyes traveled from one to the other, and his spine drew even straighter than usual, which Erin hadn't thought possible.

Her cheeks burned. At least the priest hadn't come in a few minutes earlier.

Jordan buttoned his shirt. "Sorry, padre, but Erin and I decided to stick together after all."

"You are both here. That is all that matters." Rhun turned on his heel, indicating they should follow, the stiffness never leaving his spine. "The Cardinal awaits his audience with you."

10:10 P.M.

Jordan felt disapproval rising off the priest's body in waves. He finished buttoning his shirt and tucked it in while following Erin out into the hall. She walked along with her eyes on the floor.

Korza maintained an icy silence as he led them down the passageway and up a winding staircase. Ambrose met them at the hallway at the top, greeting them with a disapproving look—or maybe that was merely his regular expression. Jordan remembered his mother's oft-repeated admonishment: *Keep making that face and it will stick.*

"While the Cardinal keeps his audiences informal," Father Ambrose said, singling Jordan out with his eyes, "do not misinterpret that for permission to be casual with His Eminence."

"Got it." Jordan tossed the guy a left-handed salute.

A trace of a crooked smile crossed Korza's lips.

Ambrose scowled, led them to a large door, and pushed it open.

Jordan followed Rhun, sheltering Erin behind him, not knowing what to expect.

A fresh breeze blew in his face, catching him by surprise. After a day spent mostly underground, it felt good to be outside again. He took a deep gulp of air, like a swimmer surfacing after a dive.

Ahead, a lush rooftop garden, illuminated by oil lamps made of clay, spread wide, inviting the eye to linger, the feet to stroll. Jordan accepted the invitation and wandered out, leading Erin.

Potted olive trees lined the parapets all around, leaves rustling in the wind.

Erin bent to inhale the spicy fragrance of a night-blooming flower. Grains of golden pollen dusted the stone tiles below.

Jordan watched her for as long as he could without getting caught. But other passions also drove him. His stomach growled as he stared over at a hand-carved wooden table, laid out with bread, grapes, pomegranates, and cheese. He really wanted a burger and a beer, but he would take what he could get.

Erin joined him, looking like a kid on Christmas morning. "This setting—from the lamps, to the plants, to the table—could have come straight out of the Bible."

Except for the electric streetlights in the distance.

At the far side of the terrace, a figure in crimson stood out against the canopy of green, his white hair in dramatic contrast with the dark sky. That had to be Cardinal Bernard.

Father Ambrose herded them away from the laden table and toward the waiting man—if he was a man. At this point, everything and everyone, in Jordan's eyes, was suspect.

Reminded of that, he looked beyond the parapet of the garden, trying to get his bearings, to figure out where they were. He spotted the giant golden cupola of a neighboring structure, what Erin had called the Dome of the Rock. She must have a pretty good idea of where they were being kept.

Father Ambrose's voice drew his attention back to the Cardinal. "May I present to you Dr. Granger and Sergeant Stone?"

The Cardinal held out his hand. The man wore a red skullcap, red leather gloves, and a cassock, like Rhun's, but his was red.

Jordan saw no ring to kiss—not that he would have—so he extended his arm. But the Cardinal took Erin's hand first, grasping her fingers between both of his palms. "Dr. Granger. It is an honor."

"Thank you, Your Eminence."

"'Cardinal Bernard' will be fine, thank you." His deep voice held a kindly tone. "We are not so formal here."

He shook Jordan's hand next. "Sergeant Stone, thank you for your services in returning Father Korza to us in one piece."

"I think we need to thank Father Korza as much as the other way around, Cardinal Bernard."

Jordan's stomach growled, again.

The Cardinal moved toward the table. "Forgive the distractedness of an old man. You need a good meal."

He led them back to the table and seated them. Only Jordan and Erin had plates.

"That will be all, Father Ambrose," Bernard said quietly.

The younger priest seemed surprised by his dismissal, but he bowed and left.

Jordan would not miss him. Instead, he happily tucked into the food. Erin helped herself to a healthy portion of cheese and bread. Bernard and Korza consumed nothing.

"While you eat, may I tell you a story?" The Cardinal raised bushy white eyebrows questioningly.

"Please," Erin answered.

"Since the beginning of recorded history, humans have feared the dark." He picked up a grape and toyed with it. "As long as anyone can remember, *strigoi* have walked among us, filling our nights with terror and blood."

Jordan swallowed the bite of bread and cheese, his throat suddenly dry. He didn't need a reminder of the danger posed by the *strigoi*.

The Cardinal continued: "The founders of the Church knew of their existence. It was not hidden in those days as it is now. The Church created a devoted sect to keep their numbers in check, not only because of the ferocity of their attacks, but also because when a human makes the transformation to *strigoi,* it destroys his soul."

Korza's dark eyes were unreadable. What must it be like to be a priest without a soul?

"How do you know that?" Erin asked.

The Cardinal smiled in a way that reminded Jordan of his kindly grandfather. "There are ways, perhaps too esoteric for this table, that it was determined."

"Maybe if you use little words," Jordan said.

Erin folded her arms. "I think you should try us."

"I meant no disrespect, only that we are pressed for time. I believe it is more important that I make certain you know that which is essential to the current situation, but I can explain about the soul of a *strigoi* after."

Erin's brown eyes looked skeptical. Jordan loved how she stood right up to the Cardinal. Not much seemed to intimidate her.

"The Sanguinists are an order of priests who draw their strength from the blood of Christ." The Cardinal touched his cross. "They are immortal in nature, but are often killed in holy battle. If killed in such a manner, their souls are restored to them."

Jordan's eyes were drawn again to Korza. So his fate was to battle evil until it destroyed him, however long that took. An eternal tour of duty.

The Cardinal's gaze settled fully upon Erin. "Many of the *strigoi* massacres are recorded falsely by history."

Erin's brow crinkled—then her eyes widened. "Herod's massacre," she said. "My dig site. It wasn't about *Herod* destroying a future King of the Jews, was it?"

"Most perceptive. Herod did not kill those babies. The *strigoi* killed them."

"But they weren't just feeding on the blood of those children. I found gnaw marks on the bones. It was a savage attack, as if done purposefully."

The Cardinal put his gloved hand atop Erin's. "I am sorry to say that is the truth. *Strigoi* sought to kill the Christ child because they knew that He would help to destroy them. As indeed it came to pass: for it was the miracle of His blood that led to the founding of the Sanguinists and started their battle against the *strigoi*."

"Sounds like the Sanguinists got a bum deal out of it all." Jordan ate a handful of grapes.

"Not at all. While it is not an easy path that we tread, our work serves humanity and opens our only path to salvation." Cardinal Bernard rolled the grape between his fingers. "For centuries, we kept the number of *strigoi* in balance, but in the last few decades, *strigoi* and some humans have formed an alliance called the Belial."

Erin pulled her arms in close, clearly recognizing that name. "Belial. The leader of the Sons of Darkness. An old legend."

Jordan stopped eating. "Great."

"We have never known why they formed." The Cardinal looked over their heads at the night sky. "But perhaps after today, we do."

Korza's eyebrows drew down. "We don't know that for certain. Even now. Don't let Bernard's love of the dramatic influence you."

"Influence us how?" Jordan asked.

"Why were the Belial formed?" Erin talked over him.

"As I believe Rhun told you, the tomb of Masada contained the most holy book ever written. It is Christ's own story of how He unleashed His divinity, written in His own blood. It is called the Blood Gospel."

"What do you mean by 'unleashed his divinity'?" Jordan asked, pushing aside his plate, the last of his appetite dying away.

The Cardinal nodded to him. "A fascinating question. As you may know, in the Bible, Christ performs no miracles early in his life. Only later does he begin to perform a whole series of wondrous acts. His first divine miracle was recorded in the Book of John, the turning of water into wine."

Erin shifted and quoted scripture. "*The first of his miraculous signs, Jesus performed at Cana in Galilee. He thus revealed his glory, and his disciples put their faith in him.*"

Bernard nodded. "Thereafter, a slew of other wonders: the multiplication of the fishes, the healing of the sick, the raising of the dead."

"But what does all of that have to do with the Blood Gospel?" Erin asked.

The Cardinal explained. "This mystery of Christ's miracles has confounded many biblical scholars. *Why* this sudden manifestation of the miraculous? *What* caused His divinity to shine forth so suddenly from His earthly flesh?" Bernard stared around the table. "Those questions are answered in Christ's Gospel."

Erin stared at him, rapt.

"Sounds like good stuff," Jordan said. "But why do the Belial care about any of this?"

"Because the book may give *anyone* the ability to touch and manifest their own divinity. Can you imagine if the *strigoi* learned this? It might help them free themselves of their weaknesses. Perhaps they could walk in daylight, like we do, multiplying their strengths. Imagine the consequences for mankind."

Korza cut him off. "But we know *none* of this for certain. It is merely Bernard's speculation." He stared hard at Erin, then Jordan. "*You* must remember that."

"Why?" Erin's eyes narrowed.

The Cardinal's face had gone stone-hard, stern. He plainly did not appreciate Korza's interruption. His next words were equally firm.

"Because you have a role to play—both of you—in what comes next. If you refuse, the world will sink into darkness. So it has been foretold."

22

October 26, 10:32 P.M., IST
Jerusalem, Israel

Erin tried not to scoff but failed. "The fate of the world depends on us? On Jordan? On me?"

Jordan muttered next to her: "You don't have to sound *so* surprised when saying my name."

Erin ignored him, hearing the sarcasm in his voice. He wasn't buying any of it either. She summarized all her questions with one word. "Why?"

The Cardinal returned the dusky grape to the empty bowl. "I cannot reveal that to you, Doctor, not at this time, not until you make your choice. After that, I will tell you all, and you may again refuse with no consequences."

"You were the one who sent the helicopter for me in Caesarea, weren't you?" she asked, picturing the whirling blades and the frightened stallion, flashing to poor Heinrich sprawled and bloody in the dig site's trench.

"I did," the Cardinal said. "I used my contacts in Israeli intelligence to have you taken to Masada, in case the Gospel was there."

"Why me?" She would keep repeating this until she got an answer that she liked.

"I have followed your work, Dr. Granger. You are skeptical of religion, but steeped in biblical knowledge. As a result, you see things that nonreligious scholars could miss. Likewise, you question things that religious scholars might not. It was that rare combination that made you perfectly suited to bring the Gospel back to the world. And I believe it continues to be true."

Either that, she thought skeptically, *or I was the closest archaeologist you could find.* It was late in the year, and most archaeologists were back teaching the fall semester. But what good would it do to point that out? So she held her tongue.

"What about me?" Jordan asked, his voice still ringing with sarcasm. "I'm guessing I'm just a random wild card, since there's nothing special about me."

Erin would have argued against that assessment, picturing his tattoo, his story of being dead for three minutes.

Could there be something to all of this?

The Cardinal favored Jordan with a small smile. "I do not know why the prophecy chose you all, my son. But you are the ones who emerged living from the tomb."

"So what are we supposed to be doing next?" Jordan shifted on his wooden chair.

Erin suspected he was accustomed to being kept in the dark for many of his missions—but she wasn't. She wanted full disclosure.

The Cardinal continued: "The two of you, along with Rhun, must find and retrieve the Gospel and bring it to the Vatican. According to prophecy, the book can only be opened in Rome." He rested his elbows on the table. "That is where our scholars will unlock its mysteries."

"And what then?" she asked. "Do you intend to hide it away?"

If the Blood Gospel existed and contained what he said, it was too powerful to leave in the hands of the Church alone.

"The words of God have always been free to all." The old man's brown eyes smiled at her.

"Like when the Church burned books during the Inquisition? Often along with the men who wrote them?"

"The Church has made mistakes," the Cardinal admitted. "But not this time. If we can share it, we shall share the light of this Gospel with all of mankind."

He seemed sincere enough, but Erin knew better. "I have dedicated my life to revealing the truth, even if that goes against biblical teachings."

The Cardinal's lips twitched up. "I would say *especially* when it goes against biblical teachings."

"Maybe." She took a deep breath. "But can you swear that you will share this book—as much as is safe—with secular scholars? Even if it contradicts Church teachings?"

The Cardinal touched his cross. "I swear it."

She was surprised by the gesture. That was something. She wasn't confident that he would keep his word, especially if the contents were antithetical to Church teachings, but it wasn't like she would get a better offer either. And if this Gospel existed, she wanted to find it. Such a discovery could in some small way pay back the debt of blood—both Heinrich's back at the camp and all those who died at Masada.

She made her decision with a nod. "Then I am—"

"Wait," Rhun said, cutting her off. "Before you pledge yourself, you must understand that you may lose your life in the search." His hand strayed to his pectoral cross. "Or something even more precious."

She remembered the earlier discussion about the souls—or the lack thereof—of the *strigoi.* It wasn't just their lives—Rhun's, Jordan's, and her own—that were at risk on the journey ahead.

A deep well of sadness shone in Rhun's eyes, something from his past.

Was he mourning his own soul or another's?

Erin silently listed logical reasons why she should not do this, why she should go back to Caesarea, meet with Heinrich's parents, and continue her dig. But this decision required more than logic.

"Dr. Granger?" the Cardinal asked. "What is your wish?"

She studied the table, spread as it had been for millennia, and Rhun, whose very existence offered possible proof of the miracle of transubstantiation. If he could be real, maybe so could Christ's Gospel.

"Erin?" Jordan asked.

She took a deep breath. "How could I pass up this opportunity?"

Jordan cocked his head. "Are you sure it's your fight?"

If it wasn't her fight, whose was it? She pictured the small child's skeleton in the trench, curled up lovingly by a parent. She imagined the slaughter that brought that baby to an untimely grave. If there was any truth to the stories told this night, she could not let the Belial get hold of that book or such massacres could become commonplace.

Jordan met her gaze, his blue eyes questioning.

Rhun bowed his head and seemed to be praying.

Erin nodded, her decision firm. "I have to."

Jordan eyed her a moment longer—then shrugged. "If she's in, I'm in."

The Cardinal bowed his head in thanks, but he wasn't done. "There is one more condition."

"Isn't there always?" Jordan mumbled.

Bernard explained: "If you enter into league with the Sanguinists, you must know you will be declared dead, listed as one of the victims atop Masada. Your family will grieve for you."

"Hold on a minute." Jordan sat back.

Erin understood. Jordan's family would miss him, would suffer for his decision. He couldn't go. Erin almost envied him. She had friends, even close friends, and colleagues, but there was no one who would be devastated if she didn't return from Israel. She didn't have family.

"There is no other way." The Cardinal held out his gloved hands palms up. "If the Belial know you live, that you seek the Gospel, they may strive to influence you through your family . . . I believe you know what that will entail?"

Erin nodded. She had seen the ferocity of the Belial firsthand in the tomb at Masada.

"To protect you, to protect those who love you, we must take you under the cloak of the Sanguinists. You must disappear from the larger world."

Jordan stroked his empty ring finger thoughtfully.

"You shouldn't come, Jordan. You have too much to lose."

The Cardinal's voice took on a kinder tone. "It is for *their* safety, my son. Once the threat is over, you will resume your former lives, and your friends and families will know you did this out of love."

"And it has to be *us,* nobody else can do this?" Jordan's eyes stayed on his fingers.

"I believe that the *three* of you together must perform this task."

Jordan glanced over to Rhun, whose dark eyes gave little away—then to Erin.

He finally stood up and paced to the rooftop's edge, his shoulders stiff. His decision was a difficult one, Erin knew. Unlike her, he was no orphaned archaeologist. He had a big family in Iowa, a wife, maybe children.

She had no one.

She was used to being alone.

So why was she staring at Jordan's back, anxious to hear his answer?

23

October 26, 10:54 P.M., IST
Beneath the Israeli desert

Bathory stirred from a nap, not knowing when she'd fallen asleep, seduced by exhaustion and the cool quiet of the subterranean bunker. It took her a moment to remember where she was. A shadowy sense of loss hung over her like cobwebs.

Then she remembered all.

As time fell back over her shoulders, an edge of panic sliced through her weariness. She sat up, rolling her legs from the reclining sofa. She found Magor curled nearby, always protecting her. He raised his large head, his eyes glowing.

She waved him to rest, but he lumbered up and padded over to her.

At her side, he slumped down again, leaving his head on her lap. He sensed her distress, as she felt the simple warmth of his affection and concern.

"I'll be fine," she assured him aloud.

But he felt what was unspoken, her fear and worry.

As she scratched his ears, she searched for the words to tell Him of her failure—if such words existed. She had lost most of the *strigoi* under her command, let a Knight of Christ escape her snare. And worst of all, what did she have to show for it?

Certainly not the book—but that was not her fault.

Someone else had stolen it long before Masada crumbled to ruin.

She even had proof of the theft: grainy photos recovered from a cell phone.

But even to her, any explanation of the night's events felt like excuses.

No longer able to sit, she gently shifted Magor's muzzle and stood. Her bare feet crossed a Persian rug that had once graced the stone floor of her ancestral castle, once warmed feet now long dead.

She reached a concrete wall. It was covered in Chinese red silk to soften the stark confines of the bunker that was her home in the desert, a home buried twenty feet under the sands. Against the wall, artfully arranged shelves displayed an antique lancet with an ebony handle and a gold bleeding bowl with rings inside to indicate how much blood had been released.

She lifted the bowl. How much of her cursed blood might He take as punishment?

Magor nuzzled her hip, and she put down the bowl and knelt, burying her face in his fur. He smelled like wolf and blood and comfort. With Hunor gone, he was her last true companion.

What if He took Magor away?

That fear drew her face up. Her gaze fell on her most prized possession—an original Rembrandt portrait of a young boy. A version of *Titus* hung in an American gallery. The boy's blond hair curled outward from an angelic face. Serious blue-gray eyes met hers, red lips curved in a tentative smile. In the American version, a gray smudge rested atop his shoulder. Art historians speculated that it was a pet parrot or monkey that had died during the weeks it took to complete the painting. To spare the boy, the lost pet had been painted over after the work's completion. Her painting revealed it was neither of those animals. A tawny owl stared back from the boy's shoulder.

But the nocturnal predator did not hold her gaze. The boy did. He looked like her brother Istvan, piquing the vague sense of loss into something more substantial.

First she'd lost Istvan.

And now Hunor.

She could not lose Magor.

The wolf rested his massive muzzle on her shoulder. She crooned him a lullaby and tried to make plans. Perhaps she should flee into the desert, disappear with Magor. She had enough money and jewels in her closet to keep them comfortable for years. Maybe she could escape at last from the silver cage that had held her for so long.

As if someone had read her thoughts, a heavy hand rapped on her door.

Magor growled, his hackles rising like a ridge along his back.

Without waiting for an answer, the thick metal door of her room swung open. Dark boots entered.

Tarek stopped just past the threshold, shadowed by his brother, Rafik. It was a daring move on his part.

She stood, lifting her chin, baring her throat and His mark.

Magor crossed in front of her, another line of defense.

"How dare you enter without my permission?" she said.

Tarek smiled, his lips stretched wide to reveal his extended fangs. "I dare because He knows of your failure."

Rafik hovered at his brother's shoulder, malicious madness dancing in his eyes.

Tarek made clear the reason for his bold intrusion, smelling a possible shift in power, declaring his intent by crossing her threshold, like a dog marking a tree. "I have received instructions from Him on how to kill you the next time that you fail."

From the glee in Rafik's eyes, she imagined such a death would be neither quick nor painless.

She kept her face impassive and met Tarek's gaze. The monsters at her door might be stronger than she was, but she was far more cunning. She let this confidence show and stared Tarek's gaze down—until she finally drove him back out the door.

Rather than making her fearful, such threats only fortified her, steeled her resolve.

As He knew they would.

She touched Magor's shoulder.

"Time we hunt again."

24

October 26, 10:57 P.M., IST
Jerusalem, Israel

From the rooftop garden, Jordan stared down at the Wailing Wall, at those praying in front of it. A young mother held up her baby, the girl's frilly pink dress shifting when her tiny hand stroked down the stone. She looked like his niece Abigail had at that age. For three years his youngest sister had dressed her little tomboy in nothing but pink. After that, Abigail picked out her own clothes—brown ones. The mother below brought the little girl back to her chest and kissed the top of her head.

The pair had no idea about *strigoi.*

They lived in a world with no monsters.

But monsters were out there, and now Jordan knew it. If this mission failed, everyone else would have to face them, too. He remembered the short work they had made of his own highly trained men.

As he watched the pair step away from the wall and head home, he fought against thoughts of his own family. Especially his mother. She had survived surgery for a brain tumor last month and was still frail, finishing off chemotherapy.

Forget the Belial, the grief of his death might do her in.

Still, he knew what she would want him to do. He was his mother's child; his belief in right and wrong had been instilled in him by her—by her words, by her actions, even by her suffering. He had signed up to serve his country, his fellow man, partly because of her. He believed in the army motto *This We'll Defend.*

Keeping *strigoi* from ruling the earth was worth a terrible price; he would not flinch from paying it. His family would expect nothing less. His team had given nothing less.

Resolved, he walked back to the table.

His reasons all sounded noble, but he knew part of his decision came from the way Erin had smiled at him when she woke up in the chopper, how she had melted in his arms downstairs. He couldn't abandon her to Rhun and the others.

He stepped to the table and dropped his dog tags. "I'm in."

"Jordan . . ." Erin stared at him, the internal war between relief and fear visible on her face.

He studied his dog tags and looked away. When his parents received them, they would think him dead.

The Cardinal nodded soberly, but his eyes shone with determination. Jordan had seen many a general wear that same expression. Usually it was after you volunteered for something. Something likely to kill you.

Korza stood so abruptly that his chair toppled backward and crashed to the tiles—then he stormed off.

"You must forgive Rhun," the Cardinal said. "In the past, he paid a terrible price in service of the prophecy."

"What price?" Jordan picked up Rhun's chair, flipped it around, and straddled it.

"It was almost four hundred years ago." Lamplit eyes stared past him toward the modern city lights. "I am certain that, should he wish you to know, he will tell you."

Jordan had half expected that kind of response. He leaned his arms on top of his chair back. "Now that we are on board, how about telling us about the prophecy and why the three of us are so special?"

Erin folded her hands in her lap like a schoolgirl and leaned forward, wanting answers, too.

"When the book was sealed away, prophecy decreed that—" The Cardinal stopped and shook his head. "Better I simply show you."

He opened a drawer in the table and pulled out a soft leather case. It didn't look like a prophecy. But when he opened it, Erin sat forward. Jordan scooted closer, shoulder to shoulder with her.

"This is it?" she asked.

The Cardinal pulled out a document sheathed in plastic. Jordan was no judge, but the parchment looked as old as the city around them. Letters written in dark ink marched along the single page. He couldn't read it but it looked familiar.

"Greek?" he asked.

Erin nodded, leaning closer to read it aloud. "*The day shall come when the Alpha and the Omega shall pour His wisdom into a Gospel of Precious Blood that the sons of Adam and the daughters of Eve may use it on the day of their need.*"

"The Alpha and Omega?" he asked.

"Jesus. I think." She returned to the parchment and continued reading, running a finger along the plastic surface. "*Until such day, this blessed book shall be hidden in a well of deepest darkness by a girl.*" She paused. "Or it might be *woman*? It's not clear. It says here a 'Girl of Corrupted Innocence.' But the last word could also mean *knowledge.* Biblical references about knowledge and good and evil often get tangled up."

Jordan's head was already beginning to spin. "How about a quick overview? Then work out the particulars?"

"Right." She continued again. "*Until such day, this blessed book shall be hidden in a well of deepest darkness by a Girl of Corrupted Innocence, a Knight of Christ, and a Warrior of Man.*"

She took another breath. "*Likewise shalt another trio return the book to the light. Only a Woman of Learning, a Knight of Christ, and a Warrior of Man may open Christ's Gospel and reveal His glory to the world.*"

The Cardinal stared at Erin. "I believe that is you, Dr. Granger, along with Sergeant Stone and our Father Korza."

Erin looked down at the parchment. "Why do you think that we are the ones?"

"The three of you came together at the original resting place of the book. Each of you played a part in defeating the creatures of darkness and returned alive to view the desert stars."

Jordan sighed—too loudly, drawing the others' eyes. It all sounded like religious crap, and he told them why. "But we didn't *get* the book. It was already gone, taken out into the world. Someone probably already opened the book a long time ago."

"No, my son, if they had opened the book, the world would have changed. Miracles would be commonplace."

"Maybe," Jordan said. "But either way, *someone* else already found it and took it. *They* must be the ones the prophecy was talking about, right?"

The Cardinal shook his head. "The prophecy does not say who will *find* it, only who must *open* it. I believe that whoever has the book cannot open it because they are not part of the prophetic trio. But I believe you three are."

"Where do we go to find the book?" Erin asked.

Cardinal Bernard shook his head. "I have no answer to that question. Rhun said that he found nothing in the tomb to indicate who had plundered it."

Erin sought Jordan's eyes, clearly asking permission. He nodded. He didn't see much point in keeping secrets now. She reached in her pocket and drew out the Nazi medallion slowly.

"This was found in the dead girl's grip. She must have snatched it off whoever stole the book, whoever killed her."

The Cardinal held out his palm. She hesitated before dropping the silver disk into his red glove.

He studied it for a full minute, closely examining the writing on the medal's edge, reading it aloud. "The *Ahnenerbe*."

"You're familiar with them?" Jordan asked.

"Our order often had similar research interests as this group. The *Ahnenerbe* scoured the Holy Lands for lost artifacts and religious items of power. Actually, the priest who once led our search for the Gospel was also tasked with observing the *Ahnenerbe*. Unfortunately, we lost Father Piers during World War Two." The Cardinal kissed his cross before continuing. "We lost so many back then."

Jordan knew how that felt.

Bernard straightened slowly, thoughtfully, and passed back the medal. "I know someone who should see this. We have a Pontifical University—one run by the Order of the Sanguines—hidden at the abbey in Ettal, Germany. They have an enormous research library. There you will find our records concerning the *Ahnenerbe* and their activities during and after the war. Perhaps that should be the first stop on your quest?"

Jordan looked at Erin. "Do you have any better ideas?"

"Better than a Sanguinist library?" She looked ready to leave immediately. "I can't wait to see it."

He grinned. No surprise there. Her excitement was contagious. "Unless Father Korza has objections, let's start there."

"I will see to the preparations. After that, I must return to Rome—to ready the Vatican if you are successful."

The Cardinal made as if to stand, but Jordan held up his hand. "Before you do that, I have a favor to ask."

"Yes?"

"I wrote letters for each member of my team." He kept his voice even, professional, trying not to think. "Letters to be delivered to their families in the event of their deaths, and mine. I left instructions with my CO about where they were and how to deliver them. Could you make sure that they are sent?"

Bernard bowed his head. "I can, my son. We have contacts with many army chaplains."

Jordan cleared his throat, speaking formally. "One more thing, Your Eminence."

"Of course."

He reached into a tiny zippered pocket in his jacket and pulled out his wedding ring. He held the ring between his thumb and finger, remembering the rainy day when Karen had put it on his finger, the moment that had been coming at him like a freight train since his senior year of high school. They'd never thought they'd be apart.

"Please see that this gets to my wife's family," he said. "I always told them that if I were to die, they would get it back. They had talked of burying it near her gravestone."

25

October 26, 11:14 p.m., IST
Jerusalem, Israel

Erin had been taking a sip of water when Jordan passed over his wedding ring. She smothered a cough of surprise.

The ring shone gold before the Cardinal's red glove closed over it. "As you wish, my son. It will be done."

So Jordan wasn't married—he was widowed.

She fought to fit this change into her overall view of him, barely hearing Jordan give instructions on where to find his letters and where to send the ring. He was *supposed* to be married. The tan line said so. She hated it when she misinterpreted evidence. He was a widower, one who had clearly loved his wife and hadn't wanted to let her go.

This changed everything. If he was single, his actions took on a different cast—as did her own. She began reviewing all their past interactions, centering back at last to that kiss in his room.

She found her fingertips touching her lips and had to force her hand down.

"Excuse me, Your Eminence." A peevish voice carried across the garden, drawing their collective attention. Father Ambrose crossed toward them. "May I clear?"

She stood, not certain of where to go.

"Of course, my son," the Cardinal said. "We are finished supping."

Wanting to keep her hands busy, her thoughts redirected, Erin helped Father Ambrose clean off the table while Jordan and the Cardinal kept talking. She hurriedly followed the fussy priest with their plates back to the stairs.

She closed the door, wanting a moment of privacy with Father Ambrose on the stairs.

"I would like to speak to Father Korza," she said.

Father Ambrose filched the lone remaining grape from the bowl and ate it. Out of view of the Cardinal, he seemed more relaxed. Or maybe he considered her no threat to his position. "You may try to speak to him, but our Father Korza is not a *communicative* man."

"I would still like to take my chances," she said.

"Very well." Father Ambrose smiled tightly, as if hiding a secret. "But you have been warned."

She followed him down to a surprisingly modern kitchen and deposited their dishes in the sink.

He then took two brass candleholders from a cabinet, inserted a candle in each, and lit them. "There is no light where we are going," he explained.

He handed her a candleholder and returned to the spiral stairs. They descended, winding deeper and deeper, passing the cells where she and Jordan had washed up, where they'd kissed. Her steps hurried past that level.

As she continued deeper, she wondered how best to approach Rhun. He had been furious when she and Jordan agreed to accompany him on the search. But why? What price had he paid four hundred years ago?

She considered his alleged age. Could he truly be five hundred years old? That would mean he'd lived through the Renaissance. His courtly, formal mannerisms made more sense now, but nothing else did.

Like why she was even heading down here?

Part of the reason was simple: *to escape*. She needed to give herself space and time to adjust to the new Jordan.

But Rhun also had answers she needed.

From the priest's reaction in the garden, she suspected Rhun would be more truthful about the dangers ahead—at least more forthright than the Cardinal. Even though her mind was made up, she wanted to know everything she could about the quest. Rhun might give her answers or, more likely, he would just stare at her with those dark eyes and say nothing. But she had to try.

Father Ambrose stopped in front of another massive wooden door. He struggled to unlock it with a skeleton key from a ring he kept on his belt. The rusty lock looked as if it had not been opened in years.

Hair stood up on her arms as a stray fear came to mind. What if Father Ambrose intended her harm? She scolded herself at such foolishness. Both Jordan and the Cardinal saw her leave with him. He wouldn't dare do anything to her. Still, her heart would not slow.

The lock finally gave and Father Ambrose pulled back the heavy door with difficulty and pointed into the dark room.

Across the chamber, Rhun knelt in front of what might have been an altar, although it was too dark to tell. A single votive candle lit the room, most of its light absorbed by the scarlet glass that held it. Its small flame revealed a distant, arched ceiling and ancient stained-glass windows that must look out upon nothing but more rock. Empty wooden pews filled the space, separated by a threadbare carpet running down the center.

Was this a Sanguinist's chapel?

Father Ambrose gestured that she enter first, and she slipped inside, moving quietly, crossing only a few steps past the threshold, not wanting to disturb Rhun in prayer.

As the door closed behind her, the wind blew out her candle. She should have thought to cup the flame. She turned to Father Ambrose—only to find he hadn't entered with her.

She went back to the door and tried the handle.

Locked.

He had trapped her alone with Rhun.

She paused, uncertain about what to do. She would not give Father Ambrose the satisfaction of pounding on the door and begging to be let out. Also she did not want to intrude upon Rhun's prayers.

For him not to notice her presence already, he must be in deep meditation. Rhun noticed everything. His senses were sharper than hers, but now he gave no outward sign that he knew she was here.

Was he so lost in his faith?

She felt a twinge of envy for such focused devotion.

In the quiet, she heard faint words whispered in Latin, words easy to translate because she'd heard them often enough during the Masses of her childhood.

"The Blood of our Lord Jesus Christ, which was shed for thee, preserve thy body and soul unto everlasting life. Drink this in remembrance that Christ's Blood was shed for thee, and be thankful."

He was giving himself Communion. For the first time, she truly understood the meaning behind the prayers. Everything she knew about the Church would have to be rethought. Beliefs she had once rejected were being proven true, supported by a history she had not even thought possible.

"The Blood of our Lord Jesus Christ keep you in everlasting life."

He put a large chalice to his lips and intoned:

"The Blood of Christ, the cup of salvation."

In the desert, he had been ashamed to drink his wine in front of her and Jordan. She crept back to the door, about to knock, but she stayed her hand.

As much as Rhun had hated her and Jordan seeing him vulnerable, it would surely be worse if Father Ambrose did.

She turned her back to Rhun, granting him his privacy. She slid to a sitting position on the floor, wrapped her arms around her knees, and waited.

11:31 P.M.

Rhun raised the cold cup to his lips, inhaling the familiar scents of gold and wine. He needed Christ's blood tonight more than he had in many years. It would help him heal, and it would still his anger. Knowing the risks, Bernard had bound the innocent woman and the soldier to him. They had accepted the quest, not understanding where it would lead. Had he been so rash when he was a fragile human?

Shame burned in him. The blame for it was not Bernard's alone. Rhun's actions had brought the soldier and the woman here. He had told them the forbidden. He had saved them when he should have let them die.

If he failed them now, they would wish that he had let them find a quick death in the desert.

He raised the cup one final time and drank. Long and deep. The liquid scalded his lips, his throat. It was not the fermented grape, but the essence of Christ's own blood that flamed against the sin that flowed through his tainted body. He set down the drained cup, then raised his arms to shoulder height and let the flames of Christ's gift burn through him while he finished his prayer. Steam rose from his lips, and he forced the last words through the agony. Then he knelt with nothing left but the memory of his sin.

Fresh rushes rustled under Rhun's boots as he crossed into the entry hall to greet Elisabeta's maid, the shy little Anna.

At Čachtice Castle, Elisabeta insisted that each fall the old rushes be discarded, the stone washed clean and dried, and new rushes be left in their place. She strewed chamomile over them, lending her house a clean, restful scent so unlike most of the other noble homes he visited.

"Do you not wish to follow me to the great room, Father?" Anna kept her eyes on the rushes and her birthmark turned from him.

"If you would, Anna, could you fetch the lady here?" Although he had visited many times, tonight he was loath to go deeper inside.

Before Anna had time to leave, Elisabeta arrived in a sumptuous dark green gown cinched tight around her slender waist. "My dear Father Korza! It is rare to see you about so late. Do come into the great room. Anna just laid a fresh fire."

"I must decline. I believe that my errand . . . my task . . . that we are best served if I remain here."

Her sculpted eyebrows raised in surprise. "How mysterious!"

She waved Anna away, then glided to a high table by the door and lit the beeswax candles. Their honey scent wafted up, reminding him of innocent summers too long past.

Flickering candlelight fell across a face lovelier than he had ever seen. Light glinted off jet-black hair, and silvery eyes danced with mischief. She clasped her hands as she faced him. "Tell me of your errand, Father."

"I come bearing tidings." His throat closed.

She stood quite still. The smile vanished from her face, and her silver eyes darkened like a storm cloud. "Of my husband, the Count Nádasy?"

He could not tell her. He could not hurt her. He gripped the silver cross of his office, hoping that it would give him strength. As usual, it only gave him pain.

"He has fallen," she said.

Of course, as a soldier's wife, she knew.

"It was with honor. In—"

She sagged back against the wall. "Spare me such details."

Rhun stood fixed, unable to speak.

She ducked her head, trying to hide tears.

As a priest, he should go to her. He should pray with her, talk of God's will, explain that Ferenc now dwelt with the exalted. He had filled that role many times and for many mourners.

But he could not do it for her.

Not her.

Because in truth, he longed to enfold her slim form in his arms, to hold her sorrow against his chest. So, instead, he backed away, letting his cowardice become cruelty, forsaking her at this hard time.

"I offer my deepest condolences for your loss," he said stiffly.

She raised grief-filled eyes to his. Surprise and confusion flickered across them, then only deeper sadness. She did her best to fix her mask of normality back in place, but she wore it crookedly, unable to fully hide the hurt of his coldness.

"I shall not detain you, Father. The hour is late, and your journey long."

He said not another word and fled.

Because he loved her, he abandoned her.

As he stumbled down the frost-rimed road that led away from Elisabeta, he realized that everything had shifted between them. Surely she knew it, too. Ferenc had been the wall that kept them both safe, kept them apart.

Without that wall, anything might escape.

Rhun returned to himself, back to the present, sprawled flat on the chapel's stone floor. As he lay there, he thought again upon that visit to the castle. He should have followed his instinct and fled forever, never to return to her side.

Then, as now, he had buried himself in the dark quiet of the Church. The bright scents in his life dissolved into nothing more than stone dust, the sweat of men, and traces of frankincense, spicy with an undertone of the conifer from which it had bled.

But nothing green and alive.

During those long-ago nights, he had performed his priestly duties. But during the days, he gazed into the Virgin Mary's clear eyes as she wept for her son, and he thought only of Elisabeta. He slept only when he had to, because when he slept he dreamed that he had not failed her, that he held her warm body against his and comforted her. He kissed her tears, and sunshine returned to her smile, a smile meant for him.

In his long years of priesthood, his faith had never wavered. But, then, it did.

He had put aside thoughts of her and prayed until the stone rubbed his knees raw. He had fasted until his bones ached. Only he and one other Sanguinist in all the centuries had not tasted human blood, had never taken a human life. He had thought his faith stronger than his flesh and his feelings.

And he had thought that he conquered them.

His hubris still ate at him.

His pride had caused his downfall, and hers.

Why had the wine shown him this part of his penance tonight?

A heartbeat thrummed through his thoughts, pulling him back to the candlelit chapel.

A human, here? Such trespass was forbidden.

He raised his head from the stones. A woman sat with her back to him, her head bowed over her knees. The angle of her head called to him. The nape of her neck smelled familiar.

Erin.

The name drifted through the fog of memories and time.

Erin Granger.

The Woman of Learning.

Rage burned inside him. Another innocent had been forced into his path. Better that he kill her now, simply and quickly, than abandon her to a crueler fate. He stood as crimson tinged his vision. He fought against the lust with prayer.

Then another faint, familiar heartbeat reached his ears, thick and irregular.

Ambrose.

The priest had locked Erin in with Rhun, either to shame him, or perhaps with the hope that Rhun's penance might cause him to lose control, as it almost had.

He crossed the room so swiftly that Erin flinched and held her hands up in a placating gesture.

"I'm sorry, Rhun. I didn't mean to—"

"I know."

He reached past her and shoved the door open with the force that only a Sanguinist could muster, taking satisfaction at the sound of Ambrose's heavy body thudding into the wall.

Then he heard the man's rushed and frightened footsteps retreating up the stairs.

He returned to Erin and helped her to her feet, smelling the lavender off her hair, the slight muskiness of her fading fear. The beat of her heart settled, her breathing softened. He held her hand a moment too long, feeling her warmth and not wanting to let go of it.

She was alive.

Even if it cost the world, he would make sure that this never changed.

26

October 26, 11:41 P.M., IST
Undisclosed location, Israel

Tommy rested his forehead against the window of his hospital room, slowly rapping his knuckles against its thick glass, listening to the dull thud. By now, he had convinced himself that this place was a military hospital or maybe even a prison.

He pulled his IV pole closer, wondering if he could use it like a battering ram to break his way free.

But then what?

If he managed to break the window and jumped, would he die? A television show he watched a couple of years ago said that any fall above thirty feet was probably not survivable. He was higher than that.

He toyed with the leads attached to his IV port. The medical staff measured everything about him—his heart rate, his oxygen saturation levels, and other random stuff. The Hebrew labels were gibberish to him. His father could read Hebrew and had tried to teach him, but Tommy had only learned enough to get through his bar mitzvah.

Reminded of his father, he pictured the blackish-orange gas rolling over his parents.

If he hadn't told them the gas was safe, they might still be alive. He knew now the gas was toxic, just not to him. *Immune* was the word he'd heard one doctor use. Maybe he could have dragged his parents to safety. That strange priest at Masada had said that there was nothing he could have done, but what else could he say?

You killed your parents, kid. You're going to Hell, but it'll be a long time till you get there.

Tommy looked out the window again. It was a long drop to the desert. Far below, the boulders' shadows looked like spilled ink against the brighter sand. It was a bitter landscape, but from this height, it looked peaceful.

A rustle jerked his attention back into the room.

A kid was standing right next to him. He looked about Tommy's age, but he wore a gray three-piece suit. He sniffed the air like a dog, his nose moving closer to Tommy with each sniff. His black eyes glittered.

"Can I help you?" Tommy asked, stepping away.

This earned him a smile—one so cold that he shivered.

Suddenly terrified, Tommy tapped his call button repeatedly, sending out an SOS of panic. He shrank back against the window as his heart rate spiked, triggering the monitors to beep wildly.

The boy winked.

Tommy was struck by the oddity of the action.

Who *winked* nowadays? Seriously, who—

The kid's right hand moved so fast that Tommy didn't even see a blur until it stopped by the angle of his jaw. A sharp pain cut across his neck.

Tommy brought both hands up to feel. Blood ran through his fingers. It pumped from his throat, soaked his hospital gown, dripped on the floor.

The boy lowered his arm and watched, cocking his head slightly.

Tommy pressed his hands against his throat, trying to cut off the flood, strangling himself in the attempt. But blood continued to pour through his fingers.

He screamed, earning only a warm gurgle as hot pain chased up his throat.

Knowing he needed help, Tommy yanked off his EKG leads. Behind him, the monitor flatlined, setting an alarm to wailing.

Immediately, two soldiers charged into the room, machine guns up and ready.

He saw their shocked expressions—then the boy winked again.

Not good.

The kid lifted a chair, moving blindingly fast, and smashed it through the thick window. Without stopping, he shoved Tommy out into the night.

Free at last.

Cold air brushed across his body as he fell. Warm blood pumped from his neck.

He closed his eyes, ready to see Mom and Dad.

He had barely pictured them—when the ground slammed against his body. Nothing had ever hurt like this. Surely it had to end soon. It had to.

It didn't.

Bullets sparked the asphalt around him. The soldiers shot through the broken window. Bullets tore electric trails of pain into his chest, his thigh, his hand.

Sirens sounded. Searchlights went up.

The boy landed lightly next to him, gray suede boots barely making a sound against the ground. Had he jumped? From that height?

The boy grabbed his arm. Tommy's bones ground against one another as the kid dragged him out of the spotlights and into the desert, running as quickly as a gazelle. He clearly did not care how the rocks cut Tommy's back, how the jouncing grated his broken bones.

All the while uncaring stars shone down on them both.

Winking as coldly as the boy.

Tommy wanted it to end. He wanted to sleep. He wanted to die.

He counted down to his death.

One. Two. Three. Four . . .

Through the haze of pain, he had the worst thought of his life.

What if I can't die at all?

27

October 26, 11:44 P.M., IST
Jerusalem, Israel

Erin kept several feet behind Rhun as he swept out of the chapel, up the stairs, and through a maze of tunnels. Even as swiftly as he moved, she knew he kept his pace slow so that she could keep up, but it scared her to be close to him. In the flickering red glow of the chapel, his rage had been unmistakable. It looked like he had barely restrained himself from attacking her.

If not for the dark maze of winding tunnels, she would have run away. But she had lost her own candle, and she needed the light of the chapel's votive candle, held in Rhun's hand, to return to safety.

Then at last, she heard voices arguing, echoing from ahead, from an open doorway glowing with light. She recognized them all: the timbre of Jordan's anger, Father Ambrose's prissy officiousness, and the sighing resignation of Cardinal Bernard.

"So where is she?" Jordan boomed, plainly wondering what Father Ambrose had done with her.

Steps away, Rhun's dark form disappeared through the doorway.

She hurried behind to discover a modern room with white-washed walls, a polished stone floor, and a long table covered with weapons and ammunition.

All eyes turned to her when she entered.

Jordan's face relaxed. "Thank God," he said—though God had nothing to do with it.

The others remained inscrutable, except Rhun.

He rushed forward, seized Father Ambrose by the neck, and slammed him against the wall. The short priest's feet dangled in the air.

"Cardinal!" Father Ambrose gasped, choking.

Rhun tightened his hand on the priest's throat. "There will come a reckoning between us, Ambrose. Remember that."

Jordan took a step toward them, his hands raised as if to intervene.

The Cardinal's face was impassive. "Let him go, Rhun. I will make sure he is properly admonished."

Rhun leaned closer.

Only Erin, standing to the side, saw the sharper points on Rhun's teeth as he snarled and threatened. "Leave my sight. Lest that reckoning come now."

Rhun dropped the priest, who had gone dead-white. So *he* had seen those points, too. Father Ambrose collected himself, scuttled a few paces away, then fled.

Jordan stepped closer. "Erin, are you okay? Where were you? What happened?"

"I'm fine."

She didn't want to talk about it, especially not until she'd adjusted to the change in the marital status of her new teammate. Still, she was more grateful than ever that he was accompanying them on the expedition. She pictured the dark rage in Rhun's face when he looked at her in the chapel, how his teeth had sharpened when he threatened Father Ambrose.

She leaned closer to Jordan's reassuring warmth. "Thanks."

Cardinal Bernard cleared his throat. "Since you are returned to us, Dr. Granger . . . perhaps now we should finish our discussion of the *strigoi*."

He gestured to the loaded table of weaponry. Erin kept to the far side of Rhun, despite the fact that he seemed calm again.

Jordan picked up a pair of goggles from the table and studied them. "These are night-vision scopes, but they look odd."

"They are of special design, made to toggle between low-light vision and infrared," Bernard explained. "A useful tool. The low-light feature allows you to discern opponents at night, but since the *strigoi* are cold, they do not glow with body heat on infrared goggles.

If you toggle between those two features, you'll be able to separate humans from *strigoi* at night."

Curious, needing to try this out for herself, Erin picked up the other pair of goggles and looked at Jordan. His hair and the tip of his nose were now yellow; the rest of his face looked warm and red. He waved an orange hand.

Definitely warm-blooded.

She remembered the heat of his kiss—and shoved that thought back down.

She hurriedly turned the goggles on Rhun. Even though the Cardinal had just told her that his body would be at room temperature, it still startled her when she saw his face in the same cold purples and deep blues as the wall behind him. When she switched to low-light vision, everyone looked the same.

"How'd it work?" Jordan asked.

"Fine."

Yet another scientific tool that showed how *other* Rhun was from them. Did he have anything in common with them at all?

"Here are silver rounds for your weapons." The Cardinal handed wooden boxes to Jordan. "It is difficult to stop a charging *strigoi* with a gun, but these bullets help. They are hollow points and expand on impact to maximize the amount of silver that comes in contact with their blood."

Jordan shook a bullet into his palm and held it up to the light. The bullet and casing glinted white silver. "How does that help?"

"Our unique blood resists mortal diseases. We can live forever unless felled by violence. Our immune system is superior to yours in every way, except when it comes to *silver*."

"But you carry silver crosses." Erin pointed to the cross atop the Cardinal's red cassock.

He kissed his gloved fingertips and touched his pectoral cross. "Each Sanguinist bears that burden, yes, to remind us of our cursed state. If we touch the silver—" He took off his leather glove and pressed a pale finger against the bullet in Jordan's hand. The smell of burning flesh drifted to Erin. The Cardinal held up his finger to show where the silver had seared his flesh. "It burns even us."

"But not as bad as it does the *strigoi*, I'd wager," Jordan said, pocketing the rounds.

"That is true," Bernard admitted with a bow of his head. "As a Sanguinist, I exist in a state halfway between damnation and holiness. Silver burns me, but does not kill me. *Strigoi* do not have the protection of Christ's blood in their veins, so silver is much more deadly to them." He drew his glove on again. "Holy objects also have some value, although not enough to kill them."

"Then how do we defend ourselves?" Jordan asked.

"I suggest that you view *strigoi* as animals," the Cardinal said. "To put them down, you must grievously wound them with traditional weapons, just like any other animal."

She looked over at Rhun, who showed no reaction to being called an animal.

Instead, the priest took a dagger and slashed his palm.

She gasped.

His eyes flicked to her face as blood pattered to the table. "You must understand fully," he said.

"Doesn't that hurt?" She couldn't help but ask.

"We feel many things more acutely than humans. Including pain. So, yes, it does hurt, but watch the wound."

He held out his open hand. The blood flowing from his cut stopped as abruptly as if he had turned off a tap. The blood at the edge of his wound even seeped back *into* his hand.

"And you are showing us this cool little trick because . . . ?" Jordan asked.

"The secrets lie in our blood. It flows on its own through our bodies, a living force. This means our wounds stop bleeding almost instantly."

Erin leaned closer. "So you don't need a heart to propel your blood? It does it on its own?"

Rhun bowed his head in acknowledgment.

Erin considered the implications. Was this the origin of the legend of the living dead? *Strigoi* seemed *dead* because they were cold and didn't have beating hearts?

"But what about breathing?" she asked, wanting every detail.

"We breathe only to smell and to speak," Rhun explained. "But there is no necessity for it. We can hold our breath indefinitely."

"More good news," Jordan mumbled.

"So now you understand," Rhun said. "As Cardinal Bernard

warned you, if you cut a *strigoi,* keep cutting. Do not assume that they are fatally wounded, because they are likely not. Be on guard at all times."

Jordan nodded.

"A *strigoi*'s only weaknesses are fire, silver, sunlight, and wounds so grievous that they cannot stop the blood flow quickly enough."

Jordan stared down at the array of weaponry, clearly more worried than he'd been a moment ago. "Thanks for the pep talk," he muttered.

The Cardinal spread his gloved hands across several daggers that had been laid out on the table. "All of these weapons are coated with silver and blessed by the Church. I think you will find them more effective than the blade you wear at your ankle, Sergeant Stone."

Jordan picked up each dagger, testing its heft. He settled on a bone-handled knife that was almost a foot long. He examined it closely. "This is an American Bowie knife."

"A fitting weapon," Rhun said. "It dates back to the Civil War and was carried by a brother of our order who died during the Battle of Antietam."

"One of the bloodiest fights of that war," Jordan commented.

"The blade has since been silver-plated." Rhun eyed Jordan. "Wear it well and with respect."

Jordan nodded, soberly acknowledging the weapon's heritage.

Erin remembered the knife battles in the tomb. She would never cower helplessly in a box again. "I want one, too. And a gun."

"Can you shoot?" the Cardinal asked.

"I hunted as a kid—but I've never shot anything I didn't intend to eat."

Jordan gave her that crooked grin again. "Think of this as shooting something that wants to eat *you*."

She forced a smile, still sickened by the thought of shooting someone, even a *strigoi*. They looked like people; they *were* once people.

"They will not hesitate to kill you or worse," Rhun said. "If you cannot bring yourself to take their lives—"

"Now, Rhun," the Cardinal interrupted. "Not everyone is meant to serve as a soldier. Dr. Granger will be traveling as a scholar. I am certain that you and Sergeant Stone can keep her safe."

"I do not share your unswerving belief in our abilities," Rhun said. "She must be ready to defend herself."

"And I will." Erin picked up a Sig Sauer pistol.

"A fine weapon." The Cardinal handed her a few boxes of silver ammunition.

She put the gun in a shoulder holster, feeling ridiculous in her long skirt, like she should be part of a Wild West sideshow. "Can I get a pair of jeans?"

"I will see to it," Bernard promised, then pointed to a pair of garments hanging on wall pegs: two long leather dusters. "And these are for you also."

Jordan crossed and fingered the larger of the two coats. "What's this made of?"

"From the wolf skin of a *blasphemare*," the Cardinal said. "You'll find such leather both stab- and bullet-resistant."

"Like body armor," Jordan said approvingly.

Erin picked up the smaller coat, clearly meant for her. It was about twice as heavy as a normal jacket. Otherwise it looked the same, textured like expensive leather.

Jordan pulled his on over his shoulders. It was the color of milk chocolate, and it suited him perfectly. He looked even better in it than he did in his camouflage.

Erin slipped into her jacket, a lighter brown than Jordan's. It reached her knees, but was full enough to allow plenty of movement. The round collar brushed the bottom of her chin, protecting her neck.

"I also want to give you this." Rhun pressed a silver necklace into her hand, a chain with an Orthodox cross.

Years ago, she had worn such a cross every day—until finally she had flung it from the horse's back as she fled the compound. After years of beating God into her, her father had succeeded only in beating God out of her.

"How is this useful?" she asked. "The Cardinal said that holy objects are not that powerful against the *strigoi*."

"It is no mere weapon." Rhun spoke so softly she had to strain to hear him. "It's a symbol of Christ. That is beyond weaponry."

She stared at the sincerity in his eyes. Was he trying to bring her back into the fold of the Church? Or was it something more?

In deference to what she saw in his gaze, she hung the cross around her neck. "Thank you."

Rhun bowed his head fractionally, then handed another cross to Jordan.

"Isn't it early in the relationship for jewelry?" Jordan asked.

Rhun's eyebrows drew together in confusion.

Erin smiled—and it felt good to do so. "Don't mind him. He's teasing you, Rhun."

Jordan sighed, put his hands on his hips, and asked one last question. "So when are we leaving?"

Bernard answered with no hesitancy. "At once."

PART III

They mounted up to heaven;
they went down to the depths;
their courage melted away in their evil plight.

—Psalm 107:26

28

October 27, 3:10 A.M., Central European Time
Oberau, Germany

With the promise of dawn still hours away, Jordan shifted in the rear passenger seat of the black Mercedes S600 sedan. He stared out the window into a dark Bavarian forest, where night still held sway. Erin sat next to him, while up front, Korza drove with a skill that demonstrated his preternatural reflexes.

Mario Andretti in a Roman collar.

Beyond the asphalt of the winding stretch of road, spruce and fir trees carved blacker lines into the murky gray sky. All around, wisps of fog stretched from the dark loam like ghostly fingers. Jordan rubbed his eyes. He had to stop thinking like a man trapped in a horror movie. Reality was freakish enough without letting his imagination run away with him.

He yawned, still jet-lagged. He had barely climbed into the luxurious private plane supplied by the Vatican before falling asleep in one of its giant seats. It was hard to believe that it was still the same night, and they had left Jerusalem only four hours before, whisking north at the jet's top speed.

When the plane had landed in Munich, Erin had an endearing, just-woken-up look, so he figured she got a bit of sleep, too.

Now she was facing away from him in the backseat, looking out her own window. She wore simple gray jeans, a white shirt, and the leather jacket the Cardinal had given her. Jordan slid his finger around his own high collar. Except for the tight neck, it was the most comfortable body armor he'd ever worn, and it looked like a regular jacket. Still, considering what they were up against, it might not be enough.

Up front at the wheel, Korza had ditched his torn cassock and wore his own leathers—black, nicer than Erin's and Jordan's, and tailored. He seemed unfazed by the long night they had spent.

Had he slept at all on the plane? Did he need sleep?

Jordan hadn't made a sound since the car started, not wanting to distract Korza from the road. Erin had kept quiet, too, but he doubted it was for the same reason.

He couldn't figure her out. Ever since he handed the Cardinal his wedding band, Erin seemed to have retreated from him. He caught her watching him occasionally from the corner of her eye, as if she dared not look him fully in the face.

If he'd known that announcing that he was single would make her less interested in him rather than more, he would have passed the ring to Bernard in private. But what did he know about women? He'd spent the year since Karen's death hiding behind the ring.

Erin stirred beside him. "There's the village of Ettal."

He leaned over to see where she pointed.

Ahead, nestled in the piney woods, glowing streetlamps revealed white buildings with brown roofs. Most windows were still dark at this early hour. The place resembled a postcard, a picturesque hamlet with the words *Enjoying Bavaria!* emblazoned on the front. It was hard to believe the humble village hid a darker secret, that it was a Sanguinist stronghold.

Rhun did not slow and swept past the town.

A few hairpin turns later, a grand Baroque structure appeared, rising high and spreading outward into two towering flanks. In the center, a domed roof thrust into the sky, supporting a massive golden cross that shone in the moonlight. Countless archways decorated the bone-white facade, sheltering statues or hiding ornate windows.

"Ettal Abbey," Erin said, awed, sitting straighter. "I had hoped to see it someday."

Jordan liked to hear her talking again.

She continued, excitement returning to her voice. "Ludwig of Bavaria chose this spot for the abbey because his horse bowed three times at this site."

"How do you get a horse to bow?" Jordan asked.

"Divine intervention apparently," Erin answered.

He grinned at her before leaning forward to talk to the priest. "Is this the monastery you were talking about, padre? The secret university?"

"It lies behind. And I'd prefer you call me *Rhun,* not *padre.*"

The car fishtailed as it rounded the corner, a plume of gravel spewing from the tires. Their headlights caught simpler buildings in the back, white with red tile roofs, more humble and austere. This seemed more like the Sanguinists' style.

Rhun drew them to a fast stop beside one of the nondescript buildings. The priest was out before the engine had fully died. He remained near the sedan, scanning the surrounding hills, moving only his eyes. His nostrils flared.

Erin reached for her door handle, but Jordan stopped her.

"Let's wait till he clears us to go. And zip your jacket up, please."

He wanted her protected as fully as possible.

Outside, Rhun spun in a slow circle, like he expected an attack from any direction.

3:18 A.M.

Rhun cast out his senses, drawing in the heartbeats of the men who were asleep in the neighboring monastery. He smelled pine from the forest and hot metal from the vehicle and heard the soft *whoosh* of an owl's wings above the forest, the quick scurry of a vole below his feet.

He found no danger.

He took one breath to relax, to become one with the night. He spent most of his life indoors in prayer or out in the field hunting, too busy with war to enjoy the natural world. When he first took the cloth of his order, the otherness of his senses had frightened him, reminding him always of his nature as one who was damned, but now he treasured these rare moments when he could stop and commune with God's creation at its fullest, at its most intimate. He never felt nearer to God than in these moments of solitude, far closer than when he was buried on his knees in some subterranean chapel.

He selfishly drew in one more breath.

Then the woman shifted inside the vehicle, recalling him to his duty.

He faced the massive structure of the main building and its two wings. He studied the rear windows, watching for any movement. It appeared no one was spying from inside. A thick door stood closed at the base of one of the smaller towers. He stretched his senses through its stout wood planking, but he heard no heartbeat on the far side—only a whisper meant for his ears alone.

"Rhun, be welcome. All is safe."

Rhun relaxed at the familiar soft voice, accented in German.

He turned and gave Jordan a quick nod. At least the man had had sense enough to stay inside the car with Erin. The pair clambered out, sounding loud and clumsy to Rhun's sharp ears.

Once they were safely in his shadow, Rhun strode toward the wood door.

Jordan kept himself between Erin and the dark forest, protecting her from the most likely direction of attack. He had good instincts, Rhun had noticed. Perhaps that would be enough.

The thick door opened before they reached it.

Rhun stepped to the side to let the other two precede him. The sooner they were out of the open, the better.

As Jordan and Erin ducked through the small doorway, he cast one final glance around. He uncovered no menace, but danger still pricked at his senses.

29

October 27, 3:19 A.M., CET
Ettal, Germany

Hidden on a forested hilltop overlooking the abbey, Bathory lay on her stomach in a bower of leaf litter, letting the cold damp soothe the fury smoldering inside her at the sight of Rhun Korza.

Bare linden branches creaked above. Through her high-power binoculars, she had watched the knight leave the sedan behind the monastery. She'd placed her post far from the monastery to stay out of range of the Sanguinist's senses. The knight's caution as he stood at a rear doorway indicated his suspicion, but he had not discovered her.

Right now her only enemy was the rising fog.

As Korza disappeared inside the abbey, she rested her forehead on her arm in relief.

The risky gamble she had played had paid off handsomely.

She had sent the photos of the Nazi medallion to three historians who were in league with the Belial. As they squabbled over the medallion's importance, she had set another course, turning to her network of spies throughout the Holy Lands. They came back with news that Korza planned to take a plane to Germany, but they didn't know where he would land, where he would go.

She did know—or at least, she had her suspicions.

Korza would not let the book's trail grow cold for long. He would take the only clue from the tomb and consult historians loyal to his order, as she had done with those loyal to hers. She knew about Ettal Monastery, the Pontifical University of Sanguinist scholars devoted to historical research, going back to the end of World War II.

Of course he would come here.

So she had acted, telling no one, knowing that waiting for permission would take too long. She gathered *all* of the *strigoi* forces out of the sands of the Holy Lands—a small army—and hunkered them down here in loam and leaf.

It had been a bold move, one supported by Tarek, who she knew secretly hoped she would fail.

Magor shifted next to her, resting his head on her shoulder. She leaned against him. Despite wearing a thick fur-lined coat against the frigid cold of the Bavarian night, she appreciated the furnace of Magor's body, and even more, the affection flowing from him, bathing her as warmly as his flesh. Likewise, he sought reassurance from her. She felt the undercurrent of unease in his breast.

This was a strange new world for the desert wolf.

Be calm . . . she sent to him *. . . prey bleeds as easily here as out on the sand . . .*

On her other side, another stirred, one who held her only in contempt. "Shouldn't I take the others and move closer?" Tarek asked. "I have no heartbeat to give me away. Unlike you."

She ignored the insult, suspecting he wanted to steal the glory of this moment from her. She reined him in. "We stay. We can't risk alerting them."

The musty smell of wet leaves filled her nostrils. Unlike Magor, she drank it in. After years in the dry Judean desert, she welcomed the familiar sounds and smells of a forest. It reminded her of her home in Hungary, and she took strength from those happier memories—the time before she took His mark.

"We have more troops this time," Tarek pressed. "We could take them, wring the information from them, and retrieve the book ourselves."

She heard the raw desire behind his words, his need to avenge those who had been lost at Masada, to slake his bloodlust. She gripped her binoculars tighter. Did he not realize she shared the same yearning for revenge, for blood? But she would not be foolish or rash—nor would she let Tarek be. That was the true strength of the Belial union: to temper the ferocity of the *strigoi* with the calculated cunning of humans.

She didn't bother to turn her head. "My orders stand. Such strongholds have protections against your kind. Just *one* of those Sanguinists took down six of you on unfamiliar ground in Masada, and we do not know how many live at the abbey. Anyone who ventures down there will not return."

Most of her troops looked cowed at the thought.

Tarek did not. He pointed toward the abbey, ready to argue, to test her. She was done with his disrespect of her authority. She needed to break him as surely as the Sanguinist had broken her family.

She grabbed his extended arm and forced his hand to her throat before he could react. "If you think you can lead," she spat, "then take it!"

As his palm touched her mark, his skin sizzled. Tarek leaped high and away with a snarl, his fingers smoking from the brief contact with Bathory's tainted blood, even through her skin.

The other men fell back—all but Rafik.

He came to his brother's defense, landing on top of her.

Magor growled, ready to join the fray.

No, she willed to him.

This was her fight, her lesson to teach.

She rolled Rafik's thin frame under her, straddling him like a lover. She grabbed a fistful of his hair and dragged his mouth to her throat. Tender flesh smoked as Rafik screamed and writhed under her.

She stared at Tarek all the while. "Should I feed your brother?"

The anger in his eyes blew out, replaced with fear—for his brother's life, but also fear of her. Satisfied, she let Rafik go and cast him away. He went whimpering on all fours to Tarek's side, his lips smoking and blistered.

Tarek knelt and comforted his addled brother.

Bathory felt a twinge of guilt, knowing Rafik's intelligence was little better than that of a small child, but she had to be hard—harder than any of them.

Magor belly-crawled to her side, both nosing her to make sure she was okay and prostrating himself to show he respected her dominant role in the pack.

She scratched behind his ear, accepting his wolfish deference.

She stared over at Tarek, expecting the same from him.

Slowly, his head bowed, his eyes averted.

Good.

She returned to her leafy bower and lifted her binoculars.

Now to break the other one.

30

October 27, 3:22 A.M., CET
Ettal, Germany

As soon as Erin stepped through the small rear door of the abbey, the familiar smell of wood smoke took her back to her days of hauling firewood and water at the compound.

The oddity of it struck her. Why would the Sanguinists need a fire? Did they enjoy the warmth, the dance of flame, the crackle of embers? Or were there humans in this part of the abbey?

Past the threshold, she stopped alongside Jordan at the entrance to a long stone hallway, the end hidden in darkness. The way was blocked by a cherubic-looking priest, no more than a boy really.

If he was a boy.

"I am Brother Leopold," he greeted them, accompanied by a slight bow, his accent strongly Bavarian. He wore a simple monk's robe and round, wire-rim glasses. "Let me switch the lights on."

He reached forward, but Rhun caught his hand. "No illumination until we are well away from the door."

"Forgive my carelessness." Brother Leopold motioned to the long hall. "We get little excitement here in the provinces. If you'll follow me."

He hustled them down the dark hallway to a set of stairs. In the darkness, Erin stumbled and almost took a header down the steps, but Rhun caught her elbow and pulled her upright, his hand as firm as it was cold.

Jordan put a pair of the night-vision goggles in her other hand. "We've got the toys. Might as well use them. Like they say, when in Rome . . ."

She slipped the glasses over her head and strapped them in place. The world brightened into shades of green. She could now easily pick out the stairs. Rather than crude stone steps, she found only worn linoleum, which remined her of the steps at any other university.

The small touch of normalcy reassured her.

Curious, she switched her goggles to infrared mode, picking out the glow of Jordan's body heat beside her. She instinctively drew a little closer to it.

A glance toward their host revealed that he had vanished—though she could still hear his footsteps on the stairs. He plainly cast no body heat. Despite his cherubic exterior, he was not a young man, not at all. He was a Sanguinist. Disturbed at the thought, she quickly toggled back to low-light mode.

At the bottom of the stairs, a steel door with an electronic keypad blocked their way.

Brother Leopold punched five digits into the keypad and the door swung inward. "Quickly, please."

Erin looked over her shoulder, suddenly fearful, wondering what danger he had sensed.

"The room is climate-controlled," Brother Leopold explained with a reassuring smile. "Nothing more, I assure you."

She hurried through the door, followed by Jordan, who did not relax his vigilant posture.

Brother Leopold reached over and flipped a switch. Light flared, bursting blindingly bright through Erin's goggles. Both she and Jordan ripped off the equipment.

"Sorry," Brother Leopold said, realizing what he had done.

Erin blinked away the residual retinal flare to discover an overstuffed office, much like her own back at Stanford. But instead of biblical-era treasures, the room was filled with memorabilia and artifacts from World War II. Framed maps from the 1940s plastered one wall; another was covered with a floor-to-ceiling case crammed with books shelved two deep; the far wall was odd, covered with black glass. The room smelled like old books, ink, and leather.

The scholar in her wanted to move in and never leave.

A dilapidated leather office chair stood at an angle to the large oak desk. The top was obscured by stacks of papers, more books, and a glass display box filled with pins and medals.

Jordan surveyed the room. "Thank God, for once, I don't see a single thing that looks older than the United States."

"You say that like it's a *good* thing," Erin scolded.

"And do not be fooled," Rhun added. "Much evil has been done in modern settings as well as old."

"No one is going to let me enjoy the moment, are they?"

Jordan moved closer to her as he let Brother Leopold pass. She again felt the welcoming and reassuring heat of his body.

"Forgive me for not tidying up," the young monk said, adjusting his glasses. "And for not making a proper introduction. You are Sergeant Jordan Stone, yes?"

"That's right." Jordan offered his hand.

Brother Leopold grasped it in both of his, pumping it up and down. "*Wilkommen*. Welcome to Ettal Abbey."

"Thanks." Jordan gave the monk a genuine smile.

Brother Leopold returned it, his expression as enthusiastic as his handshake.

After making her own introductions, Erin decided the monk seemed far more human than either Rhun or Bernard. True, his hand felt as cold as theirs when she shook it, but it was still friendlier than the usual stiff and formal gloved handshake of the others.

Maybe he was simply *younger* than his centuries-old elders.

Brother Leopold turned with a dramatic sweep of his arm over the chaos of his office. "The collection and I are at your disposal, Professor Granger. I understand you have some artifact that you wish to gain some further insight about."

"That's right." She reached under her long duster to her pants pocket and pulled out the Nazi medal. She held it out toward the monk. "What can you tell us about this?"

He held it between his pudgy finger and thumb, eyeballing it with and without his glasses. He flipped the coin over several times, finally drifting toward his desk, where he placed the medal under a fixed magnifying lens.

He read the writing along the edge of the medallion. "*Ahnenerbe*. No surprise to find one of their calling cards buried in the sands of the Holy Land. That group spent decades scouring tombs, caves, and ruins there."

He tapped the symbol on the back. "But this is interesting. An Odal rune." He glanced at Erin. "Where exactly was this found?"

"In the mummified hand of a girl murdered in the Israeli desert. We are looking for something, an artifact, that might have been stolen from her by the *Ahnenerbe*."

One of the monk's eyebrows lifted in surprise. He looked to them for further explanation, but when none came he simply sighed and concluded, "The Nazis' evil ranged far."

Erin felt guilty for not being more open with the enthusiastic monk. She knew Brother Leopold had been told nothing about the search for the Blood Gospel, only that they needed help with the medallion found in the desert.

"Do you think you can figure out whom the medal might have once belonged to?" she asked. "If we knew that, we might know where to continue our search."

"That may be difficult. I see no identifying marks."

She tried not to look crestfallen, but how could she not?

Jordan must have caught her tone because he squeezed her shoulder and changed the subject. He read a few of the titles off the maps, pronouncing the German names correctly.

"You speak German?" she asked.

"A little," Jordan said. "And a little Arabic. And a little English."

Rhun shifted, drawing Erin's attention to him. She wondered how many languages he spoke.

Jordan faced Brother Leopold. "How did you come upon such a comprehensive collection of maps?"

"Some have been in my possession since they were drawn." The monk stroked wooden rosary beads hanging from his belt. "I am ashamed to say that I was a member of the National Socialist Party, when I was human."

Jordan's eyes widened. "You—"

Equally surprised, Erin tried to picture the round monk with the open face as a Nazi.

Rhun interrupted. "Perhaps we should turn our attention to the *Ahnenerbe*?"

"Of course." Brother Leopold sat on his creaky leather chair. "I merely wish your two companions to understand that my knowledge of such matters is not esoteric. Since becoming a Sanguinist, I have learned more about the activities of the Nazis and have dedicated my continuing existence and my studies to the undoing of their evil and to ensure that such malevolence never rises again."

"To that end," Rhun asked, "have you seen any medallions like this before?"

"I've seen similar." Brother Leopold rummaged through a desk drawer and pulled out a tiny wooden box with a glass lid. "Here are some badges of the *Ahnenerbe*. Most of these were collected by Father Piers, a mentor of mine and the priest who converted me to the cloth. He knew far more about the Nazi occult practices than anyone—probably more than the Germans knew themselves."

Erin remembered Cardinal Bernard mentioning the deceased priest's name back in Jerusalem. Over the centuries, many famous historians had died, taking their undocumented knowledge with them to the grave. That kind of tragedy was not limited to human scholars.

The monk directed her attention back to the display box. "I think you'll appreciate the shape of the medal in the center."

He tapped the glass over a pewter badge in the shape of the Odal rune, with a swastika in the middle and two legs extending out from the bottom like tiny feet.

She read the words that marched around its edges. "*Volk. Sippe.*"

" 'Folk' and 'tribe,' " he translated. "The *Ahnenerbe* believed that Germans descended from the Aryan race, a people that they believed settled Atlantis before moving north."

"Atlantis?" Jordan shook his head.

Erin's eye caught on another pin in the case. The emblem appeared to be a pedestal holding up an open book. "What's this one?"

"Ah, that one represents the importance of *Ahnenerbe* in documenting Aryan history and heritage, but there are some who say it represents a great mystery, some occult book of deep power held by them."

Erin matched glances with Rhun.

Could this be some hint of their possession of the Blood Gospel?

The monk shoved aside a stack of Nazi-era documents to reveal a modern keyboard. He began typing, and the wall of glass beside his desk bloomed to light, revealing it to be a giant computer monitor. Across the large screen, data scrolled at startling speeds. It appeared the Sanguinists had their share of both ancient and *modern* toys.

"If you're looking for a lost *Ahnenerbe* artifact," Leopold said as his fingers flew over the keyboard, "this is a map of Germany. I've been working on it for the better part of sixty years. The red arrows you see represent *suspected* Nazi bunkers and repositories. Green ones have been cleared." He sighed. "Sadly there are more red arrows than green."

Erin felt a sinking in her gut. Barely an inch of the map didn't contain an arrow.

And yes, most were depressingly red.

"If all these are not cleared," Erin said, "how come you know they're even there? What do you mean by *suspected* Nazi bunkers?"

"We hear stories of them. Local folklore. Sometimes we can guess from half-destroyed Nazi documents."

Jordan squinted at the screen. "But that's not the only way you're pinpointing these places, is it?" He nodded to the crowded screen. "From the sophistication of this survey, I'm guessing you must be using satellite telemetry and ground-penetrating radar to identify hidden, underground structures."

Brother Leopold smiled. "It almost feels like cheating. But in the end, all that wonderful technology has only succeeded in adding more red arrows to the screen. The only way to know if there's anything really there—or if those hidden structures contain anything significant—is to search them in person, one by one."

Rhun's eyes flicked from side to side as he scanned the map from top to bottom. "What we seek could be in any of those hundreds of locations."

Brother Leopold pushed back his chair and crossed his legs. "I'm sorry I don't have a better answer for you."

Rhun twitched. Erin sensed his impatience. The Belial were on the trail of the book as avidly as she and Jordan and Rhun were. Every minute mattered.

Jordan tapped one of the red arrows. "Then it's grunt work from here, guys. We go through the sites and assign them high and low probabilities and work through them. Use a grid pattern. It won't be quick, but it'll be thorough."

His idea sounded logical—but it felt wrong.

3:42 A.M.

Jordan watched Erin step to the desk and remove the medallion from under the magnifying lens. He could tell she was frustrated from the pinch of her brows and the stiffness of her back. He didn't like the idea of searching hundreds of sites either, but what other choice did they have?

As Erin turned in his direction, a light flickered deep in her eyes. That usually meant things were about to change, not always for the better.

He touched her shoulder. "Erin, you got something?"

"I don't know." She rubbed the rune on the back of the medal with her thumbs.

Rhun cocked his head, his eyes fixed on Erin with an intensity that somehow rankled Jordan; as if that gaze would consume her.

Jordan shifted to stand between them. "Talk it out," he said. "Maybe we can help."

Erin's brown eyes remained far away. "Symbols were crucial to the *Ahnenerbe*. Why *that* symbol on the stolen badge?"

Leopold's chair creaked. "The Odal rune indicates *inheritance*. If the Odal rune was written next to a person's name or an object, it meant *ownership*."

"Like writing your name on your sneakers," Jordan said. He looked over at the badge with the swastika in the center of the rune. "So does that emblem mean the *Ahnenerbe* owned the Nazis?"

He knew he probably sounded like an idiot to the scholars, but sometimes an idiot's perspective ended up getting more things done.

"I think it's more like the *Ahnenerbe* thought they owned the *Third Reich*," Erin clarified. "They believed they were the true protectors of Aryan heritage."

"But what does that signify?" Rhun pressed her, leaning toward her as if trying to draw the answer from her physically.

Erin leaned back. "I'm not sure, but at the end of the war, Berlin was being bombed. The Third Reich was on the run." Her words came out slowly, as if she searched for words to a once-familiar story. "And the *Ahnenerbe* scientists would have known that the war was over long before the formal surrender."

Leopold nodded. "They would have. But they thought in terms of centuries. To them, the *present* was a pale thing of little importance. They were interested in the history of the Aryan race going back *ten thousand years*—and forward the same number of millennia."

"To the *Fourth Reich*!" Erin said, her eyes lighting up. "That group would have been planning for the long term. They would have wanted to keep their most important objects hidden until the coming of the Fourth Reich."

"Which means that they would have hidden them somewhere *unknown* to the leaders of the Third Reich," Leopold said, swinging back to his deck. "So we can eliminate any bunkers documented by the Nazi government."

The monk tapped hurriedly at his keyboard and half the red arrows vanished.

"That helped," Jordan said.

"There are still too many," Erin concluded, and began to pace the small office, plainly trying to discharge nervous energy and stay focused.

Rhun did not move, but he tracked her with his eyes.

Erin pointed at the screen but didn't glance at it. "Where would they hide their more precious artifacts to ensure that some future Aryan scientists could find them?"

"How about Atlantis?" Jordan asked with a roll of his eyes. "With the mermaids?"

She slapped her forehead with her palm. "Of course!"

All three men looked at her as if she were mad.

"Erin," Rhun warned, his voice gentle. "I must remind you that the Nazis did not know the location of Atlantis."

She waved such details aside. "Legend has it that the Fourth Reich would rise like Atlantis from the sea, returning the Aryan race to supremacy." She faced Leopold. "What if the last of the *Ahnenerbe* tried to hedge that bet, to force the prophecy to be true?"

Rhun stirred next to Jordan, as if something Erin said had disturbed him.

Erin forged on. "To match that legend, they might have hidden their most important and significant artifacts near water. Trapped and surrounded by Allied forces, the last of the *Ahnenerbe* couldn't reach the sea at the end of the war—and they would've wanted to keep their treasures buried in the soil of the Fatherland anyway. So they might have sought the next best thing."

Leopold's voice grew hushed. "A German body of water."

"A lake," Erin said.

Leopold typed in a command and all but a dozen red arrows disappeared, marking unexplored lakeside bunkers.

Jordan's fist tightened with excitement.

Even Rhun came dangerously close to smiling.

"Let me bring up a satellite view of each one," Leopold said.

In a few minutes, a checkerboard of images filled the large screen, displaying ground-penetrating images of each of the suspected bunkers.

"*Mein Gott in Himmel,*" Leopold swore, reverting to his native tongue in shock.

They all moved closer to the screen. They all saw it.

In the lower right checkerboard, one of the outlines of the subterranean bunkers was in the exact shape of the Odal rune.

And this particular one wasn't just *next* to a lake.

It lay sunken underwater.

Just like Atlantis.

31

October 27, 3:55 A.M., CET
Ettal, Germany

In front of the computer screen, Rhun stood near enough to Erin to smell the simple soap Bernard stocked at his Jerusalem apartments. Her long hair left a trace of warmth in the air when she swung it away from her face.

Jordan stepped between them, blocking his view of her again. Rhun knew it was done on purpose. The soldier kept his hands out at his sides, ready for anything, including a fight.

Irritation flashed through Rhun, but he forced it away. Jordan was correct to enforce a space between him and this young woman. Erin Granger, with her sharp mind and compassionate heart, was a very dangerous woman indeed. And Rhun needed all the distance he could muster.

Rhun turned his attention to Brother Leopold and to the task at hand. "Is there a triad in residence?"

"*Natürlich.*" The monk's rosary clacked against the desk when he rose. "Nadia, Emmanuel, and Christian are here. Shall I fetch them?"

"Nadia and Emmanuel only," Rhun said. "I will be the third."

"What's a triad?" Jordan asked, eavesdropping on their conversation.

Leopold lifted the receiver of a black telephone and explained. "Sanguinist warriors often work in groups of three. It is a holy number."

And a perfect fighting unit, Rhun added silently.

Aloud, he said, "I will go with two others to this bunker and search it."

Erin crossed her arms. "I'm going, too."

"We're a package deal," Jordan added. "Isn't that what the Cardinal said?"

Rhun drew himself up straight. "Your orders were to aid me in the search, which you have done. If we are successful, we will return here with the artifact."

Jordan gave an unconvincing smile. "I believe the Cardinal said that *we* were the trio. *Woman, warrior, and knight*. I'm all for getting reinforcements, but not replacements."

Brother Leopold dialed four numbers and spoke into the receiver—but his eyes had locked on to the soldier. He had heard what was spoken, knew what it meant, understood now what they sought.

"Rhun," Erin said. "If the . . . artifact is in this bunker, my help led you there, and maybe you'll need my help once you're inside, too."

"I have survived for centuries without your help, Dr. Granger."

She didn't back down. "If the Cardinal is correct about the prophecy, this is no time for pride. From any of us."

Rhun blinked. She had blithely named his greatest fault.

Pride.

Such a fault had once brought him low—he would not let it happen again. She was right. He might very well need their help, and he could not be too proud to accept it.

"We must all do what we were called to do," Erin said, echoing something the Cardinal had told him.

We must each humbly bow to our own destinies.

Erin added, "The book demands no less."

Rhun cast his eyes down. If the fulfillment of the prophecy had begun, the three of them together must seek the book. As much as he wanted to, he could not leave Erin behind.

Not even for her own safety.

Or for his.

4:02 A.M.

A new map covered the large computer screen, a modern road map of the mountainous terrain of Garmisch-Partenkirchen. The lake and its hidden bunker lay about forty miles into that rough terrain. On the glowing monitor, Erin traced the thin white line that threaded between dark green hills and ended at the small alpine tarn.

"Is that a road?" she asked.

"An old dirt track," Brother Leopold said. "The vehicle you arrived in cannot navigate it. But—"

The office door clicked open behind them.

Jordan's hand went to the butt of his submachine gun.

Rhun flowed back into a ready stance.

Erin simply turned. Were the others right to be so on edge, even here, where she had felt safe? At that moment she sensed her inadequacy to deal with the dangers ahead.

Two black-cloaked figures swept into the room like an icy wind: swift, relentless, and cold. Only when they stopped moving did Erin recognize them as Sanguinists.

The first, surprisingly, was a woman, outfitted in tailored leather armor, similar to Rhun's—except she wore a thin silver belt that looked like it was made of chain. She had braided her shiny black hair and pinned it up in a bun. Her severe face was darker-complected than Rhun's, but equally implacable. She rested a gloved hand on the hilt of a dagger that was strapped to her thigh.

Her eyes swept the room, then she offered the slightest bow of her head to Erin and Jordan. "I am Nadia."

The other, a man, stood two steps behind the woman.

"And I am Emmanuel," he said, his accent Spanish.

He wore a black cassock, unbuttoned down the front, revealing leather armor beneath and a silvery hint of hidden weapons. Blond hair hung loose past his shoulders, far too long for a priest, and a pink scar ran down one chiseled cheekbone.

Rhun spoke hurriedly to the two in Latin. Erin listened, not showing that she understood. Jordan maintained his usual guard, his palm resting on the stock of his shouldered submachine gun. He plainly didn't trust any of them.

Erin followed his example and feigned interest in the map on the screen as she eavesdropped.

Rhun quickly related everything in terse Latin: about the prophecy, about Erin and Jordan, about the book they sought and the enemy they faced. As he mentioned the word *Belial,* both Nadia and Emmanuel tensed.

Once finished, Rhun turned to Leopold. "You've readied what I asked?"

Leopold nodded. "Three bikes. They're already gassed and waiting for you."

Erin glanced back to the map, to a thin white track that wound through the mountains. It seemed they weren't going to be traversing that torturous route via car or truck.

"If you are ready," Rhun asked, taking Erin and Jordan in with a single glance.

Erin could only nod—but even that gesture was false. She hated to leave the familiar territory of dusty books, leather chairs, and the cold certainty of the computer screen. But she was committed.

As Leopold led them back up the stairs, Jordan hung back with her, touching her wrist, allowing his hand to linger.

He bent close to her ear, his breath chasing across her cheek. "Anything I need to know about what they just said?"

Of course, her act hadn't fooled him. He knew she had been eavesdropping. She struggled to answer his question, but her mind was too busy registering his proximity—and how a part of her longed to close the last inch.

She had to repeat the question in her head before she answered. "Nothing important. He just filled the others in."

"Keep me apprised," he whispered.

She glanced over at his eyes, then down to his lips, remembering how they'd felt against hers in Jerusalem.

"Dr. Granger?" Rhun called from the top of the stairs. "Sergeant Stone?"

Jordan gestured for her to proceed ahead of him. "Duty calls."

Rather breathless—and not only from the climb—Erin hurried toward the Sanguinists.

Once outside, she found the night much colder, the fog much thicker. She could barely make out the outline of their Mercedes sedan.

As they rounded past the car, Jordan whistled appreciatively.

Three black motorcycles, accented with red piping, sat parked on the dried grass ahead. They didn't seem like much to Erin, but Jordan was clearly impressed.

"Ducati Streetfighters," he commented happily. "With magnesium rims and what looks like carbon silencers on the exhaust. Nice. Apparently it's good to be pope."

Erin had a more practical concern, comparing the number of passengers and the number of bikes. "Who is riding with whom?"

Nadia raised the corner of her mouth in a tiny smile, which went a long way toward humanizing her. "For an even weight distribution, I shall take Sergeant Stone."

Erin hesitated. She still didn't fully understand the role of a female Sanguinist. If Rhun was a priest, was Nadia some sort of nun, equally sworn to the Church? Whatever the circumstance, the look she gave Jordan was anything but chaste.

Jordan apparently had his own thoughts on the matter, crossing to one of the bikes. "I can drive." From the edge to his voice, it was clear that he wanted to drive one of these bikes. "And I prefer that Erin and I stick together."

"You will slow us down," Nadia said, her dark eyes twinkling with amusement.

Erin bristled, but she knew, after watching Rhun drive the sedan, that her and Jordan's reflexes were no match for a Sanguinist's.

Jordan must have recognized it, too, sighing heavily with a curt nod.

Emmanuel crossed and hooked a leg possessively over one of the bikes, not saying a word. Jordan followed Nadia to another.

"You shall ride with me, Dr. Granger," Rhun said, motioning to the third motorcycle.

"I don't know if—"

Rhun stepped past her objection and crossed to the bike, mounting with a flourish of his long coat. Twisting in his seat, he patted the leather behind him with one gloved hand. "I believe you stated 'the book demands our best.' Those were your words, were they not?"

"They were." She hated to admit it and climbed behind him. "Shouldn't we be wearing helmets?"

Nadia laughed, and her bike roared to life.

4:10 A.M.

Rhun tensed when Erin's arms slipped around his waist. Even through his leather, he felt the heat of her limbs wrapped low over his midsection. For a moment he fought between elbowing her away and pulling her closer.

Instead, he stuck to the practical requirements of the moment. "Have you ridden before?" he asked, keeping his gaze fixed to the fog-shrouded dark forest.

"Once, a long time ago," she said.

He felt her heart race against his back. She was more frightened than her tone indicated.

"I will keep you safe," he promised her, hoping it was true.

She nodded behind him, but her heart did not slow.

Jordan gave a thumbs-up from the back of Nadia's bike as she throttled her engine to a muffled roar. Emmanuel simply gunned his bike and tore away, not waiting.

Nadia followed after him.

As Rhun urged his bike forward more gently, Erin's arms tightened around him. Her body slid forward until it pressed against his. Her animal warmth flowed into his back, and his body fought against leaning into it.

He must not permit baser instincts to control him. He was a priest, and with God's help, he would fulfill his mission. He murmured a short prayer and focused on Nadia's rapidly disappearing red taillight.

He sped faster—and faster still.

Black tree trunks whipped past on both sides. The blue beam of his headlight penetrated the heavy blanket of fog. He kept his eyes on the uneven road. One misjudgment, and they would crash.

Ahead of him, Nadia and Emmanuel poured on more speed. He matched it.

Erin buried her face between his shoulder blades. Her breaths came quick and shallow, and her heartbeat skittered like a rabbit's.

Not panicked yet, but close.

Despite his prayers and promises, his body quickened in response to her fear.

***4:12** A.M.*

Jordan leaned hard into the curve. Nearby trees blurred into a long line of black topped by dark green. Wind stung his eyes. His jacket flapped behind him.

Nadia opened up the throttle on the next straightaway, a rare stretch along this twisting dirt course. He flicked a quick glance over her shoulder at the speedometer: 254 kilometers per hour. That came out to a little more than 150 miles per hour.

It felt like flying.

He felt more than heard Nadia's laugh as she pushed the bike to go faster.

Unable to stop himself, Jordan matched her enthusiasm, laughing along with her, ebullient and feeling free for the first time since Masada.

Nadia leaned the bike over for another curve. His left knee skimmed a fraction of an inch above the gravel, his face not more than a foot from the rocks that tumbled by under them. One wrong move from either of them, and he was dead.

A part of him hated to be at the mercy of her skill.

No more than a spectator to her dexterity.

Still, he smiled into the wind, tucked in tight against her cold, hard form, and simply abandoned himself to the ride.

32

October 27, 4:43 A.M., CET
Harmsfeld, Germany

When the motorcycle finally slowed, Erin risked opening her eyes. For most of the journey, she had ridden blind, sheltered behind Rhun's broad back, but she was still left windburned and rattled.

Ahead, a spatter of lights revealed the reason for Rhun's slowing pace. They had reached the mountain hamlet of Harmsfeld. He slowed their pace to a crawl as he crept through the center of the sleeping village. The small Bavarian town looked like it had just emerged from a medieval time capsule, complete with dark houses with red tile roofs, stacked stone walls, and painted wooden flower boxes adorning most windows. A single church with a Gothic-style steeple marked a village square, a space that probably converted into a farmers' market during the day.

She searched past Rhun's shoulder for the other two bikes, but she saw no sign of them on the cobblestone street, a testament to the more cautious pace Rhun had set with her as his passenger.

Still, she felt like she'd left her stomach in the parking lot of Ettal Abbey.

As they left the village, a silvery expanse of lake appeared. Its still surface held a perfect reflection of the starlit skies above, the surrounding forest hugging its banks, and the craggy peaks that enclosed the valley.

Erin spotted the others, parked beside a beach next to a wooden dock. Its ash-gray pilings were darker than the waters that gently lapped at them.

Rhun roared up next to the other bikes and finally braked to a stop. She forced her hands to unclench from the front of his jacket, unhooking her arms from him and climbing off the bike on shaky legs. She tottered forward like an old lady.

Near the dock, the other three pushed a wooden dory across the mud and into the moonlit water. Jordan's excited tone echoed off the water to her, expressing how much he had enjoyed his ride. Something he said caused Nadia to laugh, the sound unexpectedly carefree.

Jordan noted Erin's bowlegged approach and called to her. "How was it?"

She gave him the shakiest thumbs-up of her life, which drew a laugh from him.

Rhun glided past her like a shadow.

Nadia eyed the two of them as they reached the shoreline, as if trying to read some secret message.

Emmanuel simply gave the small rowboat a final heave into the water, set it to floating, and climbed on board. He moved to the front, then sat there as unmoving as the figurehead on a pirate ship.

Nadia leaped as lithely as some jungle cat into the boat.

Jordan stayed on the beach to help Erin into the dory. She took hold of his hand and climbed in, noticing the white paint was peeling off the wide wooden planks of the seats. It didn't look like the most seaworthy of boats. She freed her flashlight, turned it on, and shone it at the bottom of the boat.

No water inside.

Yet.

"Did you have an enjoyable ride?" Nadia asked, and moved to the side so Erin could join her on the middle seat.

Rhun and Jordan sat on the plank behind them while Emmanuel continued his lone vigil at the bow.

"On the way back, I think I'll call a cab," Erin said.

"Or you can ride with me on the way back," Jordan said, staring longingly back toward where they had hidden the three Ducati bikes. "That is, if we're not over deadline."

Rhun dug his paddle into the water so hard that the boat lurched to the side.

Nadia glanced at him and whispered something in a teasing undertone too faint for Erin to discern. Rhun's back stiffened, which broadened Nadia's smile.

The female Sanguinist then handed Erin a heavy wooden paddle. "I believe we four must paddle while Emmanuel rests."

Emmanuel ignored her and settled back against the gunwale.

Soon Erin was stroking her paddle through the water, trying to settle into the rhythm of the others. As they glided across the surface, fog rolled thicker over the lake, swallowing them up and dimming the moonlight. The dory now bobbed through a ghostly world where Erin could see only a few yards ahead.

Jordan touched her back, and she jumped.

"Sorry," he said. "Look down."

He angled his small flashlight into the dark water. The beam stretched down through the murk like a probing finger. Far below, the mottled light traced across a human form. Erin held her breath and leaned closer to the surface. Emerald-green algae draped from an uplifted arm, the curve of a cheek. It was a statue of a man on a rearing horse. Underneath it rested the huge bowl of a fountain.

Fascinated, she freed her own flashlight and played it in a wider circle, revealing the uncanny sight of rectangular forms of ruined houses and lonely stone hearths.

Nadia explained, "According to Brother Leopold, the local Nazis—likely of the *Ahnenerbe*—had this lake enlarged, damming the river on the far side and flooding the town below. Some claim the Nazis sealed anyone who protested in their own homes, along with their families, drowning them as punishment."

Below, a school of silvery fish ghosted through Erin's light. She shivered, wondering how many people had died and were entombed down there.

Jordan's voice took on a somber tone. "They must have done it to hide the entrance to the bunker beneath the lake."

Erin had seen enough and switched off her light.

"I assume you both can swim?" Nadia asked.

Erin nodded, although she knew she wasn't the strongest swimmer. She had learned the basics in college, mostly to appease her roommate, who was convinced she would fall off a dock someday and drown. Erin conceded the practicality of the skill, took the class, but still hated the water.

Jordan, predictably, had better credentials. "I was a lifeguard in high school. Done a bit of training since. I think I'll be okay."

Erin had never thought to ask how deep the entrance was to the bunker. What if she couldn't make it all the way down and had to wait in the boat? Or what if the entire place was simply flooded?

Emmanuel spoke his first word since leaving the abbey, a command that startled Erin with its fierceness. "Stop."

He pointed into black water in front of the boat.

Jordan shifted forward and shone his flashlight into the water to reveal a rounded arch far below, its crest velvet with algae.

Emmanuel lowered the anchor into the water so slowly that it barely made a splash. Once the dory was secure, he slipped off his cassock, balled it up, and secured it under his leather armor. Then, quick as a fish, he dove and followed the anchor line down.

Blond hair streamed behind him as he sank away.

Erin watched his progress, judging the depth of the water. *Maybe twenty feet*. She could dive that deep, but what then? Would she have to explore the tunnels *underwater*?

Her throat closed up.

"You both wait here," Rhun said, and signaled to Nadia.

The pair dove overboard, rocking the boat, carrying lights down with them. Erin put a hand on each gunwale to steady it, glad to be alone in the boat with Jordan.

"Not much of a swimmer, are you?" Jordan asked with a smile.

"How could you tell?"

He threaded the paddles under the seats, then straightened. "Your shoulders inch up to your ears when you get nervous."

She made a mental note to stop doing that and gestured to the Sanguinists below. "I sure can't swim like them."

Through the water, she watched the trio try to shift what appeared to be a large metal hatch.

"They cheat," Jordan said. "They don't need to breathe, remember? Just one more weird thing to add to the list."

"You have a list?"

He ticked items off on his fingers. "No heartbeat, free-flowing blood, allergic to silver. Did I miss anything?"

"How about the way they can sit still as statues or move twice as fast as we do?"

"There's that. And the fact that they prey on humans."

"Sanguinists don't," she reminded him. "That's one of their laws."

"Law or not, I can tell they still want to. That lust is still in them." He leaned forward. "I've seen the way Rhun looks at you, like he's both fascinated and hungry."

"Quit it! He does not."

She had to turn away, hiding her lack of conviction in her words, the memory of what had transpired in the subterranean chapel in Jerusalem still fresh in her mind.

"Just be careful around him," Jordan added.

Erin glanced back again, hearing a catch in his voice. Was he right, or was he simply jealous? She wasn't sure which proposition she found more worrisome.

Just then, a sleek black head popped up next to the boat. Nadia. "The door is open. The bunker is sealed with an air lock. We must enter together, close the first door, and open the second."

She swam a yard off and waved an arm for Erin and Jordan to follow.

Always a soldier, Jordan dove immediately. He surfaced quickly, rolled onto his back, and stared at Erin with a big grin.

"Water's fine," he said, the shiver in his voice belying his words.

Nadia could read the true reason for Erin's hesitation. "If you are frightened, perhaps you had best remain with the boat."

Screw that.

Erin stood and leaped into the water. The snowmelt cold of the lake shocked her, as if trying to force reason back into her skull, to encourage her to return to the safety of the boat.

Instead, she took a deep breath and dove straight for the open door below.

5:05 A.M.

At the bottom of the lake, Rhun heard their two heartbeats change when Erin and Jordan entered the water. He stuck his head out of the archway door and shone his waterproof flashlight up, offering them a beacon to follow. Silver moonlight from the surface silhouetted their dark forms as they kicked and pawed their way downward.

The soldier swam swiftly and economically. He could have reached the bottom in seconds, but he hung back, keeping watch on Erin.

She, on the other hand, was a terrible swimmer. Her movements were jerky with panic and her heart raced. Still, Rhun respected her for having the courage to try. Without the heavy grimwolf coat weighing her down, he doubted that she would have made it.

Once she got close enough, Rhun reached out, seized her arm, and pulled her through the archway and into the small flooded air lock. Less than a second later, Nadia and Jordan swam in.

Together, the pair tugged the outer hatch closed.

Metal thudded into place. A quick clanking sounded as they spun the door lock. Rhun's flashlight revealed concrete walls surrounding them—and the frightened face of Erin.

He worried that her heart might explode, its pace barely pausing between beats. He had to get her out of the water before she panicked and drowned. If the bunker beyond the air lock was flooded, he would have to rush her back to the surface himself.

On the far side of the small chamber, Emmanuel worked at the steel dogs that locked down the inner hatch. As he twisted the last one, the door burst open on its own, shoved by the water pressure from inside the air lock. As the water flooded out of the chamber, they were all swept along with the draining torrent—and spilled into the dry Nazi bunker.

33

October 27, 5:07 A.M.*, CET*
Beneath Harmsfeld Lake, Germany

Erin stood shakily, soaked to the skin, her teeth already beginning to chatter.

Everyone else was on their feet, weapons drawn, sweeping their lights down the dark concrete tunnel ahead. She rested her hand on the cold stock of her own holstered pistol and pulled out her waterproof flashlight from the wet pocket of her long leather coat.

Her heart still thudded in her throat. She glanced back into the air lock. She did not want to ever have to do that again. She hoped there was some hidden *landward* exit to this bunker.

Clicking on the flashlight, she shone its beam on the floor, where drains were already reclaiming the water that had flooded in with the new arrivals. She swept the beam around the tunnel. Its rounded sides rose from a level floor, climbing fifteen feet, large enough to drive a Sherman tank down without scraping the concrete from the walls.

She imagined the teams of skeletal concentration-camp inmates working on this tunnel in near-total darkness, only to be killed when the structure was complete, their blood shed to keep its secrets.

She sniffed the air: dank and moldy, but not stale. She searched the ceiling. Likely some passive ventilation system was still intact.

She joined the others. Based on the satellite map, they should be standing in the right leg of the Odal rune. But where should they go from here?

"What now?" Jordan asked, mirroring Erin's concern. "We just wander around looking?"

The triad of Sanguinists formed a silent wedge-shaped shield a few steps away: Emmanuel, at the head, pulled his wet cassock back over his leather armor. Nadia and Rhun flanked him. All three were clearly casting out their senses, gaining their bearings, and judging the threat level.

Erin moved closer to Jordan, into the shelter of their protection.

She knew her role, too—as scholar, the alleged Woman of Learning.

"I think the most symbolically powerful place to store a sacred object here," she offered, "would be at an *intersection,* like where this leg intersects with the bottom of the diamond. Or maybe the top of the diamond."

"Agreed," Nadia said, and urged Emmanuel forward, to take point.

She and Rhun moved in sync behind him, as if the three were connected by invisible wires.

"You go in front of me, Erin," Jordan said. "I'll take the rear."

Erin didn't argue, happy to comply with military protocol in this instance.

Together, they all moved down the tunnel—too swiftly for Erin's taste, but likely too slowly from the triad's perspective. While the Sanguinists kept to their formation perfectly, she kept following first too close and then too far.

Emmanuel stopped at the first door they came to—a nondescript gray metal hatch on the side of the tunnel. He tried the handle. It was clearly locked, but that didn't seem to deter the stoic Spaniard. He flexed black-gloved fingers and yanked the handle out of the door. He tossed it aside with a skittering clunk.

Jordan's eyes widened, but he didn't say anything.

Emmanuel nudged the door open with one leather boot. A short silver sword appeared in his hand. He and Nadia stepped through together.

Rhun stayed outside next to Erin. She glanced up the hall, pointing her flashlight. Empty as far as her beam would reach.

"Safe," called Nadia from inside.

Erin and Jordan went in next, Rhun last.

Inside, Erin's light revealed a dusty-looking desk on which sat an old-fashioned radio assembly. A code book lay open in front of it. Next to the desk, a chair had been pushed out. Beside it sprawled the skeleton of a Nazi soldier. He had probably been transmitting or receiving when he died.

Jordan's light picked out a pewter *Ahnenerbe* pin on his lapel. The decoration was in the shape of the Odal rune, an exact match of the one etched on the Nazi medal found in the tomb at Masada.

"Looks like we came to the right place," he said.

Erin stepped over and examined the dead soldier, keeping a professional attitude.

He's just like any mummy I've encountered on digs.

That was what she kept reminding herself as she studied the dried blood staining the front of his uniform. It had run in great gouts down his chest.

What had happened?

She shifted behind the body, turned, and directed her light back at the doorway. A second body lay off to the side. She shuddered to think that she had practically stepped on it on her way in.

The Sanguinists ignored both corpses and searched the shelves next to the radio.

There wasn't room to help them, so Erin walked to the remains by the door. A neat round hole in the center of the man's skull left no question as to how he had died. His uniform differed from the radio operator's. His was khaki brown and of a rougher fabric.

She panned her light across it.

"Russian," Jordan said. "See the five-pointed red star? It's an emblem from the World War Two era, too."

Russian?

"What was he doing here?" Erin asked. "And how did he get in?"

Jordan crouched next to her and went through the soldier's pockets, setting items on the thick dust that covered the floor: cigarette pack, matchbox, an official-looking document in Cyrillic, a letter, and a picture.

Jordan held up the faded black-and-white photo of a Slavic woman holding a thin girl with pigtails in front of a haystack.

Probably the dead man's wife and daughter.

She wondered how long the woman had had to wait to learn of

her husband's fate. Had she mourned him or been relieved that he was gone? The man's wife surely must be dead by now, but the little girl might well be alive.

Erin turned to Rhun, needing to do something. "Is there any way for Brother Leopold to notify the soldier's family?"

Rhun spared her a quick glance. "Take the letter. Knowing Leopold, he will try."

She collected the note and stood up. She pictured the scene from long ago.

The radio operator at his desk, perhaps calling for help. The Russian soldier bursts in. Shots are exchanged. Afterward, someone seals the place without anyone retrieving the bodies.

But why?

Nadia stood over Jordan, holding out her gloved hand. "Show me the other document."

When he handed her the paper with the Cyrillic writing, she scanned it, folded it, and put it in her pocket.

"What did it say?" he asked.

"Orders. His unit had been ordered to deploy from St. Petersburg to southern Germany near the end of the war. To 'retrieve items of interest' from the bunker before the American invasion."

"From St. Petersburg?" Rhun asked.

He and Nadia exchanged a long glance, both their faces worried.

Then Nadia waved toward the door. "We've learned what we can here," she said. "We move on."

Erin looked around in dismay. The archaeologist in her hated that she had not photographed the room, mapped things properly, and made an inventory of the contents. "But there might be more clues to—"

"We must search as many rooms as we can before the Belial find us." Rhun stopped halfway out the door. "Brother Leopold will do a more thorough inventory later, if there is time."

Jordan stayed close behind Erin as she followed Rhun back into the long tunnel.

The Sanguinists proceeded more quickly now. Something had clearly spooked them. Erin shared an uneasy look with Jordan. Anything that made a trio with powers like theirs nervous had to be terrifying.

Moving down the tunnel, they cleared another room: sleeping quarters filled with bunks. Erin counted four dead German soldiers, two still in their bunks, two halfway to the door. Two dead Russians were slumped against the wall.

Whatever transpired here, it had been hard fought.

Metal chests next to the bunks stored folded clothes, cigarette packs, matches, a few risqué postcards, more letters, and plenty of pictures of women and children, a sad reminder of those who had sat at home awaiting word on their loved ones.

Erin collected as many letters as she could and crammed them into her pockets, hoping that the water wouldn't cause the faded ink to run.

They also discovered books—a manual on caring for a rifle, a novel in German, an instruction pamphlet on venereal diseases—but nothing that fit the description of the Blood Gospel.

Defeated and heavyhearted from all the slaughter, Erin returned to the corridor. The others filed out with her.

A heavy rustling, like the shaking of curtains, accompanied by a faint and distant squeaking filled the corridor. The hairs on the back of her neck immediately stood on end.

"Jordan?"

"I hear it, too," he said. "Rats?"

Nadia herded them behind her. "No."

A pace ahead of them, Emmanuel sniffed the air, shoulders thrown back, neck arched, and head raised, like a dog.

Or a grimwolf.

Erin drew in a deep breath, but she only smelled mildew and wet concrete. What could he smell that she could not?

"What is it?" Jordan asked.

"*Blasphemare,*" Nadia said. "The tainted ones."

"Another grimwolf?" Jordan moved his machine pistol into ready position.

"No." Nadia's eyes flashed at Erin, wholly inhuman at that moment. "*Icarops.*"

Jordan looked confused by the foreign word.

Rhun clarified, cold and matter-of-fact. "Icarops are bats whose nature has been twisted by *strigoi* blood."

Erin's heart clenched into a knot.

He was talking about *blasphemare* bats.

Erin remembered the monstrous wolf in the moonlit desert—its fetid breath, its teeth, its muscled bulk. This time, with *wings*. She shuddered.

"Just when you think it can't get any weirder." Jordan switched on the light attached to the barrel of his Heckler & Koch machine pistol. "How do we proceed?"

"Quickly, I would recommend," Nadia said. "And quietly."

They set off down the tunnel—toward the source of the noise.

Jordan kept his weapon fixed in front, readying himself.

"Will guns kill them?" Erin whispered.

Emmanuel snorted.

Not helpful.

"Even silver bullets will only enrage them," Nadia said. "A knife is a better tool."

Jordan leaned down and pulled the silver Bowie knife from his boot sheath.

Erin drew her knife, too.

"I don't like the idea of a corrupted bat getting close enough to kill it with a blade," Jordan said. "I think I'd rather take them out with an intercontinental ballistic missile."

"When they come," Nadia warned, her voice low and her tone matter-of-fact, "lie down on the floor. We'll keep them off you as best we can."

"Not happening." Jordan hefted his knife. "But thanks for the offer."

Nadia lifted her thin shoulders in a shrug.

Erin agreed with Jordan. She had no intention of lying on her stomach, waiting for a bat to chew through her spinal cord. She'd rather take her chances standing up, with a knife in her hand.

The Sanguinists were now moving so quickly that she and Jordan had to run to keep up with them.

Soon they arrived at the intersection of another cross tunnel.

"We must have reached the base of the diamond," she said, picturing the Odal rune, running a map of their progress in her head like a schematic.

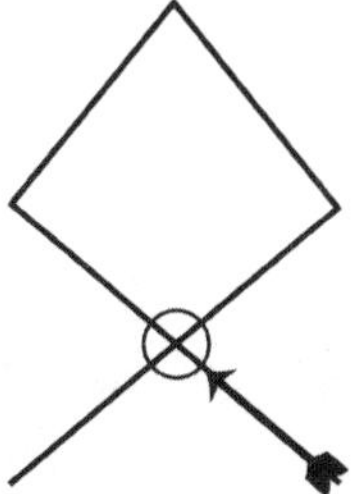

From the air, this crossing of the two tunnels must look like a giant *X*—hopefully as in *X marks the spot,* Erin thought.

"This feels like the most likely place to hide something," she said.

She cast her light across the floor but found only featureless concrete. She splashed her beam across the walls and ceiling. Nothing indicated a special or sacred hiding place at this intersection.

Jordan understood. "We'll have to check all three of these next corridors. Search every door."

Before they could take another step, though, screeches filled the air—coming from all three tunnels ahead.

There was no escape.

5:29 A.M.

The smell reached them first, thrust forward by the muscular beat of hundreds of wings. The stench threatened to knock Jordan to his knees—a foul combination of the fetid bite of urine and the bloated ripeness of corpses left in the sun. He fought his heaving stomach, wondering if this reek was as much a weapon of these beasts as their teeth and claws, meant to incapacitate their prey.

He refused to succumb.

It was more than his life in danger.

With a shaky hand he pushed Erin behind him so that she was shielded both by him and the Sanguinist triad. Her flashlight beam cut across the tunnel to the left, to the right, searching for a door.

No such luck.

Then darkness consumed the light, flowing up the tunnels on all sides. A handful of winged pieces of shadow broke from the pack and rushed forward. They swept high, over the heads of the Sanguinists, as if they had no interest in creatures without heartbeats.

Still, silver flashed through the air, slicing through wing and body.

Black blood rained.

Furred bodies fell, twisting, screeching, tumbling.

One creature made it through the silver gauntlet, diving through its dying brethren. Blinded by the light here, it struck a wall behind them and slid to the floor, flipping immediately around. It might be driven sightless by the shine, but it could still *hear.*

It hissed at Jordan, who again sheltered Erin behind him.

It was the size of a large cat, with a massive wingspan of two meters. It rushed at him, scrabbling on its hind legs and the hard angle of its wings. The bat's eyes glowed red, and its needlelike teeth shimmered in the light. A high-pitched screech burst from its slathering jaws as it launched itself at him.

Jordan lashed out with his Bowie knife, slicing across the creature's throat. Blood burst from the wound, but the bat's bulk still struck at him, knocking him back a step. He had come close to decapitating the beast in a single blow. Still, leathery wings tried to fold around him. Claws dug at his body, but the thick skin of his duster protected him.

Finally, death claimed the creature, and it fell away.

Jordan turned to find a hellish winged fury sweeping in a dark tide from three directions, breaking upon the triad in front. Each Sanguinist faced a different tunnel.

Erin stood in the center of them, her face a mask of terror.

Jordan ducked to her side, ready to defend her as devoutly as the trio.

Bats now swirled overhead in a shadowy cluster of wings, claws, and glowing eyes. The horde held back for the moment, possibly smelling the blood of their foul brothers, hearing their death cries.

Even now, the shrill squeaks set Jordan's teeth to aching.

He tried to find a single animal to focus on, but they darted back and forth too quickly.

Erin shone her light above. The bats shied from the beam, swooping away, as if it stung—and maybe the brightness did.

"*Vespertilionidae,*" she gasped, as if the word were an incantation. "Vesper bats. Never seen them more than a tenth of this size."

"How do you—"

"I work in caves a lot," she explained.

Her light jumped back and forth. Each time it struck a bat's eyes, the animal retreated.

"They're never aggressive like this."

Jordan pointed his submachine gun up, the beam from the weapon scattering them, too. "Because you work around normal bats, not friggin' tainted ones."

"They're regrouping faster each time." Erin spoke like an objective researcher, but her voice was pitched an octave higher than usual. "They're growing accustomed to the light."

"Let them come." Nadia had pulled off her silver chain belt and held it in one gloved hand. She fingered each silvery link like the beads of a rosary. "Waiting is wearing to my nerves."

"Patience," Rhun said. "Let's walk farther ahead, search for a door, somewhere to shelter. Perhaps they won't attack."

"If you can," Erin suggested, "look for a door on the *right* side of the passageway, something that might lead into the *center* of the Odal diamond."

Jordan had to hand it to her. Even shrouded within a black cloak of shrieking death, she never took her eye off the ball. She still sought the treasure that was hidden in the bunker.

Emmanuel took a step forward, one hand upraised. A dagger glinted from his fist.

Nadia moved next to him, weight balanced, graceful as a ballerina.

Together, the five of them made slow progress down the tunnel, all eyes intent on the bats massed above them.

Jordan longed to fire his weapon, but he was worried about ricochets, and concerned, too, about provoking the bats. He remembered Nadia's earlier warning that bullets would not kill them. Their best chance lay in reaching—

Without a sound, the bats dove.

Again, they ignored the Sanguinists and zeroed in on the pair at the center of the triad.

They came for Erin's face.

And Jordan's.

Overhead, Nadia twirled her belt. Jordan now recognized it as a silver chain whip. With her preternatural speed and strength, she wielded the weapon like it was a Cuisinart. Bats who came too close were shredded and torn apart.

Learning its lesson, the horde retreated.

Nadia's whip caught one last straggler across its gray back, snagging the creature from the air and smashing it against the concrete wall.

Meanwhile, Rhun and Emmanuel kept the path open ahead, continuing to fight through the shadowy forms with silver blades in both hands.

Jordan defended the rear as best he could with his Bowie knife. The high-pitched shrieking stabbed his ears. Despite the protection of his leather duster, his hands and face bore countless scratches.

It now seemed as if for every bat taken down, two took its place.

Erin plunged her knife into the belly of one that slipped past Jordan. Its sharp caninelike fangs snapped closed by her nose before it thudded to the floor.

Jordan grabbed another bat as it tried to fly past, its skin cold and dry, like a dead lizard. He swallowed revulsion and slashed at it with his knife. It pivoted its muscle-bound neck and sank its teeth into the fleshy part of his thumb. Pain shot up his arm.

He slammed his hand against the concrete wall, once, twice, three times, but the bat's teeth stayed firm. It would not knock loose. He felt teeth scrape bone, threatening to take off his thumb. Blood ran down the inside of his coat to his elbow. Another bat glanced off the side of his head, opening up a stinging wound across his temple.

Erin came to his aid. She grasped the bat attached to his hand by its ears. She thrust her knife under its chin and drew the blade downward. Black blood sprayed the wall, and the teeth finally let go.

"Forward!" Rhun called from a step away—which at the moment felt like an impassible distance. "A door ahead! To the right!"

Emmanuel drove forward, leading the charge. Bats flew at Emmanuel's face, his neck, his hands. But they seemed reluctant to bite him, not that the tall man didn't sustain wounds. His entire form dripped blood, his blond hair black with it.

Another of the horde reached past Jordan's tiring arm. Fangs locked onto his wrist. They didn't seem to have any problem biting *him*.

Rhun's knife flashed through the air, slicing through wings and fur, freeing him.

But the bats never slowed.

Jordan's arm trembled, weakening—and still the bats came.

34

October 27, 5:39 A.M., CET
Harmsfeld, Germany

Bathory knelt beside the fog-shrouded Bavarian lake.

Her finger touched drag marks left in the mud. Something wide and heavy had been hauled along the bank here—and recently. Water had seeped in to fill the lines, but no leaves or pine needles marred the surface; nor animal tracks.

Straightening, she motioned for her troops to stay back while she circled the area where the boat had entered the water. She counted footprints, recognizing American military boots, a set of Converse sneakers, and three others in handmade boots, two large and one small. Judging by the depth of the impressions, she guessed two women and three men.

But Bathory hated to make assumptions.

She followed the tracks to the water's edge. She peered into the gauzy fog, but could see no farther than a few yards, cursing the mountain mists. Earlier, she'd almost missed Rhun and his companions as they fled under the cloak of fog. Until the roar of the motorcycle engines gave them away.

She turned to her second in command. "Do you hear anything, Tarek?"

He cocked his head to the side as if listening. "Not a heartbeat out there."

But was he telling the truth, or was he lying to keep her from finding the book?

Magor? she cast out silently.

The wolf pawed the ground and ducked his head. He also heard nothing. She patted his warm flank. Her vehicle had been no match for speeding motorcycles across this harsh terrain. It had taken Magor's nose to track her quarry this far. While the wolf's keen senses had served her well, he was no more able to sense across water than she was able to see in fog.

She studied the smooth lake again. It seemed that the Sanguinists had procured a boat and had a good head start.

That presented a new challenge.

"Tarek, bring up a map of the lake."

He handed her his cell with a satellite picture. The lake had no islands. So either the Sanguinists had used the boat to cross to the other side, or they had searched for something underwater. A problem, as she had no boat, nor any idea of where to steal one. Searching would waste precious time.

Tarek growled deep in his throat, impatient. *Strigoi* hated to wait. The others caught his insolence and shifted from foot to foot.

She stared him down until he fell silent—then commanded him for good measure: "Disable the motorcycles. But stay within hearing."

Magor slumped to his haunches next to her, his reddish-golden eyes staring across the water. She rested her free hand atop his head, then returned her gaze to the on-screen image. Perhaps she could learn why the Sanguinists had chosen this place.

She zoomed in on the satellite image and scrolled around to view the terrain surrounding the lake. The picture had been taken in summer. Dark green trees obscured the ground. No clearings seemed significant.

"The bikes won't run again," Tarek called.

"Good," she answered. When they returned, the Sanguinists would have no quick way to escape.

She zoomed in tighter on the map, her eye caught by a long straight line of lighter green. The trees were different in this spot. Did that mean water? Or were the trees younger? She connected that line with another line, then another, almost too faint to see.

She smiled at her own brilliance as she recognized the pattern.

It was a corner of the design depicted on the Nazi medallion. The rest appeared to extend *under* the lake.

So that's why they came out here.

In her mind's eye, she completed the shape of the rune. On the screen, she ran one long fingernail around the diamond shape. She realized something of great interest. The two legs of the rune—one stretched and ended *under* the lake, but the other ran underground and terminated on the far side of the hill across the lake. The terrain maps showed that area to be heavily wooded. No man-made structures, just trees and boulders, but that didn't mean something wasn't still buried there.

She glanced to her small army, a force strong enough to dig for hours without tiring. She had to take the gamble. She stared across the lake to the distant hills.

If she was right, this subterranean vault might have a *back* door.

35

October 27, 5:48 A.M., CET
Beneath Harmsfeld Lake, Germany

In the echo chamber of the cavernous concrete tunnels, Rhun's senses swam and wavered, as if he were fighting underwater. Ultrasonic shrieking tore into his skull. The flurry of beating wings and writhing bodies, splattered with a rain of blood, made it near impossible to focus.

But he fought through the noise by concentrating on one face: scared, bloodied, and fierce.

Erin Granger.

Rhun reached her and swatted a bat away from her chest with all the strength in his arm, cracking hollow bones and crushing the creature's face. Although Erin's long jacket continued to protect all but her hands and head, he watched the frantic thrum of her heartbeat in her throat, heard the gasp of her breath. Their group could not last much longer.

Erin twirled before him, struggling with another icarops that clung to her back, clawing its way toward her neck.

Her flashlight jerked as she struggled, illuminating curtains of bats overhead.

Thousands.

He grabbed her, threw her across his back, and shouldered her through the dark doorway, where Emmanuel was fighting with his blade. At his side, Nadia danced amid a shimmer of whirling silver death.

"Get the soldier inside!" Rhun yelled to his sister of the cloth.

He dropped Erin roughly, deliberately, onto her back, crushing the icarops with a sharp squeal and a wash of blood. The soldier skidded across the floor next, protected by his own leathers. He rolled to bash a bat from his shoulder with his flashlight, then finished with a sharp blow of the butt of his gun.

A reverberating crash behind Rhun shook the air, telling him that Nadia had slammed the door. Emmanuel leaned his back against it. The room was square, small, but secure for the moment. An open archway at the rear of the room led into yet another chamber, but Rhun heard no heartbeats, no movement. The air smelled dead and still, tainted by old guano.

They should be safe for a few moments.

Nadia finished clearing the smattering of bats that had made it into the room with them.

The wooden door muffled the squealing of the bats outside, but claws continued to scrabble and teeth to gnaw as the horde fought to reach them.

Rhun understood that desire. Erin's heartbeat continued fast but strong. Next to her the soldier's heart still raced. The fragrance of blood wafting from her and the soldier threatened to overpower him.

He took a step back, away from the bleeding pair.

Erin stood and stumbled to Jordan's side. "Are you hurt?"

He still sat on the ground. "Just my pride," he said. "Give it a minute."

"Did the Belial do this?" Erin turned toward Rhun, bringing with her another drift of blood scent.

He swallowed and retreated another step.

Nadia answered, wiping her chain across her thigh before securing it back around her waist like a belt. "It would take years to make that many *blasphemare*. It was not those who hunted you in Masada who made these creatures."

Rhun nudged a dead bat with his toe. "She is right. Some of these icarops are decades old."

"So we are not alone down here." Emmanuel's deep voice overrode theirs. "One or more *strigoi* are using this structure as a nest."

"More good news," Jordan said, fingering his scalp. "But these bat bites won't turn us into *strigoi*, right?"

Erin aimed her light at him. Fresh blood streamed from his hands and temple. Slashes marked the top of her body, too.

Rhun flinched, having to look away from the gleaming red blood. He spoke to the wall. "No. To become a *strigoi,* you must be drained by one, then drink his blood. Or her blood. You are safe from that fate."

Nadia reached a hand down and hauled the sergeant to his feet, seeming to sense that Rhun did not dare get any closer to him. "Are your wounds serious, Sergeant?"

Jordan directed his light at the cut on his hand. "Nothing I can't fix with a big enough Band-Aid. How about you, Erin? You okay?"

"Mostly." She wiped the back of her hand on her jeans. "But why didn't the bats attack you three?"

"An intriguing question." Emmanuel's body rocked forward as bats thumped and squealed against the door. "It might be your heartbeats. Or perhaps they have been trained to attack humans."

Jordan winced. "Trained attack bats?"

"Did you prefer the wolf?" Erin pulled his miniature first-aid kit out of his pocket.

"A little," he said. "Yes."

Rhun's head was swimming with the scent of their blood. He stepped back toward the door.

"Your wine," Nadia reminded him.

He reached to his thigh, freed his wineskin, and took a quick sip, enough to steady him, but hopefully not enough to trigger a penance. Christ's blood burned down his throat, the warmth spreading through him—but thankfully no memories came.

"Hold out your hand," Erin said to Jordan. "Let me see."

The soldier pointed his flashlight at the wound on his thumb. "I think the teeth missed all the important parts. Stings like the devil, though."

"They are the devil's work," Emmanuel said, still crouched at the door. He fingered his rosary and began to pray.

Nadia flattened her back against the wall, her eyes fixed on the bats on the floor, also doing her best to ignore the small drops of fresh blood striking the concrete, as loud as raindrops on a tin roof.

Here was why humans could not be included in Sanguinist expeditions. Rhun fought down his anger, much of it directed at Bernard for forcing this pair upon them. The Cardinal did not understand life in the field.

"Did you have a recent tetanus shot?" Erin whispered.

"Sure, but not rabies."

"They're not rabid," Nadia said, not looking up.

Erin finished bandaging his thumb. "Luckily, it's your left hand."

"The expendable one?" The soldier grinned at her. "What about that gash at my hairline?"

"Put your head down." She examined it and concluded her assessment. "Bloody, but not deep."

Rhun tried not to notice how gently she wiped the scalp wound clean or how lightly her hands closed it with butterfly bandages. Every motion made it obvious that she cared for the soldier.

"Now your turn," the soldier said once she was done. He switched places with her, taking up the first-aid kit. "Let me look at you."

Jordan's bandaged hand slid along Erin's face and scalp, quickening her pulse.

She retreated and lifted her arm between them. "They only bit my hand."

With a nod, Jordan quickly wrapped her injury.

"If you two are quite finished . . . ," Emmanuel said, irritated. "Shall we discuss our next move?"

Behind him, claws continued to dig at the door.

The bats were almost through.

5:54 A.M.

As Jordan watched, a fist-size section of the door splintered and gave way. Through the opening, a scabrous head pushed into view, screeching, ears unfolding, teeth gnashing.

Emmanuel slashed out with his short sword, and the bat's head rolled to the floor.

Jordan helped Erin to her feet and backed away as another bat stuck its head through the hole.

"Bastard chewed through the door," he said. "That's dedication."

Rhun nodded toward the shadowy rear of their space. "There is an open archway back there. Seek shelter in the next room."

Jordan pointed his light, noting the dark doorway for the first time. The archway led who knew where, but at least bats weren't coming through it. And if Rhun sensed nothing of menace back there, that was good enough for him.

"Make haste." Emmanuel spoke through gritted teeth as more of the door began to disintegrate, torn apart by determined teeth and claws.

Nadia and Rhun went to his aid.

Jordan and Erin crossed and stood at the threshold, fearing to enter alone. Jordan played his light across the space, discovering that Rhun's keen senses proved true. The archway did lead to another room—a large circular space, empty and cavernous—but as he played his beam along the curved wall, an awful truth became evident.

There was no other exit.

It was a dead end.

5:55 A.M.

"There's no way out of here!" Erin called back to Rhun.

Her eyes watered from the sharp smell of ammonia in the room.

Bat guano.

She took a few steps inside, trailed by Jordan. Her flashlight illuminated a round chamber with a domed roof. She was immediately struck by two details. The chamber was the same shape and size as the tomb in Masada. But here, fine white marble covered every surface: the floor, walls, and ceiling.

She imagined it must have been a beautiful space once, but now dark guano streaked the walls and piled up in corners.

She also noted a second detail, her heart beating faster, again picturing the schematic of the Odal rune in her head.

"What is wrong?" Rhun shouted back.

Erin glanced back. Had he felt the stirring of her excitement?

She answered him, not bothering to shout this time, knowing he would hear her fine at a normal speaking volume: "I believe this chamber lies in the exact center of the diamond part of the Odal rune."

Their path here glowed in her mind's eye.

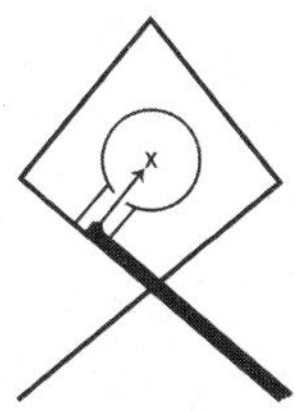

Rhun understood. "Search for the book. Time runs short! If we cannot defend this door, we may have to flee back to the tunnel and seek a more secure shelter."

Granted his permission and responding to his urgency, she hurried inside, her attention already drawn to the most dramatic object, the tallest item, in the room: a life-size marble crucifix with a shockingly emaciated Christ nailed to it, sculpted of the whitest marble. Every detail on his body was faultlessly rendered, from his perfectly formed muscles to the deep wound on his side. Unlike Christ, though, this figure was naked, hairless as a newborn, giving the image a stylized beauty, a mix of godlike innocence and human agony.

She moved her light to follow the gaze of his lowered head. The sculpture looked down upon a tall stone pedestal with a splayed top. Erin knew that shape, having just seen it hours ago. It matched the *Ahnenerbe* pin in Leopold's office, the one depicting a column supporting on open book.

The monk had said the emblem's pedestal represented an important *Ahnenerbe* goal: to document Aryan history and heritage. But he also said it could symbolize "a great mystery, some occult book of great power held by them."

Breathless, Erin knew she was looking at the source of that *Ahnenerbe* symbol.

From the way the pedestal's top was tilted toward the statue and away from her, she could not tell if anything rested there.

"We should stay by the door," Jordan warned. "In case we have to make a run for it."

She did not slow, did not hesitate. Nothing would stop her from reaching that pedestal and seeing for herself what lay there—possibly a book written in Christ's own blood.

Jordan swore under his breath and followed her deeper inside.

The cross and column rested upon a dais, a square marble base six feet across. That both objects should have been placed on a stage demonstrated their importance. But why would the Nazis erect a life-size crucifix? Were they guarding something they considered sacred and holy?

Erin had to find out.

She jumped up onto the stage, wincing when her feet ground into pieces of broken rock. Careful not to step on anything else, she circled the pedestal.

As she came around, holding her breath, her light glowed across the upper surface of the marble lectern.

Then her heart sank.

It was empty.

"What did you find?" Jordan called to her from the base of the dais, but his face remained turned toward the vestibule, where the Sanguinists fought to keep the bats at bay.

Erin stepped forward and ran her fingertips across the empty surface of the lectern. She felt the indentation along the top, as if something was meant to rest there, an object roughly of the dimensions described by Rhun.

"The book was here," she mumbled.

"What?" Jordan asked.

Defeated, she stepped back, her heel crushing another chunk of debris underfoot. She glanced down, shining her light. Fragments of gray rock lay scattered around the pedestal. Focused now, she saw that they were not natural stone, but something man-made. She knelt and carefully picked up one shard.

Most of the others strewn on the floor were less than an inch thick and ashy in hue. She retrieved a larger piece and rolled it around in her palm, judging the material.

Gray. Concrete. If ancient, probably lime and ash.

Could these pieces date to the time of the Blood Gospel? To know for sure, she would have to do a proper analysis somewhere else, but for now she improvised.

She scratched a thumbnail over one corner and sniffed at the abraded edge.

A familiar spicy scent struck her deeply, almost causing her eyes to tear.

Frankincense.

Her heartbeat sped up. There had been traces of frankincense in the tomb in Masada, common enough in ancient burials.

But not in Nazi bunkers.

She fought to keep her composure, kicking herself mentally for jumping on the dais like a lumbering ox, especially after years of scolding her students for the most minor violations of the integrity of a site.

She turned the shard over. The piece was roughly triangular, like the corner of a box. Frozen in place, as if she were crouching in the middle of a minefield, she studied the other pieces on the floor. Three other triangles rested nearby, along with other pieces.

What if the triangles were corners?

If so, maybe they had been part of a *box.*

A box that might have held a *book.*

She stared up at the empty lectern. Had the marauding Russians come upon what was hidden here? Smashed open what they found and stole what was inside?

Despairing, she looked to the crucifix for answers. The figure on the cross was as skeletal as a concentration-camp victim, thinner than any representation of Christ she had ever seen. Black nails pinned each bony hand to the cross, and a larger spike had been driven deep through the figure's overlapping feet. Burgundy paint glistened around his wounds. She moved the light up, drawn to the nearly featureless face, eyes and mouth barely demarcated by slits, the nostrils even thinner—depicted here was a perfect rendition of endless suffering.

She had an irrational urge to cut the statue down, to comfort that figure.

Then a sharp pain burst in her hand. She raised it to the light, realizing she had sliced her thumb on the shard from clenching her fist too hard.

Reminded of her duty, she turned her back on the cross and began gathering the broken pieces from the dais, scooping them up and stuffing them in her pockets. She noted that some had writing on one side, but she would have to decipher them later.

Jordan noted her work and began to climb onto the stage with her.

"Don't!" she warned, fearful of any further destruction to the clues left here by the Russians.

With enough time, she might—

Rhun's shout reached them, full of hopelessness. "The bats are through the door."

36

October 27, 6:04 A.M., CET
Beneath Harmsfeld Lake, Germany

Rhun fled from the front edge of a furious storm behind him.

Wings battered his body; claws and teeth tore at flesh and clothes.

He burst through the arched doorway, shadowed by Nadia and Emmanuel. The horde of icarops thundered past him, beating by with muscular wings. The mass fled upward and filled the arched dome of the room with fluttering shadows.

Rhun's sharp eyes took in the chamber with a glance, recognizing a dark mirror of the Masada tomb, a despoiled ruin of that sacred space. Fury stoked inside him, but fear extinguished it.

In the center of the room, he saw Erin crouching atop a stage behind a tall pedestal, her face upturned to the bats. Her guardian, Jordan, leaped atop the dais, ready to shelter her. A futile gesture. The soldier could not hope to defeat the number of icarops gathered here.

None of them could.

As if knowing this, the icarops horde crashed down upon the exposed pair.

"Arrêtez . . . !"

The single word of command shattered through the hissing screams of the bats and drove back their attack. The black horde shredded apart around Erin and Jordan and wheeled away, flapping to the streaked walls and the ceiling. There, sharp claws scrabbled for pitted roosts. Wings folded over fur, and the icarops hung from every surface. Oily red-black eyes stared down.

With his first indrawn breath, the stench hit Rhun. He drew breath again. Another smell lurked under the tainted blood of the icarops and the sharp smell of their waste.

A familiar one.

Across the chamber, Jordan scanned the room, his shoulders hunched against the fluttering mass above. "Who yelled?"

The answer came from Erin, who pointed toward the crucifix. "Look!"

There on the cross, the marble sculpture *moved.* A head lifted, revealing a ravaged face, skin shriveled tight around hard-edged bone. Erin's hand rose to cover her throat, as if she knew what hung there.

Nadia stopped still next to Rhun, and Emmanuel staggered back a pace.

The Sanguinists knew, too.

As if obeying a silent command, Rhun rushed forward, flanked by Emmanuel and Nadia.

On the cross, eyelids opened, rough slits in that leathery visage. And from those cracks, a glimmer of life still shone—the little that remained. The glassy blue stare found Rhun and settled on him with a look of bottomless grief.

Those despairing eyes left no doubt about who it was that hung on that ghastly cross.

Rhun filled out the face, crowned it with silver hair, made the sunken lips smile with the knowledge of untold ages. In his mind, he heard that once-vigorous voice explaining the mysteries of history, the destiny of the Sanguinists. In its time, this body had housed a powerful priest.

Father Piers.

A friend for centuries.

The scholar had disappeared seventy years ago on an expedition to find the Blood Gospel. When he had not returned, the Church had declared him dead. Instead, it seemed that the Nazis had captured him, then abandoned him to suffer here for decades.

Emmanuel fell to his knees in supplication. "Father Piers . . . how can it be . . . ?"

The old priest's head sagged again, as if he were unable to hold his heavy skull up any longer. Faded eyes found Emmanuel. *"Mein Sohn?"* he croaked, throat clearly unaccustomed to forming words.

My son.

Tears ran down Emmanuel's face, reminding Rhun that Father Piers had found and recruited Emmanuel into the Sanguinist fold. He was as much Emmanuel's father as his savior.

Emmanuel reached toward the blackened spike hammered through the priest's bare feet. Another nail impaled each palm. Droplets of dark, dried blood caked around his wounds.

"Careful." Nadia stood near them. "He's been secured with silver."

Emmanuel pulled on the thick spike that bound the priest's feet, burning his own fingers.

Nadia yanked him back. "Not yet."

He hissed at her, showing fangs. "Look at him. Has he not suffered enough?"

"The question," Nadia said evenly, "is *why* has he suffered? Who nailed him here and why?"

"Libri . . . verlassen . . ." It seemed that Piers struggled as much with his tongue as with his mind, tripping through various languages as madness danced behind the glaze of his eyes.

Rhun stared up at the ruins of the Sanguinist scholar. "Take him down."

Nadia looked ready to object, but Rhun knelt and gently supported the old priest's feet. Emmanuel pulled the spike from the priest's feet and tossed it aside, then stood, reaching for the hands.

Piers remained oblivious. His eyes rolled toward the arched roof and its black decorations. *"Meine Kinder . . .* they have brought you." An exultant tone threaded through his feeble words. "To save me . . ."

Nadia's face hardened. She looked in the direction of the battered priest's gaze—to the horde of the icarops. "It was Father Piers who created these unholy creatures."

"Blasphemare?" Emmanuel's fingers hesitated over the nail that lanced Piers's left palm. "But that is forbidden."

Rhun was less interested in blasphemy than he was in answers. "He had no choice. He must have had to feed to survive all those decades alone on the cross. What else would he have here to feed upon but the bats."

He pictured the priest drawing what little sustenance he could from the dark denizens of this tomb, eventually bending them to his will as the decades passed, twisting them to serve him, using their companionship to anchor what little sanity he could retain in this dark isolation.

Long ago, Rhun had starved himself almost to death in penance. He remembered the pain, and he could not fault Piers for making the icarops in order to survive. It had been the only way.

"How long has he been up there?" Erin's face had gone white.

"Since the Nazis left him, I imagine." Nadia did not move to help.

Rhun pulled the nailed spike out of Piers's right palm while Emmanuel worked on his left. Dark blood flowed down the old man's hand. Rhun tried to be gentle. The wounded priest had little blood left to lose.

"What did he do to deserve this fate?" Jordan asked.

"That is the salient question." Nadia stood in front of Piers and looked up into his gaunt face, her voice rising. "What did you do to come to be nailed here, Father?"

The memory of the tomb at Masada sliced through Rhun: the *strigoi* girl pinned to the wall by silver spikes, the old gas mask crushed under rock. Had Piers broken under torture? Had he told the Nazis where to find the book, what safeguards to expect, what they needed to do to overcome the millennia-old protections and retrieve it?

Piers whimpered with every movement of the nail. Rhun knew firsthand the pain of silver. Piers had endured the burning agony of silver for almost seventy years. Like Jesus, he had done his penance on a cross.

The last spike came free, and Emmanuel threw it across the chamber. Rhun caught Piers's slight weight against his shoulder.

Emmanuel tore off his own damp cassock, revealing his leather armor, and wrapped the cassock around the ancient priest. Rhun lowered him to the ground. Emmanuel reached for his wine flask, but Nadia stopped him.

"He's no longer holy," she said. "The wine would do more harm than good."

Emmanuel cradled Piers in his arms. "What have they done to you?"

"*Blut* und bone," the old man mumbled. "*Libri.*"

Beside him, Erin stirred. "*Libri*? That's Greek for 'book.' Does his crucifixion here have something to do with the Gospel?"

Rhun knew that it did.

Erin held out her hand toward Rhun. In her palm rested a shard of ashy stone. "I found these accretions of lime and ash, an ancient form of concrete, broken into pieces around the pedestal. It might be that the Gospel was encased in a block of such stone and someone broke it free, right here in this room. Could Father Piers have been crucified here as the guardian of it, like the little girl in Masada?"

"Only he knows," Rhun answered. "And I don't know what's left of his mind."

"Then heal him."

"Such matters may be beyond me, beyond even the Church."

Rhun took the shard and examined it. His fingertips as much as his eyes picked out the Aramaic lettering impressed on one side. If his heart still beat, it would have quickened.

The book *had* been here. Someone had found it and removed its covering. But had they opened it?

That could not be. If it had happened, the thieves of Heaven would have claimed its power. But who had taken it?

He needed the answer—and Erin was right.

Only one person could supply it.

"Father Piers?" he intoned, trying to draw a moment of lucidity from him. "Can you hear me?"

The old man's eyes slid closed. "Pride . . . shameful pride."

What was Piers talking about? Did he mean the hubris of the Nazis, or did he mean something much worse?

"How did the Nazis capture you?" Rhun pressed. "Did you tell them of the book?"

"*Es ist noch kein Buch,*" Piers whispered through bloodless lips.

"It is not a book," Jordan translated.

"They must have tortured him, Rhun," Emmanuel said. "Just as you are doing now. We must heal him before you disturb him with questions."

"Not yet," Father Piers said. "Not yet a book."

Nadia glanced at the marble walls as if they held windows. "Sunrise comes soon. Do you feel it?"

Rhun nodded. His body had begun to weaken. Christ's grace

allowed them to walk under the day's sun, but because of their taint, they were always strongest at night.

"I like the sound of sunrise," Jordan said.

"We can't take Piers out into the new day," Nadia said. "He's no longer blessed by Christ's blood. The sun would destroy him."

"Then we hunker down here." Jordan glanced uneasily at the ceiling. "It's not a five-star hotel, but as long as the bats seem calm, I think we can—"

"He will die before nightfall," Emmanuel said, and gestured toward the icarops horde rustling on the walls. "Unless he feeds off those cursed creatures."

"And I will not allow that," Nadia said. "It is a sin."

"And I will not leave Piers to die in sin." Emmanuel drew his knife, threatening her.

Rhun stepped between them and held his hands up. "If we hurry, we can still reach the chapel in Harmsfeld. We can sanctify him there. After that, he can partake of Christ's blood again."

"What if he cannot be sanctified?" Nadia practically spat out the words. "What if he was no *pawn* of the Nazis—"

Rhun held up a hand to silence her, but she would not be silenced.

"What if he *sought* them out?"

"We shall see," Rhun said. Nadia had spoken his deepest fears, that Piers's intellectual pride had led him into forming an alliance with the Nazis. Rhun knew that pride all too well—and where it could lead even a devout Sanguinist.

"Into formation," he ordered the others. "We must reach the church at Harmsfeld before sunrise."

Out of long habit, Emmanuel and Nadia stepped into their places, Emmanuel in front, Nadia to his left. Rhun met Jordan's eyes and jerked his head toward Piers.

They stepped out of the defiled chamber, through the vestibule, and back into the dark concrete tunnel.

Jordan gathered up Piers, still wrapped in Emmanuel's cassock, and followed with Erin close behind.

"Ich habe Euch betrogen," Piers whispered. *"Stolz. Buch."*

Rhun heard Jordan translate. "I have betrayed you all. Pride. Book."

Emmanuel stopped and glanced back at Piers. Tears shone in his eyes. Rhun touched his arm. Piers had all but admitted it just then, that he had betrayed their order to the Nazis.

Rhun turned away, trying to understand. Had his friend's all-consuming desire to be the first to find the book led him into his unholy alliance with the *Ahnenerbe*? Had the Germans betrayed him in the end? Rhun remembered his addled words. *It is not a book.* Did those words indicate that the Nazis had failed here somehow? As a punishment, did they crucify Piers?

No matter the outcome, if Piers had come here of his own free will, they might never be able to sanctify him enough for him to return to the Sanguinist fold.

Piers cocked his head to the left as they reached the crossroad of corridors. "*Sortie.*"

French for "exit."

Erin must have understood. He was attempting to direct them to a way out.

She knelt and drew the Odal rune in the dust with her finger. She pointed to it. "Can you show me where the exit is, Piers?"

Jordan held Piers so that he could see the rune. The old man stretched one bone-thin finger to the *left* leg of the rune. Their team had entered through the *right*.

"There's a second exit," Erin said, looking up hopefully. "In the other leg of the rune. It must be how his bats came and went."

Piers closed his paper-white eyelids, and his head fell back on Jordan's shoulder.

"If we hurry," Rhun said, "perhaps we *can* get him to the Harms-feld chapel before sunrise."

But, even so, a fear nagged at Rhun.

Was it already too late to save Father Piers's soul?

37

October 27, 6:45 A.M., CET
Harmsfeld Mountains, Germany

Bathory gathered her sable-fur coat around her slender form and waited in the dark woods. To the east, the skies had already begun to pale. From the uneasy glances of her restless troops in that direction, it was clear they knew they had only a quarter hour left before sunrise.

The air had turned bitterly cold, as if night sought to concentrate its chill against the coming day. Bathory's hot breath steamed from her lips—same as the panting wolf, blowing white into the dark forest. The same could not be said of the rest of her forces. They remained as cold and still as the forest as they waited, but not all were equally quiet.

"We must go. Now." Tarek loomed next to her, his mouth curled in a snarl.

His brother, Rafik, kept tight to his older brother's legs, his lips still blistered from the intimate moment Bathory had shared with him.

Bathory shook her head. So far, no word had been radioed from the lookout she had left by the motorcycles. The Sanguinists had not returned that way—and she didn't expect them to. She was certain this was the place where the rabbits would leave the warren.

In her gut, she knew it.

"Never follow an animal into its burrow," she warned.

She kept her eyes fixed on the bunker door. Magor had discovered the hole nestled among some boulders. It was little larger than a badger den, but the sharper senses of Tarek's men revealed the source of the scent that drew her wolf.

Icarops.

She pictured the foul flock squirming out of that hole each night. Something must have created that horde, something that might still be down there.

Her men had set about widening the hole, digging out the earth that the Nazis had used to bury the hidden door. Once it was cleared, they discovered where the bats had clawed through stone around one edge of the hatch to make their nightly sojourn.

With the way unblocked, it would be easy to push open the hatch from the inside, an invitation to her quarry to make their escape this way.

"We'll kill them as soon as they step out the door," she said.

"What if they're waiting for dawn?" Tarek's eyes swept the eastern sky, already turning steel gray.

"If they are not out by sunrise, we will enter the bunker," she promised. Her men would fight best if they knew they must take the bunker or die. "But not until the last moment."

Her six crossbowmen stood rock-still, three to each side of her, silver arrows at the ready. The larger bolts of a crossbow delivered a deadlier dose of silver than a simple bullet, plus the arrows had the tendency to remain impaled in place rather than passing harmlessly through.

She was not taking any chances with Rhun Korza.

Tarek's head swiveled to the door. All her troops went on alert.

She heard nothing, but she knew they must.

The bunker door moved forward, pushing its way along the path they had carefully cleared for it.

Three Sanguinists stepped into the forest, Rhun Korza among them.

Bathory counted three more figures behind them, still in the bunker, one carried by another, apparently wounded. But that made no sense—and she didn't like surprises. Only *five* had left the abbey, and only *five* tracks were found at the water's edge.

So who was this *sixth*?

Had Korza found someone alive in the bunker?

Then she remembered the icarops.

Was this the mysterious denizen of the bunker?

She kept her hand held high, telling her troops to wait until everyone was out of the bunker. But the last three stayed inside, plainly suspicious.

Korza looked at the ground and knelt, clearly noting where Bathory's men had disturbed the soil. Before any further suspicions could be raised, she slashed her arm down.

Crossbow bolts whistled with a *twang* of taut strings. The volley struck the Sanguinist in the lead, nailing him to the large bole of an ancient black pine.

He struggled to free himself, smoke already steaming from his wounds into the cold night.

The bowmen shot another volley, all the bolts striking true, piercing chest, throat, and belly.

The Sanguinist writhed in a fog of his own boiling blood.

That took care of one priest.

Now to kill Korza.

38

October 27, 6:47 A.M., CET
Harmsfeld Mountains, Germany

"Stay inside!" Rhun shouted, diving through a rain of deadly silver.

A crossbow bolt struck his arm, embedded itself into his forearm. Its touch burned deep into his flesh with the poison of silver. He had known the danger as soon as he found the fresh loam turned at the foot of the door—but he had reacted too slowly.

Someone had been waiting in ambush.

Someone who had expected to fight Sanguinists.

He reached the shelter of a thick linden tree and rolled behind it.

Safe behind the broad trunk, he yanked out the crossbow bolt. More blood than he could spare flowed from the wound, trying to purge his body of the silver's taint.

He sagged against the tree and glanced left.

As he had hoped, Nadia had reached the shelter of a boulder next to the doorway.

But not Emmanuel.

A dozen silver bolts had skewered him to a pine a few yards away. Smoke boiled from his wounds, enfolding him in a ghostly shroud of his own pained essence.

Rhun knew he could not reach him—and even if he could, death had already laid claim to his old friend and brother of the cloth.

Emmanuel knew this, too. He reached an arm back toward the bunker.

Piers's voice rasped from out of the darkness. "My son."

"I forgive you," Emmanuel whispered.

Rhun hoped that Piers had heard the words and cast a silent prayer to his dying friend.

Then Emmanuel slumped, only the cruel bolts holding him upright.

Behind the boulder, Nadia wiped the back of her hand across her eyes. Like Rhun, she had to accept that Emmanuel was dead, but with that grief came a sliver of joy. He had met the most honorable end for any Sanguinist: death in battle.

Emmanuel had freed his soul.

When he was finished with his prayer, Rhun's attention snapped to the sound of a single human heart beating out in the forest. There was a human among the *strigoi* attackers, revealing the true nature of those who attacked them.

The Belial.

But how had they come to find Rhun and his party here?

And how many were hidden in the woods?

Behind him, Erin's and Jordan's heartbeats echoed out of the bunker, where they remained sheltered with Piers. They were safe, at least for another moment.

Rhun reached to his thigh and pulled out his wineskin. He needed Christ's blood to replace what he had just lost. Without it, he could not continue to do battle. But with such a drink, he risked being thrust into the past, helpless and exposed.

Still, he had no choice. He lifted the skin and drank.

Heat burned through him, fortifying him, pushing back the burn of silver with the purity of Christ's fire. Crimson crept into the edges of his vision.

He fought against the looming threat of penance.

Elisabeta in the fields. Elisabeta by the fire. Elisabeta's rage.

He tightened his hand around his pectoral cross, begging the pain to keep him present. The world became a shadowy mix of past and present. Images flashed:

. . . a long bare throat.

. . . a brick plastered in a closing wall.

. . . a young girl with a raspberry blemish screaming silently.

No.

He fought to focus on the woods, on the pain of the cross in his burning palm, on the sounds of breaking twigs and snapping branches as *strigoi* burst out of hiding and surged toward the bunker. He risked a glance around the trunk, catching movement too quick for human eyes to track.

Six to ten.

He couldn't be sure.

Jordan and Erin would have no chance against them. He brought his gun up into firing position with trembling hands.

More images assaulted him, reminding him of his sin, unmanning him when he needed to be at his strongest.

. . . a spray of blood across white sheets.

. . . pale breasts in moonlight.

. . . a smile as bright as sunshine.

Through the spectral glimpses of his past, he aimed and fired, hitting two *strigoi* on the right, each square in the knee, dropping them, slowing them, if nothing else.

Nadia picked off another two on the left.

Behind him, Jordan's submachine gun crackled as the soldier fired and strafed from the bunker's door. He heard the *pop-pop-pop* of Erin's pistol.

The first wave of *strigoi* scattered to the side, trying to flank them. More came behind them. He counted a dozen, four wounded, but not badly. One was older than Rhun; the others youngsters but still dangerous.

Memories continued to wash over him, thicker now, pulling him away, then back again.

. . . a crackling fire, listening to the soft voice of a woman reading Chaucer, struggling with the Middle English, laughing as much as reading.

. . . a twirl of a gown in moonlight, a figure dancing by herself under the stars on a balcony, as music echoed from an open window.

. . . the pale nakedness of flesh, so stark against a crimson pool of blood, the only sound his own panting.

Please, Lord, no . . . not that . . .

A crossbow bolt grazed his cheek, snapping him back to the present. The arrow winged off the edge of the tree and buried itself in dirt behind him.

He fell back, knowing none of his party could last out in the open, especially not in the state he was in.

They were too exposed.

"Take them farther inside!" he gasped out, waving to Nadia, who was closer to the bunker door. "I'll hold them off—"

"*Stop!*" called a voice so familiar Rhun clutched for his cross again, unsure if he was in the past or present.

He listened, but the forest had gone dead quiet.

Even the *strigoi* had gone to ground—but with the sun nearly up, they would not wait long. They would rush at any moment, swarming over them.

He strained, wondering if he had imagined the voice, a broken fragment of memory come to life.

Then it came again. "*Rhun Korza!*"

The accent, the cadence, even the anger in that voice he knew. He struggled to stay in the present, but the calling of his name summoned him into the past.

. . . Elisabeta climbing from horseback, an arm outstretched for his aid, baring her wrist, exposing her faint pulse through her thin pale skin, her voice amused at his hesitation. "Father Korza . . ."

. . . Elisabeta weeping in the garden under bright sunlight, hiding her face from the sun, grief-stricken, but finally seeing him, rising to meet him, her simple joy shining through tears. "Rhun Korza . . ."

. . . Elisabeta coming to him, barefoot, across the rushes, her limbs naked, her face raw with desire, her lips moving, speaking the impossible. "Rhun . . ."

Those arms lifted toward him, inviting him at long last.

He went to them.

A gun blast tore into his chest, the blossom of pain tremendous, shredding away the past and leaving only the present.

He stood still with his arms outstretched toward her.

She stood before him—only transformed. Her dark black hair had turned to fire. He heard her heartbeat, knowing there should be none, not here, not now.

Downslope from him, she kept her distance, sheltered by an alder. But even from here, he recognized the same curve of her cheek, the same dance to her quicksilver eyes, the same long curls tumbling to her shoulders. She even smelled as she always had.

His vision swam, overlaying two women.

Pink lips curved into the smile that had once seduced him. "Your deeds brought us here, Father Korza. Remember that."

She lifted her smoking Glock and fired, fired, fired.

Bullets tore into his chest.

Silver.

Every one.

The world darkened, and he fell.

6:50 A.M.

Jordan fired a volley over Rhun's body as the priest dropped. The redhead who had shot him ducked behind a tree.

Why the hell had the fool stepped out into the open like that?

Rhun had looked like he was in a daze as he stumbled out of hiding, his arms stretched out toward the woman, his hands empty, as if surrendering to her.

Jordan kept firing his Heckler & Koch submachine gun, offering Nadia cover so she could reach Rhun. *Strigoi* crawled forward toward them, clearly not eager to stand up and be shredded apart by silver. He hoped he had enough bullets in the extended magazine to get the pair back inside.

Erin knelt on the other side of the door, her Sig Sauer in hand. She didn't have the same firepower he did, but she was a surprisingly good shot. She shot for legs, wounding rather than killing, just as Rhun had done. For the moment it was easier to slow them than to kill them.

Nadia hooked a hand under one arm and dragged Rhun back toward the bunker.

She took a crossbow bolt in the back of her thigh, but didn't even flinch until she had hauled Rhun's body inside and slammed the bunker door.

"Emmanuel?" Jordan asked.

"Lost." She clenched her jaw and yanked out the bolt. Blood boiled out and smoked down her thigh. The stench of burnt flesh drifted up.

Erin swallowed hard. Jordan understood how she felt.

"Can you walk?" he asked. "I can give you a shoulder to—"

"I can walk."

Nadia hurried them away from the door and pulled a wineskin from her belt. She took a small, cautious sip.

A heavy object thudded against the locked door behind them, echoing inside.

Nadia ignored it, but she finally stopped and lowered Rhun to the floor. She quickly freed Rhun's *karambit* and used the hooked blade to slice off the leather armor covering his chest.

"We must work swiftly. The Belial will come through that door at any moment."

Erin knelt next to her. "How do you know they'll do that?"

"They have to. They're *strigoi.* When the sun rises, they'll all die. They will need to go to ground."

Nadia dug a slug out of Rhun's chest with his *karambit*'s tip. The bullet had deformed into a grotesque five-petal flower.

"Silver hollow point," Jordan said, immediately understanding.

The attackers had known what to expect.

Nadia dug out the other slugs, none too gently, hurrying. Six total. A human could not live with that much damage. Maybe not even a Sanguinist.

Blood pumped out and ran across the floor.

Erin put her palm on Rhun's chest, plainly concerned. "I thought he would stop bleeding on his own."

Jordan remembered Korza's demonstration back in Jerusalem with his sliced palm.

Nadia pushed Erin's hand away. "His blood is purging the silver. If it doesn't, he'll die."

"But then won't he bleed to death?" Erin asked.

Nadia's face tightened. "He might," she admitted, and glanced back at the door.

The *strigoi* had ceased pounding. Jordan didn't trust the silence and apparently neither did Nadia.

She stood, hauling Rhun over one shoulder.

Erin joined her. "What do we do? Try to use the water exit?"

"It's our only chance," Nadia said, and pointed her free arm. "We must reach sunlight."

They took off at a dead run. Jordan hauled Piers along in a fireman's carry, but Nadia outpaced him. They reached the intersection of passageways—when a thunderous explosion erupted behind them.

Jordan jolted, ducking from the noise. The enemy had set charges against the door.

Without breaking stride, he turned to check on Erin. She was behind him, *too* far behind. Snarls echoed down the tunnel from the blasted doorway.

The monsters were inside—and they were pissed.

39

October 27, time unknown
Undisclosed location

Tommy shifted in his new bed, trying to find a more comfortable position. He had no idea where he was, when he was, but he didn't think it was another hospital. He studied his new home, which he suspected was what this prison was supposed to be.

He filed that disturbing thought away for now.

But he had to admit that the *box* in his head was growing more and more crammed.

Something eventually had to give.

He stared around. The walls were painted silver, with no windows, but the room came equipped with three different kinds of video-game consoles and a flat-screen TV, fed by satellite and carrying American channels.

Across from the foot of his bed, a door led to a bathroom stocked with familiar brands of soap and shampoo. Another door led to a corridor, but he'd been unconscious when he was brought in, so he didn't know where that went.

Some faceless doctor must have set his bones, patched his wounds, and cranked him up on pain relievers. His mouth still felt full of cotton that no amount of water could soothe. But his neck had already healed, and his bones were knitting fast, too. Whatever had happened at Masada, it had sped up his healing, curing him from far more than just cancer.

Since he'd woken up, they brought him food, whatever he asked for: burgers, fries, pizza, ice cream, and Apple Jacks cereal. And he was surprisingly hungry. He could not get enough to eat; likely his body needed the fuel to help heal itself.

Nobody told him where he was or why he was here.

He spent one entire hour crying, but no one seemed to care, and he finally realized the futility of tears and turned to more practical thoughts: thoughts of escape.

So far, he had no good plan. The walls were made of concrete, and he imagined that something in the room was a camera. The guards shoved his food through a slot in the door that led out to the corridor.

Suddenly that door opened.

Tommy sat up. He couldn't stand very well yet.

A familiar figure strode inside, sending a chill through Tommy. It was the boy who had kidnapped him from the hospital. The strange kid walked in and flung himself into bed, sprawling next to Tommy, as if they were best chums.

This time he wore a gray silk shirt and a pair of expensive-looking gray pants.

He sure didn't dress like a normal kid.

"Hello." Tommy twisted to face him and held out his hand, not knowing what else to do. "I'm Tommy."

"I know who you are." The boy's accent was strange and stiff.

Still, he shook Tommy's hand, pumping it firmly, formally. He had the coldest hands that Tommy had ever felt. Had he been shipped to some country above the Arctic Circle?

The boy let go of his hand. "We are friends now, no? So you can call me Alyosha."

Friends don't try to kill friends.

But Tommy kept silent about that and asked a more important question. "Why am I here?"

"Is there somewhere else you would rather be?"

"Anywhere else," he admitted. "This feels like a prison."

The boy turned a thick gold ring around on his white finger. "As cages go, it is a gilded one, no?"

Tommy didn't bother pointing out that he didn't want to be in *any* cage—gilded or not—but he didn't want to offend the kid, nor did he want to chase him off by being rude. To be honest, Tommy didn't want to be alone again. He'd even take this weird kid's company at the moment—especially if he could learn anything.

"When I was your age, I lived in one of the most gilded cages in the world." The boy's soft gray eyes traveled around the room. "But then I was set free, as you are."

"I don't call this *free*." Tommy gestured around the room.

"I meant *free* of the prison of your flesh." The boy sat up, crossed his legs, and reached for a game controller. "Many aspire to that."

"Are you free?" Tommy reached over and picked up the other controller, as if this were the most natural thing to do.

The boy shrugged and started an Xbox game on the screen. "After a fashion."

"What does that mean?"

Alyosha faced him as the game bloomed to life on the screen. "You are immortal, no?"

Tommy lowered his controller. "What?"

Alyosha prompted the game—*Gods of War*—to start. "You know this now, no? It was what I tried to teach you. Out in the desert. So you would understand."

Tommy struggled to understand, seeking some frame of reference as the game's theme music began, full of drumbeats and brass chords. "Are you immortal, Alyosha?"

"There are ways that my life can end. But if I avoid them, yes, I will live forever. So we will be friends for a very long time."

Tommy heard a hint of the loneliness in that voice.

He spoke softly, despairing. "So I'm like you, then?"

Alyosha shifted as if this part of the conversation bothered him. "No, you are not. In all the long history of time, there has only ever been *one* other like you. *You,* my friend, are very special."

"Is this other one still around?"

"Yes, of course, he is still around. Like you, he cannot die or take his own life."

"Ever?"

"Until the end of time."

Tommy took another long look around the room. Would he be a prisoner here forever? He wanted to laugh at the absurdity of it, but some part of him knew that Alyosha had told him the truth—but maybe not the full enormity of it.

Tommy understood that on his own.

Immortality was not a blessing.

It was a curse.

40

October 27, 6:55 A.M., CET
Beneath Harmsfeld Lake, Germany

With Piers hauled over his shoulder, Jordan ran several steps sideways, chased down the concrete tunnel by the screams of pursuing *strigoi,* feral and terrifying.

He yelled back to Erin, who trailed twenty yards behind.

"Hurry!"

"Keep going!" she called back, both irritated and scared.

That was Erin.

To hell with that.

By now, Nadia had reached the far leg and vanished down it, aiming for the air lock with Rhun, limp and poisoned, in her arms. Apparently she felt no obligation to wait for the two, slower humans. And she didn't seem too fond of Piers either. She probably wasn't coming back.

Jordan lowered Piers to the concrete and freed his submachine gun. "Sorry, old man."

Piers opened faded blue eyes. "*Meine Kinder.*"

My children.

"I'll come back." Jordan hoped he'd be able to keep that promise.

Before Jordan could come fully to standing, Piers seized his hand, his grip incredibly strong, still capable of breaking bone. "Icarops. *Sie kommen*. To help. I send them."

From the broken doorway of the neighboring vestibule, a black cloud of bats burst forth into the tunnel, churning, squealing, and swooping over their heads.

Thousands poured into the passageway.

Jordan ducked under the wings, overwhelmed by the creatures' stench, tasting it on the back of his tongue. He crouched with Piers against the wall.

Erin had almost reached him, one arm shielding her face against the winged onslaught.

But this time their fury was not directed at her.

She forged through them, ducking low.

Behind her, the black horde struck the *strigoi* like a raging torrent. Bats battled monsters in a kaleidoscope of black blood, fur, and pale skin. Amid the chaos, silver flashed like lightning. Some of the icarops fell, but more swooped in to take their places.

Jordan saw one huge bat sweep up and wrap its wings around one *strigoi* like a monstrous cloak.

Screams rang louder.

Then a jetting flame burst upward in the heart of that dark storm. A *whoosh* and a crackling filled the air, followed by a terrible screeching. A cloud of foul smoke rushed toward the three onlookers.

Burnt flesh and petroleum.

Flamethrower.

Piers moaned in sympathy for his children as the chorus of screams threatened to burst Jordan's ears.

But Erin finally reached him.

Jordan grabbed her arm and pushed her around the corner. "Make for the air lock! I'll be right behind you!"

She nodded, breathing hard.

He collected up Piers and sprinted after her. He prayed that the remaining bats could buy them enough time to get free of this cursed place. After that, the sun ought to protect them.

At least, it was a theory.

They fled toward the open air lock. Out of the darkness ahead, Nadia came rushing toward them, empty-handed. She must have left Rhun at the air lock and come back to help. So she hadn't abandoned them after all.

"Hurry!" the woman shouted, reaching Erin and grabbing her, almost lifting her off her feet.

A feral scream from behind drew Jordan's attention. A *strigoi*—bloody, burned, and missing an eye—came charging around the corner at them, moving too fast, half climbing the walls in its haste to reach them.

The air lock loomed mere yards away.

But he'd never make it.

6:57 A.M.

Erin ground her heels against the inevitable force of Nadia's pull toward the air lock. She twisted in her grip and lifted her Sig Sauer pistol.

"Jordan! Drop!"

From farther down the tunnel, he obeyed, sprawling headlong, rolling with Piers, keeping the priest protected.

She aimed her pistol at the monster as it leaped toward Jordan.

She took a single steadying breath, not holding it, and squeezed the trigger.

The blast of the pistol cracked like thunder, stinging her ears, setting them to ringing.

The back of the *strigoi*'s skull burst, smoking from the silver she had sent through its remaining eye. The creature's momentum carried its bulk past Jordan. The body hit the ground and skidded to Erin's feet.

She leaped back, but Nadia pronounced its sentence.

"It's dead."

Jordan hauled back up, lifting Piers. "Nice shooting."

There was no condescending grin. He meant it. A surge of satisfaction warmed through her.

Together, they charged into the damp air lock.

Erin hurried over to Rhun, fearful at the sight of his white complexion—whiter than usual. His bared chest still seeped blood. Nadia and Jordan slammed the air lock with a resounding *clank* and dogged it shut.

The two went to open the outer hatch, hurrying.

Nadia rushed across the tiny room and spun open the handle for the outer door. As it cracked open, cold lake water surged inside before Erin had time to snatch a breath. In seconds the water rose above her head. Jordan switched on his waterproof flashlight, crouching by Piers.

Erin did the same, keeping one fist curled in Rhun's jacket.

Nadia shouldered the door open as pressure finally equalized, and motioned them all out. She swam over to Erin and Rhun, grabbing her fellow Sanguinist by a wrist.

Freed of responsibility for him, Erin kicked off through the hatch and swam upward. She fought the weight of her leather duster—not to mention the pockets full of concrete fragments. She began to sink, but she refused to give up what had cost her so much to gain. In the distance, she made out the shimmering form of the fountain statue, a man on a rearing horse, draped in algae.

Would she join the others who had drowned in this flooded town?

Then Jordan was by her side. He gathered a fistful of her jacket's collar and pulled, kicking and dragging both Piers and her toward the silvery promise of dawn above.

What felt like an eternity later her head broke the surface.

She gasped.

Overhead, the sky had lightened to a dove gray. Sunrise was approaching, but it would be too soon for Piers. They would never reach the sanctuary of the Harmsfeld church in time.

Jordan pushed her toward the boat.

Nadia was already aboard with Rhun and helped pull Father Piers's unconscious body into the stern. Jordan hauled up by himself, coming close to capsizing the dory.

Erin clutched the wooden gunwale near the bow and waited her turn. She took deep shuddering breaths, her body shaking. She had never been so cold in her life, but she was alive.

Balancing, Jordan stripped off his grimwolf leather coat and spread it over someone in the boat. He then reached a warm hand down to Erin and pulled her, one-armed, into the dory, causing her to land in a sprawl.

"Your coat," Nadia said. "Hurry."

Jordan helped peel off her sodden duster as if she were on fire.

She was shivering so hard she nearly fell over.

Jordan and Nadia worked quickly, arranging both coats over the wounded Sanguinists so that no sun would touch them. Sunlight would kill Piers, and Erin guessed Rhun must be too weak to withstand it as well. He had lost so much blood at the bunker door.

Once she was done, Nadia knelt and bowed her head. She shuddered and fell to one arm.

"Are you okay?" Jordan asked.

"I'll be fine," the woman whispered, sitting back but not sounding fine. She had a hole the size of a quarter in her right thigh, and it went clean through. Yet despite her wound, she had saved everyone.

Jordan raised the anchor and dropped it in the middle of the boat.

Feeling like a weakling, Erin fumbled with her paddle and helped Jordan row toward shore. Her hands shook so that she could barely hold the shaft.

From under one of the cloaks, a weak, muffled voice gasped. "Please. Take it off."

It was Father Piers.

Nadia stared down at his covered figure, her face a study of agony. "You'll die."

"I know," he said. "Release me."

Nadia's hand hovered over the coat, but she did not pick it up. "Please, Piers, don't."

"Can you grant me absolution?" His frail voice barely rose above the splashes of their paddle blades.

Nadia sighed. "I have not yet taken Holy Orders." She lifted the other coat and peered under it. "Rhun cannot grant you absolution either in his state. I'm sorry."

Beside Erin, Jordan raked his paddle through the water, methodical and fast. She paddled harder, her hands cold claws on the wood.

"Then please, let us pray together, Nadia," Piers pleaded.

As Erin and Jordan worked slowly toward shore, the two Sanguinists prayed in Latin, but Erin did not translate the words. She stared straight at the water, orange in the rising sun, and she thought of Rhun, dead or dying under Jordan's coat. Why had she acceded to this quest? The search for the Gospel had already cost so many lives, just as Rhun had warned her. They had gained nothing and lost much.

As they neared the shoreline, Nadia gently lifted the coat off Piers and drew him up, cradling his gaunt form against her. For the first time, she looked frightened.

Piers's filmy blue eyes searched the landscape of the shore.

Erin followed his gaze to dark pines, to the silver trunks of lindens bared by fall, a lake turned copper, and the golden rays of light breaking through fog.

Piers raised his face to the sun. "Light is truly the most beautiful of His creations."

Tears streamed down Nadia's cheeks. She didn't wipe them away, instead tightening her grip on Piers. "Forgive me," she said in Latin. "You are blessed."

Jordan's face was set like stone. He did not break the rhythm of his paddling.

Piers's face glowed iridescent in a wash of sunlight.

His back arched. The flush spread to his neck and hands.

He screamed.

Nadia held him close. "Lord our God, You are our refuge from generation to generation. Year and days vary, but You remain eternal."

Piers grew silent, slumping in her arms and going still.

"Your mercy sustains us in life and in death," Nadia continued. "Grant us to remember with thanks what You have given us through Piers and Emmanuel. Receive them together into Your kingdom after their long years of service to You."

Erin finished with her, using a word she hadn't spoken in years and doubted that she ever truly meant, until now.

"Amen."

41

October 27, 7:07 A.M., CET
Harmsfeld, Germany

Jordan dug deeper with the paddle, working slowly across the lake's surface. He stared up at the sun, marking a new day after the longest night of his life—but at least, he still had a *life*.

He pictured the faces of his men . . . of Piers . . . of Emmanuel.

When Jordan had spread his coat over Rhun, he could tell that the priest might not be far behind the others. And for what? They'd come out of their long nightmare empty-handed.

At the bow of the boat, Nadia removed the duster from Piers's body and handed it to Erin. The priest no longer needed its protection, but Erin was shivering in the early morning chill.

Nadia laid Piers out in the boat as best she could and crossed his arms over his thin chest. Her hands lingered above the terrible wounds on his feet and hands, but she refused to touch them. She drew Emmanuel's cassock over his lifeless form, tucking it lovingly around him, then bowed her head in prayer.

Jordan did the same, owing Piers that much.

Once this was done, Nadia made the sign of the cross.

The woman looked to the sun for a long breath, then scooped up Piers, lifted him over the gunwale, and gently rolled his body into the lake. He sank out of sight in the green water, a trail of bubbles rising from the black cassock.

Erin gasped at the unceremonious end of Father Piers.

"He cannot rest in hallowed ground, nor can his body be found," Nadia explained, then she sat back down, picking up a paddle. "Let him find his peace and eternal rest in these highlands he loved so much."

Erin shivered, her blue lips pressed into a thin line, but she kept paddling.

Jordan checked behind his shoulder. The shore loomed out of the fog. He spotted the dock to the right. In the forest ahead, a bird called, greeting the morning, and another answered.

It seemed that life went on.

He did not slow the boat as the bank swept up to its bow. He used their momentum to shove the boat into the mud.

"Wait here," he warned.

Erin shivered and nodded.

Nadia did not respond.

He drew his Colt and vaulted off the side. Mud sucked at his boots, but it felt good to be on land, outside in the sunlight.

He hurried to the spot where they'd hidden their Ducati bikes. They could be back at the abbey in less than an hour. Maybe Brother Leopold had some kind of medicine to help Rhun heal.

But as Jordan stepped behind the sheltering tree, he stopped, staring down at the wreckage of the trio of bikes. He tensed, searching around. The *strigoi* were surely hiding from the sun, but he knew that the Belial also employed humans.

At that moment he realized a horrible truth.

They were still not safe—even in the brightness of a new day.

7:12 A.M.

Standing on the muddy shore, Erin pulled her leather duster tightly around her body. She turned her gaze at the trees that had swallowed up Jordan. She saw no movement out there, which burned an ember of worry in her chest.

To the side, Nadia unstrapped the wineskin from her leg and ducked under the coat covering Rhun, still keeping the sunlight off his body as she checked on him.

Erin longed to peek beneath, too, and see how Rhun fared, but she didn't dare. Nadia knew best how to care for him. She had probably known him longer than Erin had been alive.

Jordan's familiar form reappeared out of the woods, and Erin let out a deep breath. But she could tell by the slump of his shoulders that he had bad news. Very bad. It took a lot to defeat him, and Jordan looked crestfallen.

Nadia sat back up, one hand resting on Rhun's covered head.

"Someone destroyed the bikes," Jordan said, casting her an apologetic look, as if it were his fault.

"All of them?" Nadia asked.

Jordan nodded. "Not fixable without parts and tools and time."

"None of which we have." Nadia's hand stroked her wounded leg. She suddenly looked frail. "We'll never get Rhun back to the abbey alive if we have to walk."

"What about the Harmsfeld church?" Erin pointed to the steeple poking above the forest. "You thought it could offer Piers sanctuary. What about Rhun?"

Nadia leaned back. She stroked a hand along the coat covering Rhun.

"We must pray it has what we need."

7:14 A.M.

From the shoreline, Jordan watched the fog disperse in tatters in the early morning sunlight. Once it was gone, they'd be exposed beside the lake: three adults with a stolen dory and a badly wounded man.

Not easy to explain that one.

Nadia stepped over to the beached boat and began to haul the unconscious Rhun up in her arms. It was a short hike to the picturesque hamlet of Harmsfeld.

Jordan stepped in to intervene. "Please give him to me."

"Why? Do you think me too weak for such a task?" Her dark eyes narrowed.

"I think that if anyone sees a woman as small as you carrying a full-grown man as easily as if he were a puppy, it'll raise questions."

Reluctantly, she allowed Jordan to hoist Rhun on his shoulder. The priest was deadweight in his arms. If he were a human, he'd be simply dead: cold, no heartbeat, and no breath. Was he even still alive?

Jordan had to trust that Nadia would know.

The woman led them through the surrounding forest at a punishing pace. Jordan soon wished he'd let her carry Rhun until they got within sight of the village.

But in less than ten minutes, they were traipsing across the frost-coated paving stones of the main street. Nadia led them in a seemingly haphazard fashion, stopping occasionally to listen with her head cocked. She probably heard people long before Jordan and Erin could and sought to avoid running into any.

He glanced over at Erin. Like him, she was soaked to the skin. But unlike him, she wasn't working up heat from carrying a heavy weight. Her blue lips trembled. He had to get her inside and warmed up.

Finally, they reached the village church in the square. The sturdy structure had been constructed out of locally quarried stone centuries ago, its builders forming bricked archways and framing stained-glass windows along both flanks. The single bell spire pointed toward Heaven with what seemed like an unquestioning resolve.

Nadia sprang up the steps and tried the double front doors. Locked.

Jordan eased Rhun to the ground. Maybe he could pick the lock.

Nadia drew back a step, lifted her leg, then kicked the thick wooden doors. They slammed open with a *crack*. Not the quietest way in, but an effective one.

She rushed inside. Jordan picked up Rhun and followed, with Erin close behind. He wanted everyone out of sight before someone noticed that they had broken into a church while carrying a dead man.

Erin tugged the doors closed behind them, likely fearing the same.

Nadia was already at the altar, rooting around. "No consecrated wine," she said, and in her frustration, she elbowed an empty chalice and sent it crashing to the stone floor.

"Maybe a little quieter?" Jordan hated to upset her.

She uttered something that sounded blasphemous, then stormed toward a wooden crucifix behind the altar. The resemblance of the carved oak figure to Piers was so uncanny that Jordan stepped back a pace.

What was Nadia planning on doing?

42

October 27, 7:31 A.M., CET
Harmsfeld Mountains, Germany

Bathory stood before the dead Sanguinist's body. It was still spiked by crossbow bolts to the trunk of an ancient pine, like some druidic sacrifice.

She gripped one of the bolts by its feathered end and yanked it out of the dead arm, freeing the limb to hang limp and broken. She studied her handiwork with a sigh.

Bright sunlight suffused the glade, melting frost from the yellow linden leaves. There was little evidence of the battle that had been fought here: some torn earth, more than a few rounds of ammunition that peppered tree trunks, and dark splotches of blood soaking into the ground. A good rain, a couple weeks of new growth, and no one would have any clue as to what transpired here.

Except for this damned body bolted to the tree.

She yanked out another bolt, wishing that she could have assigned this job to Tarek, but she couldn't, not during the day. Even Magor had suffered too much in the sunlight, his body smoking, until she had forced him to retreat into the bunker with the others.

She continued yanking out spikes, slowly freeing the body.

Too bad it wasn't Korza impaled here. But she had seen him fall after putting six silver slugs into him. He wouldn't last long in that state. She savored the look of surprise on his face when she shot him. He had thought her Elisabeta—Bathory's long-dead ancestor, somehow come back to forgive him.

As if that would be enough to atone for his sins.

She pulled the Sanguinist free from the last spike. If the man had been a *strigoi,* the sunlight would have burned him to ash and saved her the trouble.

Resigned, she hurried with this last bit of bloody business as a plan took shape in her mind.

The book was still lost—but she knew where to go to find it.

And more important, *who* could help her.

43

October 27, 7:35 A.M., CET
Harmsfeld, Germany

Erin accompanied Jordan as he placed Rhun down in front of the altar. The limp priest lay on the stone floor as if dead.

"Is he still alive?" she asked.

"Barely." Kneeling, Nadia dribbled wine from her flask into his mouth.

He did not swallow.

That couldn't be good.

"How can we help?" Jordan asked.

"Stay out of my way." Nadia cradled Rhun's head in her lap. "And stay quiet."

Nadia sorted through the items she had gathered from behind the altar, settling first on the sealed bottle of wine. She pushed in the cork with one long finger.

"I need to consecrate this wine," she explained.

"You can do that?" Jordan looked at the door, plainly worried about someone coming into the church and interrupting whatever was about to happen.

"Of course she can't," Erin said, shocked. "Only a priest can consecrate wine."

Nadia sniffed derisively. "Dr. Granger, you are enough of an historian to know better, are you not?" She wiped blood off Rhun's chest with the altar cloth. "Didn't women perform Mass and consecrate wine in the early days of the Church?"

Erin felt chastened. She *did* know better. In a knee-jerk reaction, she had leaned upon Church dogma, when history plainly contradicted it. She wondered how much she was still her father's daughter at heart.

That thought stung.

"I'm sorry," Erin said. "You're right."

"The human side of the Church took that power away from women. The Sanguinist side did not," Nadia said.

"So you can consecrate wine," Jordan said.

"I did not say that. I said that *women* in the Sanguinist Church can be priests. But I have not yet taken Holy Orders, so I am not yet a priest myself," Nadia said.

Jordan stared back at the door. Again. "Why don't we just take this bottle of vino and do whatever you're planning somewhere else, away from where someone might come barging in at any time? You don't need to do this in a church, do you?"

"Wine has its greatest healing powers if consecrated and consumed in a church. Holy ground lends it additional power." Nadia put a hand on Rhun's chest. "Rhun needs as many advantages as we can give him."

She poured the last drops of wine from her flask into one of Rhun's bullet wounds, raising a moan from him.

Erin's heart leaped with hope. Maybe he wasn't as bad off as she thought.

Nadia unfastened Rhun's silver flask from his leg. She trickled more wine down his throat. This time he swallowed.

He drew in a single breath. "Elisabeta?"

Nadia closed her eyes. "No, Rhun. It's Nadia."

Rhun looked around, his eyes unfocused.

"You must consecrate this wine." She wrapped his fingers around the bottle's green neck. "Or you will die."

His eyelids drifted closed.

Erin studied the unconscious priest. She didn't see what could rouse him. "Are you sure that you need to consecrate the wine? Maybe you can just tell him it's blessed."

Nadia gave her a venomous look.

"I've been wondering, since our time in the desert, if the wine needs to be truly consecrated or if Rhun just needs to *think* it is.

Maybe it's about faith, instead of miracles." Erin couldn't believe that these words were coming out of her mouth.

She had seen firsthand what happened when medical care was left to faith and miracles, first with her arm, and then with her baby sister. She shut her eyes, as if doing this would shut out the memory. But the memory came, like it always did.

Her mother had been having a hard birth. Erin and the other women in the compound had watched her labor for days. Summer had come early, and the bedroom was hot and close. It smelled of sweat and blood.

She held her mother's hand, bathed her brow, and prayed. It was all she could do.

Eventually her sister, Emma, came into the world.

But Emma was feverish from the first. Too weak to cry or suckle, she lay wrapped in her baby quilt, held against her mother's breast, wide dark eyes open and glassy.

Erin begged her father to take the baby to a real doctor, but he backhanded her, bloodying her nose.

Instead, the women of the compound gathered around her mother's bed to pray. Her father led the prayers, his deep voice confident that God would hear, and God would save the child. If not, God knew that she wasn't worth saving.

Erin stayed by her mother's side, watching Emma's heartbeat in her soft fontanel, quick as a bird's. She ached to pick her up, load her on a horse, and take her into town. But her father, seeming to sense her defiance, never left her alone with the baby. All Erin could do was pray, hope, and watch the heartbeat slow and stop.

Emma Granger lived for two days.

Faith did not save Emma.

Erin touched the fabric in her pocket. She had cut it from Emma's baby quilt before she was wrapped in it for burial. She'd carried it with her every day since, to remind herself to honor the warnings in her heart, to ask the impossible questions, and then, always, to act.

"Nadia," Erin said. "Try drinking the unconsecrated wine. What have you got to lose?"

Nadia lifted the bottle to her own mouth and took a deep gulp. Red liquid erupted from her throat and sprayed across the floor.

Jordan grimaced. "Guess it doesn't work that way."

Nadia wiped her mouth. "It's about miracles."

Or maybe it was simply that Nadia didn't *believe* the wine was Christ's blood.

But Erin remained silent.

7:44 A.M.

Rhun longed for death, wishing they'd never woken him.

Pain from his wounds paled in comparison to what he had felt when he saw Elisabeta again in the forest. But it had not truly been her. He knew that. The woman in the forest had red hair, not black. And Elisabeta had been gone for four hundred years.

Who was the woman who had shot him? Some distant descendant? Did it matter?

Darkness folded back over him like a soft cape. He relaxed into it. Silver did not burn him in the warm blackness. He floated there.

Then liquid scalded his lips, and he tried to turn his head away.

"Rhun," ordered a familiar voice. "You *will* come back to me."

It wasn't Elisabeta. This voice sounded angry. Also frightened.

Nadia?

But nothing frightened Nadia.

He forced his heavy eyelids open, heard heartbeats. Erin's quick one, the soldier's steady rhythm. So they had both made it out alive.

Good.

Content, he tried to drift away again.

But cold fingers grabbed his chin, pulling him to Nadia's dark eyes. "You will do this for me, Rhun. I have given you all of your wine—and *mine*. Without it, I, too, will die. That is, unless I break my oath."

He strove to keep his eyelids open, but they slid closed again. He pushed them open.

"You force this upon me, Rhun."

Nadia released his head and stood, a quick flash of darkness. She wrapped an arm around Erin's waist and yanked her head to the side. Erin's heartbeats sped until each muscular squeeze flowed into the next in one continuous thrumming.

Jordan brought up his submachine gun.

"If you shoot me, soldier, know that I can kill her before the second bullet strikes," Nadia hissed. "So, Rhun, can you do this?"

Erin's amber eyes stared into his, pleading for her life, and for his.

To answer that look more than Nadia's question, Rhun found the strength. He roused himself to grasp the wine, to pull the bottle to his heart, to recite the necessary words.

The ceremony stretched into a sacrament—all the while Nadia held Erin, her teeth at her throat.

Finally, Rhun ended with "*We offer to Thee this reasonable and unbloody sacrifice; and we beg Thee, we ask Thee, we pray Thee that Thou send down Thy Holy Spirit on us and on these present gifts.*"

Nadia answered, "Amen. Bless this Holy Chalice."

"*'And that which is in this chalice, the Precious Blood of Thy Christ.'*"

He dropped his hands to his lap, the ritual complete, his strength fleeing his limbs, his only desire a wish for unconsciousness.

But Nadia refused to let him rest. She poured Christ's blood into his wounds, into his mouth. His body took in that fire, and it burned him completely this time. He knew where it would take him, and he quailed at the prospect.

"*No . . . ,*" he begged—but this prayer wasn't answered.

"Turn away." Nadia's ragged command to the humans faded as his sins carried him away into penance.

Bernard had sensed the blackness in Rhun's heart and sent him to Čachtice Castle to cut ties with Elisabeta. Rhun told himself that he could do it, that he felt nothing more for her than the duty to serve her as a priest.

Still he prayed as he lingered on the long winter road to her door. Snow hid fields and gardens where they had once walked together. Among long dried stalks of lavender, a raven pecked at a gray mouse, the tiny scarlet stain of its lifeblood visible even from so far away. He tarried until the raven finished its repast and flew away.

He reached the castle at twilight, hours later than he had planned. Yet he stood long in front of the door before he could bring himself to knock. Snow dusted the shoulders of his cassock. He did not feel cold anymore, but he brushed the snow away as a man would do. He would not show his otherness in this house.

Her maid, Anna, answered, her hands reddened with cold. "Good evening, Father Korza."

"Hello, my child," he said. "Is the Widow Nádasy at home?"

He prayed that she was far away. Perhaps he should request that she meet him at the village church. His resolve was strongest there. Yes, the church would be better.

Anna curtsied. "Since the death of the good Count Nádasy, she walks late in the evenings, but she will return before dark. You may wait?"

He followed her thin figure into the great room, where a fire crackled in the immense hearth. Chamomile sprinkled atop the floor rushes lent the room the familiar smell of summer. He remembered gathering leaves of it with her on a sunlit afternoon before Ferenc's death.

Rhun refused Anna's offer of refreshment and stood as close to the fire as he dared, drawing its heat into his unnatural body. He prayed and thought of Ferenc, the Black Knight of Hungary, and the man to whom Elisabeta had been bound. If Ferenc were still alive, all would be different. But Ferenc was dead. Rhun pushed away thoughts of his last visit, when he had told her of Ferenc's passing.

Elisabeta entered wearing a deep burgundy cloak, snow melted to darkness on the shoulders. Rhun straightened his spine. His faith was strong. He would endure this.

She shook water from her cloak. Dark droplets spattered the floor. A servant girl took the heavy woolen garment from her outstretched hand and walked backward from the room.

"It is good to see that you are well, Father Korza." Black skirts swished against rushes as she walked to join him at the fire. "I trust you have been offered wine and refreshment?"

Her tone was light, but her racing heart betrayed her.

"I have."

In the firelight, she looked thinner than he remembered, her features harder, as if grief had tempered the softness from her. Even so, she was achingly beautiful.

Fear flashed through Rhun's blood.

He longed to flee, but he had promised Bernard, and he had promised himself. He was strong enough to do this. He must be.

"I imagine that you are here collecting for the Church?" Her bitter tone told him that she knew how he had failed her when he left her to grieve for Ferenc alone, that she did not forgive him for deserting her in her hour of deepest need.

His mind screamed at him to run, but his body would not obey.

He stayed.

"Father Korza?" She leaned closer, her dark head tilted in concern, her heart slowing in sympathy instead of speeding up in anger. "Are you ill? Perhaps you should sit?"

She guided him to a straight-backed wooden chair, then sat across from him, their knees a mere handsbreadth apart. The fire's heat cooled in comparison to the warmth of her body.

"Have you been well, Father Korza?"

He roused from the song of her strong red heart. "I have. How have you fared, Widow Nádasy?"

She shifted at the word widow. *"I have been bearing up—" She leaned forward. "Nonsense. We have known each other too long and too well to be untruthful now. Ferenc's death has been both a great burden and a freedom to me."*

A freedom?

He dared not ask. He raised his head.

"You look as if you have been ill," she said. "So tell me the truth. How have the past months served you?"

He fell into her silver eyes, reflecting orange from the firelight. How could he be apart from her? She alone of all he knew he had trusted with memories of his mortal life, only keeping secret his unnatural state of being.

A ghost of a smile played on her soft lips. Her hand brushed water from her bare shoulder, then fell coyly to her soft throat. He stared at her fingers, and what they covered.

She stood and took his hand between hers. "Always so cold."

The heat of her hand exploded under his skin. He must move away, but instead he stood and put his other hand over hers, drawing more of her warmth into his chilled body. Just that. A simple moment of connection. He asked for nothing more.

Her heartbeat traveled from her hands through his arms and up to where his heart had once beat. Now his blood moved to the rhythm of hers. Scarlet stained the edges of his vision.

Her eyelids fell closed, and she tipped her face up toward his.

He took her flushed cheeks in his marble-white hands. He had never touched a woman before, not like this. He caressed her face, her smooth white throat.

Her heart sped under his palms. Fear? Or did something else drive it?

Tears coursed down her cheeks.

"Rhun," she whispered, "I've waited so long for you."

He traced the impossibly soft redness of her lips with one fingertip. She shivered under his touch.

He longed to press his lips against hers, to feel the warmth of her mouth. To taste her. But it was forbidden. He was a priest. Chaste. He must stop this at once. He drew his hands a finger's width away from her and toward the silver cross that lay over his cassock.

She cast her eyes on the cross and let out a quiet moan of disappointment.

Rhun froze, fighting the warmth of her skin, the scent of snowmelt in her hair, the pulse of her heart in her lips, the salt smell of her tears. He had never been so terrified in his mortal and immortal life.

She leaned forward and kissed him, her lips light as the touch of a butterfly.

And Rhun was lost.

She tasted of grief and blood and passion. He was no longer a priest or a monster. He was simply a man. A man as he had never been before.

He pulled his head back and stared into her shadowed eyes, dark with passion. She pulled off her cap and black hair tumbled free around her shoulders.

"Yes, Rhun," she said. "Yes."

He kissed the inside of her wrist. Her heart pounded strong against his lips. He unfastened her sleeve and kissed the crook of her elbow. His tongue tasted her skin.

She buried her hands in his hair and pulled him closer. He chased her pulse up her bare neck. As she swooned in his embrace, he tightened his arms around her back. Her mouth found his again.

God and vows fled. He needed to feel her skin against his. His hands fumbled with the lacings of her dress. She pushed him away and undid them herself, her mouth never leaving his.

Her dress fell heavy to the stone floor, and she stepped out of it, closer to the fire. Orange flames shone through her linen chemise. He released her long enough to tear the garment in half.

And she stood naked in his arms. Skin soft and warm. Her heart racing under his palms.

Her hands flew across the impossibly long row of buttons on his cassock. Thirty-three, to symbolize the thirty-three years of the earthly life of Christ. The cassock fell to the floor atop her dress. His silver cross burned against his chest, but he no longer cared.

He swept Elisabeta up in his arms, crushing her against him. She gasped when the cross touched her bare breast. He reached up and broke the chain. The cross clattered to the stone next to his robes. He should care, he should gather up its holiness and hold it against his body, hold it between them like a wall.

Instead, he chose her.

Her lips found his again, and her mouth opened under his. Nothing separated them now. They were two bodies craving only union.

She called out his name.

Rhun answered with hers.

He lowered her to the fire-warmed floor. She arched under him, long velvet throat curving toward his mouth.

Rhun lost himself in her scent, her warmth, her heart. No man could experience what he felt; no Sanguinist could withstand it. Never had he felt so content, so strong. This bliss was why men left the priesthood. This bond was deeper than his feelings for God.

He joined with her. He never wanted to be separate again.

Red consumed him. Then it consumed her. He pulsed in a sea of seething red.

When the red cleared, both their souls were destroyed.

44

October 27, 8:02 a.m., CET
Harmsfeld, Germany

A few feet away from Erin, Nadia knelt next to Rhun, whispering in Latin while he wept. Whatever happened when they drank consecrated wine, it was more unpleasant than being shot six times in the chest. She ached for Rhun, trapped in such a state for eternity, consigned to an unimaginable Hell for the sin of being attacked by a wild *strigoi*.

Erin walked back to the broken church doors and stared out at the early morning. Jordan joined her, leaned next to her. How did he stay so warm? She was freezing. First they had both been dunked in that snowmelt lake, and now they stood in an unheated church.

Once Rhun quieted, she heard Nadia gasp as she also consumed a draft of consecrated wine, but she did not weep as Rhun had done.

For a long moment silence filled the church.

"He is awake," Nadia finally called out, returned again to her calm, even state. "With luck, he will be fit to travel before nightfall. But he will be weakened for the next few days. Christ's blood does not heal us as quickly as human blood would."

"Why is the wine not as difficult for you to drink as it is for Rhun?" Erin glanced over at the priest, lying on his side, facing away from them, covered with the altar cloth.

Nadia stared over at him, too. "I did not have so far to fall."

8:22 A.M.

Jordan looked around the small room of the inn that Nadia had rented for him and Erin in Harmsfeld. The quaint residence stood across the town square from the church.

Nadia shared a room with Rhun, right next door, but Jordan still surveyed the room as if he were preparing for a coming siege. The hotel door was made of stout oak. A check of the window revealed a trellis below their second-story room. A difficult entry point. He did a quick assessment of the bathroom. The window there was too small to admit anyone. The rest of the space was typical of European accommodations: white tiles, a utilitarian shower, sink, toilet, and bidet.

When he returned to the main room, Erin hadn't moved from her spot on the bed, perched at the edge of a plump duvet. The space contained a double bed, two nightstands with lamps, and an odd metal contraption he thought might be used for cleaning boots.

Erin looked paler than he'd ever seen her. Dark circles shadowed her eyes; dirt smudged her face.

"Do you want the first shower?" he asked.

" 'Shower,' " she said, standing and stretching. "Best word in the English language right now."

Jordan watched her leave, closing the door. He thought that the best two words in the English language right now might be *shower together,* but he knew better than to say so. Instead, he sat on the other side of the bed and opened the room-service menu.

He selected three breakfasts with coffee and tea because he had no idea what Erin ate or drank. He picked up the phone and dialed, but before anyone answered, Erin turned on the water for the shower. Jordan pictured her stepping over the tile threshold, her hair loose and falling halfway down her bare back, water tracing its way down the curves of her—

"Darf ich Ihnen behilflich sein?" said the voice on the other end of the phone.

Jordan turned his back to the bathroom door and ordered breakfast in German.

While he waited, he spread their coats to dry over the radiator, trying not to think about Erin in the shower, face upturned to the water and steam rising around her.

He had to find something else to do. He sat on the bed and

cleaned his weapons, one at a time, keeping the other always near to hand. After that, he cleaned Erin's Sig Sauer.

Nadia knocked on the door and thrust a paper bag into his hands without a word. As he closed the door, he opened the bag to find basic toiletries and a change of clothes for both of them.

Warm sweaters, so he guessed he wasn't flying back to Jerusalem.

Room service arrived, and Jordan started his breakfast before Erin finished her shower.

Moments later, the flow of water shut off with a clunking sound. He kept glancing at the door, trying his best not to picture Erin buffing her naked form.

He failed.

He waited for her to come out. When she finally did, she stepped into the room in a cloud of steam. She wore a white terrycloth robe she must have found in the bathroom and had rebandaged her hand. Her face and neck were flushed from the hot water. He wished he could see how far down her body that flush extended.

As she approached, Jordan adjusted the napkin on his lap.

"I tried to save you some hot water," she said.

"I . . . um . . . tried to save you some breakfast." Jordan took a big sip of his steaming coffee.

Erin walked over and looked down at the remains of the food. She smelled like soap and clean laundry. "Here's hoping I did a better job than you."

He kept his eyes studiously averted from the front of her robe and hurried to the bathroom. He showered and shaved quickly. After he brushed his hair and pulled on a clean pair of khakis and a long-sleeved shirt, he felt ready to take on the world.

Or at least to take a long nap.

Erin was just finishing up breakfast when Jordan came out of the bathroom. He lay down on the bed and sighed. A real bed.

"I could sleep on the floor," Erin said.

"Neither of us is taking the floor," Jordan answered. "I promise to stay on my side, if you promise to stay on yours."

Erin looked at the floor, as if considering the other option.

Jordan rolled back to his feet and retrieved his dry coat from the radiator. "During times of dire need, didn't maidens once sleep with a sword between them and their knight protector?" He spread the coat across the middle of the bed and held up three fingers. "Scout's honor, I won't cross this moat of leather unless you ask me to."

She eyed him skeptically. "Were you ever a Boy Scout?"

He flopped down on the side of the bed closest to the door. "Eagle Scout."

After a short time, they both settled to their respective sides of the bed. Jordan thought he'd be awake thinking about Erin lying inches away, but he fell asleep almost immediately, still in his clothes.

He awoke sitting up, one hand on his gun. He took in the sunlit room with a single glance. Nothing out of place. Door closed. Window closed. Bathroom empty. What had woken him up?

Next to him, Erin whimpered.

He turned to check on her. Still in her robe, she lay on her side facing him, her hands clasped under one cheek. She gasped in her sleep. He wanted to reach over the coat and touch her, but he didn't want to break his promise. One wrong move with Erin, and he would be finished.

"Hush," he whispered, as if she were his niece Abigail, famous in the family for her nightmares about giant tarantulas.

Erin let out one long breath and seemed to sink deeper into sleep.

She had plenty of food for bad dreams: *strigoi*, bats, and—

With a scream, Erin sat bolt upright.

"I'm right here," Jordan said, sitting up with her. "We're safe."

She looked over at him, eyes wide.

"It's Jordan, remember?" he said.

She drew in a ragged breath and scooted back to lean against the headboard. "I remember."

Careful to stay on his side of the coat, Jordan did the same. "Bad dreams?"

"Bad reality."

"Should I be insulted?" Maybe that would lighten the mood.

"I didn't mean you. You're . . . well . . . fine. But the rest of the situation . . ."

Jordan *was* insulted at being relegated to merely *fine*, but decided this wasn't the time to make a smart-aleck comment about it. "At least we got some sleep and food. I haven't felt so good since before Masada."

He stopped talking. Masada. Where his team had died. All of

them. He named them in his head, intending to never forget them: Sanderson. McKay. Cooper. Tyson. All of them, except McKay, younger than he. Tyson had a two-year-old daughter who would never see her mother again. McKay had three kids, an ex-wife, and a dog named Chipper. Cooper used his army pay to support his frail elderly mother and a long string of girlfriends. Sanderson hadn't even had time to start a relationship. He was just a kid. Jordan rested his head against the headboard. "It's been a very long twenty-four hours."

"I wonder what comes next," Erin said.

"Another field trip with our fun tour guides, Rhun and Nadia."

"Nadia's not much fun." Erin pulled the covers up past her waist. "I think she would've killed me in that church."

"I thought she was bluffing."

Erin put one hand up to her throat. "I don't think Nadia bluffs."

Jordan didn't think so either. "I get the feeling that if she wanted to, she could just crush us like bugs and hire someone to clean up the greasy spots."

Erin grinned. "That's supposed to be reassuring?"

He glanced over at her. "At least we have each other." It sounded so cheesy he wished he could take it back.

"But I barely know you," she said.

"What do you want to know?" He stuck a pillow behind his head. "I'm human. Thirty-five. Career army. Born in Iowa. Third son. My mom had five kids. My favorite color is green."

Erin smiled and shook her head.

"Not good enough?" Jordan decided to go for it, just tell the truth. "My wife—Karen—was also in the army. She died about a year ago. Killed in action." His voice tightened around that knot of grief, but he forged on. "No kids, but I wanted three. Now your turn. Kids? Husband? Siblings?"

"I can't play this game." He saw a quick flash of pain in her eyes before she glanced away.

Family was off-limits. Got it. He picked an easier question. "Not even your favorite color? That's not a state secret, right?"

She turned back with a slight smile, as if she appreciated the effort. "Sepia."

"Sepia?" He looked over at her. "That's brown, right?"

"It's a brown gray. It was originally made from the ink sac of a cuttlefish. *Sepia* is the Latinized form of 'cuttlefish.' "

Her earnest amber eyes stared over into his. Or were they *sepia*?

"See. That's a start." He shifted on the bed, trying to come up with another question. "Let's say today was Saturday, and you were home. What would you be doing?"

She looked down at the grimwolf jacket, almost as if she were embarrassed. "I'd be eating Lucky Charms and watching cartoons."

"I didn't see that answer coming." He imagined her sitting in pajamas with a bowl of cereal in her lap and cartoons on TV. Not a bad way to start a weekend.

"My roommate in college, Wendy, got me into it. She said I had a lot of cartoons to catch up on."

After her freaky childhood, it sounded like Wendy had a point.

"So," Erin said. "Your turn. What would you be doing on a lazy Saturday morning?"

"Sleeping." He wished he had a cooler answer.

She looked sheepish. "I'm sorry I woke you up."

"I'm not." He reached over and smoothed a damp strand of hair back from her cheek, ready to back off if she gave any sign that she wanted him to stop.

Instead, she closed her eyes and rested her head against his hand.

He leaned across the grimwolf leather jacket and kissed her. He did it without thinking, as if his lips were meant to be there.

She let out a tiny sigh and slid her arms around his neck.

10:04 A.M.

Rhun awoke to the lemony smell of chemical cleaning fluid. He laid a palm against his aching chest, remembering.

He pushed himself up on an elbow. He was in a bedroom with white curtains drawn against the light. A few steps away a woman was lying on the wooden floor. Nadia. He remembered now. Nadia. Emmanuel. The bunker. He listened for Erin's and Jordan's heartbeats, heard them on the other side of a wall. The soft rumble of their voices comforted him.

He used the headboard to lift himself to his feet.

Nadia stirred, stretching like a waking cat. "Better?"

Rhun stood, swaying. "Were you hurt?"

"Only my leg." She stood, too, more easily than he had. "It will mend."

Rhun envied her. "Were the others wounded?"

"The soldier has luck," she said. "The woman is a talented shooter, even with a pistol, and she had the sense to stay low."

"Piers?" Rhun looked around the darkened room.

"Gone." Nadia explained all that had happened since Rhun was shot in the forest.

Rhun circled to the most disturbing question. "How did the Belial know where we were, where to ambush us?"

His team's departure from Jerusalem had been known only by the Cardinal and his innermost circle.

Nadia sighed, concerned. "I think the best course of action is for me to return to the abbey with news of Emmanuel's death, to claim you and the others died, too. That will give you time to operate outside the range of the Church and any spies, to hide your next steps on the way to the Blood Gospel."

Rhun nodded. They needed to keep their search secret from the Belial. "What about Piers? What will you say about him?"

"I'll tell them what I found," she said. "A shame that I only noticed *German* soldiers in the bunker. And *strigoi,* of course."

"So you will not tell them of the Russian soldiers?"

"If the Church learns that Russian soldiers from St. Petersburg had been in the same bunker as the Blood Gospel, they will send more than a *team* to Russia. It will be all-out war."

Rhun nodded. No Sanguinist had ever returned from St. Petersburg alive since the traitorous Vitandus took command there. To retrieve anything from Russia, the Church would have to send an army. And every casualty would weaken their order in the battle they must eventually fight against the Belial.

"We must go alone," Rhun said. "Both to prevent a war and for any hope of recovering the book."

"And what about the humans? It will be dangerous to bring them."

"The Vitandus may hate our order, but he maintains a strange sense of honor. It may be enough to keep them safe."

From the other side of the wall, Rhun heard Jordan's and Erin's hearts beat faster.

"I can plainly see your affection for them, Rhun," Nadia said. "Do you think that the Russian will not?"

"I can't leave them here." He tried to block out the sounds of Erin and Jordan. "If the Belial have agents within the Sanguinist ranks, their lives might be more at risk here than if I took them to Russia."

"Then the matter is settled." Nadia stood and put on her chain belt.

"I will need papers for us all," Rhun added.

"I will get them for you in secret."

Rhun considered the path on which he was about to embark. For the first time in his long, long life, he was about to be sundered from the Church, even if only for a time. He felt bereft.

Nadia headed toward the door. "And I will bring you something you can trade for safe passage. Something precious to the ruler of St. Petersburg."

Even Nadia did not dare to speak *his* name.

He had once been a Sanguinist, but he had broken the Church's laws so violently that he had been excommunicated—and not an ordinary excommunication, but a banishment that could not be undone, one so severe that all who knew him must shun him forever after.

In the end, his name had become his curse: Vitandus.

10:08 A.M.

Erin smiled when Jordan lifted her over the leather jacket and onto his lap. She now straddled him, staring down at his impish smile. "What happened to staying on your side?"

"You're the one who came over to my side." He kissed her lightly on the lips and a shiver ran down her spine.

She couldn't argue with that. With one foot, she kicked the grimwolf jacket onto the floor.

Jordan grinned up at her. "Problem solved."

She stroked a hand across his jaw. Smooth from his recent shave. She kissed him again. He smelled like eucalyptus shaving cream, and he tasted like coffee.

She pulled back and gazed into those beautiful blue eyes. "Your eyes are Egyptian blue, like the sun god Ra."

"I'm taking that as a compliment."

He slid one warm palm around the small of her back, then pulled her so tightly against his chest that she felt his heartbeat against her breast.

She relaxed against him, feeling safe.

Then he shifted his lips, found her mouth, and kissed her hard. A yearning urgency flowed from his lips to hers. She moaned between them and threaded her fingers through his hair, pulling him even closer.

She wanted to forget everything that had happened in the past twenty-four hours, blot out every bad memory. The only thing she had room for in her head was the two of them. He stroked his hands along her body.

With one arm around her back, he used the other to ease her around and under him on the bed.

She stretched under his weight, feeling his muscular bulk settle upon her. Her hands stroked down his broad back. She slid them under his shirt, felt the smooth warmth of his skin. He pulled his T-shirt over his head in one quick movement, revealing the blaze of his tattoo down one side, the branching fractal marking the lightning strike, a testament to his brief experience of death.

Her finger traced one of the forking lines, raising a shiver over his flesh.

He was far from dead now: his breath heaved, heat radiated from him, his eyes shone deep into hers.

Never breaking from her gaze, he undid the belt of her robe and smoothed back both sides. Only then did his eyes drift down, devouring her body, leaving heat in their wake without him even touching her.

"Wow," he silently mouthed.

She drew him down to her, gasping when his bare skin touched hers. His mouth found hers again. Erin lost herself in the kiss. Her heart raced against his, and her breath caught, held, then sped, too.

He raised his lips from hers, just a finger's breadth, and she lifted up to meet them again. He kissed down her throat. She tilted her neck and arched her head back against the pillow, feeling strands of wet hair fall across her face but not wanting to take her hands from his body for even a second to brush them away. His lips moved lower, grazed along the top of her collarbone, ending on the hollow of her throat.

"Erin?" His question brushed soft against her neck.

She knew what he asked, and she knew what she wanted to answer. But she didn't speak. "Wait." The word came out breathless. She pushed him away and pulled the robe closed. "Too fast."

"Slower," he said. "Got it."

She tied the robe. Her heart raced, and she wanted nothing more than to flee back to the warmth of his arms. But she didn't trust that. She couldn't.

A fist pounded the door.

A voice called through.

Nadia.

"Time to go."

45

October 27, 10:10 A.M., CET
Munich, Germany

As the jet lifted off, Bathory settled into the plane's soft seat with a sigh. In the darkness of the cargo hold, she felt Magor relax.

Sleep, my darling, she told him. *We are safe.*

For the first time in years, she was flying during the day, and without her *strigoi*. Where she was going, they had more to fear than just sunlight; their very existence put them at risk. It was a dangerous destination, but she felt safer without them.

She had chartered a plane, one whose pilot did not question her when the ground crew loaded the wolf into the cargo hold. He had stayed silent in his covered crate, as ordered, but they must have smelled him, known that he was a huge beast. For the right price, they had said nothing. She stretched luxuriantly in the wide seat of the jet. She had the plane to herself. The only others on board were the captain and the copilot.

How long since she had been so alone? Far from Him and His tools? Years.

She stroked the leather seat appreciatively and pulled up the window shade. Sunlight flooded into the cabin, falling across her legs, warming them. She held her hand palm up to the light, as if she could grasp hold of it. When she tired of that, she turned her attention to the bright landscape below.

The city of Munich gave way to farms, forests, and tiny, one-family homes that spread ever farther apart as the jet headed east. In each house, a family had just had breakfast. A father had kissed a mother good-bye, a child had gathered up a schoolbag and left. Those houses were empty now, but later they would fill again.

What would it be like to live in one of them?

Her destiny had been fated at birth. No simple life of husbands and children and domesticity. She usually felt only contempt for those living such a simple existence, but today she was drawn to its humble charm.

She shook her head. Even if she were free, she would not settle into another prison as a wife and mother. Instead she and Magor would hunt. They could range as far as they liked, living alone, never having to worry that He would punish her, that Tarek would finally have the revenge he had so long sought, not fighting every day for respect, for the right to live to see another sunrise.

Just thinking about it made her tired.

Magor stirred in the cargo hold, sensing her worries.

Rest, she told him, and he settled back down.

Her fingers stroked the black mark on her neck, the proof that set her apart from others. It would take a miracle for her to erase it, to escape Him.

What if the book could show her just such a miracle?

PART IV

Cursed shalt thou be in the city, and cursed shalt thou be in the field.
Cursed shall be thy basket and thy store.
Cursed shall be the fruit of thy body, and the fruit of thy land . . .
Cursed shalt thou be when thou comest in,
And cursed shalt thou be when thou goest out.

—Deuteronomy 26:16–19

46

October 27, 4:45 P.M., Moscow Standard Time
St. Petersburg, Russia

Erin had trudged through Russian customs half asleep, but she woke up fully when she and the two men reached the freezing sidewalk in front of the St. Petersburg airport. Rhun hustled them into a taxi with a broken heater and a driver who obviously had no fear of death. She was too scared to be cold as the driver careened through the thickening snowstorm, talking all the while in Russian.

Eventually the cab slid to a stop in front of what looked like a city park, a large space that was probably green in summer, with tall trees lining both sides. Right now the trees had naked limbs, and the frozen grass would soon be buried under thick white snow.

She could not believe how far she had come from the searing heat of Masada. Yesterday morning, her biggest weather worry had been sunburn; today it was hypothermia. As she climbed from the taxi, the St. Petersburg wind cut through her grimwolf leather coat and sucked warmth from the marrow of her bones. Instead of sand, gritty snowflakes stung her cheeks.

Overhead, the sun had changed into a pearly disk struggling to cast a white glow through banks of cloud, providing little light and less warmth.

Jordan walked close at her side as they crossed under a stone arch and into the park. She suspected that he wanted to take her hand, but she punched her fists deep in her pockets and kept walking. He looked hurt, and she couldn't blame him, but she didn't know what to do with him. She had been very close to making love to him back in Germany and was terrified by what would have happened if she had. She liked Jordan far too much already.

With each step, her sneakers slipped on the ice-glazed stone tiles of the path. To either side, the earth had been raised into knee-high grassy mounds. She eyed them, wondering what they were for.

Jordan had turned up his collar, his nose and cheeks already red. She remembered the feel of his jaw under her lips, the heat of his lips against her skin, and quickly looked away.

A few steps ahead, Rhun hadn't bothered with a coat and strode in a billowing black cassock, white hands at his sides, looking as comfortable as he had in hundred-degree heat atop Masada. In one hand, he carried the long leather cylinder that Nadia had left for them in Germany. Erin had no idea what it contained and suspected that Rhun didn't either. Before Nadia had given it to him, she had sealed the cylinder with golden wax and imprinted it with the papal seal—two crossed keys tied with a band and topped by the triple crown of the pope.

"Okay, Rhun." Jordan stepped up on the priest's right side. "Why are we here? Why did we come to this freezing park?"

Erin moved to Rhun's other side to hear the answer. He had told them only that their destination was St. Petersburg, that Russian forces might have brought the book to the city after the war. Erin had already surmised as much, picturing the dead Russian soldier in the bunker, remembering Nadia reading the Cyrillic orders. The soldier had been dispatched from this city.

Erin also knew the man had a wife and a child, a daughter who might still be alive, living in St. Petersburg, unaware that some strangers knew more about her father's death than she did.

Erin was glad that she had given Nadia the letters from the bunker to pass along to Brother Leopold. Maybe their efforts would bring the woman a small measure of peace.

"Rhun?" Erin pressed him, wanting to know more, deserving to know more.

The priest stopped and looked across the snow-covered mounds toward a copse of skeletal trees. Wind rattled stubborn and ragged leaves. "We have come here to ask permission to seek the book on Russian soil."

"Why?" Jordan said. "I thought Sanguinists didn't ask for permission."

Rhun's poker face concealed his emotions, but Erin sensed fear from him. She hated to imagine something terrible enough to frighten Rhun.

"St. Petersburg is not in our domain," he answered cryptically.

"Then whose is it?" Jordan asked. "After the fall of the Berlin Wall, the Catholic Church has a renewed presence here."

Erin stuffed her hands deeper into cold pockets and stared at the path's end, where she saw a large bronze statue of a woman in a broad skirt holding an object up into the air. Erin squinted, but couldn't quite make out what it was. She searched around the space. She had thought this was a city park, but an air of sadness permeated the air. She could not imagine children ever playing here.

"The Vitandus rules this land," Rhun answered Jordan. The priest touched the leather cylinder slung over his shoulder as if to reassure himself that he had not lost it. "And he has no love for the Church. When he comes, tell him nothing about our mission or yourselves."

"What's a Vitandus?" Jordan asked.

Erin knew that answer. "It is a title given as a punishment. There is no worse religious condemnation from the Church. It's worse than excommunication. More like a permanent banishment and shunning."

"Great. Can't wait to meet the guy. Must be a real charmer."

"He is," Rhun added. "So beware."

Jordan made an involuntary move for his holster, but they had been forced to leave their weapons in Germany. They flew here by commercial airlines, using false papers prepared by Nadia. But there was no way to smuggle in their weapons.

"What did this Vitandus do?" Erin asked, stamping her cold feet against the stone as if that would warm them. "Who is he?"

Rhun kept his gaze on the bare trees, watchful, wary, with a frightened cast to his eyes. He responded matter-of-factly—though the answer stunned her.

"You know the man better as Grigori Yefimovich Rasputin."

4:52 P.M.

Moving slowly down the tiled path, Rhun fingered his icy rosary and offered a prayer that Grigori would not order them immediately slaughtered, as he had murdered every Sanguinist sent to Russia since 1945. Perhaps the tube that Nadia had handed him offered some hope. She had instructed him to give it to Grigori unopened.

But what was it?

Did he bear a gift or a weapon?

Erin broke into his worries. "Rasputin?" Disbelief rang in her voice, shone in her narrowed eyes. "The Mad Monk of Russia? Confidant to the Romanovs?"

"The same," he answered.

Such details were what most historians noted about Grigori Yefimovich Rasputin. He had been a mystic monk rumored to have healing powers, his fate tied to Czar Nicholas II and his family. In the early 1900s, he had used those powers to ingratiate himself with the czar and his family, seemingly the only one capable of helping their son through his painful illness of hemophilia. For such tender care, they had overlooked his sexual eccentricities and political machinations, until eventually a British secret-service agent and a group of nobles had assassinated him.

Or so it was thought.

Rhun, of course, knew far more.

He drew in a deep breath of cold air. He smelled the fresh tang of snow, the underlying carpet of frostbitten leaves, and the faint tinge of old death.

Here was Russia.

He had not breathed its scent in a hundred years.

Jordan, meanwhile, surveyed the park, ever vigilant as he strode at Rhun's side.

Rhun followed his gaze. The soldier's eyes lingered on the dark tree trunks, the low stone wall, the plinth supporting a statue, all places where enemies might hide. He appreciated Jordan's wariness and suspicion, two valuable traits while standing on Russian soil. But their adversary had not yet arrived. For perhaps another few moments they were still safe.

They stopped at the grim dark statue of a woman staring into the distance, proffering a wreath to the lost citizens of St. Petersburg: the symbol of a mourning motherland.

Jordan blew into his hands to warm them, a gesture that spoke to his humanness and the fire burning inside him. He faced Rhun. "I thought Rasputin died during World War One?"

Erin answered him. "He was assassinated. Poisoned with cyanide, shot four times, beaten with a club, wrapped in a rug, and thrown in the Neva River, where he supposedly drowned."

"And this guy survived all that?" Jordan said with thick sarcasm. "Sounds like a *strigoi* to me."

Erin shook her head. "There are plenty of pictures of him in daylight."

Rhun tried to focus past their endless chatter. He heard a creature rustle among the trees a few yards off. But it was only a field mouse searching for grain before winter buried everything in snow. He hoped that the creature might find some.

"Then what is he?" Jordan asked.

Rhun sighed, knowing only answers would silence them. "Grigori was once a Sanguinist. He and Piers and I served as a triad for many years, before he was defrocked."

Jordan frowned. "So your order defrocked this guy, then punished him with eternal banishment?"

"An order of Vitandus," Erin reminded him.

The soldier nodded. "No wonder this guy doesn't like the Church. Maybe you need to work on your PR."

Rhun turned his back on them. "That is not the entire reason for his hatred of the Church."

He touched his pectoral cross. Grigori had *many* reasons—hundreds of thousands of reasons—to hate the Church, reasons that Rhun understood far too well.

"So why was Rasputin excommunicated?" Erin asked.

He could still hear the doubt in her voice as she spoke Grigori's name. She would not believe the truth until she could touch it. In this case, she might regret needing such reassurances.

Jordan pressed Rhun with more questions. "And what happens to an excommunicated Sanguinist? Can he still perform holy rites?"

"A priest is said to have an indelible mark on his soul," Erin said. "So I'm guessing he can still consecrate wine?"

Rhun rubbed his eyes—with such short lives, their impatience was understandable, their need for answers insatiable. He wished for silence, but it was not to be.

"Grigori can consecrate wine," Rhun answered tiredly. "But unlike wine blessed by a priest from the true Church, it does not have the same sustaining power of Christ's blood. Because of that, he is forever trapped in a state between cursed *strigoi* and blessed Sanguinist."

Erin brushed her hair out of her face. "What does that mean for his soul?"

"At the moment," Jordan said, "I'm more concerned about what it means for his *body*. Like can he come out during the day?"

"He can and does and will."

And soon.

"So why do we need his permission to be here?" Jordan asked.

"We need his permission because he has not let a Sanguinist leave Russian soil alive for many decades. He knows we are here. He will have us brought to him when it is time."

Jordan turned on him, his heart spiking with anger. "And you couldn't have told us this sooner? How much danger are we in?"

Rhun faced his fury. "I believe that we stand a good chance of leaving Russia alive. Unlike the others who have come here, the Vitandus and I have a more nuanced relationship because of our shared past."

Jordan's hand strayed to the side where his weapon usually hung. "So the men in the black rattletrap who have been following us since the airport . . . they belong to a Russian *strigoi* mobster with a shoot-on-sight order for all Sanguinists?"

Erin jerked her head toward the distant street. "We're being followed?"

Jordan simply glared. "I had hoped they were Rhun's people."

"I have no people," Rhun said. "The Church does not know we are here. After the attack at Masada and then the events in Germany, I suspect the Belial have a traitor in the Sanguinist fold. So I had Nadia declare us all dead."

A muscle twitched in the soldier's jaw. "Oh, this just gets better and better."

A new voice interrupted, scolding in tone but amused nonetheless. "Such vehemence is unbecoming here."

They all turned as a man in the long dark robe of a Russian Orthodox priest circled around the bronze statue and approached on stocky legs. The edges of his robe swept the tiles. Around his neck he wore a pectoral cross, a triple-barred crucifix of the same Church.

He smiled as he closed upon them. His once-long hair had been cut an inch above his shoulders and was combed back to reveal a broad face and cunning blue eyes. His sable-brown beard was neatly trimmed, which it had not been during the years Rhun had spent with him.

Erin smothered a gasp.

Grigori, Rhun realized, must still look enough like his century-old photographs to put an end to her lingering doubt. He prayed that she and Jordan would remember his admonition to tell Rasputin nothing.

Rhun greeted him with the slightest bow of his head. "Grigori."

"My dear Rhun." Grigori inclined his square head toward Erin and Jordan. "You have new companions."

Rhun did not introduce them. "I do."

"As usual, you have chosen a wise meeting place." Grigori gestured toward the mounds to either side of the path with one powerful hand. "I might have killed you elsewhere, but not here. Not among the bones of half a million of my countrymen."

Jordan swiveled his head around, as if looking for those bones.

"He did not tell you where you are, perhaps?" Grigori clucked his tongue. "Ever the poor host, Father Korza. You are at Piskariovskoye Cemetery. It commemorates the lives of those lost during the siege of Leningrad. These mounds you see are mass graves. Precisely one hundred and eighty-six of them."

Erin stared aghast at the spread of grassy hummocks.

"They contain the bones of half a million Russians. Four hundred and twenty thousand civilians. They died during the years that the Nazis surrounded our city. When we fought and prayed for help. But help did not come, did it, Rhun?"

Rhun said nothing. If he said anything, it would fan to life the flame of Grigori's smoldering temper.

"Four years of unending slaughter. And yet do any of these graves weigh on your Cardinal's conscience?"

"I am sorry," Erin said. "For your losses."

"Even the child can apologize, Rhun. Do you see?" Grigori pointed back toward a car idling near the entrance to the cemetery. "Shall we move your poor companions out of the cold? I can see that they suffer under its bite."

Rhun spared Erin and Jordan a quick glance. They did, indeed, look very cold. He had so little to do with humans that he often forgot their fragility.

"Will you guarantee our safety?"

"No more than you will guarantee mine." Wind whipped Grigori's dark hair across his white face. "You must know that the time of your death is at my choosing now."

5:12 P.M.

Jordan wrapped an arm around Erin's shoulder. She didn't lean into it, but she didn't move away from it either. He faced Rhun and Rasputin, sensing between them the tension of old hostilities mixed with a measure of respect, maybe even dark friendship.

He kept his tone light. "How about we all talk about our imminent demise someplace *warm*?"

Rasputin's eyebrows rose high at his words, then he threw back his head and laughed. It sounded deep and merry and completely out of place in a snowy graveyard, especially after the threat to kill them. Jordan could see why they called him the *Mad* Monk.

"I like this one." Rasputin clapped a broad hand on Jordan's back, almost knocking him off his feet. He smiled at Erin. "But not quite as much as the beauty here."

Jordan didn't like the sound of that.

Rhun stepped between them. "Perhaps my companion is right. We could find a more amenable location for our conversation."

Rasputin shrugged heavily and led them back down the path to the waiting car. Once there, he indicated that Jordan and Erin should take the front seat. He and Rhun took the back.

Jordan opened the door to a wave of warmth. It smelled like vodka and cigarettes. He climbed in before Erin, to sit between her and Rasputin's driver.

The driver held out his hand. He looked around fourteen, and his snow-white hand felt colder than Jordan's.

"Name's Sergei."

"Are you old enough to drive?" It slipped out before Jordan could stop it.

"I am older than you." The boy spoke with a slight Russian accent. "Perhaps older than your mother."

Jordan suddenly missed his submachine gun, his dagger, and the days when all his enemies were human.

47

October 27, 5:15 p.m., MST
St. Petersburg, Russia

As the large sedan wound away from the cemetery, Erin held her outstretched fingers over the car's heater vent. Jordan had one arm across the back of the seat behind her. He was the only one in the car whom she trusted—and in truth, she barely knew him.

But at least he was *human*.

Right now that meant one hell of a lot.

Rhun and Rasputin spoke in measured tones in the backseat. As civil as they sounded, she could tell that they were arguing, even if she didn't understand a word of Russian.

The car screeched through the late-afternoon streets, bright Russian facades peeking like fairy-tale houses through plumes of swirling snow. They had at best another hour of daylight. If the Belial had followed them to Russia, would they attack again after nightfall? Was Rasputin at war with them, as he seemed to be with the Sanguinists?

Any answers would have to wait until she could get Rhun away from Rasputin.

After another ten minutes, the car slowed to a stop in front of a magnificent Russian-style church. Erin pushed her face closer to the window to see.

Onion-shaped domes topped with golden crosses soared into the sky, each dome more fantastical than the last—two gilt, one with bright swirls of color, others blue and encrusted with designs of gold and white and green. The facade sported columns, raised squares, arches, and an enormous mosaic of Jesus bathed in a golden light. Such fanciful opulence stole her breath away.

"Wondrous, yes?" the driver said with reverence.

"Stunning," she answered honestly.

"You see here the Church of the Savior on Spilled Blood," Rasputin said, leaning forward from the backseat. "Erected over the spot of Czar Alexander the Second's assassination in 1881. But he would not be the *last* Romanov to fall to the wrath of the people. Inside that church, you will see cobblestones once stained with Alexander's blood."

Despite the church's rich history, it lost some of its splendor in Erin's eyes as she listened to Rasputin's words. She had seen enough stones stained with blood, enough to last a lifetime. Still, she pushed open the car door and stepped into cold wind, more frigid than even the cemetery. She stared at dirty gray snowdrifts pushed up along the wall of the church by the stiff wind coming off the nearby river.

Jordan moved close enough to her to block the wind. He stared up at the elaborate construction. "Looks like someone had a gingerbread kit and a lot of spare time."

Rhun scolded in a low voice, "He is proud. Do not insult him."

Rasputin's answer carried through the wind and across the car. "They could do no more to insult me than you and those whom you love have done already, Rhun. But they would be wise not to anger me themselves. For now, I am feeling generous enough to grant them immunity because they are not Sanguinists."

"Guess it's good to be human," Jordan muttered with a crooked, wry smile.

Proving this, he reached down and threaded warm fingers through Erin's cold ones.

Together, they followed the two black-clad priests toward the twin arches of the church's entrance.

5:27 P.M.

Once they passed the entrance vestibule, Rhun stepped into the main nave. He knew what to expect, but what he saw still struck his senses deeply—as Grigori knew it would.

His gaze was immediately drawn to the mosaics covering every surface inside the space. Bright blues and golds and crimsons swam in Rhun's vision. Tiles depicting biblical stories shouted from every wall and ceiling: Jesus and the apostles, the stylized brown eyes of saints, the brilliant wings of angels. Millions of minuscule tiles formed and re-formed into biblical scenes. He closed his eyes, but they burned anew when he opened them.

His stomach roiled from the smells here, too: warm humans in the nave, incense, wine, old death seeping from the floor and cracks, and, somewhere, fresh human blood. He struggled against an urge to flee.

Rhun turned back toward the entrance, his eyes falling upon a vast mosaic over the doorway. Hundreds of thousands of small tiles depicted the greatest moment of Sanguinist history. He knew that Grigori himself had commissioned this very work, showing the rising of Lazarus from his tomb, the first of the Sanguinist Order to greet Our Lord, making his pact to serve Christ, to partake only of His blood.

Except for Rhun, Lazarus was the only member of the Order who had been converted before ever tasting human blood, before ever taking a single life.

How far I have fallen . . .

Rhun cast his eyes down. The majesty of the story of Lazarus helped him find his center amid the din and clamor of the vibrant church.

"Wondrous, is it not?" Grigori beamed at the monstrous home he had created.

"The mosaics are masterful," Erin agreed, striding past him, her head tilted up, studying all.

"Yes, they are."

Grigori clapped his hands, and shadowy figures appeared from doorways and alcoves, whirling into activity.

Rhun returned his attention to the room, noting that those who did Grigori's bidding had no heartbeats; most looked like their driver, so very young in face but so very old in years. These were *strigoi* who had made a pact with Grigori as their pope, creating a dark version of the Sanguinist order on Russian soil.

Upon Grigori's orders, the tourists in the church were hustled out the doors, which thudded closed and locked. Within minutes, only two human hearts still beat in the church.

Besides Rhun and his companions, the church held only Grigori's followers, fifty in all: men, women, and children whom he had turned into his own dark congregation, forever trapping them between salvation and damnation. They were not as feral as most *strigoi,* yet neither were they striving toward holiness like the Sanguinists.

A new shade of darkness had been brought into the world by Grigori.

Wooden pews were carried into the nave and lined up facing the altar. Electric lights were switched off, and long yellow beeswax candles flamed to life. The summer scent of honey fought the tainted odors of the dark congregation.

Erin and Jordan stayed close to Rhun near the back of the church. Jordan shifted warily from side to side, as if he expected an attack at any moment. Erin turned her focus to one fantastical mosaic after another. Even here, they each amply demonstrated their roles as Warrior of Man and Woman of Learning.

Rhun kept between them and Grigori's congregation, filling his own role.

Knight of Christ.

But his head whirled at the deep sense of *wrongness* here, as sacred images looked down upon Grigori's profaned flock.

Accompanied by young acolytes, Grigori climbed the black marble stairs to the altar with a stately tread. Ornate bloodred columns, lit by tall candles, flanked him. Behind his shoulder, the last light of day, a feeble orange glow, shone through high windows onto a mosaic of Christ feeding the apostles with the host and the wine, while angels beamed from above.

In this space, Grigori intoned his dark Mass.

The choir chanted ancient Russian prayers, clear voices soaring to faraway ceilings in rhythms and tones that humans could never attain, would never hear.

At last, hands led Rhun and the others to a pew. He followed, still unable to adjust to the bone-deep wrongness of this spectacle.

Then a warm hand touched his bare wrist.

"Rhun?" whispered a voice.

He turned and looked into Erin's questioning eyes. Their naturalness, their humanity, helped to ground him.

"Are you all right?" She tilted her head as they took seats in the pew.

He put his hand atop hers, closed his eyelids, and concentrated on the quick, sure beat of her heart, letting it blot out the profane music. One true human heartbeat was enough to keep it all at bay.

The singing stopped.

For a heartbeat, silence swallowed the church.

Then Grigori called everyone forward to accept the Eucharist, holding high a golden chalice. Disciples filed forward to receive their wine, their boots soft on the dark marble floor. Rhun remained seated with Jordan and Erin.

When the consecrated liquid touched their lips, smoke rose from their mouths as if they had just breathed fire. With bodies too impure to accept Christ's love, even the pale version of it that Grigori could offer, they moaned in agony.

Erin's heart squeezed to a faster beat, in sympathy with their pain, especially that of those who seemed no more than children.

Rhun stared at a young girl, who in life had been no more than ten or eleven, step away, her lips blistering, each breath a steaming gasp of agony and ecstasy. She crossed back to her pew and knelt with her head bowed in supplication.

Here was Grigori's greatest evil, his willingness to convert the young. Such an act stole their souls and cut them off from receiving Christ's love for all eternity.

Grigori's voice cut through Rhun's musings. "And now, Rhun. You, too, must accept my Communion."

He remained seated, refusing to take such darkness into his body. "I will not."

Grigori snapped his fingers, and Rhun's party was suddenly surrounded by a group of Rasputin's disciples, fouling his nostrils with the odors of wine and burnt flesh.

"That is my price, Rhun." Grigori's words boomed through the church. "Accept my hospitality. Drink of the sacred wine. Only then will I listen."

"If I refuse?"

"My children will not go hungry."

The disciples moved closer.

Erin's heart raced. Jordan's hands formed fists.

Grigori smiled paternally. "But your companions will fight, won't they? It will be no easy death. The man is a soldier, is he not? Dare I say, he is a *warrior*?"

Rhun flinched.

"And the woman," Grigori continued. "A true beauty, but with hands callused from work in the field, and also, I suspect, from holding a pen. I believe that she is most *learned*."

Rhun glared across the dark congregation toward Grigori at the altar.

"Yes, my friend." Grigori laughed his familiar mad laugh. "I know that you are here seeking the Gospel. Only prophecy would send you to my doorstep. And perhaps I will even help you—but not without a price."

Grigori cupped the tainted chalice in his palms and raised it.

"Come, Rhun, drink. Drink to save your companions' souls."

With no choice, Rhun stood. On stiff legs, he walked between the pews, mounted the hard stone stairs, and opened his mouth.

He braced himself against the pain.

Grigori came forward, lifted his chalice high, poured from that height.

Bloodred wine struck and filled Rhun's mouth, his throat.

To his surprise, this black sacrament did not burn. Instead, a welcoming warmth coursed through his body. Strength and healing surged within him, quickening even his still heart to beat—something it had not done in many centuries. With that quiver of muscle in his chest, he knew what was mixed in that wine, but still he did not turn his face away from the flowing chalice.

It filled him, quieting that endless hunger inside him. He felt the wounds that had been opened in the bunker pull closed. But best of all, he was enveloped in a deep contentment.

He moaned at the rapture of it.

Grigori stepped back, taking his chalice with him.

Rhun struggled to form words as the world around him wavered. "You did not—"

"I am not so holy as you," Grigori explained, looming over him as Rhun slumped to the marble floor. "Not since my excommunication from your beloved Church. So, yes, any wine that I give my followers must be fortified. *With human blood.*"

Rhun's eyes rolled back, taking away the world and leaving only his eternal penance.

At Elisabeta's throat, Rhun swallowed blood. In all his long years as a young Sanguinist, he had never tasted its rich iron against his tongue, save that first night when he became cursed, feeding on tainted strigoi *blood.*

Panic at the blasphemy gave him strength to swim against that bloodred tide, to pull his vision clear. The beating of his own heart, quickened by her surge of blood through him, slowed . . . slowed . . . and stopped.

Elisabeta lay under him, her soft body golden in the firelight. Dark hair spilled over her creamy shoulders, across the stone floor.

Silence now filled the room. But that could not be.

Always he heard the steady beat of her heart.

He whispered her name, but this time she did not answer.

Her head fell to the side, exposing the bloody wound on her throat. Rhun's hand rose to his mouth. For the first time in many years, he touched fangs.

*He had done this. He had taken her life. In his blind lust, he had lost himself, believing himself strong enough—*special *enough, as Bernard always claimed—to break the edict placed upon those of his order, to maintain chastity lest they free the beast inside them all.*

In the end, he had proven to be as weak as any.

He stared down at Elisabeta's still form.

Pride had killed her as surely as his teeth.

He gathered her cooling body into his lap. Her skin was paler than it had been in life, long lashes soot black against white cheeks. Her once-red lips had faded to pink, like a baby's hand.

Rhun rocked and wept for her. He had broken every commandment. He had loosed the creature buried within him, and it had devoured his beloved. He thought of her vibrant smile, the mischief in her eyes, her skill as a healer. The lives she would have saved now withering as surely as hers had.

And the sad future of her motherless children.

He had done this.

Under the fire's hissing a faint thump *sounded. A long breath later, another.*

She lived! . . . But not for long.

Perhaps only long enough to save her. He had failed her so many times and in so many ways, but he must try.

The act was forbidden. It defiled his most basic oaths. Already he had defiled his priestly vows, at a terrible cost. The cost would be even greater if he also broke the vows of a Sanguinist.

The penalty for him would be death.

The cost for her would be her soul.

The first law: Sanguinists may not create strigoi. *But she would not be* strigoi. *She would join him. She would serve the Church as he did, at his side. As Sanguinists, they would share eternity. He would not fall again.*

Fainter, her heart throbbed.

He had little time. Almost none. He slashed his wrist with his silver knife. The hissing and burning were stronger, now that he was no longer holy. His blood, now mixed with hers, welled out. He held his wrist over her mouth. Drops splattered onto bloodless lips. Gently he parted those lips with his own.

Please, my love, he begged.

Drink.

Join me.

Rhun woke to hunger on the cold marble, the points of his fangs sharp on his tongue.

Grigori's cursed wine had been spiked with human blood. Rhun fought against that treachery. But his body, even now, demanded more, insisted upon release.

His ears picked out the twin heartbeats at the back of the church.

He staggered to his feet, shaking with desire, turning inexorably toward the thrum of life, like the face of a flower turning to the sun.

"Do not deny your true nature, my friend," Grigori whispered seductively behind him. "Such measures of control must always snap. Release the beast within you. You must sin greatly in order to repent as deeply as God demands. Only then will you be closer to the Almighty. Do not struggle to withstand it."

"I *shall* withstand it," Rhun gasped out hoarsely.

His ears rang, his vision dimmed, and the hand at his cross trembled.

"You didn't *always,*" Grigori reminded him. "What did you see when you drank my wine? Perhaps the defilement of your Elisabeta?"

Rhun turned and lunged for him, but Grigori's troops fell upon him, ready for such an assault. Two boys held each of his arms, two encircled each leg, another two pulled at his shoulders.

Still, he fought, dragging them all across the marble floor.

Paces away, Grigori laughed.

"Rhun!" Erin called to him. "Don't!"

He heard the fear in her voice, in her heart—for them all.

Grigori heard it, too. Nothing escaped him.

"Look, Rhun, how she knows to fear you. Perhaps it will save her, as it did not save your Lady Elisabeta Bathory."

Rhun heard the gasp behind him, one of recognition, coming from Erin.

Shame finally drew him to a stop, down to his knees.

Grigori smiled over him. "So even your friend knows that name. The woman whom history would curse as the Blood Countess of Hungary. A monster born out of your very love."

48

October 27, 5:57 p.m., MST
St. Petersburg, Russia

Cold hands clutched and held Erin to the rear pew. Frigid bodies pressed from all sides. She forced herself to stay still, not to yield to fear, and most of all, not to provoke an attack. Jordan leaned against her, his body as tense as hers.

The next moment would determine everything.

Rhun turned from his pursuit of Grigori. He met her gaze. She read the raw hunger there, his eyes almost aglow with it. In the pain of his grimace, the points of his fangs punctured his own lips. He clearly fought a battle against his bloodlust.

From Rhun's reaction, she assumed that Rasputin had tainted the wine with human blood.

Resist it, she sent silently to him, keeping her eyes locked upon his, refusing to look away, to face the beast inside him and his shame.

At last, Rhun's shoulders sagged and he sank to his knees. He raised his folded hands before his nose. Past his fingers, he still locked gazes with her. His mouth moved in a silent Latin prayer. She read those bloody lips, knew that prayer of atonement from her days spent kneeling in the dirt as punishment.

She shook off those who held her and sank to her knees at her pew.

In unison with Rhun, she recited that Latin plea for forgiveness.

All the while she stared into Rhun's eyes.

At the end, his head finally bowed—when he raised it again, his fangs were gone.

He whispered to the church: "You have failed, Grigori."

"And you have triumphed, my friend. God's will be done." Rasputin did not sound disappointed. If anything, he sounded awed and reverential.

Grumbling, the congregants retreated from the pew, from behind Erin and Jordan.

Sergei patted Jordan's shoulder before stepping away. "Perhaps later."

Once Jordan was alone with Erin, he turned to face her as she rose from her knees and returned to her seat. His breath whispered warm against her cheek. "Are you all right?"

Not trusting herself to speak, she simply nodded.

She watched Rhun slowly regain his feet, still wobbly.

If she understood what Rasputin implied, it sounded like Rhun had defiled Elizabeth Bathory. Erin knew that name, one that echoed from the bloody legends of the dark forests of Hungary and Romania.

Elizabeth Bathory, also known as the Blood Countess, was often referred to as the most prolific and cruel serial killer of all time. In the 1600s, over the course of decades, the wealthy and powerful Hungarian countess had tortured and killed many young girls. Estimates of the number of her victims ranged well into the hundreds. It was said that she bathed in the blood of her victims, seeking eternal youth.

Such stories smacked of vampirism.

Did Rhun create that monster? Did he have those young girls' blood on his hands? Was that what haunted him every time he drank his transubstantiated wine?

A tragic sigh drew Erin's attention to the altar, back to the present. "You mentioned a *gift* on the car ride over here," Rasputin said, pointing to the leather tube over Rhun's shoulder. "Let me see it, and we shall see what it buys you."

Rhun pulled the tube from his back.

Rasputin motioned to Erin and Jordan like an excited schoolboy. "Come, let us *all* see."

As Erin left the pew with Jordan, Rasputin's acolytes cleared the altar, stripping it down to bare marble. Once finished, they were waved away to make room for Rhun, Erin, and Jordan.

She climbed the altar, the air richer in incense and the scent of burning candles.

Once they were all gathered around the altar, Rasputin rested his fists on his hips and looked avidly at the long brown leather tube. "Show me," he ordered.

Rhun ran a sharp nail through the papal seal and lifted the top off. He stared inside, his brows pinching together, then shook the contents onto the marble surface. A rolled-up piece of old canvas slid out and landed on the altar, unfurling slightly.

Rasputin leaned closer, and with gentle care, respecting the age of the canvas, he rolled it wide for all to see.

Erin gasped at the painting revealed under the candlelight. She recognized the work immediately. Painted by the deft hand of the Dutch master Rembrandt van Rijn.

It was an original.

It depicted Christ performing his most powerful miracle.

Raising Lazarus from the dead.

6:04 P.M.

Grigori dropped to his knees in supplication before the altar, before the oil painting, and one by one, his dark congregation followed suit.

Rhun remained standing, staring down at the image of Lazarus in his stone tomb.

It was a stunning rendition of that moment, a secret known to Rembrandt and recorded in his painting. The work was one of three known to exist.

In beautiful, evocative strokes, Rembrandt revealed Lazarus, clad in his death shroud, rising from his granite sarcophagus. To the side, family members started back in horror. These spectators to the scene held up their hands as if to protect themselves from the man they had once loved. To them, this was not a joyous moment of resurrection. For they knew what had killed Lazarus.

"The first Sanguinist." Erin's whisper carried across the now-silent church.

Yes, those beside the tomb had witnessed the birth of the Order of the Sanguines. Lazarus had been attacked and turned to a *strigoi*, but his family had found him and sealed him into a crypt before he was able to feed on a human victim. There they doomed him to a slow death by starvation. But Christ arrived and set him free. For on that day Christ offered Lazarus a choice that no *strigoi* before could ever have been offered. Lazarus could not change his nature, but he could use Christ's love and blood to struggle against it. He could choose to serve Christ, and perhaps someday see the resurrection of his own soul.

This pact of duty, of service as a Knight of Christ, was represented in the painting by weaponry—the sheathed sword and sheaf of arrows—hanging above Lazarus's crypt, ready to be taken up in service of the new Church.

From that moment onward, Lazarus had accepted his burden and formed the Sanguinist side of the Church. Fresh from his crypt, he had never tasted human blood. He had always found sustenance simply in the blood of Christ. Only one other Sanguinist, since the dawn of time, had started his next existence ready to follow in Lazarus's footsteps; only one other had been turned before his first kill.

Pure. Untainted.

Long ago, Rhun had been that Sanguinist. He had thought himself worthy of prophecy. Had believed in his goodness. Had taken solace in his pride. Until the day he tasted Elisabeta's blood. The day he created a monster.

In that moment he had fallen. Only the One had ever kept himself undefiled.

Lazarus.

Their true father.

Even Grigori recognized that role. He traced the holy form of Lazarus on the painting, his finger slowing as it crossed a thin line of red dripping from the corner of Lazarus's mouth.

How could anyone look upon this painting and not recognize the truth revealed by Rembrandt? The scared spectators, the blood on the lips, the weapons on the wall. Rembrandt had been privy to the Sanguinists' secrets, one of the few ever allowed such knowledge outside the inner circle of the Church. To honor that trust, he produced this masterwork of light and shadow, to hide a secret in plain sight as a memorial and testament to their order.

Grigori regained his feet, his eyes lifting from the painting to a mosaic in his own church, sprawled above the entrance. It depicted

Lazarus in his shroud, standing alive at the door to his tomb, his hood up to protect his face from the sunlight. Christ stood before the risen man, his hand outstretched toward his new disciple as his followers looked on in wonder, much as Grigori's followers looked to him.

Tears shone in Grigori's eyes as he faced Rhun.

"I will help you search for your book, my friend, and, unless God wills otherwise, no grievous harm shall come to you while you are within the borders of my land."

October 27, 6:08 P.M., MST
St. Petersburg, Russia

Jordan stood a few steps from the altar, watching the others.

He didn't trust any of them. Not Rasputin with his crazy laugh and his games, not the waiflike congregants who had finally retreated into the shadows, not even Rhun. He pictured that glowing bloodlust in his eyes, the way he stared at Erin, locked on her like a lion on a fatted calf.

Worst of all, Jordan could have done nothing if she had been attacked. Grigori's minions had him trapped, weighing down his every limb, his strength useless against them.

Voices drew his attention away from the altar. Rasputin's children spoke in hushed tones as they carried a wooden table and four clunky chairs into the nave. Although the dark chairs had to be heavy, the boys lifted them as if they were made of balsa wood.

Unlike Rasputin, his acolytes wore regular street clothes instead of priestly garb. Jeans or black pants and sweaters. If he hadn't known what they were, he'd have assumed them to be pasty Russian schoolchildren and their parents.

But he did know.

"Come." Rasputin strode from the altar to the table, leading the others and collecting Jordan in the wake of their passage. The Mad Monk sat quickly, straightening his robes like a fussy old lady. "Join me."

Erin found a seat, and Jordan took the one next to her, leaving the last for Rhun.

Sergei set a giant silver samovar in the middle of the table. Another of Rasputin's minions brought in tea glasses that fit into silver holders with handles.

"Tea?" Rasputin asked.

"No, thanks," Jordan mumbled.

After seeing what happened to Rhun, Jordan had no intention of eating or drinking anything Rasputin had touched. He'd rather not even breathe the air.

Erin declined, too, but from the way she pulled the ends of her sweater down over her hands, she was probably cold enough to want something hot to drink.

"Your companions don't trust me, Rhun." Rasputin bared square white teeth. His fangs were retracted, but Jordan didn't find him any less dangerous for it.

None of them responded. Apparently the subject of Rasputin's trustworthiness would never take up a lot of conversation.

Rasputin turned to Rhun. "Pleasantries aside, then. What makes you think the Gospel might be here in my city?"

"We believe it may have been brought back by Russian troops at the end of the Second World War." Rhun kept his palms flat on the table, as if he wanted to be ready to push back and stand, either to fight—or possibly to flee.

"So long ago?"

Rhun inclined his head. "Where might they have taken the book?"

"If they knew what they possessed, they would have taken it to Stalin." Rasputin rested his elbows on the table. "But they did not."

"Are you certain?"

"Of course. If they had taken it anywhere of significance, I would have known. I know everything."

Rhun rubbed his index finger where his *karambit* rested when he fought. "You have changed little in the last hundred years, Grigori."

"I assume you refer to my sin of pride, which always made you worry so for my soul." Rasputin shook his head. "Yet it is *your* pride which needs looking after."

Rhun inclined his head. "I am aware of my sins."

"Yet, every day, you suffer the foolishness of penance."

"And should we not repent our sins?" Rhun's fingers found his pectoral cross.

Rasputin leaned forward. "Perhaps. But are we forever defined by our sins? How is a moment or two of weakness so large a crime when weighed against centuries of service?"

Though inclined to agree with him, Jordan suspected Rasputin might have had more than a couple of weak moments in his time.

Rhun tightened his lips. "I am not here to discuss sin and repentance with you."

"A pity." Rasputin looked at Erin. "We've had many enlightening discussions about that over the years, your Rhun and I."

"We are here for the Gospel," Erin reminded him. "Not enlightenment."

"I have not forgotten." Rasputin smiled at her. "Tell me from where was it taken and when?"

Rhun hesitated, then spoke the truth. "We found evidence that the book may have been at a bunker in southern Germany, near Ettal Abbey."

"Evidence?" Rasputin fixed his intense eyes on Jordan, as if he were more likely to answer than Rhun.

Jordan tensed. His instinct was to hide everything from Rasputin that he could. "I'm just the muscle."

"Russia is a big land." Rasputin looked to Erin. "If you do not help me, I cannot help you."

Erin glanced at Rhun. She tugged at the cuff of her sweater.

"Piers told us," Rhun answered. "Before he died."

Rasputin's face drooped. "Then he turned to the Nazis after all?"

When Rhun did not answer, Rasputin continued: "He came to me early in the war. I was not as comfortable as I am now." He paused and gazed around at the church, smiling at the silent followers lined up against resplendent walls. "But even then I had my resources."

Surprise flickered across Rhun's face. "Why would he go to you?"

"We were close once, Rhun. Piers as first, you as second, and I as third. Do you honestly not remember?" Hurt was plain in his voice, with an undercurrent of anger. "Where else could he go? The Cardinal threatened to excommunicate him if he continued searching for the book. So after visiting me, Piers went next to the Nazis, seeking help that I could not provide. He refused to give up the hunt. Obsessions are hard to forsake, as you can attest with Lady Elisabeta."

Rhun turned away. "Cardinal Bernard would have done no such thing to Piers."

But Jordan heard the lack of conviction in Rhun's words. Even with the little experience Jordan had with the Cardinal, he knew how much importance the man placed upon the prophecy of the three. To the Cardinal, Father Piers had no role to play.

How wrong he was . . .

Grigori continued: "Rhun, you do not know your precious Cardinal so well as you think. Remember, he excommunicated *me*. For committing a sin no greater than your own. And I did not take the life of the one I sought to save."

"What are you talking about?" Jordan asked, feeling like he'd walked into the theater in the middle of a movie.

Erin sat straighter, guessing the truth. "You're referring to Czar Nicholas's young son, aren't you? The boy named Alexei."

Rasputin favored her with a sad smile. "The poor child suffered. Finally, he lay near death. What was I to do?"

Jordan now remembered the history. The czar's son was once Rasputin's young charge. Like many of Queen Victoria's grandchildren, he had suffered from what was known as "the Royal Disease" of hemophilia. According to history, only Rasputin could bring him relief during his episodes of painful internal bleeding.

"You should have let him die a natural death," Rhun said, "within the grace of God. But you could not. And afterward, you would not repent for your sin."

Jordan pictured Rasputin turning the boy into a monster rather than letting him die.

"That is why you could not be forgiven," Rhun said.

"What makes you think I wanted the Cardinal's forgiveness? That I needed it?"

"I think we have gotten off topic here," Jordan cut in. Rhun and Rasputin's old arguments did not advance their cause. "Will you help us find the book?"

"First tell me, how did Piers die?" Rasputin took Erin's hand. She looked like she wanted to take it back, but she didn't. She should have. "Please."

She told him of the cross in the bunker, of the moment in the boat when Piers passed on.

Rasputin dabbed at his eyes with a large linen handkerchief. "How can you explain that, Rhun?"

"God's grace." Rhun's words were simple and fervent.

"Explain what?" Erin asked, looking between them.

"Tainted as Piers was for breaking his vow, for creating and feeding upon *blasphemare* creatures, he should have been burned to ashes by the sunlight." Rasputin folded the handkerchief and secreted it away in his robes. "That is what happens to *strigoi* who do not drink the blood of Christ. Has Rhun told you nothing?"

He hadn't told them much. Just that sunlight killed them, not that they burned up. Jordan remembered how Nadia had carefully lifted the coat from Piers's face, and her fear as she held him against her side so that he might see the sun one last time. His death had seemed peaceful, not violent, more of a letting go. Had God somehow forgiven his sins at the end or was there enough of Christ's blessing still within Piers's veins to keep him from burning? He suspected they would never know the true answer, and at the moment they had a more important concern.

"The book," Jordan said. "Let's get back to the book."

Rasputin straightened, visibly drawing back to the matter at hand. "The German bunker was far south. Do you know *when* Russian troops might have reached it? If I had a time line . . ."

Jordan tried to remember his history, expecting Erin to interrupt with the answer. "The last major German unit in the south surrendered on April twenty-fourth, but the Russians were probably still mopping up until the formal surrender of Germany on May eighth."

He counted off dates in his head. "By mid-May, though, the Russians were formalizing the division of Germany and the whole of the Iron Curtain. I would guess the Russian smash-and-grab teams peaked around May twentieth, although there were probably Russians clearing out bunkers before and after."

Rasputin eyed him with what might be respect. "You indeed know your history."

Jordan shrugged, but he kept talking, eager to find the book and get the three of them out of Russia alive. "I've studied a lot about the World War Two era, heard a lot more from my grandfather who fought during it. Anyway, *that* bunker was far south and isolated. Calculating travel time back then, plus a buffer to get out before American troops began their patrols, I would guess the most likely time for the Russians to have hit the bunker would have been between May twenty-eighth and June second. With a wide margin of error, of course."

Erin gave him a surprised look, as if she hadn't expected him to know anything useful. Which was getting old.

"Impressive, Sergeant." Rasputin leaned back. "That information is valuable. Although it will still take time to find the book."

How did Rasputin know that Jordan was a sergeant? That was worrisome.

"Why is it valuable?" Erin asked. "Why do the dates matter?"

"First, tell me what you are hiding in your coat, my good doctor."

So he knew Erin had a Ph.D., too, Jordan realized, and that she had the pieces of concrete that had surrounded the book in her pockets. What didn't he know?

"I can smell it," Rasputin said.

Erin looked to Rhun. He nodded, and she drew out a piece of the book's encasement. "We believe this might have been covering the book."

Rasputin held out his hand, and Erin slowly dropped the gray fragment into his palm. His thumb followed the thin lines of soot that showed where the stone had been blasted apart.

Jordan snapped upright. He should have thought of this before. "If you get me an explosives sensor, I can use that piece as a control and find anything else with the same chemical signature. If this was wrapped around the Gospel, the book would have the same chemical breakdown products on its cover. Assuming it wasn't destroyed in the blast."

Rhun touched his cross again, looking shocked. Apparently the priest hadn't considered the possibility that the book might have been destroyed, that they might be risking their lives to search for something that had been blasted to fragments and ashes.

Rasputin nodded to Sergei, who stepped forward. "Go with my personal assistant. He will help you procure the item that you need."

Jordan stayed seated. "We move as a team."

6:17 P.M.

Rasputin frowned, then laughed. Erin hadn't thought that she could hate that laugh more than she had the first time she heard it, but she did.

"Very well," Rasputin said. "Write down the details for Sergei."

Sergei produced a spiral-bound notebook and pencil stub from his back pocket.

Erin took the concrete piece off the table and slipped it back into her pocket, worrying that Rasputin might steal it. He was clearly an opportunist and not one to underestimate. He already knew too much: that she was a doctor, that she and Rhun and Jordan searched for the book, and that they were possibly the trio of prophecy. And from the greedy glint in his eyes when Jordan had listed the likely dates the bunker had been breached, she also suspected that he already had a good idea about the book's location.

Clearly, Rasputin enjoyed making them dance like trained monkeys, but was it more than malicious pleasure?

Their host rose and gestured toward a black tabernacle at the rear of the church. "Shall we view the very cobblestones where the czar fell? The namesake for this church."

She pushed back her chair. Jordan and Rhun stood, too. They walked behind Rasputin's slope-shouldered form like a Sanguinist trio, Rhun in front, Jordan flanking the right, and Erin the left.

Rasputin stopped in front of the tabernacle. Four polished black columns supported an ornate marble canopy carved in Russian folk-art style, with jet-black stone flowers and flourishes. Behind a small gate lay a simple section of gray cobblestones. Its utilitarian nature clashed with the church's elaborate grandeur, reminding Erin why this giant building had been constructed—to memorialize the murder of the czar. She contrasted the soaring ceilings and rich gold tiles with the simple mounds of earth in Piskariovskoye Cemetery.

Some deaths were marked better than others.

A handful of Rasputin's followers came and stood in a semicircle behind them, as if bound to their leader by invisible cords.

"I came here often during the siege of Leningrad," Rasputin said, resting his hands on the wooden edge of the tabernacle. His sleeves rode up, displaying thick black hair on his wrists and lower arms. "The church was deconsecrated. The holiness stolen back by Rome.

But the building was good enough for the dead. They used this nave as a morgue in winter. Piled bodies against the walls."

Erin shivered, imagining frozen corpses stacked like carcasses in a slaughterhouse, awaiting a spring burial.

"As the siege stretched and the hunger grew worse, the bodies were brought here by wooden carts pulled by living men. The horses had been eaten by then. The dead came as they were born: naked. Every scrap of cloth had to be saved to warm the living." Rasputin's voice sank to a hoarse whisper. "I lived in the crypt. No one thought to check the dead. There were too many. Nights I came up, and I counted. Do you know how many children died in the siege? Not just from the cold, although it was bitter and claimed its share. Not just from the hunger, although it drove many to their death. Not even from the Nazis and the death they rained from the sky and the land all around. No, not even them."

Erin's throat closed. "*Strigoi?*"

"They came like a plague of locusts, devouring the weak and starving souls huddled here. I escaped to Rome and begged for help." Rasputin turned to Rhun, who lowered his eyes. "The Church was neutral in the war, but never had Sanguinists forsaken their war against *strigoi*. Until then."

Erin hugged her chest. *Strigoi* would have found easy prey in the besieged city.

"So I came back alone from Rome. I fought through troops until I was back inside the charnel house that the city I loved had become. And when I came upon dying children, I saved them, brought them into my fold. With my own blood, I built an army to protect my people from the curse."

Rasputin gestured to those acolytes nearby with one black-clad arm. "You see before you only a few of the lost children of Leningrad. Angels who did not die in filth."

They shifted their feet, pale eyes fixed on him, in worship.

"Do you know how many people died here, Doctor?"

Erin shook her head.

"Two million. Two million souls in a city that once housed three and a half million people."

Erin had never confronted someone who had seen the suffering, counted the Russian dead. "I'm sorry."

"I could not stand aside." Rasputin clenched his powerful hands into fists. "For *that,* I was shunned. A fate harsher than excommunication. For saving children. Tell me, Doctor, what would you have done in my stead?"

"You did not save them," Rhun said. "You turned them into monsters. Better to let them go to God."

Rasputin ignored him, deep-set blue eyes focused on Erin's. "Can you look into the eyes of a dying child and listen to a heartbeat fade and do nothing? Why did God give me these powers, if not to use them saving the innocent?"

Erin remembered watching her sister's heartbeat slow and stop. How she had begged her father to let them go to a hospital, how she had prayed for God to save her. But her father and God chose to let an innocent baby die instead. Her own failure to save her sister had haunted her entire life.

She slipped her hand into her pocket and touched the scrap of quilt. What if she'd had Rasputin's courage? What if she had used her anger to defy her father, renounced his interpretation of God's will? Her sister might still be alive. Could she fault Rasputin for doing something she wished she had done herself?

"You corrupted them." Rhun touched her sleeve, as if he sensed her sorrow. Rasputin's eyes dropped to follow his hand. "You did not save those children. You kept them from finding eternal peace at God's side."

"Are you so sure of this, my friend?" Rasputin asked. He turned from the tabernacle to face Rhun. "Have you found any peace in your service to the Church? When you stand before God, who will have a cleaner soul? He who saved children or he who created a monster out of the woman he loved?"

Rasputin's eyes fell upon Erin at that moment.

She shivered at the warning in that dark gaze.

50

October 27, 6:22 P.M., MST
St. Petersburg, Russia

Before Rhun could respond to Grigori's contempt, they were interrupted. All eyes—except for Erin's and Jordan's—swung toward the entrance to the ornate church. Again Rhun's senses were assaulted by the reflection of flickering candlelight off millions of tiles, patterned marble, and gilt surfaces.

Past it all, he heard a heartbeat approach the outer door. The rhythm sounded familiar—*why?*—but between Erin's and Jordan's own throbbing life and the head-swimming sensory overload, he could not discern what set his teeth on edge.

Then a knock.

Now Erin and Jordan turned, too, hearing the strong, demanding strike of knuckle on wood.

Grigori raised his hand. "Ah, it seems I have more visitors to attend to. If you'll excuse me."

His dark congregants surrounded Rhun and his companions, driving them toward the apse.

Rhun continued to stare toward the door, casting out his senses toward the mysterious visitor, but by now the smell of blood and burnt flesh wafting from Grigori's acolytes had engulfed him, too. Frustrated, he took a deep breath and offered up a prayer for patience in adversity. It did nothing to calm him.

Grigori slipped away with an insolent wave and vanished into the vestibule and out the door into the cold night.

"I'm getting tired of being herded around," Jordan said as he was elbowed closer to Erin.

"Like cows," Rhun agreed.

"Not a cow," the soldier said. "Like a *bull*. Let me keep my dignity. Such as it is."

As they waited, Erin crossed her arms. She seemed the calmest of the three. Did she trust that Grigori would keep his word, that they would come to no harm? Surely she was not so foolish. Rhun tried to shut out the sound of her heartbeat and listen, straining at the door, but Grigori and his late visitor had moved too far away.

"Do you think he knows where the book is?" she asked, making it plain how little she actually did trust Grigori.

"I don't know. But if it is in Russia, we will never find it without his cooperation."

"And after that?" Jordan asked. "What then? What will he do—to you, to us? I imagine that won't be fun either."

Rhun relaxed fractionally, relieved that Jordan had seen through the monk. "Indeed."

Erin's voice remained resolute. "I think Rasputin will keep his word. But that may be as worrisome as if he didn't. He strikes me as someone who plays many levels of a chess game while always wearing a smiling face."

Rhun nodded. "Grigori is a man of his word—but you must listen carefully to each utterance from his lips. He does not speak casually. And his loyalty is . . . *complicated*."

Jordan glanced at the silent congregation, who kept their guard as they all waited. "Things would be easier here if the Church had kept *its* word. They should have helped during the siege, especially if *strigoi* came here to feed. Maybe then we wouldn't have Rasputin as our enemy."

Rhun fingered the worn beads of his rosary. "I pressed his case with Cardinal Bernard myself, told him that Christ had not saved us to show neutrality in the face of evil, that He made us to fight it always and in all of its forms."

Rhun did not tell them that he had considered following Grigori back to St. Petersburg during the war. He believed his inability to convince Bernard to help the besieged city was one of his greatest failures as a Sanguinist, possibly rivaling what he had inflicted upon Elisabeta.

One of the congregants stepped closer. It was Sergei, his eyes hard as glass. "So you admit that he was right?"

"Even a broken clock is right twice a day." Jordan folded his arms. "And *right* doesn't always mean *good*."

There, the argument stalled.

Erin seemed to spend the next hour studying the jewel-like mosaics, stopping to feel them where she could, as if she made sense of them through touch. Rhun could not stand to look at them. It was an affront to God to have such beautiful works of religious art in such a profane den.

Like a good soldier, Jordan returned to the table, sat down, and rested his head on the top, catching sleep when he could do nothing else. Rhun admired his practicality, but he could not settle to such calmness. He stretched his senses outside the church, listening to the rhythms of a city moving into night, the rumble of cars quieting, the muffled footfalls, the voices passing away, and underneath it all, the soft whisper of falling snow.

Then Rhun heard feet and a frantic heartbeat approaching the church's outer entrance. Heads turned, but Grigori's acolytes seemed to have already recognized the visitor, because they did not bother to herd Rhun and the others into hiding again.

Sergei disappeared into the vestibule and returned with a small greasy-haired man with a pointed nose. The stranger brought with him the icy smell of snow.

"It wasn't easy to get, what you asked." The man handed Sergei a sealed plastic case about the size of a shoe box.

Sergei gave him a roll of bills, which he counted with one nicotine-stained finger. He pocketed the roll, nodded once to Sergei, and on quick, furtive feet, disappeared back out into the night.

Sergei turned to them, to Jordan. "Now it is our turn to give gifts, *da*?"

6:38 P.M.

Jordan accepted the case, undid the small latch, and lifted the lid. He whistled appreciatively at what he found. Christmas had come early.

"What is it?" Erin brushed his elbow. The fresh laundry scent of the German hotel's shampoo drifted up, and he remembered that first kiss. "Jordan?"

It took him an extra second to collect himself.

"It's what I asked for earlier." He tilted the box to reveal a blue electronic device packed into gray foam cushioning, along with battery packs, carrying straps, manuals, and sampling tools. "It's a handheld explosives detector."

"It looks like an oversize remote control." She touched the blue casing with one bare finger. "One without enough buttons."

"This has enough buttons," Jordan said. "If it works properly, it can detect trace levels of explosive materials in the parts-per-quadrillion range. Anything from C-4 to black powder to ammonium and urea nitrates. Actually pretty much anything it can sample, it can search for."

"How does it work?" Erin looked like she wanted to take it right out of his hand to see.

"It uses amplifying fluorescent polymers." He pulled the detector out of the foam, earning a twinge from his bat-gnawed thumb. "The detector shoots a ray of ultraviolet light out and sees what happens in the fluorescent range after the particles are excited."

"Is it dangerous?" Rhun asked, eyeing it with suspicion.

"Nope." Jordan inserted the battery and turned on the device while they were talking. "May I have that piece of the book's concrete jacket?"

Erin fished it out of her pocket and put it in his hand, her cold fingers stroking across his palm. He didn't know if she did this on purpose, but she could keep doing it all day long.

Rhun cleared his throat. "Will it suffice for our needs?"

"It should help."

Jordan examined the scorch marks along one side of the crumbling lime-ash concrete. Once satisfied that it should offer a decent test sample, he set everything down on the table and got to work.

"I should be able to calibrate the device to match whatever explosive was used to shatter the cement jacket. It'll turn this little unit into our own personal electronic bloodhound."

He had only just finished his calibrations when Rasputin returned, beaming. Jordan tensed, glancing up at him. Anything that made Rasputin that happy could not be good for them.

6:46 *P.M.*

Erin turned to Rasputin as Rhun hovered nearby.

Jordan returned to doing some final adjustments on the explosives detector.

"Good evening!" Rasputin strode across to them. He seemed energized and overly enthusiastic, even for him. "I trust that the equipment we obtained is satisfactory?"

"It is," Jordan admitted grudgingly. "And it's ready to go."

"As am I." Rasputin rubbed his hands together and smiled. He looked greedy and happy, like a child about to go to an ice-cream store.

"You have a lead on the book?" Erin asked.

"Possibly. I know where it *might* have been taken if it was brought back to St. Petersburg on the dates specified by the sergeant."

Rasputin stepped closer, touched the small of Erin's back, and guided her toward the center of the church. She reached behind her and tried to pull his hand away. He left it there for a second, as solid as if it were made of stone. Then, with a tiny smile, he let her shift his arm aside. The message was clear: he was stronger than she was, and he would do with her as it suited him.

Seeing this, Jordan collected the detector, stood, and moved to her side, sticking close, either jealous or worried. She found that this thought didn't bother her as much as it had in Jerusalem. Body heat radiated across the small space between them.

Jordan's eyes darkened as it warmed him, too.

Rasputin drew them to a halt in the center of the church. He knelt on a stone mosaic and pulled out a single tile from the center of a flower. Sergei handed him a metal rod with a hook on the end like a crowbar. Rasputin wedged it in the hole and lifted out a circular section of the floor one-handed, revealing a dark shaft leading down.

With a gentlemanly flourish, he gestured to a metal ladder bolted in place on one side.

Erin leaned over and couldn't see the bottom, but it smelled rank. She bit back a sigh.

They were going underground.

Again.

Rhun slipped around Jordan and mounted the ladder first, climbing down swiftly.

Jordan dropped his detector into his pocket and waited for Erin to go second. He plainly intended to act as a buffer between her and Rasputin.

And she was happy to let him.

After first slipping her hand into her pocket to reassure herself that her flashlight was still there, she followed. Cold from the metal seeped into her fingers and palms as she grasped the rungs and began the longest ladder climb of her life.

Jordan followed, clambering down one-handed. Was he showing off or favoring his bitten hand? The wound ran deep, but he hadn't complained.

Above him, Rasputin and his congregants flowed down after them.

She turned her attention to the long journey down, counting the rungs. She had reached more than sixty when her toe stretched down and touched the icy floor.

Rhun helped her off the ladder. She didn't refuse. By now, her fingers had gone numb. She stepped aside to get out of Jordan's way, jamming her hands in her pockets.

Jordan gave her a quick grin as he hopped off the ladder. "When this is over, let's spend a week at a sunny beach. *Above*ground. And margaritas are on me."

She smiled back at him and fought down the urge to pinch her nose against the stench down here. It reeked of human waste.

Russian voices from above directed their attention back to Rasputin, his figure outlined in the circle of light as he climbed down. Behind the monk's shoulder, ten of his congregants followed him. Then someone replaced the metal cover over the hole and plunged them into darkness.

A half second later, Jordan's flashlight flared brightly, and Erin followed suit with her own.

Their twin beams showed them enclosed by a dingy gray concrete tube, with a ceiling so low that Jordan's head almost touched it. Green-and-brown frozen slime covered the floor and climbed the walls.

Erin fought against gagging. The reek of waste filled her mouth and crawled down her throat. She told herself she could stand it. It must be much worse during the summer.

Rasputin smiled grimly. "Not so pleasant as an ancient tomb, is it?"

Erin shook her head.

"This warren continues to serve as a tomb, I'm afraid," he said. "Each winter, the homeless children of St. Petersburg flee to the sewers. Tens of thousands of them. We bring them hot food and keep the sewers free of *strigoi,* but it is not enough. Innocents still die here in the dark, and still your precious Church does not care, Rhun."

Rhun tightened his lips but did not speak.

Rasputin lifted the hem of his robes with one hand, like a lady with a ball gown, and led them forward. Five of his acolytes trailed at his heels and another five brought up the rear behind Rhun, Erin, and Jordan.

Erin concentrated on watching where she stepped and on not slipping. She shuddered to think of any part of her touching the floor. It was comforting to have Rhun on one side and Jordan on the other, although the three of them could not hold their own against the ten who accompanied them—eleven if she counted Rasputin.

Rhun stumbled and caught himself against the wall.

Jordan shone his light toward him. "Are you all right?"

The acolytes pushed them forward, keeping them moving.

Rhun sniffed the air, as if to double-check something. He called up to Rasputin: "Is that an *ursus* I scent? Down here?"

Erin sniffed, but didn't smell anything.

"Not just *any* ursus." Rasputin's answer boomed down the tunnel. "*The* Ursa herself. Since we're down here, I think we should pay her a visit, for old time's sake."

The monk turned abruptly into a side tunnel, forcing them to follow.

Erin caught Rhun rubbing his right leg. She read worry there, along with fear.

Jordan must have seen it, too, because he took her hand again.

After trudging a few minutes more, she then smelled it, too. She had grown up in the California woods, and she recognized the familiar musky odor.

Bear.

Jordan's grip tightened on her fingers.

Ahead, Rasputin stopped at the crossing of two tunnels.

Like in the bunker, *X* marked the spot.

The tunnels came together in a chamber about fifty feet square. Wrought-iron gates blocked each of the four ways into the intersection, forming a massive cage. The metal had been worked into fanciful trees with connecting branches and leaves, like a forest. The pattern continued on the concrete walls with glass mosaics of trees and birds. The deep jewel tones and artistic renderings reminded Erin of the mosaics in the church far above.

In spite of the beauty, she fought down bile. A fouler stench underlay the musk of bear—the stench of rotting meat and old blood.

Jordan played his flashlight's beam into the cage and picked out a black mound of fur curled atop a nest of gray bones and spruce boughs.

Rasputin smacked both palms against the gate blocking them. "My dear Ursa! Awake!"

The blackness shifted into life—cracking branches and bones underneath it—as it rolled lugubriously to its stomach.

A scarred muzzle rose and sniffed the air. Then the creature lifted itself onto four unsteady legs and lurched upright.

Erin gasped at its sheer size. Its shoulders scraped the arched roof inside. She put the creature's height at around seven feet at the shoulder, probably fifteen feet when upright, if it could stand.

It shook itself once and came fully awake, turning the black wells of its eyes toward them, revealing a deep crimson glowing out of the bottomless depth. The shine spoke to its corruption and raised all the hairs over Erin's body.

Then in one lightning-fast leap, it charged at them.

Rhun swept in front of Erin, his arms raised, ready to protect her. She appreciated the gesture, but it would be futile if the bear broke through that gate.

"Darling Ursa," Rasputin crooned as the bear skidded to a halt before him. "One more meal before your winter's sleep?"

Erin's heart raced. Did he intend for *them* to be that meal? A quick look at Jordan and Rhun told her that they were thinking the same thing. Even the acolytes hung back, maintaining a healthy distance.

Reaching the gate, the bear rubbed its massive head against the iron, revealing gray fur interspersed with black. It was old.

Rasputin reached through the bars and fondled its ears. The bear huffed at him warmly, then swiveled its head toward Rhun, fixing him with those unnatural red eyes—and growled.

"Ah, see, she *remembers* you!" Rasputin chucked the bear under the chin. "After all these years. Imagine!"

Rhun ran his hand again down his leg. "I remember her, too."

Based on his expression, it was no happy memory.

"Your leg seems to have healed well," Rasputin said. "And you should not have been so careless."

"Why is she here, Grigori?" Anger hardened Rhun's voice.

"There was no safe place for her to overwinter in the wilderness," he said. "Humans might find her den. At her age, she is slow to wake. She deserves a quiet place to spend the cold months."

Rasputin rolled up his long black sleeve, drew a short dagger from his robes, and slit his own wrist. Dark blood welled out. He slipped his muscular forearm through the gate. The creature huffed again, sniffed, and licked his wrist. A long pink tongue wrapped around the monk's arm with each stroke.

All the while Rasputin murmured to the bear in Russian.

Erin covered her mouth in disgust, and Jordan swallowed hard.

As the bear nuzzled Rasputin's arm, its huge front foot kicked a round object through a gap in the gate's ornamentation. The sphere rolled to a stop in front of Erin's sneakers. She shone her light on it.

A human skull.

Judging by the tiny strips of flesh still clinging to it, it had come from a recent kill.

She danced back in horror.

Rhun spoke, his voice thick with command. "Enough, Grigori."

Rasputin withdrew his white arm from the fawning bear and tugged his sleeve down. He glanced back at the others. "Does the time press at you so, Rhun?"

"We are here to find the Gospel and leave." Rhun's dark eyes never left the bear. "As you promised."

"So I did." Rasputin drew a handkerchief from his sleeve and wiped his palms. "Follow me."

He headed back down the tunnel, slipping past the others, smelling of blood and bear.

They resumed their journey. Erin needed no urging to put distance between herself and the bear.

"Rhun?" she asked, keeping next to him. "What was that about you and the bear?"

He sighed impatiently. "The Ursa was once known as the Bear of Saint Corbinian. Do you know the story?"

Erin nodded. During her youth, she'd been forced to memorize all the saints and their stories. "Saint Corbinian, on his way back to Rome, encountered a bear who ate his mule. Afterward, Corbinian forced the bear through the will of God to accept a saddle, and it carried him home. But surely the monster here can't be *that* bear. That story goes back to the eighth century."

"The beast is a *blasphemare,* and they can live very long lives. Corbinian encountered the monster on the road and got it to serve him, a very rare event for a *blasphemare* creature to bow to the will of a Sanguinist."

Erin thought about Piers and the bats but remained silent.

Jordan glanced back over his shoulder. "That bear definitely looked big enough to ride."

"How did you encounter it?" she pressed.

"Eighty years ago there was word of a huge bear, one that was devouring peasants in Russia. Piers, Grigori, and I were sent to dispatch it."

"Looks like you didn't," Jordan said.

Rasputin dropped back and joined in the conversation, clapping a hand on Rhun's shoulder. "Not for want of trying. Rhun tracked her to her winter den. Piers was displeased by the mission and refused to help. But the Father proved most helpful after she nearly took off Rhun's leg."

Rhun touched his leg again. "That took over a decade to heal."

"The Ursa was merely frightened," Rasputin said. "She is a gentle soul."

Erin thought about the pile of human bones in her cage.

"She didn't look too gentle to me," Jordan added.

"After Piers and I removed Rhun from the Ursa's playful embrace, she escaped into the forest." Rasputin shook his head. "We never found her. Eventually we were recalled to Rome."

"But you found her now," Rhun said. "How?"

"She called to me," Rasputin said. "Once I left the Sanguinists and embraced my true nature, *blasphemare* began to seek me out."

"Abominations seeking kinship." Rhun sounded bitter.

"We are what we are, Rhun. Accepting your fate instead of fighting it grants you more power than you can imagine."

"I do not seek power. I seek grace."

Rasputin chuckled. "And, in all these centuries of striving, have you found it yet? Perhaps the *grace* you seek is within your *heart,* not within the walls of a church."

Rhun clamped his jaw closed tightly.

No one spoke for several minutes. They hurried along. The only sounds were the crunch of shoes against foul ice.

They passed several other tunnels leading off in both directions, also ladders leading up and down to other levels. Erin usually had a good sense of direction underground, but she would never be able to find the church again. Jordan seemed to be counting, so she hoped he had a better sense of where they were.

Finally, Rasputin stopped and mounted a metal ladder. Erin shone her light up, but couldn't see the end.

"Up we go," Jordan said, craning his neck. "Is it too much to hope that this takes us to a Starbucks?"

In short order, they all mounted the rungs and climbed.

The ladder emptied out into a clean concrete room. Erin was glad to leave the stench far below. She took a deep breath of the fresher air, clearing her lungs. The only feature in the small space was a gray metal box on one wall connected to cables running into the ceiling.

Rasputin ignored it and crossed to a gunmetal-gray door. He used a huge old-fashioned key to unlock it and led them into another room. Another door blocked the way from here, this time guarded by a modern keypad on the wall. His fingers darted across the keys, entering digits so quickly that Erin could not keep track.

The thick steel door, like a bank vault, trundled open.

Rasputin crossed gingerly over the threshold and waved them all into a darkened corridor with ocher walls. Other hallways branched off in many directions. It felt like stepping into a giant labyrinth.

Rasputin's pace hurried from there. Soon even Jordan gave up counting as they delved deeper into the maze.

After another ten minutes of traversing halls, climbing short staircases, and crossing dusty rooms, Rasputin stopped before an unremarkable wooden door with a black glass doorknob. It looked no different from a hundred others that they had passed.

Rasputin pulled free a massive key ring out of the folds of his robes. He fumbled through what must have been fifty keys before finally selecting one.

As he inserted the key, Rhun stationed himself between Erin and Rasputin. Jordan stood on her other side. The congregants from the Russian church stood in a semicircle behind them.

Rasputin twisted the key with a tired creak and pushed open the door. "Come!"

They followed him into a shadowy room that smelled of rust and mildew. Erin's throat itched, drawing a cough out of her. She wondered how long it had been since the room had been aired out. The scientist in her wanted to ask for a dust mask.

A few steps away, Rasputin pulled a string attached to a bare bulb hanging from the ceiling. Dim flickering light fell on piles of junk stacked against the walls. It looked like a hoarder's living room.

"Here we are!" Rasputin turned to his followers. "Wait outside. I think we are already too many for this space."

"Where are we?" Jordan asked as the lightbulb buzzed overhead.

"We are beneath the Hermitage," Rasputin said. "One of the largest and oldest art museums in the world."

Jordan glanced around the crowded room. "It doesn't look like much."

"These are the museum's storage areas," Rasputin said with a glare. "Above, the actual museum is quite lovely."

Erin felt a twinge of professional irritation. Like most academics, she had heard of the sorry state of the Hermitage's long-buried and decaying collection, but never had she imagined it would be *this* neglected. As she stepped forward, mice erupted from a pile of mildewed quilts.

She stumbled back, aghast. "This is where and how the museum stores its extra collections?"

Rasputin merely shrugged, as if to say, *What is history to someone who has lived centuries?*

She wiped her hands on her jeans and looked around in dismay. A framed picture leaning against the wall behind the quilts looked like an original Dürer woodcut of the Four Horsemen of the Apocalypse. The priceless woodcut had been tossed in haphazardly with broken tools and old rotting tapestries. Overhead, a black bloom of mold stained the roof, marking an old leak.

"This can't be the right place," she insisted.

Rasputin chuckled and nudged Rhun good-naturedly. "She is endearing, isn't she? This Woman of Learning of yours."

Rhun simply turned to Jordan. "You should try the detector in here."

As Jordan set about booting up the explosives sniffer, Erin refused to let it go. "Why has none of this been cataloged?"

Rasputin pulled what looked like a dirty dishcloth off a sculpture, like someone rummaging through a garage sale.

"Careful!" Erin touched the top of the exposed sculpture's downturned head, ran a finger along an extended leg. "This is a Rodin. A dancer. It's priceless."

"Likely," Rasputin agreed. The monk moved to a stack of leather-bound books, picking through them. Scraps of paper fluttered out of his hands to the ground.

Erin closed her eyes. She couldn't watch, and she hated to think of the damage that had been done to the artifacts in the museum and to the historical record.

Rhun sifted through a crate. "Why do you believe this is the right room, Grigori?"

"The date." Rasputin fingered a yellowed card affixed to the wall by a rusty nail. "This is one of the rooms where Russian forces, those returning in late May, warehoused the treasures plundered from Europe."

"How many other rooms are there?" Jordan had finally booted up his detector and swept it from side to side.

"Several," Rasputin said.

A piece of plaster fell from the ceiling, narrowly missing Erin's head.

"Are they all this disorganized?" Her head throbbed in time to the flickering bulb.

"Many are worse."

Sighing in defeat, she joined Rhun in his search.

It took them an hour to go through the first nest of rooms. Rasputin's minions did not help. They stood out in the corridor and smoked. *Smoking* wasn't doing the artifacts any favors either, but Erin supposed it was just another grain of sand in the hourglass marking the inevitable decay of these treasures.

Rasputin remained as gratingly cheerful as ever.

"One down, but more to come!" he announced, and led them down a damp corridor.

The next room, like the first, was crammed to the ceiling with a mishmash of useless and priceless objects, but here there was at least a theme—a martial or military one. Erin stared across the panoply of old Russian flags, piles of helmets, bayonets stacked up like cordwood, and what looked like a giant propeller stretching across the room.

The space was cavernous. They could search a lifetime in just this one room and never find something as small as a book.

Then Jordan's machine beeped.

51

October 27, 7:18 P.M.*, MST*
The Hermitage, Russia

Jordan whooped with delight.

Now we can get down to business—and soon, hopefully, get the hell out of here.

"Is the book here?" Erin hurried to his side, looking over his shoulder. Her breath brushed the back of his neck.

He had to step away. "Maybe. I don't know. But at least it's a positive reading. Something with a chemical signature equivalent to Nobel 808 is close. That's what I picked up on that chunk of rock in your pocket."

He swung the detector from side to side, almost bumping her. The sniffer led him to a tattered tapestry. He lifted it and it disintegrated under his finger, tearing apart with a quiet sigh.

This time Erin didn't scold him. She stuck close to his side.

Jordan stepped past the tapestry, following each beep of the detector deeper into the room. It led him toward the giant propeller that rested atop a wooden crate in the center of the room.

"I think that's from a MiG-3," he said, stroking a hand along the smooth metal. "Only a few thousand were ever made, but they kicked butt in dogfights on the eastern front."

"Is that what's setting off your detector?" she asked.

"Noooo . . ." He slowly knelt, pointing the tip of the device forward. "Whatever is triggering the detector is *underneath* the propeller. Probably in that crate."

"We will move the propeller," Rhun said, nodding to Rasputin.

Jordan glanced over his shoulder at the other men. It would normally take six or seven guys to lift this steel monstrosity. But then again, there was nothing *normal* about the pair.

The two men crossed to either side of the giant propeller, each shouldering himself under one of the steel blades. At a silent signal, they both straightened, lifting the massive hunk of aeronautics with a groan of metal. From the strain on their faces, the weight was taxing even their strength.

Jordan wiggled under the blades, trusting them not to drop it on his head. He reached the exposed crate and stared into its straw-filled depths. His heart thudded into his throat.

Oh, God . . .

"Anything?" Erin called.

To either side of him, Rhun and Rasputin struggled with the sheer mass of steel. Overhead, the propeller began to shake in their weakening grips.

"Freeze!" Jordan yelled. "Nobody move!"

7:22 P.M.

Hearing the panic in the soldier's heart as much as in his words, Rhun went dead still, as did Grigori. A fleeting fear passed through him with razored wings, cutting through his resolve: *had the propeller crushed the book?*

"What is it?" Erin asked. "Should I help you?"

"No!" The salty scent of fear wafted from him. "Stay where you are. And I mean everybody. Or we'll all die."

The soldier crawled backward away from the wall, his heart skittering.

Rhun waited, the propeller growing heavier in his hands.

Grigori gave him a mischievous grin. "Here we are, working side by side, one step from death, my *droog*. Just as in the olden days."

Jordan slowly rose to his feet. "You can't put the propeller back down. There's an unexploded ordnance stored in that crate. The detector did what it was designed for. Unfortunately, it found a bomb, not a book."

"Are you sure it's a bomb?" Erin asked.

"It's a Soviet antitank missile. And yes, I'm sure."

As always, Erin kept arguing. "Maybe the book is *under* the missile—"

"If it is, I'm not getting it out." Jordan pointed to the hall. "Sorry, guys, but I think you're going to have to take that to the far side of the room. If so much as a pound of weight presses on that missile, we're all dead."

"Did you hear that, Rhun? We must be *cautious*." Grigori gave a carefree laugh.

The sound took Rhun back decades. Grigori had been the most foolhardy member of the trio, unconcerned about the prospect of death—not for himself, not for others. His blithe bravery had saved Rhun's life many times, but it had also endangered it.

"Should the two of you evacuate before we attempt to move it?" Rhun asked.

"It wouldn't help," Jordan said. "If that missile goes off, it'll take out the building and half a city block around it."

Erin's heart sped up.

"I suggest everyone make their peace with God, then." Grigori's lips curved into a familiar half smile. "On three, Rhun?"

Together they lifted the propeller higher and inched toward the back of the room. Jordan and Erin ducked under the blades and helped clear the path for the others' burdened legs.

Once he was far enough away, Jordan waved them to lower the propeller to a mound of crates near the back of the space.

"What if there are bombs in these crates, too?" Rhun asked, his voice strained by the sheer weight of the engine blades.

Jordan swore, and Erin's face paled.

"Life is always a risk." Grigori began lowering his end. "I see no point in perishing while holding this."

With no choice, doubting he could carry the weight another foot anyway, Rhun followed Grigori's example. Together, they safely sat the propeller on the pile of boxes.

They all waited, as if expecting the worst.

But the crates held.

Satisfied, Grigori called to one of his acolytes, telling him to seek out the museum curator in the morning and explain what they had found. Rhun was grateful that Grigori had assumed the responsibility to ensure that the missile would be removed.

Over the next long, tense hour, they continued to search this room and others, hitting a series of false alarms, including a rusted truck muffler that Jordan's detector sniffed out, which must have been exposed to a bomb long ago.

At some point, Erin's hair had come loose from its fastening and dusty grime now streaked her cheeks. Rhun could see that the chaos around them weighed on her. She seemed to be more upset that so many precious objects were hidden away than that they had made no progress toward finding the book.

Grigori searched with his usual dogged patience, a counterpoint to his reckless daring. The Mad Monk was more careful and cunning than most believed.

Jordan's detector beeped again.

Erin walked to his side. "Another car part?"

"Let's hope it's not another *missile.*" Jordan moved closer to the room's corner.

Rhun followed.

The device led them to a crumbling wicker basket holding linens that might have once been white. Thick dust had settled on the top, and black mold ate at the basket's sides.

Rhun pulled off the top sheet. A tablecloth. He set it atop a Louis XIV–era writing desk and reached for the next one.

"The readings are getting stronger," Jordan said. "Be careful."

Rhun lifted off another tablecloth, a pile of napkins, and a red Nazi flag.

Grigori tensed when the flag was unfurled to reveal the black Nazi swastika. How many of his countrymen had died under the waving of that flag? Rhun crumpled the cloth and tossed it aside.

Erin lifted out a linen pillowcase stuffed with oddly shaped objects. She set it on the floor and searched through it, item by item. She pulled out a book, but it was only a German code book.

Rhun closed his eyes. Was it the Gospel's destiny to remain hidden? Perhaps things were better so. Perhaps the best outcome would be if they *never* found the book. He opened his eyes. No. They must find it, if only to keep it from the hands of the Belial.

Erin pulled blackened sardine tins out of the pillow sack—then she tensed.

"Jordan! Rhun! Look!" She lifted out a gray concrete fragment identical to the ones that had encased the book.

Jordan ran the sensor across the top. It chirped.

Excited, she removed more fragments until the pillowcase was empty. She shook her head. No book.

Rhun clutched his cross, attempted to hold back the tide of despair that accompanied the pain of burning silver.

Had they come this far only to be disappointed again?

Jordan poked through to the remainder of the basket with his device.

The sensor began to beep again, steady as a heartbeat.

8:31 P.M.

Erin pulled the last threadbare sheet from the basket. She lifted it like a burial shroud, holding her breath, fearful of what she might discover, yet just as excited. But what she found both disappointed and confounded her.

What is it?

Resting at the bottom of the basket was a featureless block of dull gray metal about a foot in width and a little more in length. She lifted it carefully. It felt heavy, like lead.

Jordan ran the explosives detector over it, sagging a bit. "This is definitely what set off my sensors. See the scorch marks? It must have been caught in the same sort of blast."

Rhun turned away, bowed over his cross in frustration.

Erin refused to succumb to defeat. If nothing else, the oddity of the artifact intrigued her. Could this still be what they were searching for—not a book written by Christ, but a symbolic relic, a piece of ancient sculpture?

She recalled the words of Father Piers, spoken first in German, then translated by Jordan.

Es ist noch kein Buch.

It is not a book.

Is this what Piers meant? Or was this artifact just a piece of lead that had been contaminated by the fragments when it was tossed into the pillowcase with them?

Something about the fragments also nagged at her, something she'd never really had a chance to investigate. But now that she had more pieces of the puzzle . . .

She turned and handed the lead block to Jordan. "Hold this. I want to try something."

She then gathered the broken bits of rubble into one of the ancient sheets and took them out into the hall, where she had more room. With the fragments still in her pockets, she might have enough pieces to reassemble the casing more fully. Maybe then she could read the Aramaic lettering impressed on one side of the fragments. At the moment it seemed like a better idea than poking through more piles of rotting junk.

She gestured for Rasputin's forces to move aside, then spread the sheet across the floor. Grigori's acolytes gathered around, watching her. She ignored their presence and lifted out the fragments. As she set about arranging the pieces into their original form, concentrating fully on her task, the sounds of Jordan and the priests rummaging next door receded.

Her world became the puzzle.

Sometime later, a hand touched her shoulder, making her jump.

"We found nothing else in there," Jordan said. "We're ready to move on to the next room."

"I need another minute."

Jordan crouched down beside her. "What do you have there?"

Bare overhead bulbs illuminated the fragments. She had organized them into a square of about one foot by one foot. Fitted together, they revealed a bas-relief of a drawing and impressions of Aramaic letters.

The left side of the bas-relief depicted what looked like a skeleton topped by the Alpha symbol. The right showed the profile of a well-fleshed man with the Omega symbol crowning his head. The two figures were crossed together in an eternal embrace, while a braided rope looped from around the man's throat to the lower vertebrae of the skeleton, binding them together.

"What does that mean?" Jordan asked.

Erin blew out her breath in frustration. "I have no idea."

Jordan traced it with his finger, his voice sharpening. "I've seen this skeleton."

"What? Where?" She ran back over the places they had been together: the tomb in Masada, the bunker, and the Russian church.

"This way!" He uncoiled like a spring. He sprinted back into the room he had just vacated, almost bowling over Rasputin in his haste.

Erin rushed after him, drawing both Rasputin and Rhun with her.

"Such a volatile pair." Rasputin spoke from behind her. "So hot-blooded."

She hoped that blood would stay right where it belonged.

Jordan crossed back to the basket and lifted that strange block of lead. Black blast marks covered its surface. He rubbed the scorched area with his leather sleeve. "Look!"

Erin leaned at his shoulder, only now seeing a faint pattern underneath the blast marks.

He spat on his fingers and used them to rub away a circle of the soot.

A skull grinned back at them from the lead, its backbone trailing down at an angle.

It matched the picture on the fragments. Erin pictured a slurry of lime and ash being poured over this lead sculpture and drying like clay, hardening to create an impression of the design on the lead box's top.

Jordan stared up at her, laying a palm atop the lead surface. "Is this another box? First concrete, now lead. Could the Gospel be inside of that?"

8:47 P.M.

Rhun heard Jordan's words, wanting to disbelieve. It seemed impossible. He reached one tentative hand toward the block, realizing he was acting just like Erin—needing to *touch* it to make it real.

Did this truly hold the Gospel of Christ*?*

After so many centuries of searching, he had thought he would never find it, had assumed his sin with Elisabeta had made him *unworthy* of finding it.

Jordan passed the heavy leaden block to Erin's outstretched hands. She polished away more of the soot with a grimy tablecloth.

"I don't see any seams." She hefted it. "And it feels solid. It looks more like a sculpture than a box."

Rhun longed to take it from her and test the truth for himself, but he kept still.

"I bet the Germans believed there was something in there." Jordan tapped the blast marks. "It looks like they tried to blast it again and again. That's why the sensor readings are so high."

Grigori jostled against Rhun, wanting to examine the object himself. If the book was still encased within this block of lead, Grigori must not have it. He placed himself between Grigori and Erin.

"Have no fear, Rhun," Grigori said. "I have no illusion that I am part of the prophecy."

Only now did Rhun even remember the prophecy. He had never truly believed its words, especially after Elisabeta. Yet now . . .

"All three of you touch it," Grigori said. "See if it reveals itself to you."

"Could it be that simple?" Jordan put a palm on the block.

Erin rested her smaller hand next to his.

Rhun hesitated, loath to attempt such an act in front of Grigori.

As if reading his thoughts, Grigori beckoned with one hand. His dark followers crowded into the room. Their threat made real.

Rhun placed his hand next to Jordan's and Erin's.

8:50 P.M.

Erin stood, afraid to move.

The cold of Rhun's hand chilled one side of her hand; the warmth of Jordan's bathed the other. She couldn't believe that she, who had devoted her life to science, was standing with her hand on a block of lead expecting miracles. What had happened to her over the last day and a half? If Jordan and Rhun hadn't been standing next to her, she would have taken her hand off the block and jammed it into her pocket.

But they were there, so she stayed put, trying to convince herself that she was just humoring them, even though she knew better.

As she waited, icy cold seeped into her palm. It felt dead, like a corpse. The irrational thought would not leave her mind. The book was *dead,* and it would not come back to life on Russian soil.

She remembered the Cardinal's words: *The book can only be opened in Rome.*

"Well, that was disappointing," Jordan said, taking his hand back, the first to break the circle and admit defeat.

Rhun followed suit, and Erin hefted the block back against her chest. Would something miraculous have happened if she had only had faith?

She shook her head.

Enough of that.

"I figured it wouldn't be that easy," Jordan said.

"Indeed." Rasputin gave his personal assistant, Sergei, a meaningful look and the young acolyte backed out the door.

Erin didn't like to think where he might be going.

"Let's gather up the stone pieces," Rhun said. "And be on our way."

"Where does your *way* lead?" Rasputin blocked their exit.

"Do you mean to break your word, Grigori? Steal the book and kill us?"

Rasputin's feet stayed planted. "If God chose you, there is nothing I could do to stop him."

"Great!" Jordan stepped close. "Thank you for your help and—"

Five acolytes glided up swiftly and surrounded him.

"Don't be a fool," Rhun warned Rasputin, his tone as calm as if they were discussing travel arrangements. "You must know that you do not have the resources here to open the Gospel."

"I do realize that, my dear Rhun." Rasputin smiled. A chill ran up Erin's back that had nothing to do with the Russian weather. "Larger forces are at play than you or I."

Sergei returned to the room.

A massive beast padded in after him, the dead come back to life.

The grimwolf growled, its ears flattened menacingly, its hackles spiked along his back.

Here was a twin to the one they had killed in the desert.

From behind the wolf, a woman stepped forward, running her fingers possessively along the flank of the monster. She tossed aside a mane of fiery hair to reveal a pale and familiar face—the woman from the forest in Germany.

The one who shot Rhun.

52

October 27, 9:01 P.M., MST
The Hermitage, Russia

As Rhun stared, fire lanced through his chest, igniting with the memory of the silver rounds exploding into him. The woman looked so much like his Elisabeta—the silvery-gray eyes, the high cheekbones, the perfect skin, the same tilt to her chin, even the knowing smile.

But it could not be her. Rhun closed his eyes, listened to her heart. Each beat told him that this woman was not his Elisabeta, could not be her.

Rage replaced remorse. She had used her resemblance to his beloved to trick him, to try to murder him. Her forces had killed Emmanuel, had almost killed them all.

Jordan spoke, but Rhun caught only the end of the sentence. "... the visitor who pulled you away from the church earlier today?"

"I am ever a polite host," Rasputin said.

Rhun opened his eyes and studied the impostor. The resemblance was uncanny, but false. Like everything in Rasputin's realm, the fair face hid an evil core.

Rasputin's followers seemed frightened of her. They crowded against the walls, leaving a circle around her, as if they did not dare to touch her.

"I see that you are quite restored, Father Korza." The redhead smiled coldly.

Her icy eyes flicked over Erin and lingered on Jordan. Rhun heard his heartbeat quicken under her gaze.

The grimwolf at her heels snarled, its red eyes fixed on Rhun with deep hatred. It looked enough like the one in the desert of Masada to be its littermate. If so, did it know that he had killed its brother?

Masada.

The woman with the wolf must have been there, too, Rhun realized. She had more than Emmanuel's blood on her fair hands.

As if reading his thoughts, she nodded. "This sudden restoration of health. Was it perhaps the blood of your companions that fortified you so?"

"I drink only the blood of Christ."

"Not always," she said. "Long ago, you defiled one of my ancestors."

"I've heard our guest's story," Rasputin said, shaking a finger at Rhun. "She has good reason to be angry at you. Since your tragic mistake with Elisabeta, one woman of each generation of the Bathory line is cursed to a lifetime of pain and servitude. Each must bear a mark to prove it."

The stranger bared her long throat, revealing a black handprint.

Still, Rhun searched for some trickery here. Did this woman truly come from the line of Bathory? Was she a descendant of the first woman believed to be the Woman of Learning?

Reading portents of that time, Cardinal Bernard had thought Elisabeta was the prophesied Woman of Learning. In the end, he was proven wrong, but had someone believed Bernard was on the right path? Had they taken command of the Bathory lineage as a precaution? Or was there some other purpose here?

The redheaded woman shifted her attention to Rasputin, but she never took her eyes off Rhun. "Let me take *him* as well as the book. I will double your fee."

Rhun's eyes narrowed. *Whom did this strange woman serve? Who gave her that black mark on her throat? And why?*

Rhun could think of only one person powerful enough to receive favors from Rasputin. The mysterious head of the Belial. The very last person who should ever receive the book.

He studied the mark on the woman's throat. Was he staring at the shadow of the man's own hand, the true puppet master of the

Belial? A shiver traveled through him. He prayed that Cardinal Bernard was right, that the Belial could not open the Gospel. The Nazis had not been able to. Nor had the Russians. Perhaps the book was its own best protector.

But he hated to leave that to chance.

Rhun calculated the odds. Ten *strigoi,* Rasputin, and the wolf. He could not win here, and if he tried, Erin and Jordan would likely be killed. But an opportunity could present itself later. If he let Bathory take him now, he could remain near the book, try to get it free. Knowing he had no other choice, he inclined his head in agreement.

Rasputin studied his face for several seconds before speaking, his blue eyes calculating. "No, my dear. He is too willing. I promised you the book as a gesture of goodwill toward those whom you serve. But Rhun is *mine.* You may, however, take *one* of the humans, if, in return, your master grants me the life of my choosing later."

"That was not your promise to us, Grigori." Rhun kept his voice calm, but still his minions tightened their grip on him. "But if someone must be taken, why not me?"

"Yes," Bathory said. "Why not him?"

Rasputin motioned to his remaining followers, and they reluctantly stepped closer to her. "My counsel is my own. Do not try my patience further."

"You gave us your word, Grigori," Rhun said. "We were not to be harmed."

Bathory ignored him. "My apologies, Father Rasputin." She studied first Erin, then Jordan. "I will accept your kind offer, but you have left me with a hard choice. Whom will I choose?"

"Take me." Jordan winked at her. "I'm a lot more fun."

"I'm sure you are." Bathory's lips curved into a wicked-looking smile. Her silver eyes met Rhun's. A malicious glint flared. "But I believe I will take the woman."

Rhun dove for Bathory, but a crowd of *strigoi* bore him to the ground before he could take a single step, pinning him with their sheer weight. Three others immobilized Jordan.

"Now, Rhun." Rasputin kicked him lightly with the toe of a black boot. "I always keep my word. *Every* word, in fact."

Rhun struggled to fight free. Next to him, Jordan tried, too. But it was pointless. Erin's eyes had grown wide. *Strigoi* held her by each arm. She could not escape either. Rhun cursed himself for foolishly trusting Grigori. This, too, was his fault.

Rasputin rested his hands on his hips. "Bathory, my dear, I gave my word that the woman would not be harmed *while in Russia*. And you will adhere to that promise. But that protection dies as soon as she crosses our borders. Once beyond Russian soil, you may do with her as you wish."

9:04 P.M.

Erin fought the hands that restrained her, but she couldn't budge an inch. More of Rasputin's people swarmed into the room, filling it with the smell of death.

Rhun thrashed against the *strigoi* who were holding him, lashing out with teeth and nails. Blood spattered the nearby wall. More figures piled on top of him.

Jordan struggled with his attackers, too, but suddenly went limp. Erin gasped. Was he dead? Knocked out cold?

She struggled to get close to him, but it was impossible.

Hands snatched the lead block. Others cuffed her hands in front of her.

A cold collar encircled her neck, and Grigori's minions stepped back a pace. As she hurled herself toward Jordan's prone form, sharp points dug into her throat. Blood ran down her neck.

Gasping for air, she stopped short. Her neck throbbed. The collar was spiked, like a dog's collar, although the points must have been sharpened to make it more painful. Someone ran a finger under the collar, pulling the spikes out of her flesh. She clenched her jaw to keep from crying out.

A moan ran through the *strigoi* who were gathered around her. All eyes fixed on her neck. The one holding her licked his lips.

"Enough!" Rasputin called.

He pushed himself to Erin's side. In his hands he held a leather leash. He clipped one end to the back of Erin's collar and handed the other end to Bathory.

"Thank you." Bathory looped it around her wrist. With the other hand, she yanked the leash tight.

Erin choked, the tightness of the collar keeping her from coughing. She couldn't breathe. Her cuffed hands rose to her throat, fingers trying to loosen it. Cold hands pulled her limbs down. She would die.

"Just so we understand each other." Bathory stuck her face right next to Erin's. "You can come very near to a painful death in Russia without me breaking my word to Rasputin."

Her knees buckling, Erin looked into those cool silver eyes. Would they be the last things she ever saw?

"I hope that you understand that, too, Father Korza." Bathory glanced at the pile of forms that were burying Rhun.

Erin's vision closed in dark.

9:06 P.M.

Buried under a mass of Grigori's acolytes, Jordan struggled to breathe against the sheer weight of them, squeezing the air from his chest, slowly choking him. Teeth sliced into his arms and legs.

Please, God, don't let me die like this . . .

His prayer was answered from the most unlikely source.

Distantly, he heard Rasputin shout. *"Enough!"*

At that command, the pressure eased; bodies rolled off of him. Hot blood seeped from the bites on his arms and legs. His head swam; his vision whirled, but finally settled.

Impossibly strong hands hauled him to his feet. Grigori's minions yanked Rhun upright, too. One acolyte still lay on the ground, bleeding profusely.

It seemed Rhun had put up a better fight than Jordan had.

"Wh-where did that woman take Erin?" Jordan swayed with dizziness. How much blood had he lost?

"Away." Rasputin smiled his crazy smile. "If Bathory doesn't kill her en route, I have an idea where they will end up."

Rhun spat blood and wiped his chin with the back of his hand. "Why did you let the Belial take her—and the Gospel? They are godless. You must know the consequences if they open the book."

"Would the consequences be any worse for me if Sanguinists had the book?" Rasputin's face relaxed into planes of sorrow. "Your beloved Church has possessed countless holy tomes, Rhun—filled their precious Secret Archives with them—and they have never used any of them to help me and mine."

"But the world will suffer, Grigori. The entire world that God created."

"The world suffers now." Rasputin ran his hand through his long hair. "And your God does nothing. Your Church does nothing. Your humans do nothing."

Rhun took a step toward Rasputin, but the Russian's acolytes surrounded him again, forcing him to halt.

"If it doesn't matter," Jordan said, "then let us go."

Rasputin chuckled. "He is charming, your warrior."

"What do you plan for us, Grigori?"

"What I have always planned." Rasputin turned to leave the cramped room. He snapped his fingers, and his dark flock herded Jordan and Rhun along behind him. "I intend to let your God save you, Rhun. Has not that been your eternal prayer, my friend? Salvation at His hand."

9:12 P.M.

Gasping, her throat on fire, Erin trailed down the dark corridor at Bathory's heels, dragged like a dog. The woman released the choke chain enough to allow her to breathe—but barely.

Rasputin's words rang in her ears: *Once beyond Russian soil, you may do with her as you wish.*

If she didn't get away before they left Russia, Bathory would kill her.

And what about Jordan? Was he already dead?

She refused to believe it.

Rhun was clearly alive, fighting desperately against overwhelming odds, when she was hauled away, but Jordan had not moved, buried and being bitten on all his limbs.

He cannot be dead . . . he cannot.

Erin lifted her chin in an effort to ease the pressure of the spikes at her throat. Even that small movement caught her neck in a fiery noose of agony, narrowing her vision. She suspected the spikes were made of silver, the collar likely meant to imprison Sanguinists. She tried not to imagine how much worse it would feel if the silver acted as a poison in her body as it did in those of the Sanguinists.

Bathory threaded through corridors with no hesitation, trusting her grotesque wolf to lead the way. It loped ahead, occasionally dropping its nose to the floor and snuffling along like an ordinary dog. Erin found the naturalness of the gesture unsettling, as if this creature had no right to behave like a normal animal.

"Why do you hate Rhun Korza?" Erin's voice sounded hoarse and unnatural, echoing in the corridor.

The leash twitched, and her throat closed in fear, but Bathory did not pull.

"That creature ruined my family."

Erin took a fast step to keep up. "Then it's true. You are descended from *the* Elizabeth Bathory? But how exactly did Rhun ruin her?"

"He killed her and turned her. As a *strigoi,* she abused peasants to satisfy her needs, something which would have gone unremarked during that time, but then she turned to noble girls, and the Hungarian king stripped her of her wealth, her nobility, and sent the Church after her. Since that time . . ."

Her voice trailed off and she touched the mark on her throat.

Erin took a few more steps before prompting, "Since that time . . . ?"

Bathory's fingers dropped from her neck. "We were penniless, persecuted. Then a stranger came offering a path to survival, to lost riches, and also to revenge." She held up her hand, one finger of which bore a large ruby ring. "He even returned some of our family treasures and heirlooms, rescued them in secret before they were lost forever. But such noble generosity came with a stiff price: one woman from every generation had to be bound in servitude to a hard master, chained to His painful will. I am the only woman of my generation. So it fell to me, whether I wished for it or not."

This last was said with a bitterness that stung.

Aghast, Erin fell silent for several steps. They reached a closed door, and Bathory unlocked it to reveal a dingy stairwell. She took a flashlight from her pocket and shone it up. Steps ascended for several stories. It would be a long climb.

"Come."

Bathory pulled Erin into the stairwell behind her as the grimwolf bounded ahead. With each step, the collar pinched against Erin's throat. Fresh blood dripped down her neck. She tried to block the pain out of her mind, struggling to think of some way to escape.

The grimwolf had reached the next flight. The landing ahead had a door. This might be the only chance she would get.

As they reached the next landing, she took a deep breath, then slipped into a quick crouch, sweeping out with her leg, catching Bathory across the knees.

As the woman fell back toward the steep stairs, Erin yanked the leash free from her grip. Bathory went tumbling and crashing below. Erin twisted to the side. The spikes still dug painfully into her neck, but she didn't care. If she could get through that door and somehow seal it, she might be able to lose her captors in the maze of the Hermitage.

Higher up on the stairs, the wolf yelped, as if feeling his mistress's pain.

Glowing red eyes turned to stare down at Erin.

She fell back against the door and fumbled at it with her cuffed hands. She struggled to turn the doorknob—and despaired.

Locked.

9:16 P.M.

Forced down the hallway by a squad of Grigori's acolytes, Jordan smelled the giant, reeking bear. As he marched, he pictured the human skull that had rolled out of its cage, and glanced sidelong at Rhun.

The priest nodded. He knew the truth, too.

Rasputin planned to feed them to the bear.

Jordan had been waiting for a clear moment, but the bastards surrounded him like a wall, less than a step away on all sides. He knew their strength, and his own weakness. He'd lost too much blood to put up much of a fight. Hell, he could barely walk.

Was this how he was going to die, as bear chow? He recalled his desperate plea not to meet his end at the fangs of Grigori's minions. That prayer had been answered, and he was, oddly, still grateful. He would take the maw of the bear over the fangs of a *strigoi* any day.

Then he pictured Erin's face, remembered her lips, her heated hands on his skin. He had to get free. He had to find her. Every second that passed, Bathory dragged her farther from Rasputin's domain and closer to her death. He'd seen that look in Bathory's eyes. She intended to kill Erin the minute she could do so without disobeying Rasputin.

All to hurt Rhun.

The tunnel ended a short way ahead, the stench of bear overpowering. Jordan spotted the elaborate gate depicting a woodland forest. He and Rhun were pushed forward until they were pressed against its fancy iron scrollwork.

Inside the cage, the bear slumbered on. Maybe it would be too tired to eat them.

Rasputin banged the flat of his palms against the gate, sounding the dinner bell.

The creature lumbered to its feet.

It was feeding time.

9:18 P.M.

Fueled by raw fury, Bathory tucked into a roll as she tumbled headlong down the stairs, pushed by that damned archaeologist. She felt each sharp step against her back, until she finally hit a landing and sprawled out.

Above her, two thuds sounded. She heard a low growl, knew it was aimed at the cursed archaeologist, and felt a wash of satisfaction emanating from Magor, the pleasure of a predator who had cornered its prey.

"Easy!" Bathory called out, sharing in the wolf's joy. It helped dull the pain as she climbed to her feet. She would have some nasty bruises, but nothing serious. She had lived so long with pain she barely noticed it.

She climbed with determination to the landing above. Magor had pinned the woman against the battered door, a paw on either side of her shoulders, his teeth bared at her neck. She felt his longing to tear out her throat. His claws scored the concrete wall.

The archaeologist watched him with wide eyes. She looked ready to faint.

In fact, Bathory was surprised she hadn't.

"Not yet, my pet." She retrieved the end of the leather leash and drew the collar tight. "When we can, I promise you can play with her as long as you like."

Cowed and on shaking legs, the archaeologist trudged after her up the next flight of stairs, her shoulders low.

"Such despair and hopelessness," Bathory taunted. "This isn't what you expected when you started out on this bold quest in Jerusalem, is it? You thought your life might have value because of the prophecy?"

They reached a side door, and she unlocked it before pulling the woman out onto the empty street. Wind ruffled the sable fur of Bathory's coat.

"What prophecy are you talking about?" the archaeologist asked, feigning ignorance . . . *badly.*

Lying took practice, and her prisoner clearly hadn't had much of that.

Moving suddenly, Bathory grabbed her shoulder and slammed her against the side of a silver SUV that was parked roadside.

Magor growled.

"Don't even try to lie to me. I am not a fool. I don't believe in prophecy. So don't think your life has value to me because of a thousand-year-old poem."

The woman struggled to keep her feet on the icy cobblestones. Hauling the leash up, Bathory forced her higher up onto her tiptoes. If the woman should slip, the choke collar might kill her.

Bathory glanced up and down the empty street. No witnesses. But Rasputin would still know. She was not safe from him until she was well off Russian soil.

She loosened the leash, opened the SUV's door, and shoved the archaeologist into the backseat. Magor jumped in after her, pushing his muzzle close to the prisoner's throat. A tongue, frothing and thick with drool, licked the blood dribbling from under the spiked collar.

The archaeologist smothered a scream. She was a brave one, Bathory thought, but she had limits, too.

"Easy, Magor. If the Cardinal believes that she has a special destiny, she might have some use for us yet as a pawn in the game to come."

The woman twisted her face away from the wolf, her voice tight and hard. "I don't think the Cardinal cares that much about me."

"Then you don't know this Cardinal very well." Bathory smiled. "Either way, remember that the prophecy never specified the *condition* you must be in when the book opens."

Bathory read the understanding, the fear, in the archaeologist's eyes.

Smart.

Maybe she was indeed the Woman of Learning.

"We will probably need you *alive,*" Bathory cruelly acknowledged. "But *unwounded*?"

She shook her head and smiled.

No.

53

October 27, 9:20 P.M., MST
Under St. Petersburg, Russia

Standing in the tunnel outside the cage's gate, Rhun watched the Ursa, and the Ursa watched Rhun. Her red eyes glinted with old malice, her hatred of him undiminished across the past century. Drool slavered from her muzzle, and her impossibly long tongue slid across lips as black as rubber.

He suspected she remembered how he tasted. His leg throbbed and threatened to buckle. His limb remembered her, too.

Grigori wrapped his fingers around the branch of a wrought-iron oak sculpted into the gate. "If God loves you, Rhun, He will help you to escape the bear. Remember the lesson of Daniel and the lions? Perhaps your belief will close her mouth."

Rhun didn't think it would be that simple.

He studied the tiles that covered the chamber where the tunnels met, finding no break, no other way out. He shifted his attention to the iron gates.

When unlocked, they parted down the middle into two halves, opening like French doors. Two thick iron rods, one on each side of the gateway, had been drilled into the concrete and attached each side of the gate to the floor and ceiling. Less than an inch of a gap surrounded the gateway, and the elaborate patterns woven through the bars left openings no bigger than a few inches.

Once Rhun went into the room, there would be no escape.

Jordan dropped a warm hand to his shoulder. Rhun met his

questioning blue eyes. The soldier glanced surreptitiously to Grigori and the *strigoi.* It was plain that he was asking if they should make their stand here, go down fighting before Rhun could be thrown in with the bear.

Affection rose in his breast. Jordan was a true Warrior of Man to the end. "Thank you," Rhun whispered. "But no."

Jordan stepped back, his eyes scared—but less for his own safety than for Rhun's.

Unable to face that raw humanity any longer, Rhun turned to the gate. "I am ready, Grigori."

Acolytes grabbed Jordan's arms; others held Rhun in place while Grigori unlocked the thick steel lock and wrenched open the door.

Rhun was shoved bodily through the gate and into the cage.

The Ursa's head swung toward him.

"Yes, my love," Grigori called. "Sport with him as long as you like."

Keeping back and staying low, Rhun circled her. The room was large, about fifty feet by fifty. He must use that space wisely. Overhead, the creature's shoulders brushed the ceiling. Rhun could not jump over her.

A twig cracked under his shoe, releasing the sharp smell of spruce, the only natural scent in the cavern. He drank it in.

Then the Ursa lunged.

Her giant paw drove through the air with unnatural speed.

He had expected it. Long ago, she had always led with her left paw. He dove under her claws and rolled. The movement took him to the center of the room.

Ahead, a glint caught his eye. He ran forward and snatched it from the floor. *A holy flask.* Another Sanguinist had been sacrificed here. As he searched, he discovered other evidence: a pectoral cross, a silver rosary, a scrap of black cassock.

"May God have mercy on your soul, Grigori," Rhun called out.

"God forsook my soul long ago." Grigori rattled his gate. "As He did yours."

The Ursa spun to face Rhun.

He swept the chamber swiftly with his eyes. If the murdered Sanguinist had been armed, perhaps his or her weapons remained. If he could—

The Ursa charged again.

He stood his ground.

The floor shook under her paws. He listened as her old heart stirred to passion again, beating hard.

When her carrion breath touched his cheek, he dropped flat to his back, letting her momentum carry her across his body. The sea of dark fur passed inches from his face. He lifted his own cross and let it drag across her stomach, setting her fur to smoldering.

She shrieked.

He had inflicted no serious damage, but he had given the bear a reminder that he was no mosquito to be squashed.

Jordan cheered from outside the gates.

Rhun rolled across the floor, his hands seeking the objects he had spotted before the attack. Two wooden staffs lay on the floor, both ends tipped with silver. He knew those unique weapons. His brother of the cloth—Jiang—had died here. Rhun had watched him practice with those staffs for hours, deep below the necropolis of Rome, where the Sanguinists made their home.

Still addled by the burn, the Ursa swept her head from side to side.

Rhun crouched perfectly still and measured the sides of his prison with his eyes.

With the hint of a plan in his mind, he darted to the iron gate that was farthest from Grigori.

The Ursa caught his movement and barreled toward him.

Leaping and twisting at the last moment, he cracked one of the staffs across her muzzle and rolled to the side.

Her enormous bulk plowed straight into the gate, knocking one of the two iron support rods loose from the floor. That corner of the gate bent, creating an opening too small for Rhun to squeeze through, but such an escape was not his intent.

He led her around toward where Grigori and Jordan watched the blood sport.

She came after him. He performed the same maneuver, but this time she skidded and stopped less than an inch from the gate. Her paw swatted through the air and caught him across the back as he leaped away. A glancing blow, but it cut through his leather armor and ripped into the flesh of his back.

A gasp escaped him, equal parts pain and defiance.

The Ursa sank onto her rear haunches and pulled her bloodied paw to her maw. With tiny eyes watching him, she licked each drop of his blood from her claws, huffing with pleasure.

He waited at the far side of the room, next to the damaged gate. The iron smell of his own blood coated his nostrils. He slid one staff down his bleeding back and through his belt, hooking the top through his priestly collar. That left him a staff in one hand, and the other hand free.

He broke the staff across his knee and set both pieces on the ground.

Then he dropped to that same knee, bowed his head, and muttered a prayer, calming his mind. A holy kiss on his pectoral cross burned his lips. His pain drew to a single point, centering him.

He touched his forehead with his index finger. "*In nomine Patris . . .*"

He touched his breastbone. "*Et Filii . . .*"

He touched first his left shoulder, then his right. "*Et Spiritus Sancti.*"

Then he crossed his thumb across his index finger and kissed it.

He gathered up the two pieces of the staff.

The bear came.

He whispered, "By the sign of the cross, deliver me from my enemies, O Lord."

The Ursa thundered toward him, almost upon him.

At the last moment he leaped straight toward the ceiling, flattening his body against the roof as only a Sanguinist could, sliding between the bear's back and the roof. He found narrow passage, only inches to spare.

Below him, the Ursa hit the gate with a tremendous crack. The *second* rod holding it to the floor broke away, and the gate was now bent more than a foot. If Rhun had been willing to abandon Jordan, he could have escaped.

Instead, he twisted in midair and fell back down upon the dazed beast. Before the Ursa had time to shake her stunned head, he stabbed one half of his broken staff toward one shaggy paw.

His aim was true.

His weight and momentum thrust the silver-tipped piece of the staff through her paw and deep into the hole that had been drilled into the concrete long ago for the gate's iron rod.

She bellowed in pain, from the wound and the precious silver.

Before the beast had a chance to move, Rhun leaped onto her back and rolled across to her other side, shifting the second piece of the broken staff into his right hand.

He drove it through her other paw and into the other hole on the floor, imprisoning both limbs.

The Ursa collapsed forward, her muzzle knocking under the broken gate into the tunnel. With her forelegs splayed to each side, her body formed the sign of a cross.

Rhun had crucified the bear.

She howled.

He jumped atop her head and drew the unbroken staff from behind his back. Kissing the silver end first, he jammed it through her eye and deep into her brain. She twitched and heaved, dying. He read her demise in the vast chambers of her ancient heart.

Dominus vobiscum.

He bowed his head and made the sign of the cross over the beast's massive form. As he finished his prayer, the red glow faded from her remaining eye, leaving it black.

After centuries, she was finally freed of her tainted servitude.

Rhun turned to this nemesis, his face defiant, triumphant in his glory.

9:33 P.M.

Jordan's arms were let free. He stared around, surprised. He swiped his hand down his jacket, as if dusting off the places where Rasputin's congregants had touched him. Would that Russian monk keep his word and let Rhun and him go? If not, he intended to go down fighting side by side with Rhun.

Rasputin stepped back from the cage's gate, his blue eyes wide. "God truly loves you, Rhun. You are indeed His most chosen one."

Rhun knelt down and gathered a rosary, a silver cross, and a flask. Jordan bet they had belonged to another Sanguinist, someone killed by the bear.

Rasputin unlocked the cage.

Rhun's hatred for Rasputin burned so palpably that the monk fell back a step. His minions retreated as if blown by a fierce wind.

"Where has Bathory taken Erin?" Rhun asked, biting off each word.

Rasputin's voice cracked. "To Rome."

Rhun glared, searching the other's face for the truth. "Are we done here with your challenges to God, Grigori?"

Rasputin tilted his head. "Why do you scold me so, Rhun? Your dear Bernard sought to *force* the prophecy. He thrust you next to Elisabeta in the past, his alleged Woman of Learning . . . and her husband, that mighty Warrior. Look how that meddling turned out." He lifted his hands in supplication of forgiveness. "I merely sought to *test* the prophecy here today. If you were truly one of the prophesied, God would spare you from the bear."

"And here I stand," Rhun said. "But your test is not over, is it? That is why you sent Erin off. You sundered the trio, to test if the three of us would find one another again and fulfill our duties. In this way, you continue to challenge God, as you once challenged the Church."

Rasputin shook his head. "Not at all. I challenge only you, my friend. The one whom the Church loves as much as it hates me."

Turning on a heel, Rasputin swept his minions aside with a wave of his hand, opening up a path to freedom.

Jordan waited for Rhun to reach him. Together, they walked through the gauntlet of Rasputin's dark flock. With each step, Jordan's bite wounds throbbed. The hair stood up on the back of his neck. He tensed, waiting for an attack from behind, a final betrayal by Rasputin.

None came.

"Find your woman, Rhun," Rasputin called after them. "Prove that the Church placed its faith in the correct bloodstained hands."

Rhun swept down the tunnel toward the Church of the Savior on Spilled Blood, not seeming to notice that his own blood pattered onto the frozen ground behind him.

PART V

And they sang a new song, saying, Thou art worthy to take the book, and to open the seals thereof: for thou wast slain, and hast redeemed us to God by thy blood . . .

—Revelation 5:9

54

October 28, 2:55 p.m., Central European Time
Rome, Italy

Erin jerked awake, chased by nightmares. She batted at the darkness around her, but it wouldn't go away. Only now did the full desperation of her plight wash back over and fill her with an icy dread that did little to settle her waking panic. She stretched her eyes wider—not that it did any good. The place where they had imprisoned her was so dark that it made no difference whether her eyes were open or closed.

She pressed her palms against her cheeks, surprised that she had fallen asleep. But the exhaustion and total sensory deprivation here must have finally overwhelmed her.

How long have I been asleep?

She remembered the flight from St. Petersburg by private jet last night. They had kept her hooded the entire time, but she had overheard enough of the conversation around her to know that the destination was Rome. The trip had taken about four hours. Once they had landed, another hour's ride brought them into the predawn city. Erin could hear the sound of honking horns and the shouts and curses in Italian, and smell the Tiber as they crossed one of the city's major bridges.

If she wasn't mistaken, they were heading in the general direction of Vatican City.

What was Bathory planning?

What does she want with me?

The SUV that had shuttled them from the private airstrip eventually stopped and Erin had been dragged, still hooded, into a cold early morning. She could see enough under the lower edge of the hood to determine that it was still before sunup.

Then back underground they went, using stairs, tunnels, and ladders—the last especially difficult when blindfolded. They must have traversed the subterranean world of Rome for a full hour. She was familiar enough with the city to know that a good portion of the ancient world still existed below its surface, in a series of interconnected catacombs, wine cellars, tombs, and secret churches.

But where had she ended up?

At the end of the journey, she had been thrust into this dark cell, with the bloody collar still clamped around her neck. She had sat against the wall for ten minutes, hugging her knees, hearing no one, before she tugged off the hood and discovered the collar unlocked. She removed it and tossed it aside gladly. Shortly after that, she must have fallen asleep.

She raised her fingers now and felt the ring of scabs around her neck.

She always had a good internal clock, and now she wagered it must be somewhere around midafternoon in the world above.

She stretched out her other senses and heard the slow drip of water, the echoing giving her some indication that the space beyond her cell was cavernous. The air smelled old and stale, with a hint of mildew. She reached out and slid her palm along the floor. Stone. Her fingertips picked out chisel marks.

A tomb?

Erin's hands slipped into her jacket pockets, searching. Of course, they had taken her flashlight, but she discovered the scrap of quilt in her pants pocket. At least they let her keep that.

Scooting up onto her hands and knees, she swept her hand from left to right in bigger and bigger arcs, stirring up a thick carpet of dust that made her eyes water and drew several sneezes. When she rubbed the dust between her fingers, it felt like wood slivers and rock dust.

Continuing on in a wider sweep, her fingers bumped against a rounded object. She picked it up and brought it to her lap. Bone. Her fingers filled in what her eyes could not see. A skull. She gulped, but still blindly examined its surfaces: an elongated nose, a small brainpan, long curved incisors.

Not human. Not even *strigoi*.

A giant cat. Probably a lion.

She sat back, pondering the implications of her discovery. She must be in some sort of Roman circus, an arena where gladiators and slaves fought one another and wild beasts. But the beast to which this skull had belonged had been buried with the remains of the spectacle in which it lost its life.

She paired that information with her knowledge of the path she had just taken through the city.

Toward Vatican City.

She knew of only one cavernous circus in that region. The Vatican itself had been built over half of the blood-drenched place.

The Circus of Nero.

Almost two thousand years ago, Nero had completed the circus started by Caligula. He had built enormous tiers of seating for the audience to watch his brutal games. At first, he sacrificed lions and bears to cheering crowds. But slaughtering animals hadn't been enough for the ancient Romans, so he moved on to gladiators.

And eventually Christians.

The blood of Christian martyrs soon drenched the soil of the arena. They weren't just ripped apart by animals and gladiators. Many were crucified. Saint Peter himself had been nailed upside down on a cross, near the obelisk in the center of the arena.

The circus was also famous for its vast network of underground tunnels, used to shuttle prisoners, animals, and gladiators to and fro. The builders had even installed crude elevators for delivering wild beasts or warriors directly to the sands above.

Erin stared up, picturing how St. Peter's Basilica sat partly on top of this cursed place. During her postgraduate studies in Rome, she had read a text written a century ago—*Pagan and Christian Rome* by Rodolfo Lanciani. It depicted a map of the two overlapping structures—the horseshoe-shaped Circus below, the cruciform Basilica above.

In the dark, the schematic glowed again in her mind's eye.

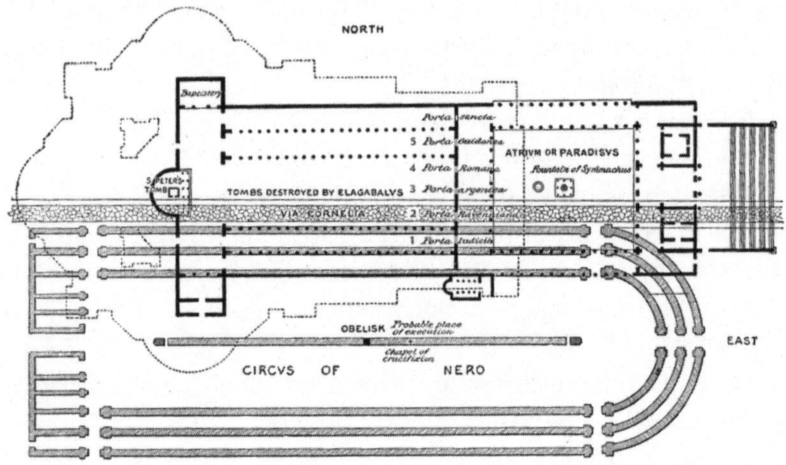

If she could get free of her cell, climb up, and reach the outside, she should be very near to St. Peter's Basilica.

With help close at hand.

With renewed determination, she explored the edges of the room. It was about eight by ten feet, with a modern steel gate installed at the front. No weaknesses that she could detect.

She needed help. Two faces flashed before her: one as pale as his eyes were dark, but always shining with noble purpose; the other grinning, with flushed cheeks and laughing eyes the color of the sky.

What might have happened to Rhun and Jordan in that time?

She shied away from that thought.

Not in the dark.

After what seemed an eternity, Erin noticed a light approaching. She jammed her face next to the bars. Four figures and what looked like a huge dog were walking toward her down a stone tunnel, one carrying a flashlight. The dog walked next to a woman with long hair.

Bathory and her grimwolf.

Behind them, two taller figures who looked like brothers dragged along a third man, his arms slung over their shoulders. At the sight, her throat closed up. Was that Jordan? Or Rhun?

Reaching the cell without a word, Bathory unlocked the door and swung it open.

Erin tensed. She wanted to charge out, but she wouldn't make it two steps down that tunnel.

The grimwolf padded into the cell.

Bathory and the two men followed the wolf in. A blast of cold air came in with them. The two brothers were both *strigoi.*

They dumped the man at her feet. He moaned and turned over. A mass of bruises covered his face, his eyes were nearly swollen closed, dried blood soaked his shirtsleeves and a pant leg.

"Professor Granger?" asked a cracked, familiar voice, with a slight Texas twang.

She fell to her knees next to him, taking his hand. "Nate? Are you okay . . . *why* are you here?"

She knew the answer to both questions and despaired as she realized the result of her own shortsightedness. She had never considered that the Belial would go after her innocent students. What did they know? Then it all tumbled together. She had sent the *pictures* of the tomb, of the Nazi medallion. No wonder Bathory knew to track their team to Germany.

What have I done?

She didn't know the answer to that one, nor another. "Amy?" she whispered.

Nate stared up at her, tears welling in his eyes. "I . . . I wasn't there to protect her."

Erin rocked back as if she had taken a blow to the face. She heard a sob escape Nate.

"It's not your fault, Nate."

It had been *her* fault. The students had been left in *her* care.

Nate's voice was hoarse. "I don't know why I'm here."

A rush of affection rose in Erin for the tough Texas kid. She squeezed his hand.

"How touching," sneered Bathory.

"Why did you take him?" Erin turned and glared at her, earning a threatening growl from the grimwolf. "You got the photos, I imagine. He knows nothing else. He has nothing to do with any of this."

"Not quite," said Bathory. "He has something to do with *you.*"

Guilt washed across Erin. "What do you want?"

"Information from the *Woman of Learning,* of course." Bathory displayed her perfect white teeth in an unpleasant grin.

"I don't believe in that damn prophecy," Erin said, and meant it. So far, the trio seemed to have bungled more things than they got right. It didn't feel like they had divine prophecy on their side.

"Ah, but others do." Bathory stroked the grimwolf's head. "Help us."

"No." She would die before she assisted the Belial in opening the book.

Bathory snapped her fingers. The grimwolf leaped and pinned Nate to the floor with his front paws, knocking his hand loose from Erin's. The wolf bent his muzzle low over Nate's throat.

The message was clear, but Bathory drove it home anyway. "I don't need your cowboy."

Bathory trained her flashlight on Nate. Erin tried not to look at him. She stared instead at the rough stone walls, the newly installed barred steel gate, and the black ceiling of the cell that seemed to extend upward forever.

But her gaze returned to Nate. He had closed his eyes, quaking, but looking so brave she wanted to hug him. Clearly terrified, he still didn't ask for help. He just waited.

"What do you need?" Erin asked Bathory.

"Your thoughts about opening the lead casing that holds the book." Bathory put both hands on her hips. "To start."

"I don't know."

The dog lowered its head toward Nate's exposed throat and snarled.

"But maybe *we* can talk it through, you and I." Erin spoke as fast as she could. "But first, call off the grimwolf."

As if obeying a silent command from its mistress, the wolf raised its head.

Nate shuddered with relief.

Erin had to give the woman something. "The lead box had a design on it. A skeleton and a man bound together by loops of rope."

"Yes, we know. Along with the symbols for the Alpha and the Omega."

Bathory turned to the taller of the two brothers, his flesh punctured and tattooed, his eyes hungry upon her. He shrugged off a satchel, pulled free the heavy artifact, and held it out to Erin.

"What else do you see?" Bathory asked.

Erin took the cold metal object, careful not to touch the fingers of the tattooed man. She wished she had something significant to add. What did she know about the book? She stroked the two figures carved into the front: the human skeleton and the naked man, crossed and locked in an embrace, bound together by a braided cord.

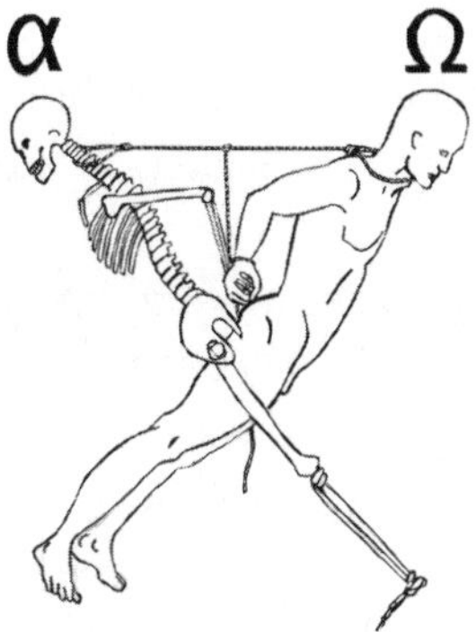

"The book is about miracles," Erin started. "Christ's miracles. How He harnessed His divinity."

The wolf shifted its weight from paw to paw.

"We know that," Bathory snapped. "How do we *open* it?"

Erin ignored her and tried to think. "Miracles. Like changing water to wine. Bringing the living back from the dead . . ."

She stopped, surprised.

Bathory understood at the same time. "All the major miracles are about *transformations*."

"Exactly!" Erin was surprised at how quickly Bathory had made the connection. "Like transubstantiation, changing wine to the blood of Jesus."

"So, perhaps this block of lead *is* the actual book." Bathory crossed over and crouched next to her, like two colleagues conferring. She touched the lead, too. "Alchemists were always trying to find a way of turning lead to gold."

Erin nodded, understanding the woman's hypothesis. "Maybe that quest has its roots in this legend. Some old hint about the Gospel traveled up through the ages. Turning lead to gold."

Bathory's silver eyes locked on hers. "Maybe the Gospel needs to be transformed in the same way. From dull, worthless lead to the golden glory of the book?"

Erin suddenly remembered Piers's words in the bunker.

The book is not yet a book. Not yet.

Had the old priest figured out the puzzle as he hung for decades on the cross with nothing else to ponder as he suffered?

Erin nodded. "I think you're right."

"It's an interesting idea. But what are the alchemical ingredients needed to cause this transformation?" Bathory tapped the figure of the skeleton inscribed on the lead jacket. "I suspect the answer may lay in our bony friend here?"

"But what does the Alpha symbol above his head mean? It has to be a clue." Erin stared at the skeleton under the Alpha symbol, then glanced at the naked man and the symbol above his head. "And what's the meaning of the Omega symbol?"

"Alpha skeleton, Omega man." Bathory slipped her finger into two small divots at the top of the block.

Erin hadn't seen those before. They looked like tiny receptacles, meant to hold something, maybe something like those alchemical ingredients Bathory mentioned. She tried to get a better look at them.

Before she could, Bathory sprang to her feet, understanding flashing across her face. She ripped the lead block from Erin's hands.

"What?" Erin asked. "What did you see?"

Bathory snapped her fingers, and the wolf abandoned Nate.

The young man sat up shakily, rubbing his throat.

The eerie silver eyes smiled at Erin. "Thank you for your help."

With that, she and the *strigoi* brothers left the cell. The lock clicked closed, and light retreated down the tunnel. Erin leaned forward to watch it disappear. Bathory had figured out something, something important.

Nate drew in a shaky breath. "She'll be back."

Erin agreed, adding, "But we won't be here."

***3:35* P.M.**

Rhun pulled his dark hood lower over his eyes, hiding from both the tourists and the late-afternoon sunlight that inundated St. Peter's Square.

Here he waited with Jordan.

Across the travertine square rose St. Peter's Basilica, its dome the highest point in all of Rome. To either side, Bernini's double colonnade swept out in two wide arcs, framing the keyhole-shaped plaza between. According to Bernini, the colonnade was supposed to represent the arms of Saint Peter reaching out to embrace the faithful into the fold. Atop these arms, a hundred and forty stone saints perched and stared down upon the spectacle below.

Rhun hoped they didn't see him. He had chosen this place for a rendezvous, out in the open, under the sun, to hide in plain sight, so that if Bathory had reached Rome, her *strigoi* wouldn't be able to overhear any words he spoke. Possibly he was being too paranoid, but after the events in Russia, he dared take no chances.

Jordan rolled up his sleeves. The edge of a *strigoi* bite showed just above his elbow. The man had an incredible constitution. He'd been battered and bitten, but his obvious worry for Erin kept him going. *A fine Warrior of Man,* Rhun thought, and tried to be grateful that she had such a champion.

Humans swirled around him. A mother bounced a fat infant on her hip. Next to her, a young man watched her breasts, his heart rate giving away his response. A group of schoolgirls in navy-blue uniforms chattered under the watchful eye of a middle-aged teacher wearing brilliant red-framed eyeglasses.

A woman in long jeans, a tight-fitting black shirt, a floppy straw hat, and sunglasses meandered around the crowded square. She snapped a few pictures, then stuck a tiny camera into the backpack that dangled by one strap on her shoulder. She looked like a tourist, but she wasn't.

Nadia.

At last.

Rhun waited, not daring to cross the square until she signaled it was safe. He hated skulking around Vatican City. Rome had been his home for centuries. It had been the one place in the world where he had always walked freely—until now. Before this quest had started, he had considered retreating from the world, ensconcing himself in the meditative world that existed deep below the Basilica. Would such peace ever be afforded him again?

He strolled along the curved colonnade toward the ancient three-tiered fountain. Like many things in Rome, it was older than he was. A young girl played hide-and-seek among the Doric columns, chased by an energetic mother. They probably sought to get in one more game before heading home for their dinners.

Rhun's sharp eyes picked out the red porphyry stone set among the sea of gray cobblestones. The red stone had been placed there to mark the spot of Pope John Paul II's shooting thirty years before. The bloodred stone reminded him of the cobblestones enshrined in the Church of the Savior on Spilled Blood, a thought that seemed to call the specter of Rasputin into this holy place.

Rhun stopped next to the tall stone obelisk. This very pillar had witnessed the crucifixion of countless Christians in Nero's Circus, even Saint Peter himself. But since the late 1500s, it had watched over the center of the Christian world. He calculated the time by the long shadow it threw across the square. They had less than two hours before sunset. If the Belial had *strigoi* stationed in Rome, they must act before then.

Nadia paused next to him.

"Where is the woman?" She angled her head back as if studying the cross that topped the obelisk.

"Erin," Jordan said. "Her name is Erin."

"She was taken, along with the book." Rhun filled her in on the events in Russia, ending by handing her Jiang's rosary and flask. She could bring them to the sanctuary beneath the necropolis of St. Peter's Basilica, where the Order of the Sanguines made their home.

Nadia's hands lingered on the flask before she slipped it into her backpack. She had often worked with Jiang. "The Cardinal has returned to Rome from Jerusalem. He's been with the Cloistered Ones since he received word of your alleged death. Praying."

Guilt wormed its way into Rhun's gut. He hated having lied to Bernard. He had known that after Nadia told him of his death, Bernard would grieve. He would be furious and hurt when he found out how Rhun and Nadia had deceived him. But there had been no other way to conceal their actions from the Belial spy in their midst. Still, it would not get any easier to face Bernard. Rhun glanced toward the imposing stone Apostolic Palace rising above the colonnade. A few windows had been left open to let in the light and air.

"Can you take us to Bernard? We have no time for secrecy now that the Belial have the book."

"And Erin," Jordan put in. "They have Erin, too."

55

October 28, 3:40 P.M., CET
Circus of Nero, Rome, Italy

"What do you mean we're getting out of here?" Nate asked.

Erin stumbled over to him in the oily darkness and caught his hand to reassure him. "We're going to *climb* out."

"What? How?"

She told him.

Earlier, when Bathory had waved her flashlight around the cell, Erin had spotted a possible way out. They certainly could never breach the stone walls, and the new steel bars looked strong, and the floor had been carved from solid rock. They wouldn't be leaving by any of those ways.

But the ceiling!

Under the glow of Bathory's flashlight, she had noted that the cell had no roof. It was just a sheer-walled black shaft that headed straight up.

Erin knew what that meant. In ancient times, Roman slaves used long poles to push caged animals down the stone tunnel that Bathory had sauntered along before. They were animals meant for the arena, but first their cages had to be pushed into the very cell that she and Nate now occupied.

Back then, a wooden platform would have covered the cell's stone floor. Over the centuries, the platform had disintegrated into the slivers Erin had felt when she first woke up in the cell. Originally, planks had been nailed together in the shape of this room. Chains would have been attached to both sides of the platform and run up to pulleys at the top. Those chains would have traveled up slots on either side of the black rectangle above her.

Slaves rolled the caged animals on top of the platform. Later, on cue from above, other slaves used an elaborate rope-and-pulley elevator system to lift the platform and the cage from deep under the earth to the ground-level arena.

Erin and Nate had to hope that this shaft led to someplace safer than the prison they were stuck in now.

"Come over here," she urged Nate, taking him by hand. "We can climb the steel gate to reach the shaft above."

She helped him mount and clamber up the horizontal braces. Still, he trembled. Beaten and poorly fed, he was noticeably weak.

"Now for the interesting part." Erin held him against the bars with one arm. "I saw a small vertical slot running up one wall of the shaft. Once upon a time, the slot held the pulley chains used to lift the elevator platform up that shaft. With any luck, we can climb that slot all the way to the surface. I'm going to go first. You come up after me."

"Yes, ma'am." Nate's voice had a sarcastic tone, and she was glad to hear it.

Her fingers explored the shaft overhead and found the slot. It was wide enough to jam into: legs on one side, back on the other. The climbing technique was called chimneying.

She pushed off with her legs from the cell's gate and lifted herself up into the slot. Before she could fall back down, she jammed one leg against the side. Her back rested hard against the other side. She was in.

She moved up one foot, then another. "Okay, Nate. Your turn."

Blind in the dark, she heard him hoist himself off the bars toward her—then fall back down to the stone floor with a *thud*.

She jumped down. "Are you hurt?"

"I'm fine." He didn't sound fine.

"This time, *you* go first."

Erin found his hand and directed him back to the bars. Nate climbed up again, fell again.

"Leave me," he said. "I can't do it."

"You mean to tell me that a strapping Texas boy like you doesn't have the guts to outclimb a scrawny old lady like me?"

"It's not about guts." His quiet voice sounded defeated.

She hated to poke him again, but she did. "Damn right it is. Stop whining, and get your ass up that shaft. I am not going up there just to tell your kid sister that you were killed here because you were too lazy to climb out of a hole."

Nate stood back up. "I used to like you."

"Up you go."

This time she supported his feet when he pushed himself upward. Once braced across the slot, he didn't need to use his wounded arms, just his back and his legs.

Dirt and stone chips rained down on her as Nate made slow progress upward. She followed, straightening one leg, lifting it up a few inches, then forcing herself to pry the other foot off the wall. Over and over. Inching upward. She had done chimneying before, but always with a rope belay and a flashlight.

"How're you doing, Nate?"

"Best time I've had in days." He shifted up another few inches.

She smiled grimly. Probably true.

A few more precious feet, and then he slipped.

She caught his calf, forcing it against the wall. He pushed out and stopped his slide.

Her heart raced. She and Nate had almost fallen all the way back down to the cell. With any luck, they would have died on impact. If not, they'd have had the fun of being torn apart by the grimwolf.

But at least they would have died trying.

Dim gray light shone up the shaft.

Someone was coming.

4:05 P.M.

In a private room in the Apostolic Palace, Jordan gritted his teeth. Naked from the waist up, he was lying on his face on a thick wool rug covering a polished wood floor.

Nadia played nursemaid, swabbing the bite wounds on his arm and back—and none too gently.

"Strange tattoo," she said, noting the Lichtenberg design from the lightning strike.

"I know," he said, wincing. "You got to die to get one."

Nadia had sneaked him and Rhun out of St. Peter's Square through some secret doorway into the Apostolic Palace, where, apparently, the pope lived. She'd rushed them into this simple room with whitewashed walls. The room held an old-fashioned, long wooden table, six heavy chairs, and a macabre crucifix on the wall. After his meeting with Piers, he could hardly stand to look at crucifixes anymore.

Instead, he kept his eyes on the rug. It smelled like a wet sheep.

Nadia wrung out a brown washcloth into a copper basin, its water stained pale pink from Jordan's blood.

"Where is Bernard?" Rhun paced the room, stopping only long enough to peer out the window into the courtyard below.

"I've sent word." Nadia poked Jordan again.

Ouch. Now she was just being mean.

She drew a glass jar from her backpack. "This might sting."

"That's not what you're supposed to say," Jordan groused. "You're supposed to lie."

"Lying is a sin."

"Like telling the Cardinal we died."

Nadia unscrewed the top of a jar that smelled like pitch mixed with horse manure.

"What's *in* that stuff?" he asked, changing the tender subject.

She scooped the goop onto her index and middle fingers. "It's best you don't know."

He opened his mouth to insist—then thought better and shut it again. If something made Nadia squeamish, he didn't want to know.

She slathered the balm into a bite wound on his back. Fire followed in its wake.

He gasped, immediately breaking out into a sweat. "Feels like napalm."

"I know." She worked fast, sealing each wound.

He studied a bite on his arm. It had been oozing blood since they'd left Russia, but the stinking salve had stopped the bleeding. He took deep breaths, hoping that the burning would subside. "What's the plan for finding Erin?"

Rhun kept pacing, his steps quiet on the old rug. "Once the Cardinal arrives, we will put together a team to search for her and the book. The Sanguinists have a wide net of informants, especially in Rome. We'll find them."

Near as Jordan could tell, the Sanguinists' net of informants had been useless so far, but saying that wouldn't help. He stayed quiet as Nadia roughly bandaged his wounds. She had no future as a nurse.

Nadia tossed him a clean gray T-shirt, and he sat up to put it on. He now looked like a normal guy with a couple of big Band-Aids, instead of the survivor of a *strigoi* attack.

Progress.

Someone tapped on the door. Before anyone could reach it, it burst open.

The Cardinal stood in the doorway. Scarlet cassock and all.

He was flanked by men wearing blue pantaloons tucked into high black leather boots, blue long-sleeved shirts with flat white collars, white gloves, and black berets. They looked like they had stepped out of another century.

But the Sig Sauers in their hands were plenty modern.

4:12 P.M.

Erin froze as the light grew brighter below. She didn't want anyone to hear—then realized how ridiculous that was.

The cell had a single exit, and she and Nate were jammed in it, about ten feet up. The *strigoi* could hear heartbeats, so hiding was useless. The only chance of escape lay in flight.

Above her, Nate scrambled faster. His labored breathing expressed how much this effort cost him. And, since neither he nor Erin knew the length of the shaft, she had no idea if it made any difference. She kept close behind him, hoping for a miracle.

The grimwolf barked up the shaft.

The sound bounced off the stone, as if a pack of hellhounds were coming to get them.

Nate slipped.

Erin braced herself hard against both sides of the slot.

No use.

The impact of his body knocked her loose. She and Nate hurtled downward. Her head and arms glanced off the sides as she tried to slow them.

Then she dropped through empty air, Nate on top of her.

Her back struck not stone, but a figure that crashed to the floor underneath her.

She tried to push Nate off to roll free, but he was too heavy.

A woman snarled Slavic-sounding curses and with sharp elbows drove Erin to the side. Erin rolled off Bathory with no small amount of grim satisfaction.

A hulking *strigoi* picked Erin up in his left hand, Nate in his right. He must have been seven feet tall, bald, with beady eyes. He was dark-skinned, for a *strigoi,* and wore dirty cargo pants with a stained white T-shirt. The shirt hugged the contours of his muscular chest. He definitely didn't have a weapon on his upper body. She looked lower. A dagger in a leather sheath was strapped to his waistband.

He tossed Nate against the wall, then reached a hand down to Bathory.

And stopped.

He jerked his hand back.

Blood was seeping from a wound in Bathory's arm. A dirty white bandage had slid down to her elbow. Erin must have knocked it off when she hit her. Stitches had pulled out of a cut across her triceps. Blood trickled down her arm. Bathory glanced down and swore, then yanked the bandage up. It slid back down.

The grimwolf nuzzled her leg and whimpered.

"Back." Bathory pushed the wolf away roughly, almost frantically. "Magor, stay away."

The creature retreated a pace and sat.

Erin's eyes narrowed. *Interesting.*

Bathory struggled to her feet unaided. A drop of blood fell from her arm to the floor. The color looked strange, but Erin couldn't bend to look closer because the *strigoi* held her arm fast.

"You are an enterprising one." Bathory dusted off her pants.

"The first duty of any prisoner is to escape," Erin said.

With wide eyes, the *strigoi* stared at Bathory's wounded arm.

Erin had never seen a *strigoi* react to blood with fear rather than excitement. Clearly, injuring Bathory was a bad thing to do.

"I shall get my wound seen to." Bathory picked up her flashlight. "And return."

What would happen then?

Bathory turned to the *strigoi* who was holding Erin. "Mihir, stay and watch them. Don't let them even think of escaping."

Mihir bowed his head.

Bathory whistled for the grimwolf and headed down the tunnel. Another *strigoi* waited outside. He closed the door and tugged on the bars, probably to make sure that it was locked before following Bathory.

Erin was trapped in the cell again, but this time with an angry *strigoi* for a roommate. He tossed her to the side, and she twisted to keep from landing on Nate.

Mihir played his flashlight up the shaft and along the slot from which Erin and Nate had just fallen.

Erin bent over Nate. "You okay?"

His eyelids fluttered open. "This is the worst dig ever."

She smiled. "When we get out of this, I promise to write you one hell of a recommendation."

Mihir walked over, giving the single drop of Bathory's blood on the floor a wide berth. He loomed over them. "No more talking."

His eyes lingered on the fresh blood that oozed down Erin's neck. She, too, had torn open her wounds in the fall. She could see the hunger rise in his eyes.

She clenched her jaw. She would not be afraid. Her heart ignored her comforting words and raced. Afraid or not, she would use his bloodlust for her own advantage.

Instead of shrinking back like she wanted to, she stepped toward Mihir, tilting her neck to the side, knowing that he could smell the blood, hear the frightened heartbeat behind it. Rhun had barely been able to restrain himself when faced with flowing blood. Surely Mihir was weaker than the priest.

His eyes stayed locked on her neck, and his breathing roughened. She kept her left hand low. She would have only one chance—if she was lucky.

Mihir licked his lips, but he held back.

He needed a better invitation. Steeling herself, she dragged her fingers across her wounded throat. Never taking her eyes off his, she brushed her bloody fingertips across his lips.

Lightning-fast, Mihir reached a hand for her throat. Nate called out a warning, drawing the monster's attention for a flicker.

A flicker was long enough.

Erin dropped to one knee, jerked the *strigoi*'s dagger from its belt sheath, and drove it under his sternum.

He staggered forward. Blood spread across his shirt.

Nate pushed past her. He wrenched the knife from Mihir's body and, in one quick movement, slashed it across the *strigoi*'s throat. Mihir collapsed to the floor, dark lifeblood spurting wet across the stone. A puff of smoke rose in the air when his blood touched the drop of Bathory's.

Nate stood over him with the weapon, shaking from head to toe.

Mihir's eyes went glassy and dead. Blood pooled around him.

"Nate?"

He spun on her, knife high.

"Nate," she said soothingly. "It's me."

He lowered the dagger. "Sorry. What he did to me . . . with his teeth . . ."

"I know," she said. She didn't know, not really, but Nate needed to hear the words. "Let's get up the shaft before that witch comes back."

This time she took the lead, playing the beam of Mihir's flashlight along the walls. Nate tucked the bloody knife into his waistband and followed with greater strength than before, apparently fueled by the adrenaline from the battle.

Erin shone the light straight up. The shaft didn't lead to the arena, as she'd hoped. It ended in what looked like a metal plate, trapping them inside. They couldn't climb straight out.

She sagged back against the wall, catching herself before she slipped onto Nate.

Then she checked the walls of the shaft and her eyes lit upon a secondary shaft that opened off the side. It had probably housed a second tier of animal cages. It might lead somewhere.

And even that slim hope was better than staying here.

"Nate!" she called, and pointed the beam toward the secondary shaft. "Look!"

He smiled. "Let's get going."

With proper illumination and renewed determination, they chimneyed up the vertical slot and reached the side passageway. It was more like a small anteroom than a cross shaft.

She played her light around the cell. Bars had once sealed the way out, but now only piles of rust and the stumps of rods remained.

Erin climbed over them into the next passageway.

She squinted and covered her hand over the flashlight to darken the way.

Far ahead, a thin line of pale yellow light beckoned.

A way out.

56

October 28, 4:30 P.M., CET
Vatican City, Italy

Cardinal Bernard swept through the halls of the Apostolic Palace like a thundercloud.

Rhun followed, herded by a cadre of Swiss Guards with their weapons drawn. Nadia walked on his left, seemingly unconcerned; Jordan tromped on his right, looking more angry than worried. Rhun was grateful to have them both beside him.

Cardinal Bernard's straight back conveyed his wrath. His scarlet cassock twitched behind him. He was no doubt furious that Nadia had lied to him about Rhun's death.

Rhun looked back at the line of Swiss Guardsmen. At the tail end marched Father Ambrose, not bothering to hide his gleeful smirk.

With Nadia's help, Rhun could have easily overpowered them all, but he had no wish to escape. He wanted to make Bernard understand what had happened and to enlist his aid in recovering Erin and the book. He prayed that there was still time.

Bernard unlocked the door to a receiving room and led them in.

The Cardinal crossed and dropped heavily at a round mahogany table, then gestured for Rhun to sit at his right, his usual place. Perhaps he was not so angry, after all, Rhun thought as he pulled out a spindly antique chair, its cushion covered in amber fabric, and sat.

"Rhun." Bernard's stern tone dispelled that momentary hope. "You lied to me. To *me*."

"*I* lied to you," Nadia corrected. "The blame rests on my shoulders."

Bernard waved a hand at her dismissively. "He allowed it to happen."

"I did." Rhun bowed his head. "I take full responsibility."

Nadia folded her arms. "Very well. If I bear no responsibility, may I leave?"

"No one leaves until this situation is explained to my satisfaction."

"Do you want a confession?" Rhun asked. "None of that matters now. The Belial have the book."

Bernard sat back in his chair. "I see."

"The Belial are in Rome." Rhun placed his palms on the gleaming table as if to stand. "We must search for them."

"Stay," Bernard ordered, as if Rhun were a dog. "First, tell me how this came to be."

Rhun bristled. He fingered his rosary, seeking to calm himself before he recounted the events in Russia. He spoke quickly, but Bernard slowed him down with question after question, picking at the story for flaws. His theologian's mind sought inconsistencies, tried to uncover lies.

And all the while minutes ticked away.

No longer able to sit as he told the story, Rhun began to pace, stopping to stare out the window at the darkening square below. Out on the plaza, people were reaching for jackets, gathering up belongings. Sunset was close, another half hour or so away; then the *strigoi* would be free. Every second decreased the chances that Rhun and Jordan would find Erin alive or recover the book. Still, the Cardinal pressed him.

"If you're going to interrogate us all day," Jordan broke in, "how about you send out a team to look for Erin and the book, just in case we haven't come all this way simply to spin you a tale?"

"You do not speak to the Cardinal that way!" Ambrose glared at him.

"Don't I?" Jordan pushed back from the table, clearly ready to make short work of Ambrose. Nadia shifted in her seat. If Rhun gave the word, both she and Jordan were ready to fight.

Rhun held up a restraining hand. "Calm yourselves. We—"

A light knock sounded on the door.

Rhun listened. Five men and a woman. He smiled as he recognized one of the heartbeats. He had to resist falling to his knees and giving thanks to the Lord. That would come later.

Nadia heard it, too, catching his eye.

Jordan looked from one to the other, his handsome face contorted with confusion.

Ambrose put on his most supercilious expression and opened the door.

In walked Erin.

Bathory's collar had left wounds and trails of dried blood on her throat. Dirt smudged her face and hands, and she looked exhausted. The young man following her looked worse.

But she was alive.

4:40 P.M.

Jordan swept Erin into the best hug she'd had in a very long time. She closed her eyes and leaned her head against his chest. She wished that she could rest there for a very, very long time.

"How did you get here?" Rhun spoke. "And who is your companion?"

Erin disentangled herself from a grinning Jordan. "This is Nate Highsmith. He was part of my team in Caesarea. Bathory captured him and brought him to Rome."

Nate shook hands all around, casting a suspicious, jealous glare at Jordan after that unmistakably warm hug.

Jordan didn't seem to notice, remaining all smiles. He kept looking at Erin, and she couldn't help but smile back. When Bathory had dragged her away and left Jordan and Rhun in Rasputin's clutches, she had feared she might never see either of them again.

Jordan quickly caught her up on what had happened in the past few hours.

In turn, she explained how she and Nate had escaped by following the tunnels out of Nero's Circus and into Vatican City. Once here, she had demanded to see Cardinal Bernard, whereupon the Swiss Guard took them into immediate custody.

"The ruins of the Circus!" Rhun said. "Of course. That cursed warren of tunnels would offer the perfect shelter for the Belial."

"Why?" Jordan asked.

"It's underground, and protected from the light, so Bathory's *strigoi* can roam freely during the day," Rhun said. "But more important, the circus is the most unholy place in Rome, its sands forever tainted by the blood of the Christians who were martyred there. That unholiness would strengthen her forces and weaken ours."

Cardinal Bernard gestured to one of the guardsmen and Ambrose. "Send troops to the circus. Sanguinists and humans. They must sweep the tunnels and retrieve the book. And inform His Holiness."

The soldier and the priest nodded and left.

The Cardinal walked Erin and Nate through the events again, matching details. It took him a long time, but eventually he looked like he believed they were telling the truth.

"Describe the book to me again." The Cardinal closed his eyes and steepled his fingers.

"It's better if I draw you a sketch," Erin said, and waved for paper and pen.

Nodding, the Cardinal passed her some papal stationery and a pen. Working quickly, she began drawing a crude representation of the images atop the book.

"It's a block of lead about the size of a Gutenberg Bible," Erin said, and quickly described the strange imagery that was etched into it: the skeleton and the man, embracing each other and bound by a braided rope, along with the inkwell-like indentations and the Greek symbols.

"Alpha and Omega," the Cardinal muttered as she finished. "That stands for Jesus, of course."

"I'm not so sure." Erin hated to pick a fight, but something told her that the Cardinal was wrong.

"Of course it does! *I am the Alpha and the Omega, the first and the last.* From the Book of Revelation." His brown eyes looked angry.

"But Alpha and Omega are also the first and last letters in the Greek alphabet." Something moved around in the shadows of her mind. "The *first* and the *last*."

As she finished her sketch, something nagged at her about the drawing—then she suddenly knew the answer. A cold certainty spread through her. She had seen a similar image as the one depicted on the book throughout the Apostolic Palace. That iconic symbol was found everywhere—even at the top of the piece of stationery in her hand.

She stared at the others, her eyes widening. "I think—"

Just then, a Swiss Guardsman slammed open the door behind her, making her flinch. He came running inside, his cheeks bright with panic. "Your Eminence, someone has broken into the papal tomb in the necropolis!"

Erin twisted around, meeting the guard's eyes. "And they did something with the bones of Saint Peter, didn't they?"

He took a full step back in surprise. "S-someone stole them."

The Cardinal gasped, while Rhun and Nadia leaped to their feet.

"Of course they did!" Erin practically shouted, her heart racing. "Of course!"

All eyes turned to her.

"I know how to open the book!" she exclaimed.

She remembered the look on Bathory's face when they had been talking about the transformation of the book, and about how alchemical ingredients were needed in order to catalyze the transformation of ordinary lead into the golden word of Christ.

Bathory had already figured out the Alpha and Omega.

All heads turned to Erin.

"Go ahead," Jordan said.

"The book has the clues to open it on the cover." Her voice trembled. "And Bathory figured it out."

"You'd better explain quickly," Jordan said.

Erin bent to the stationery and circled the papal seal at the top.

It depicted two keys—the gold and silver keys of Saint Peter—crossed at the middle and bound by loops of crimson rope. The papal seal and the image on the book bore an uncanny resemblance to each other—but instead of *keys* representing the popes, the book had two *figures* crossed in a similar fashion.

Erin explained: "Saint Peter hid the book two millennia ago. He must have seen the design on the Gospel, a design that was to become better and better known as the centuries passed—moving out of secrecy into the open sometime during the twelfth century when the crossed keys began to appear as heraldic symbols of the popes. But the source for that design must have come from the images inscribed on the Blood Gospel and borne by Saint Peter."

She tapped the papal seal. "The keys represent the papacy. So do the figures. The skeleton and the man." She pushed hair back off her face. "*Alpha* stands for *first*. Under that is the drawing of a *skeleton*."

"Yes?" Rhun leaned in close, dark eyes staring at her as if he could read the answer in her face.

"That symbol represents the *bones* of the *first* pope."

"Saint Peter!" the Cardinal said. "That's why they stole his bones."

"To be used as the first ingredient in opening the book. I believe some of Saint Peter's ground-up bone is meant to fill that first inkwell-like hole on the cover."

Jordan stirred. "Piers might have been trying to tell us that in Germany. He kept saying 'book'—and 'bones.' "

"Exactly." She tapped the other half of the picture. "This depiction of a *living* man represents the current pope. The Omega pope. The last pope."

"So they need the current pope's bones, too?" Jordan asked, looking squeamish.

She shook her head.

"Then what do they need?" Rhun asked.

"What does a man have that a skeleton doesn't?" She started listing. "Life. Flesh. Blood."

"Blood?" Jordan interrupted. "Piers mentioned that, too, but in German. *Blut*."

"The second ingredient . . ." Erin's hands turned to ice as the full realization dawned on her. She looked at the others. "They need the *blood* of the current pope."

4:48 P.M.

Rhun and Nadia ran behind Bernard, flanking him, forming their own triad. No longer concerned about revealing their unnatural heritage, they moved at top speed, shadows sweeping the halls of the Apostolic Palace. The humans fell behind. But this was no affair of theirs.

Rhun sprinted down the long hall that led to His Holiness's bedroom. Walls covered in rich wood flashed by. Crucifixes and dark religious paintings hung throughout the hall. A fortune in art, but that would not be enough to save an old man's life. Only they could do that.

Grant, O God, Thy protection, and in protection, strength.

The pope's bedroom door stood open, spilling light into the dark hall.

Shadows flickered inside.

Bernard ran into the room without pause or a knock, he and Nadia in formation close behind him. A wave of blood assaulted his senses. They were too late.

His Holiness lay on his side on the floor. Blood flowed from his opened neck onto his holy white cassock. On the floor next to his body lay a straight razor, probably his own. Near his old white head were his red papal shoes, neatly lined up next to his bed. His usually carefully combed hair was tousled, his lined face pale with shock, his warm blue eyes closed.

Ambrose was kneeling by him. Blood coated his palms. He was trying, ineffectually, to stanch the wound.

Bernard joined Ambrose on the floor, Nadia stepped into the adjoining bathroom, and Rhun assessed the bedroom for threats. Thick velvet curtains were drawn tight, the simple brass bed rumpled and empty, the chair pushed straight into the antique desk, bookshelf orderly behind it.

Rhun understood.

They had taken him in his bed as he rested, and with little struggle.

Rhun closed his eyes and reached out with other senses. The only heartbeats in the room belonged to Ambrose and His Holiness. The only smells were familiar ones: Ambrose, His Holiness, the other Sanguinists, paper, dust, and a trace of incense. And, overlying it all, the old man's spilled blood.

He returned his attention to His Holiness. His face had lost even the small amount of color it had when they'd arrived. His breath rasped out through his partially opened mouth.

"I came to tell him and he . . . he . . ." Ambrose stuttered. "He needs a doctor. Get him a doctor!"

Bernard pressed a firm palm on the pope's wound. Nadia nodded once to let the Cardinal know that the bathroom was clear, then ran from the room, as fleet as the wind.

Ambrose wiped his hands down his black cassock. His heart tripped along in fear or shock. He looked so pale and lost that Rhun pitied him.

Rhun dropped his hand to Bernard's shoulder. "We must take him to the surgery. Perhaps his physician can help him there."

Bernard's shocked eyes met his.

"Bernard!" he said sharply.

The Cardinal's eyes cleared. "Of course."

Bernard kept one hand tight against His Holiness's throat and slid the other under his shoulders. Rhun put his own arms under the pope, too. The slight weight would be easy to bear. The old man's heart stumbled, weakness in every beat. Without help, he did not have long to live.

Rhun and Bernard lifted the wounded man and bore him toward the emergency surgery. Nadia would bring the physician there.

This time their progress down the hall was slow. Rhun had time to see the ancient paintings, framed in heavy wood. This was the wall of saints, and each picture told a story of pain and martyrdom.

Swiss Guardsmen pounded down the hall, arriving with Erin, Jordan, and Nate.

"His Holiness is grievously wounded." Bernard spoke in the formal Italian of his long-ago boyhood. Rhun had not heard that accent for many years. Bernard must be still in shock.

The guards parted like water to let them through.

As Rhun had hoped, Nadia waited at the surgery, a disheveled man in a white coat next to her. He looked as if she had dragged him from his bed, running every step.

He blanched when he saw whom they carried.

They stepped past him into the sleek modern surgery. Stainless-steel surfaces gleamed and modern machines waited under plastic covers. On the wall was only a simple round clock and a heavy iron cross.

Rhun and Bernard laid His Holiness gently on the clean white bed. Bernard still held his wound closed. "A razor did this," he explained.

A second doctor rushed in.

"Everyone must leave," the first doctor said. "Only medical staff allowed."

As the physicians began to administer to His Holiness, Rhun prayed that they would find a way to save him. There was nothing more for the Sanguinists to do.

He stepped out into the hall. Drops of the pope's blood gleamed against the wooden floor. "Where did Nadia go?"

"She took a division of the guardsmen back down the hall," Jordan said. "To look for the guy who did this."

If the attacker could be found, Nadia would find him. Rhun leaned against the wood paneling. Bernard reached an arm around his shoulders, and he leaned against him. A successful papal assassination had not occurred in centuries.

"What does this mean for Bathory, Erin?" Jordan asked.

Her eyes told Rhun all he needed to know. "It means that Bathory has both ingredients necessary to open the book."

57

October 28, 5:05 P.M., CET
Vatican City, Italy

Standing outside the surgery room, Erin wished that she had better news. The Belial had the book and the means to open it. Would that be enough for them to transfigure it? Had evil already won?

Nate slumped and sat on the floor next to her. Fresh blood soaked his pant leg. She had never seen him so pale. He leaned his head back against the wall.

Jordan pulled a water bottle out of his coat pocket and pressed it into the kid's hands.

Nate downed it in one long swallow. How long had it been since he'd had a drink? It had never even occurred to Erin to ask if he was thirsty, and she'd basically had him sprinting from the moment he had been tossed into her cell.

Bernard made eye contact with a Swiss Guardsman. He pointed at Nate. "This man must be taken to medical care. The woman, too."

"Take Nate now," Erin said. "I'll follow along in a minute."

Bernard hesitated, then nodded in agreement. The guardsman helped Nate to his feet.

"I'm fine." Nate pulled himself up straighter, but his back began to slide down the dark oak paneling.

"Of course you are," she said. "So am I. But let's just humor them. I'll be right behind you."

Nate raised a skeptical eyebrow but didn't protest as two guardsmen herded him down the hall. The kid was tough. He'd be fine. She tried not to think of watching Heinrich being carried away. She would see Nate again soon.

Jordan pulled out his first-aid kit. "Sure you don't want to go with the kid?"

"The neck looks more dramatic than it is," she said.

"Looks pretty dramatic." Jordan pulled out an alcohol wipe, the smell all too familiar to Erin.

She gritted her teeth when he reached for her, but the touch of his hands on her neck was featherlight.

"So what's next?" His familiar blue eyes looked into hers.

Her heart sped up. "Next?"

"What will Bathory do now? Where will she open the book?" From the way he asked, it sounded as if he thought she knew the answer.

She tried to talk, not to think about how close he stood, how gently he touched her throat. "The book cares very much about how it is to be opened and where."

"You make it sound like a person." Jordan stroked hair back from her neck and cleaned the side, stroking the wipe down from her jawline to her collarbone.

She shivered and shifted her feet to cover the movement. "I wonder if it doesn't have some kind of awareness, some part of its maker tied to it."

"I agree." Bernard straightened the scarlet zucchetto he was wearing atop his white hair. "Always that has been my interpretation of the prophecy. And the book must be opened in Rome. But where in Rome?"

"If holy ground is important to the Sanguinists," Erin said, sensing she was onto something, "it matters to the book, too. What's the holiest place in Rome? Saint Peter's tomb." She stepped away from Jordan. She needed to think, which meant moving clear of his warmth, his musky scent. "But if the Belial wanted to open the book down there, they would have taken the pope's blood first, then the bone so they could open it right there where the bones are."

"Makes sense," Jordan said. "Why break in twice, once to steal the bones and once to open the book?"

A bell tolled. Rhun and Bernard exchanged a glance.

"What does that mean?" Jordan pulled out a roll of gauze.

"The Swiss Guard are sounding the alarm," Bernard answered. "They are evacuating tourists from Vatican City."

"Then Bathory doesn't have much time." If only she had a better idea of where that witch might be. Then a ray of hope dawned. "Wait! The basilica. It's built *above* Peter's tomb. The holiest part of the holiest church in Rome."

Before she even finished her sentence, Rhun and Bernard vanished from her side, like a pair of apparitions. They fled down the hall with eerie speed. No one watching them would think for a second that they were human.

Jordan shook his head. "Guess they're giving up the secret identity thing." He lifted an eyebrow and held out a hand. "Feel like one more run?"

She nodded and let him pull her to her feet.

He broke into a jog after collecting his Heckler & Koch submachine gun, which Nadia had been kind enough to return from Germany, along with his Colt pistol. Erin followed Jordan through the spacious halls of the Apostolic Palace and toward the square. No one tried to stop them.

They bounded down a flight of stairs, taking two at a time, to the wide hall that led to a bronze door and out to St. Peter's Square.

Ahead, two Swiss Guards in formal blue-, red-, and yellow-striped tunics and tights swung the doors open for Rhun and the Cardinal.

Jordan sped up, trying to catch them.

"We're with those two!" Jordan yelled.

"Let them pass," the Cardinal called over his shoulder, already out onto the square.

The guardsmen stood aside as the couple ran through.

Behind them, the doors slammed closed with a resounding *thud*. No one would be allowed to enter again so easily.

Erin hurried down the steps, already out of breath. Marble pillars rose on either side of her, climbing more than twenty-five feet into the air. The scale of everything made her feel like a child who had broken into the home of a giant.

They raced down into the open square, where Jordan skidded to a halt.

The plaza teemed with people. They streamed from the basilica and the colonnades; they parted in riptides around the obelisk and the fountains, all heading for the exit and the streets. The setting sun washed their faces a warm orange.

Swiss Guard troops jostled them forward, as if they were herding cattle.

Far ahead, Bernard and Rhun's progress had slowed as they tried to force their way forward against that current of humanity.

"Grab my belt!" Jordan yelled over his shoulder.

Erin wrapped her fingers around the thick leather.

Jordan pushed himself out into the square like a fullback. Instead of cutting straight through the crowd like the Sanguinists, he hugged its edges, one arm up. The crowd rippled to the side around him.

Erin kept pace, trying to match his stride. Jordan's left shoulder knocked against a fleeing tourist. It was his wounded side, but he didn't even flinch.

Reaching the basilica, he cut left toward the door. Just ahead, Rhun and the Cardinal sprinted through the entrance in a flash of scarlet and black.

Erin glanced up. Above the massive dome of the basilica, the sky glowed amber orange.

The sun had set.

Distracted by what that implied, she didn't see the monk until it was too late. He slammed into her, knocking her hand off Jordan's belt. The monk muttered what sounded like an apology in Polish, his hands reaching to pat her shoulder.

"It's okay," she said.

Jordan didn't seem to notice that she was gone as he pushed through the door ahead of her. The two Swiss Guardsmen manning the doors were too distracted by the tourists coming out, but they collected their wits enough to collar her when she tried to follow.

Already inside, Jordan turned back.

"Go on!" she called. He could do more good against Bathory than she could anyway.

He nodded and hurried deeper into the basilica.

"The building is being evacuated, miss." The guardsman's polite words contrasted with the hard fingers digging into her arm. "I'm afraid I'm going to have to ask you to—"

A flash of gold radiated from inside the basilica, bursting with the blinding brilliance of a supernova. Along with it came a sweet scent, and a hint of music just beyond hearing, causing the ear to strain toward it.

The guard dropped her arm and turned to stare inside.

It's happening . . .

Needing to bear witness, Erin quickly sidestepped the guard and slipped over the threshold. Once inside, she raced through the portico, knocking aside a tourist who stood as transfixed as the guard.

She hurried through the inner doors and into the main nave. A forest of massive stone pillars rose ahead, holding up the elaborately decorated roof of the basilica. She stared across the expansive floor to the distant papal altar in the center of the church. Golden light flowed from beneath the massive black-and-gilt baldachin that sheltered the altar. The bronze structure seemed to tremble within that glow, like a shimmering mirage above hot desert sands. Or maybe the power behind that brilliance was too much for any man-made structure to contain within it.

Without thinking, Erin ran toward that light, dodging straggling tourists heading in the opposite direction. But already most of the basilica had emptied out, leaving the way open.

It was like sprinting across a football field, except that she was indoors. She knew that St. Peter's Basilica had the largest interior of any church in the world. She had visited it many times in the past, but she had never *run* through it. As she did so now, her eyes remained fixed on the glowing brilliance flowing out from under the baldachin.

As she got closer, she was struck by the sheer size of the baldachin. Marble plinths as tall as a man supported twisted black Solomonic columns that rose sixty feet into the air. They held up its massive bronze canopy, edged with fanciful borders and topped by statues and a cross.

Under that canopy, in the very center of the basilica, stood Bathory.

Her red hair blazed in the golden light that was blasting from the object in her hands. The brilliance illuminated every alcove and corner of the church. All the statues and frescoes pulsed with a deep, mystical light as if they sought to merge with the radiance flowing from the baldachin.

In Bathory's hands, the book had transformed from lead to gold.

Transfiguration, Erin thought.

I was right.

She sprinted past the last of the statues lining the nave. Ahead, Jordan slowed to let her catch up. He caught her hand, and they ran together down the aisle toward the light.

Farther ahead, Rhun and Bernard stood frozen at the edge of the baldachin.

Stopped by a holiness that frightened even them.

58

October 28, 5:11 P.M., CET
Vatican City, Italy

Bathory's blood sang with joy as golden light bathed her body.

She breathed in warmth and love. The pain that had flowed through her veins since she had reached womanhood began to recede. She felt the black mark on her throat fading, washed away by the brilliance. How could any darkness withstand this light?

The lead block warmed within her palms. It pulsed with its own heartbeat, like any living thing. With each passing second, it weighed less and less, until it felt as if it were floating above her fingers.

In her hand, the block had been replaced by pure golden light.

The radiance mesmerized her. It lit her eyes but did not burn them. She could gaze upon it forever, dwell forever in its light, explore its mystery for all time. Far above, the golden sun painted on the bottom of the baldachin outlined the painting of a white dove. The dove flew, free, in the light.

As did she.

But not for long.

The archaeologist and the soldier rushed toward her. The knights circled, closing in. Swiss Guard troops rushed down the nave. She was trapped. They would kill her, spill her blood on the book, steal its light from her.

As if sensing her fear, the radiance died away, fading until only an actual book rested in her palms, weighing down her hands.

She stared at the book, transfixed.

The tome was bound in ordinary sheepskin, its surface unadorned. Her fingertips caressed the worn leather while the scent of ancient sands rose up to her nostrils.

How could such brilliance shine from something so simple and ordinary?

Then she knew the answer.

She pictured Christ's visage—an ordinary man's face, hiding a wellspring of divinity.

Tears ran down her cheeks as a heavy ache returned to her blood.

Without touching her throat, she knew that the black mark had returned.

She shook her head to clear the glow that still filled her mind. It felt as if she had just awakened from a deep dream. But she did not have the luxury of distraction.

She stared out across the basilica, knowing what she had to do. She needed a way out and intended to create her own exit.

Moving swiftly, she leaped away from the altar into the apse behind her and retreated back toward the giant black marble throne high on the wall. It was the throne of Saint Peter, surrounded by popes and angels and rays of golden light that seemed cheap in comparison to what she had just witnessed.

Once far enough away from the altar, she reached into her pocket, found the transmitter she had hidden there, and pressed the detonator button.

The blast was a distant echo, like a clap of thunder beyond the horizon. The floor jolted under her feet. She'd planted charges deep in the necropolis below, beneath the very altar where she had been standing.

She watched with satisfaction as the marble floor shattered in front of her, cracking like broken ice under the heavy baldachin. The massive bronze canopy shook—then, as she watched, the entire structure crashed under its own weight through the floor, dropping cleanly through the hole.

Its base struck the floor of the necropolis below with the resounding *boom* of Heaven's gate slamming shut.

So be it.

She waved rock dust and smoke from her eyes and watched as the baldachin came to a shuddering rest, sunk most of the way through the floor. Only the canopy still remained visible in the nave, tilted crookedly.

Her charges had worked perfectly.

On the far side of the hole, a Swiss Guardsman fell screaming into the crater as the edge broke under him.

To the left, the Sanguinists jumped back like startled lions, leaping into the transept on that side. The archaeologist and soldier took shelter to the right. More Swiss Guardsmen came rushing down the center of the nave toward the site of the destruction.

But the *strigoi* army below in the necropolis did not wait. With the sunset here, they swarmed up the twisted columns of the fallen baldachin, a horde of demons rising out of the Stygian darkness. They swarmed over the metal canopy and boiled into the basilica like ants fleeing from an anthill. Even weakened by the holiness of the sanctuary, they would make short work of the Swiss Guards and buy Bathory time to escape.

She leaped from the broken edge of the floor onto one of the huge angels atop the baldachin's canopy. Holding the book in one hand, she wrapped the other around a gilded wing.

Gunshots cracked at her.

She swung, keeping the angel between herself and the sniper. She quickly tucked the book into the front of her shirt to free her hands—then stretched out on her stomach and lowered her legs over the edge of the canopy, her feet searching for toeholds in the ornamented capital of a column. With all of its fanciful decorations, the baldachin made a lovely hundred-foot-tall ladder leading down into the tunnels of the necropolis, the city of the dead that lay beneath the basilica.

Finding her footing, Bathory clambered down a twisted column of the baldachin, finding additional handholds among the metal garlands sculpted on the surface.

Far below, Magor howled for her.

She smiled, feeling the weight of the book against her breasts.

Together, they would escape Rome—and maybe even Him.

59

October 28, 5:15 P.M., CET
Vatican City, Italy

Jordan rolled off Erin. Had he hurt her? He had knocked her to the marble floor with some force when the explosion hit.

"Erin?"

She pointed behind him.

A cloud of dust obscured most of the basilica behind him, but Jordan swung his Heckler & Koch submachine gun out of his coat as he turned. He fired once, striking a *strigoi* in the shoulder as it stepped free of the pall of smoke. Dark blood sprayed against white stone. The *strigoi* backed off, more slowly than Jordan had expected, like it was walking through water. He trained his gun on it, but he hated to let loose in the basilica.

Had all the civilians gotten out?

He couldn't see far through the dust to be sure, but he did spot the gaping hole with the black sculpture resting crookedly down its throat. He had to admire the skill of the enemy's demolitions expert.

With his left hand he pulled Erin to her feet and handed her his Colt 1911 pistol.

She took it, her eyes on the wounded *strigoi*. "They seem dazed."

"Must be the sanctified ground weakening them." He kept his gun up and ready to fire. "But dazed or not, they're blocking our way to the exits."

"What do we do?"

He pulled her with him. "Let's get into a corner where nobody can circle behind us."

Erin resisted, pointing to the smoking crater in the floor. "We have to follow Bathory. She can't escape with the Gospel."

He sighed, resigned, knowing Erin would go after the woman anyway if he balked. "You're the boss."

She smiled at his tone.

Using the dust from the explosion as cover, the two of them circled around to the apse, edging closer to the hole. Erin kept one step behind, her pistol up, moving in tandem with him.

Most of the *strigoi* forces were concentrating their attention on the Swiss Guardsmen racing into the basilica with their guns blazing. Their lack of caution suggested that the civilians had been cleared out.

Good to know, Jordan thought.

He and Erin reached the back of the crater without drawing any attention. The entire baldachin leaned drunkenly before them, the canopy canted to one side. From the basilica floor, the bronze structure had appeared to be a hundred feet tall. Now only twenty feet stuck out, which meant an eighty-foot climb down into the darkness—with *strigoi* waiting at the bottom.

The dust to the right swirled, revealing two black-cloaked figures. Rhun and the Cardinal.

"Take that woman out of St. Peter's," Bernard ordered.

"You try telling her that," Jordan said.

Proving the impossibility of ordering "that woman" to do *anything,* Erin jumped from the crumbling marble edge out onto the bronze canopy. She teetered backward, then clutched at one of the smaller angels, one who held a crown aloft.

Jordan and Rhun jumped at the same time, landing to either side of her, both reaching to steady her. The Cardinal landed an instant later, higher up the canopy, next to the sphere that was topped by a cross. That seemed fitting.

"If you follow," Rhun warned, "stay behind me."

Without waiting for a response, the priest clambered down one side of the canopy.

Jordan gripped Erin's shoulder before she moved, catching her eye. "As soon as you're over the edge, get to the *inside* of the columns. Use that bronze bulk to shield you as much as possible if there is any shooting."

She leaned forward and kissed him quick on the lips—then freed her grip on the angel, slid down the tilted bronze surface, and vanished over the edge.

With his heart in his throat, Jordan stood still for a moment, shocked, then hustled after her. No matter what, he had to keep her safe.

Reaching the edge, he flipped to his belly, lowered his legs, and discovered plenty of footholds and handholds. In moments, he was leaving the light above for the blackness below. Once this was over, he vowed to climb the tallest building he could find, sit up on its roof, and spend an entire day staring at the sun and enjoying a clean breeze on his face. But for now, he kept climbing *down,* again, following the blond crown of Erin's head. She heeded his advice and got to the inside of the column.

He fitted his fingers into the shallow golden swirls decorating the column, moving fast, hoping to get as far down as he could in case he his lost his grip and fell.

Then a dark shadow, tinged with red, stormed past him.

The Cardinal.

"Be warned!" Bernard yelled as he passed. "The enemy is on all sides!"

Great.

Moments later, Jordan's boots hit the stone floor. He clicked on the flashlight attached to his machine pistol. All around, black shapes converged upon him, boiling out of the dark passageways of the necropolis.

To the right, he spotted Bathory—shadowed by her massive grimwolf. The pair rounded a corner and disappeared into a black tunnel.

"Over there!" Jordan yelled, and pointed.

Rhun and the Cardinal stepped into formation, with Bernard at the head. Jordan took the left side, pushing Erin between him and Rhun. It wasn't much, but it was the safest place for her. She brought her pistol up and fired once into the darkness.

Jordan turned and opened up with his machine pistol.

Dark blood splattered rough stone walls.

Ahead, the Cardinal grappled hand to hand with three *strigoi,* proving his spryness.

But at this rate, they'd never reach that tunnel.

Then a voice spoke at his ear, seemingly arriving out of thin air.

"I bring reinforcements."

He turned to discover the cherubic, bespectacled Brother Leopold at his shoulder. Beyond his small frame, a cadre of Sanguinist monks—twenty strong—fell like rain from the baldachin and landed in a circle around Jordan's group, already fighting before their feet hit the floor.

Leopold joined Jordan, pushing his eyeglasses higher on his nose, looking more like a kid brother than an undying warrior of Christ.

As if zeroing in on a weaker target, a *strigoi* lunged out of the darkness behind the short scholar; the flash of sword was the only warning.

Jordan reacted on pure muscle memory. He jerked his machine pistol up and caught the blade, deflecting it from Leopold's neck. The edge still grazed a bloody line across the young Sanguinist's shoulders.

The scholar's eyes grew round.

Angered, the *strigoi* turned toward Jordan. He was a hulking figure with dark skin and pale tattoos, studs puncturing his nose and ears. Jordan remembered seeing the guy in Germany, at Bathory's side. He figured him to be some sort of lieutenant for the Belial—which meant he must have helped orchestrate the attack on Jordan's men in Masada.

The beast smiled, showing teeth.

"Get back, Leopold," Jordan warned, ready to square off with this bastard, who only kept smiling.

The young monk's eyes became huge as he stared at Jordan—or rather *behind* Jordan.

Caught in the reflection of Leopold's eyeglasses, Jordan spotted movement.

He twirled, his American Bowie knife appearing in his fingers.

A gaunt, skeletal version of the larger lieutenant lunged at him, impossibly wide jaws going for his throat.

Jordan continued his spin and drove the silver-plated blade between those snapping jaws, punching it hilt-deep.

Chew on that.

The creature screamed, jerking straight up into the air like a jack-in-the-box, ripping the knife's haft from Jordan's fingers. As it flew high, smoke and boiling blood erupted from its mouth, from the back of its skull.

The body fell and struck the stone, already dead.

A scream of rage erupted behind him. "Rafik!"

Feral, grief-filled eyes fixed on Jordan.

"Hurts, doesn't it?" Jordan growled. "Losing someone you love."

The *strigoi* launched himself at Jordan, flying through the air, his cloak billowing wide, like a man-size icarops.

Jordan dropped to a knee, tilted his submachine gun up, and unloaded at full auto, shredding the monster in the chest with pure silver. "That's for my men."

The *strigoi* lieutenant clattered to the stone, his body steaming. But he was still alive, in agony, dragging himself toward the impaled Rafik.

Leopold scooped up the monster's abandoned sword, the very weapon that had come close to killing him. He strode to the struggling *strigoi.*

The creature had almost reached his goal, extending a bloody arm, his fingers scrabbling to reach the one called Rafik, to touch him one last time.

Mercilessly, Leopold swung the sword in a blurring flash.

The *strigoi*'s head flew off his body, and the stretching arm fell limply to the floor.

The fingers dropped short, never reaching the other, the two remaining forever separated.

Leopold turned and stared around the cavern, his brow pinched in confusion. "Where did everyone else go?"

Jordan spun, searching the spot where Erin had been a half minute ago.

She was gone.

And Rhun with her.

60

October 28, 5:34 P.M., CET
Necropolis below St. Peter's Basilica, Italy

Erin twisted to the side as a *strigoi*'s blade thrust toward her.

Then Rhun was there. He yanked her nearly off her feet and hauled her behind him. With one quick step forward, he slashed his blade across the *strigoi*'s throat, felling him like a sapling.

She stared around, realizing they were momentarily alone in the tunnel down which Bathory had fled. She glanced back. Out in the main necropolis, Sanguinists were flowing down the columns to join the subterranean battle.

"Return to Jordan when it's safe," Rhun said fiercely, brooking no argument as he nodded back to the fighting. "I shall overtake Bathory."

With a swirl of his cassock, he disappeared down the dark tunnel.

With no choice, Erin faced the battlefield, heard the screams, smelled the blood. She searched the carnage until she spotted Jordan. He stood with his back to one of the metal plinths, firing at another tunnel that disgorged a flow of *strigoi*.

It was chaos, a hellish Bosch painting come to life.

She would never make it through that gauntlet. If the *strigoi* didn't get her, friendly fire might. She turned back toward the empty tunnel that Rhun had taken. It seemed the safest choice.

She kept her light low and to the left, running her right hand along the side of the tunnel, feeling for a side tunnel. If she came to a crossroads and she didn't know which direction Rhun had taken, she'd have to turn back.

Shots echoed ahead of her, coming from a place where a gray light flowed from around a bend in the tunnel.

She hurried forward—then a fierce, guttural growling flowed back to her, slowing her feet to a more cautious pace.

She brought up Jordan's Colt, loaded with silver ammunition. She moved more warily as she reached the turn in the tunnel. Step-by-step, she edged around the bend.

The *crack* of a pistol made her jump.

A short way down the tunnel, she watched Rhun leap with unnatural speed past the bulk of the grimwolf, his gun smoking. Landing beyond it, he lunged down the tunnel, away from the wolf, ready to continue his pursuit of Bathory, who was nowhere in sight—but then he skidded to a stop, turning as he did so with incredible grace.

Over the bulk of the wolf, his eyes found her. No doubt he had heard her heartbeat or noted the shift in shadows as she arrived with her flashlight.

He wasn't the only one.

The grimwolf jerked around, facing her, its teeth bared, its muscles bunched to spring.

"Erin, run!"

The beast's ears twitched toward Rhun, but it didn't turn from Erin.

Rhun came sprinting back, his pistol up, firing at the monster's hind end.

That got its attention.

With a deafening howl, it surged around, and with a heave of its back legs, bowled into Rhun. Erin lost sight of him, blocked by the body of the wolf.

More shots were fired.

She pointed her Colt but didn't fire, fearing she might strike Rhun with its silver bullets.

Then the wolf tossed its thick neck—with Rhun clutched in its jaws. The massive beast shook him like a rag doll. Blood sprayed the walls of the tunnel. Rhun lost his handgun and struggled to free a knife.

Knowing she had to help, Erin fired her pistol at the wolf, striking it in the shoulder. It twitched, but otherwise remained unfazed. She fired over and over, hoping that the cumulative load of silver might affect it. Pieces of fur ripped off its hide, but still it ignored her and slammed Rhun to the floor, its jaws clamped around his neck.

Rhun didn't move.

Erin began to run forward—when she heard a high-pitched whistle slice down the tunnel.

Bathory.

The grimwolf dropped Rhun, shook blood from its muzzle, and bounded off down the dark tunnel.

Holstering her useless pistol, Erin rushed forward and skidded on her knees to reach him. Blood soaked her jeans—but it was not her own.

She shone her flashlight on Rhun. Blood wept down both sides of his torn throat. It bubbled from his lips as he tried to speak.

She pressed both hands against his wound. Cold blood covered her palms and seeped between her fingers.

He coughed his throat clear enough to issue a command: "Go back."

"When you stop the bleeding." The wounds were so deep that she did not see how he could do so, but she remembered how he had controlled his blood back in the Cardinal's residence in Jerusalem.

He closed his eyes, and the blood from his neck slowed to a trickle.

"Good, Rhun, good." She fumbled for the wineskin that was tied to his thigh.

"Not enough . . ."

The flask slipped from her blood-slicked hands and thumped to the floor. She picked it up, wiped one hand on her pants, and twisted the cap. It took three tries before it opened. Should she pour it on his wounds? Have him drink it? She remembered that Nadia had put it on his wounds first.

Following her example, Erin doused the wound.

Rhun groaned and seemed to fade away.

She shook his shoulder to keep him conscious. "Tell me what to do. Rhun!"

He opened his eyelids slowly, but his gaze slid past hers, staring at the ceiling before his eyes rolled back in his head.

Back in Russia, Rasputin had mixed human blood with the wine.

That concoction had seemed to heal Rhun better than the holy wine alone.

Erin knew what he needed.

Not wine.

Not now.

Rhun needed human blood.

She swallowed. Her hand ran across the puncture wounds left by the collar Bathory had forced her to wear.

She looked down the tunnel. No sign of Bathory or the wolf. Erin knew she could never catch the woman. The best hope to secure the Gospel was still Rhun. If Bathory escaped Rome with the book, the world would be forever changed.

But was she ready to do this? To risk everything on her faith that her blood would cure Rhun? Every fiber of her scientific mind rebelled at the thought.

After escaping the compound, she had refused to succumb to superstition, finding no value in mere faith. She knew too well what had happened when her father and mother had stopped thinking logically. They had placed the fate of her infant sister, Emma, in the hands of an indifferent God—and Emma had died for those blind beliefs.

But over the past days, Erin had seen *extraordinary* things. She could not discount them; she could not explain them with logic and science. But was she ready to trust her life to a miracle?

She stared down at Rhun.

What choice did she have?

Even if she could fight her way back to Bernard and the other Sanguinists, to warn them, Bathory would be long gone by the time Erin fetched them here.

Bathory must not escape with the book. The stakes for the world were too high for Erin not to try everything—even the power of *faith*.

She leaned over Rhun, baring her neck to his cold mouth.

He did not move.

Reaching up, she raked her fingernails across the soft scabs on her throat, ripping them away. Blood began to flow. Again she pressed her bleeding throat against his open lips.

He snarled and turned his head, refusing to drink.

"You have to."

His voice was a pained whisper. "Once I start, I might not . . ."

She finished his sentence: *once started, he might not be able to stop.*

Might was the important word.

It seemed, in order to do this, that she must put her trust not only in faith, but also in Rhun.

If I do not try, then the Belial will have already won.

She tilted her head, lowered her throat to his mouth.

Her blood pattered onto his lips.

He groaned deep in his throat, but this time he did not turn away.

Erin's heart raced. She was still animal enough to want to run away—but in the end she wasn't an animal. She remained steadfast, her mind flashing to Daniel entering the lion's den.

I can do this.

Shifting her gaze, she forced herself to look at Rhun. His eyes grew alert, as if those few drops of blood had revived him.

He ran his tongue over his lips and swallowed. He took her by the shoulders and gently pulled her down.

She tensed, knowing she could still stop him in his weakened state. Her body continued to scream for her to flee. Instead, she took a deep breath and gave in to her *faith.*

Rhun shifted, laying her down on the stone floor beside him while he raised up on one elbow, a question glowing in his dark eyes.

She trembled from her bones outward.

"Erin." He lingered on the *n* at the end of her name. "No. Not even for this price."

She pleaded, "I can't catch Bathory and the grimwolf. Only you can save the Gospel."

She read defeat in his eyes, knew he could not fault her logic.

"But—"

"I know the consequences," she said, repeating the same words she'd spoken before climbing down into the fissure in Masada. These *were* the consequences. "You must do it."

His lips slowly lowered toward her, his face softened by tenderness. She marveled at his expression.

Still, he stopped. "No . . . not you . . ."

"It serves your vows." She clenched her hands into fists. She thought of all those lives that would be destroyed if either of them balked from this act of duty. "The book is more important than the rules."

"I understand . . . were you someone else, perhaps. But." He tightened his hand on her shoulder. "I can't feed on *you*."

She stared into his face, seeing what was hidden behind that collar, behind those hidden fangs—a *man*.

He stroked strands of hair off her face, his fingers cold but very gentle, his hand cupping her cheek.

She had no words to convince him to break his vows as a priest.

She had no actions that would stir his bloodlust as a Sanguinist.

She had only one recourse.

To treat him as a man.

And she a woman.

She lifted her head from the stone, her eyes fixed on Rhun's dark ones. She read the sudden flash of fear in their depths. He was as frightened as she was, perhaps even more. She ran her fingers through his thick hair, drew his mouth to hers. Rhun closed his eyes, and she kissed him. His cold lips brought the taste of blood into her mouth.

As she drew him to her, she felt the last of his resistance give way—the hardness in his lips softening and letting her come closer. His mouth parted, as did hers, as natural as a flower opening at dawn.

He shifted farther over her, his weight settling on top of her.

He should have been cold, but the heat in her was enough to warm both of them.

Her tongue found his, encouraging him. He moaned between their lips—or maybe the sound came from her. She felt the slow push of sharpness within his mouth, like a gate closing against her, but she held fast. Her tongue reached, punctured so sweetly on a point as sharp as a thorn.

Her blood welled, filling both their mouths.

But rather than tasting iron and fear, her senses burst with the essence of her life, a sweetness and burning heat that swept aside all fear. She could almost taste her own divinity—and she wanted more.

She pulled him tighter.

He clung to her, with the promise of cold iron and ecstasy.

The intensity of the sensation stunned her. Her body could not hold it, arching under him, with the rapture of life coursing between them, quick and rhythmic as her heartbeat.

He lifted his lips from hers, exquisitely close but not touching. Even such a slight distance left her feeling an aching emptiness.

He moaned as if he felt it, too. His breath whispered across her lips.

He stared down, his eyes larger and darker than she'd ever seen them, offering glimmers of what lay beyond the grave.

Rather than feeling fear, she glowed against that darkness with the blaze of her own light, with the heat of her body.

She arched her neck, offered him her throat, daring him to drink from that blazing font—desiring it with every fiber of her being.

He took it.

A prick of fangs, testing—then plunging deep.

Heat flowed out of her, warming those cold lips at her throat.

She writhed beneath him, opening herself to the pleasure. Darkness closed around the edges of her vision. With each pulse, he swallowed her into his body.

Ecstasy filled those empty spaces between her heartbeats. Shatteringly fast at first as her body gave itself over to pure sensation. Then time slowed, and the pleasure expanded and grew even more intense. She waited for her heart to stop so that she could dwell in that feeling forever. Nothing else mattered.

Only bliss.

Then slowly, a soft light surrounded her, enveloped her—along with a love unlike any she had ever known. Here was the love she had wanted from her mother, from her father, from a baby sister who never had a chance to grow.

Somewhere far back, Erin knew she was dying—and she was so grateful for it.

She breathed in that light, as if taking her first breath.

Then she saw them.

Her mother stood in the tunnel of light. A little girl stood next to her. Emma. She had her baby quilt slung over her arm, the missing corner facing Erin. Her father stood behind them wearing his old red flannel shirt and jeans, as if he had just come back from the stable. He raised his arm and beckoned to her to join them. For the first time in many years, she felt no anger when she saw him, only love.

She reached her arms toward them all. Her father smiled, and she smiled back. She forgave him—and herself.

He had been bound by his *faith,* she by her *logic.*

At this moment they were beyond both.

Then that innocent light fractured.

And cold darkness rushed in.

She opened her eyelids. Rhun had pulled away from her. He rolled off of her and leaned against the wall, shaking. With the back of his hand, he wiped his mouth. Wiping away blood.

Her blood.

Her eyelids drifted closed, feeling a sting of rejection.

"Erin?" His chill fingertips brushed her cheek.

She trembled from cold and loneliness, consumed by the ache of all that she had lost.

"Erin." Rhun lifted her into his lap and rocked her, his hands stroking through her hair, running along her back.

She forced herself to open her eyes, to look into his, to say the impossible. "Go."

He held her so tightly that it hurt.

"Go," she insisted.

"Will you be all right?"

He heard her heartbeat. He knew that she wouldn't be. "Don't waste my blood, Rhun. Don't let this be in vain."

"I'm sorry," he said. "I couldn't—"

"I forgive you," she breathed out. "Now go."

He tore off his pectoral cross and laid it upon her chest. She felt the weight of it over her heart. It felt warm.

"May God protect you," he whispered. "As I could not."

He lowered her onto the filthy stone floor, covered her with his cassock, and left her.

61

October 28, 5:44 P.M., CET
Necropolis below St. Peter's Basilica, Italy

On the hunt, Rhun ran.

Erin's blood pulsed warm and strong through his veins. Her life sang within him. He had never felt such power surge through his limbs. He could run forever. He could defeat any foe.

His shoes skimmed the stone floor, not seeming to need even to touch it. Fast, and faster still. Air caressed his face, tendrils of wind stroked through his hair.

Even in his rapture, he grieved for Erin. She had given everything for the Gospel. And for him. Her learning, her compassion—they lay waning behind him. It should have been his darkness dying on the floor, not her light.

He would not waste her sacrifice.

Mourning would come later.

The musky odor of grimwolf painted the trail before him. In that scent, he read each heavy-pawed footfall, smelled each drop of blood, even as the creature healed and the drops grew smaller.

It could never escape him.

He would find them. He would retrieve the book. He would honor Erin's sacrifice.

She would not be forgotten, not for one of all his endless days to come.

5:55 P.M.

Jordan jogged along the tunnel, searching for Erin.

Leopold kept close behind.

The two had fought their way through the first wave of *strigoi* in order to open a path to this tunnel. Jordan hoped that Erin and Rhun had reached Bathory and retrieved the book.

After all of this bloodshed and horror, he just wanted to go home.

And when he pictured home—he pictured Erin's face.

"There!" Leopold said, pointing ahead, spotting with his sharper eyes a body crumpled along the side of the tunnel.

Don't let it be Erin. Don't let it be Erin.

Jordan hurried forward, for once outpacing a Sanguinist. He led with his flashlight, sweeping his beam across the still figure.

Oh no . . .

With his heart thundering in his ears, he crashed next to her, reaching immediately for her throat to take her pulse. Her skin was cold, but a weak heartbeat throbbed in her neck.

"She's alive," he told Leopold.

"But barely."

The young monk knelt and tore open Erin's grimwolf jacket. Blood stained her white shirt, running down to her waist. Leopold drew a balm from his robes. As he opened the container, Jordan noticed that it stank like the ointment Nadia had used on his own bite wounds.

But would it be enough?

Leopold intoned a prayer in Latin as he spread it over Erin's wound.

Jordan watched, holding his breath, shaking all over.

Within seconds, the bleeding slowed, then stopped.

Still, Erin lay unconscious on the ground, ghost white against the dark stone.

Leopold examined her arms and legs, probably looking for more bites. "Only her neck."

Jordan shrugged off his coat and spread it over her body to warm her. He rubbed her cold hands. "Erin?"

Her eyelids fluttered as if she were dreaming—then slowly opened. "Jordan?"

"Right here." He caressed her icy cheek. "You're going to be fine."

Her lips curved up ever so slightly. "Liar."

"I never lie," he said. "Eagle Scout, remember?"

But he did lie. She wasn't going to be fine at all.

Leopold reached Jordan and touched a bite on his arm from which blood was oozing; the bite was from one of Rasputin's minions and the wound had been torn open again during the struggle in the basilica. "Your blood type?"

"O negative. Universal donor." Jordan's heart leaped and he turned to the monk. "Can you do a direct transfusion from me to her?"

Leopold pulled his first-aid kit out of his pocket, muttering instructions. His hands moved with impossible swiftness, breaking apart a syringe, hooking it up to a tube, and placing a second tube on the other end.

As the young monk worked, Jordan stroked wisps of hair off Erin's face. His hands lingered on her forehead, her cheeks. "Hang in there."

He couldn't tell if she heard him or not. *What* had attacked her? And where was Rhun? He looked up the tunnel, expecting to see the priest's body. But the tunnel was empty. Had Rhun been taken?

Leopold ripped open an alcohol patch and swabbed Erin's arm, then used another for Jordan's.

"I must ask you to be silent, Jordan." Leopold's tone was no-nonsense. "I must hear both your heartbeats to see how much blood passes between you. I don't want to kill you in this process."

"Just save her." Jordan leaned against the stone wall, watching Erin's pale face.

Leopold stuck a needle in her arm, then Jordan's. He barely felt it.

Time passed, interminable, in the dark.

To the side, Leopold attached a bandage to Erin's neck. "We are fortunate. It's a simple wound. *Strigoi* are not usually so careful when they feed."

Jordan shivered at the thought of one of those monsters at Erin's throat.

I should have been guarding her better.

After several minutes, Leopold pulled the needle from Jordan's arm and taped a cotton ball over the hole. "That is all you can spare."

"I can spare whatever she needs." He pushed up straighter. "Do this right."

Light glinted off Leopold's round glasses as he shook his head. "You cannot bully me, Sergeant."

Before Jordan could come up with a better argument, Erin opened her eyes; she looked bleary but still she seemed stronger than she'd been a few minutes ago. "Hey."

Jordan slumped next to her against the wall and smiled. "Welcome back."

"Her pulse is strong," Leopold said. "With a little rest, she should be fine."

Jordan asked a question, knowing the answer. "Who did this to you?"

Erin closed her eyes, refusing to speak.

Jordan lifted his hand, revealing what he'd found as Leopold ripped off her coat. He showed her the pectoral cross. "Rhun?"

Leopold flinched, aghast.

"Erin?" Jordan tried to control his anger so she wouldn't hear it. "Did Rhun do this to you?"

"He had to." Her fingertips traced the bandage at her neck. "Jordan, I begged him to."

He barely heard her words as fury engulfed him.

That bastard had drained Erin and left her alone to die.

She struggled to sit up, to explain.

Jordan scooped her up in his arms and cradled her against his chest. He wrapped her in his arms. She was still so cold but had a little color back.

"We had to do this, Jordan, to heal him so he could keep Bathory from getting away with the Gospel. Rhun was almost dead."

Jordan pulled her closer as she dropped her head against his shoulder.

Leopold readjusted the coat over them both, then turned his back. Crouched next to them, he swung his head from one side of the tunnel to the other.

Jordan rested his chin on top of Erin's head. She smelled like blood. Under the coat, she curled up to nestle closer against his chest. He took in a shaky breath and let it go.

Leopold stood—a bit too swiftly.

"What is wrong?" Jordan asked.

Leopold faced him. "More *strigoi* are coming. It is not over."

***6:24** P.M.*

Erin winced when Leopold hauled her upright. With the other arm, he hoisted Jordan up onto his feet as if he weighed no more than a doll. Jordan staggered a step and caught himself. He was weaker than he let on. The blood transfusion had cost him.

Jordan pulled Erin's arm over his shoulder and wrapped his other arm around her waist. She wanted to argue that she could walk on her own, but she suspected that she wouldn't make it more than a few steps. This was no time for false pride.

"Go forward." Leopold pushed them ahead, his eyes fixed on the tunnel behind.

She struggled to stay on her feet. She and Jordan did their best to run, but even by human standards they were slow.

Leopold guarded their rear, his blade drawn.

Echoing snarls grew louder behind them.

"There's a bend up ahead," Jordan said. "We can face them there."

Leopold herded them forward—then waved them onward. "I stay. You go on."

"No." Jordan's stride broke.

"You are the prophesied trio," Leopold said simply. "My duty is to serve you. Find Rhun. Retrieve the book. That is *your* duty."

Jordan set his jaw, but he said nothing.

"Go with God." Leopold stopped at the bend in the tunnel, his sword flashing silver as he turned to face the enemy.

With no other choice, Erin fled with Jordan, chased by guilt at leaving Leopold. But how many others had already given up their lives to keep them moving forward? They had to honor that debt of blood by not giving up.

Savage screaming rose behind her, accompanied by the clash of steel.

Behind her, the boyish scholar was facing down the savage *strigoi* alone—but how long could he keep them at bay?

She concentrated on moving each heavy leg, refusing to surrender.

Jordan's flashlight jolted up and down as they walked, illuminating the smooth stone floor, the massive blocks on the bottom of the tunnel, the rough stone arch that curved above their heads.

She lost track of time and distance. Her world narrowed down to the next step.

Far ahead, a light appeared, glowing dimly.

Jordan pulled her forward, drawing her toward it.

The light grew brighter.

The source appeared as they rounded a corner. It came from a flashlight, attached to the barrel of a pistol. Silhouetted against that light was the lithe form of Bathory, her red hair loose around her shoulders, her back to them.

She was pointing the weapon at Rhun.

Yards away, Rhun fought the grimwolf—pinned under its bulk.

The beast growled into his face, throwing slather, ready to tear his throat out. Only this time Rhun was strong enough to hold it back, the two now equally matched. But it took all of the priest's renewed power to do so.

Riveted by the fighting, Bathory remained oblivious to Jordan and Erin's sudden arrival. She stalked toward the warring pair with her pistol, intending to end the impasse between priest and wolf with a barrage of silver.

Trembling with weakness, Erin nudged Jordan with a silent command.

Help him!

Jordan's face stayed hard. He stood, rigid, and did not reach for his gun.

Enough of this . . .

Erin slipped behind him and yanked out the Colt pistol. Earlier, she had fired almost an entire magazine at the grimwolf. The bullets had barely made it twitch. She couldn't kill it with a pistol.

But she had to do something.

With her back still to them, Bathory stepped near the wolf, aiming her pistol at Rhun's face.

"Now to set us both free."

Erin noted the bandage on Bathory's upper arm. It glowed white in the gloom.

The sight made her flash back to the Circus of Nero. She remembered the reopening of Bathory's wound, how she pushed the wolf away from her in a panic, and how Mihir had kept his distance from the dripping blood. Erin had never seen a *strigoi* react in such a way to blood. Mihir had been afraid to step on even a single drop. Then she pictured Mihir's blood smoking when it touched that silvery-crimson drop on the floor of the cell.

She knew what she had to do.

Erin shifted away from Jordan, putting Bathory between her and the wolf, calculating angles. She held the pistol steady in front of her with both hands, lined up the sights, and took a deep breath.

On the exhale, her left index finger squeezed the trigger.

The shot blasted loudly.

Bathory lurched forward, and the grimwolf howled in agony.

Jordan turned in surprise, but Erin kept her eyes on Bathory and lined up a second shot.

The grimwolf hurled its body away from Rhun and ran in a circle, snapping at its shoulder. The bullet had passed through Bathory's body before it struck the wolf, carrying her blood with it. The wolf's coat rippled, smoke boiling out from the bullet wound.

Bathory's blood was toxic to the *strigoi*—and the *blasphemare* created by them.

Bathory swung around to face Jordan and Erin. Blood seeped through her shirt, low, above her right hip. Her eyes fastened on her enemies. Her lip raised in a sneer. She lifted her gun toward them.

Holding steady, Erin squeezed the trigger three more times.

The cluster of shots struck Bathory through the chest—and from there into the grimwolf's flank.

Bathory fell backward, stumbling against the wall, crimson spreading across her chest. She slid to the floor, her silver eyes wide with surprise. Her gun clattered to the floor next to her limp arm.

The grimwolf collapsed with a mighty shudder. Blood smoked from its body and frothed from its mouth. Unable to stand now, it dragged itself on its belly, whimpering. A dark smear of blood trailed behind it.

The wolf reached Bathory and dropped its head into her lap. She lifted her arms and wrapped them around its head.

Beyond them, Rhun struggled to his feet and retrieved Bathory's gun.

Straightening, he turned in Erin's direction. When he saw her, his lips moved into a shadow of a tired smile, relieved to see her—

and maybe something more. Either way, it was the first genuine and honest smile she had ever seen him give.

He looked young, vulnerable, and very human.

She stumbled toward him, but Jordan pulled her back. "That's close enough."

His gun was out and pointed at Rhun.

That smile fled Rhun's face.

And the world was darker for it.

October 28, 6:54 P.M., CET
Necropolis below St. Peter's Basilica, Italy

Magor . . .

Bathory cradled the wolf's huge head in her lap. She felt his agony, heard his moan, poisoned by her blood. More silvery crimson flowed down her chest, pooling on her lap where he lay, boiling his skin, burning him in agony.

Please go . . . don't die like this . . .

She tried to push him away, but he nuzzled closer into that pain so he could be with her.

Too weak to fight him, she leaned over as he rolled one eye up at her. She sang him a final lullaby. It had no words. She had no breath to form them. Her song came from somewhere deeper than language, where summer suns still shone on a little boy catching butterflies in a white net among tall green grasses. Her song was laughter and love and the simple warmth of one body holding another.

The world darkened at the edges, until it was reduced to just that pained eye staring lovingly up at her. She watched that crimson glow within it fade, becoming only a soft gold as the curse inside him faded, and Magor became, again, just wolf . . . leaving all the grimness behind.

The pain also faded from his great, loving bulk as she sagged over him.

The pain fled her blood, too, leaving only peace.

As darkness consumed them both, she willed one last message to her friend.

Let's go find Hunor . . .

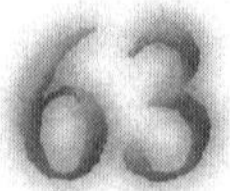

October 28, 6:57 P.M., CET
Necropolis below St. Peter's Basilica, Italy

Rhun knelt before the ghost of Elisabeta.

He held the Gospel in his lap and prayed for her soul. How soft and young her face looked in death, the fire of hatred snuffed out, leaving a purity and innocence that had been corrupted in part by his act centuries ago.

He stared at the paleness of her long throat.

A black mark had once marred its beauty, a strangling imprint from some unknown hand. Rasputin's words in the Hermitage came back to him, words about one woman from every generation of the Bathory line who was sentenced to a lifetime of pain and servitude.

Going back to the time of his defilement of Elisabeta.

But who could do such a thing? The Belial? If so, what interest was Elisabeta's line to them; surely it could not just be to torture him? What was he not seeing here? Why prey upon the descendants of Elisabeta Bathory?

To what end?

Now, with this woman dead, he realized that he might never know the answers to these questions, that perhaps the chain had finally been broken.

As he stood, his prayers done, he stared down at the humble book that he'd taken from her.

Though a creature whose life was damned, he had brought this great goodness into the world. Perhaps the Gospel held the secret to restoring his own soul. He feared even wishing for such a thing, to be human again, with a heartbeat and warm flesh to share.

Erin stood several paces to his right, waiting, Jordan beside her, his machine pistol up and ready. After what the Sanguinist himself had done to her, he could not blame the man.

"Aren't you going to open it?" Erin asked.

Rhun opened the book and turned it around so that Erin and Jordan could see the pages. "I have," he said.

The first page contained only a single paragraph, written in Greek. The rest of the pages remained empty, possibly awaiting further miracles before more text would come to light. But what was there was frightening enough.

The two came closer, drawn by the curiosity that burned so brightly in those with the shortest lives.

"What the hell?" Jordan groaned. "All of this for one paragraph. It had better be good."

Erin stared at the page as if she might cause more words to appear by force of will alone. She translated what she saw. *"A great War of the Heavens looms. For the forces of goodness to prevail, a Weapon must be forged of this Gospel written in my own blood. The trio of prophecy must bring the book to the First Angel for his blessing. Only thus may they secure salvation for the world."*

"You're supposed to be a priest." Jordan shifted back a pace. "If the book needs a *blessing*, then go ahead and bless it."

"I am not the *First Angel.*" Rhun ran his hand down the smooth leather cover, longing to know what else might be revealed, sensing he held only the beginning of a greater truth. "The book must be blessed by the *first* one, someone pure in heart and deed. Only then will more be learned."

"That leaves you right out, doesn't it?" Jordan said.

"Jordan!"

"He is correct." Hating to part with it, Rhun handed the book to Erin. "I am not pure. Even today my actions showed this to be so."

"If we had not done what we did, then the book would be gone."

Rhun watched a blush rise to Erin's cheeks and heard her heart beat faster. What had it been like for her when he'd fed on her, that it shamed her so to think of it? He thought back to the long-ago night when he had been turned.

"I don't approve of the price Erin paid." Jordan glared at him.

"It wasn't your choice." Erin hugged the book and turned away. "It was ours."

She walked back the way they had come, one steadying hand on the wall. Rhun wanted to pick her up and carry her, but he did not trust himself to touch her.

7:04 P.M.

Jordan fought the urge to shoot Rhun.

As if he knew, Rhun held out his hands. "She needs us both now."

The bastard was right; he and Erin needed Rhun's protection to get out of this subterranean charnel house. Jordan could not protect her down here. Rhun could.

He lowered the gun. "But not forever."

Rhun nodded. "When she is safe, you must follow your conscience."

Jordan went after Erin. She stumbled forward, sliding along the wall. He pulled her arm over his shoulder and slid another one around her waist.

She tensed, displaying her anger.

Why is she mad at me? I didn't leave her to die.

He gritted his teeth and started walking. She leaned against him, probably because she couldn't help herself.

Rhun ghosted past them and settled into a position a few yards in front. He looked fresh, ready to take on a pack of *strigoi* single-handed. If Erin was right and he had been near death, her blood had definitely given him a shot of energy.

Jordan's head throbbed, his wounds ached, and his arms and legs were done for the day. He'd come out on the short end of this transfusion party.

Rhun sped up, and Jordan lost sight of him.

Jordan tightened his grip around Erin and tried his best to follow Rhun, cursing his damnable speed.

The reason for Rhun's haste became clear as they rounded a corner.

Rhun was kneeling next to a prone black-clad figure.

Brother Leopold.

Rhun reached out and pulled him upright. Leopold looked terrible, but he was still alive.

"The book?" Leopold croaked hoarsely.

"Safe," Rhun assured him.

Upon hearing that single word, the monk collapsed. Rhun lifted him in his arms and trotted down the tunnel toward the necropolis.

At the end of the tunnel, he was greeted by the sight of corpses that littered the ground around the sunken baldachin. *Strigoi* and Sanguinist blood ran slick across the floor, making for treacherous footing as they worked their way across the killing field. A handful of Sanguinists searched and patrolled, but apparently the war was over.

So many casualties for the sake of the book Erin carried.

How could it possibly be worth it?

Jordan drew in a deep, shuddering breath. Erin tightened her arms around him, pulling him close to her. The book in her hands pressed against his back. When he lowered his head to her shoulder, his cheek brushed the bandage on her throat.

He would never forgive Rhun for that.

64

October 29, 5:44 A.M., CET
The sanctuary below St. Peter's Basilica, Italy

Half the night later, Erin walked between Jordan and Rhun as they descended beneath Rome, far deeper than the necropolis where the battle had been fought and won. The remaining *strigoi* had been slaughtered or driven away. One of the enemy had even been converted to the order, beginning his long road to donning the cloth of the Sanguines.

Erin continued down the steps, carrying the book. A soft glow had begun to shine again from its leather cover, illuminating the smooth stone walls. Its light grew brighter the deeper they went, as if it were drawn toward a power source. But where were they headed? Rhun had yet to reveal their destination.

As they continued ever deeper, she felt stronger than she had in days. She and Jordan had spent a few hours being nursed back to health, learning that the pope had pulled through his surgery and was expected to make a full recovery. The old man was tougher than he looked.

Nate, too, was doing well.

Erin had eaten, napped, showered, and now finally wore clothes that were not saturated with blood. Next to her, Jordan looked revitalized. Was it the rest or the grace of the book's golden glow that suffused them now? With each step, strength surged through her. Warmth and light spread not just through the hall, but through her body and, maybe, her soul.

Still, she remembered Bathory, bent in death over her wolf. Though her death had been necessary, Erin could not escape a measure of guilt at taking her life, sensing that Bathory was less villain than pawn. But she kept such thoughts pushed back for now and focused on the task ahead.

Golden light bathed the limestone walls around her, walls that had been cut through the earth with ancient hammers and chisels, forming an arched point high above, like a Gothic cathedral that stretched down for miles. This must have taken lifetimes to build.

Underfoot, the floor was ice-smooth, worn down the center by the passage of many soles. Here was a *new* kind of ancientness, neither that of a deserted tomb nor that of an old street that now supported cars where it had once supported only hooves and feet. Down in this subterranean cathedral, the slow rhythms of the air seemed changeless but alive.

The tunnel ended at a vast chamber. The vaulted ceiling soared fifty feet above them, reminding Erin of St. Peter's Basilica.

But this room had none of the opulence of the church far above. This place was unadorned. Its beauty came from the simplicity of its lines, the smoothness of the curves that drew the eyes ever upward. No man-made objects strove to distract or to glorify.

Torches guttered in wrought-iron holders were fastened to the stone. Far above, lines of soot streaked the ceiling.

Rounded alcoves lined the walls. Each space held a simple round plinth. On most of the bases stood detailed statues of men and women, most as emaciated as Piers had been, but these looked peaceful and beatific, not anguished.

Erin paused to stare at one. Gold light from the book washed across a beautiful woman, her hair loose to her waist, eyes closed, cheekbones high, with an enigmatic smile and slender hands folded in prayer beneath her chin. A silver cross around her neck caught the book's light.

Erin had never seen anything more beautiful. The expression etched on that face reminded her of her mother when she sang a lullaby late at night, her father long since gone to sleep, and she and her mother cuddled together in Erin's bed.

The book pulsed against her, drawing away her sense of loss, reminding her that nothing was ever truly lost.

As she stared at the woman, she knew then that it was no statue; it was a Sanguinist in deep meditation. Rhun had mentioned such people in passing.

The Cloistered Ones.

She smiled and moved forward again, heading deeper into the cathedral.

"We should stay near the exit," Jordan said, his wary suspicion shining in the dark.

She glanced to him. He had not spoken to Rhun since they found Leopold.

"I want to learn about the First Angel." She turned to Rhun. "That's why we're down here, isn't it?"

Rhun bowed his head in acknowledgment. "We seek the oldest of all. The only one who can bless the book. The Risen One."

Erin's heart skipped a beat. Even Jordan looked shaken.

The Risen One?

She had seen enough miracles in the past few days not to dismiss Rhun's words. She pictured the crucifix that used to hang above her bed at the compound.

Could she be about to meet the figure on that cross?

The one who rose from the dead three days after his crucifixion?

5:52 A.M.

Rhun fingered his rosary, running through prayers to calm his mind. He was in awe of the Risen One, the one who had made their order possible, the one who had taught those such as Rhun that even the damned could seek forgiveness. Without him, Rhun would have become no more than a tainted animal.

He pushed forward into the sanctuary.

Jordan started when a figure in one of the alcoves moved, the face turning toward them. "The statues are alive. Like Piers."

"No." Rhun shook his head. "Not like Piers. They are not trapped and suffering. They have sought out this sanctuary."

Erin's eyes took in the scene. "Why?"

"After many long years of service, many choose to retire here, to spend their eternal existence in contemplation."

He knew some had been here a millennium, sustained by no more than the smallest sips of sacramental wine.

Jordan's eyebrows lifted.

Rhun smiled. "I, too, sought to shed the world in this place."

"What happened to that plan?" Jordan didn't sound pleased that Rhun hadn't abided by that choice.

"Cardinal Bernard called me to service."

Rhun was grateful that he had answered the call. He had discovered the book, yes, but he had also found Jordan and Erin, and a new life. Perhaps, with the aid of the book, he might shed his curse, walk in sunlight without pain, partake of simple meals, and live the life of a mortal priest.

Erin shifted, warm next to him.

Or perhaps he could live the life of a mortal *man,* outside the walls of the Church.

The book glowed brighter in her hands.

Rhun knelt and bowed his head in supplication.

The book knew his deepest desires.

Then footsteps approached out of the darkness ahead, out of the blackness of time.

The Risen One had come.

5:53 A.M.

Erin dropped to her knees next to Rhun, and Jordan followed suit. The book trembled in her arms. She wasn't ready.

"Rise," commanded a hoarse voice.

As one, all stood, heads still bowed.

"Thou hast brought me the book, Rhun?"

"Yes, Eleazar."

Erin smothered a gasp. *Eleazar?* She remembered that this was the name of the one who had first hidden the book in Masada. Here was not the risen Jesus Christ, but a different miracle come to life.

Someone else who had *risen* long ago.

Jordan tilted his head to look at her, his eyes asking a question. He didn't know who faced them.

She did. They did not stand before Christ.

Eleazar was the ancient form of a name now translated as *Lazarus.*

Here was the spiritual leader of the *Sanguinist* branch of the Catholic Church, just as the pope was the spiritual leader of the *human* branch of the Catholic Church.

Keeping her head bowed, she offered him the book, and he took it.

"Ye all may look upon it."

She raised her head, still afraid to look upon *him*. But she did. The figure before her was tall, taller than Jordan. Long white hair flowed back from an unlined face. Deep-set eyes were dark brown, like olives, and his stern face smiled at her.

He turned the book so that all could see it, then opened the cover.

Golden light flowed from the page, but the crimson letters, written in ancient Greek by Christ's own hand, could be easily read. Erin had them already memorized.

A great War of the Heavens looms. For the forces of goodness to prevail, a Weapon must be forged of this Gospel written in my own blood. The trio of prophecy must bring the book to the First Angel for his blessing. Only thus may they secure salvation for the world.

Lazarus seemed to take the words in at a glance. "As you see, the book is safe. Ye have done well. This battle is won, and without that victory all hope would have been lost."

"That sounds promising," Jordan said.

"But war still looms. To prevail, ye must seek out the First Angel."

Erin stared at him in disbelief.

"Isn't that you?" Jordan asked.

"No," Lazarus said. "It is not."

Erin looked around the vast cavern. "Then who is the First Angel?"

Unknown time
Undisclosed location

Tommy fiddled with his bootlaces. Alyosha had promised that today he could go outside. He'd only been cooped up for a few days, but it felt like forever. He wanted to see the sky, feel the wind, and he wanted to *escape*.

A pearl-handled knife had dropped from Alyosha's pocket when he was playing video games a few days ago. Tommy had covered it with a pillow, then hid it under his mattress. It was in his pocket now. He didn't know if he could hurt anyone. He'd never even been in a fight at school.

His parents had always taught him that violence didn't solve anything, but he thought it might solve this problem. Asking politely sure hadn't helped.

The door opened. Alyosha stood there, holding a snow-white fur coat. The strange kid wore only pants and a light shirt, not bothering even with a jacket. Probably why he was always so cold.

Tommy shrugged into the unusual coat. "What's it made of?"

"Ermine. Very warm."

Tommy stroked his hand along the front. It was the softest thing he'd ever felt. How many little creatures had been killed and skinned to make it?

Alyosha led the way down a long hall, up a flight of stairs, and through a thick steel door painted black. Paint flaked off into the snow when Alyosha slammed it behind him.

Tommy spun in a slow circle. They were in a city, in a deserted parking lot. Dirty snow had been crossed by many feet. The sky was overcast and dark gray, as if a storm or night threatened.

Seeing his chance to escape, Tommy made a break for it, but Alyosha was suddenly in front of him. Tommy cut to the right, hoping to get around him and run along the side of the building. Alyosha jumped in front of him again. Tommy dodged left.

But Alyosha stopped him yet again.

Tommy pulled out the knife. "Out of my way!"

Alyosha threw back his head and laughed to the uncaring gray clouds.

Tommy tried to turn, to flee, but he slipped on the ice and caught himself before he fell into the dirty snow. Alyosha had just been playing with him. He would never be able to escape. He'd be stuck here forever, eternally bound to this cruel kid.

Alyosha's gray eyes glittered with malice. He reminded Tommy of a shrike. Shrikes were cute little birds, but they survived by impaling their prey on thorns and waiting for them to bleed to death. Skeletons of smaller birds and mice littered the ground around their nests.

"You won't let me go, will you?" Tommy asked.

"He cannot let you go," boomed a voice from behind them.

Tommy spun around so fast he fell. Gray slush stained his coat. Alyosha dragged him up painfully by one arm.

A priest in a black robe crunched across the snow toward them. At first, Tommy thought it was the priest from Masada because he wore the same kind of uniform, but this one was taller and broader, and his eyes were blue instead of brown.

"I have been waiting a very long time for you, Tommy," the priest said.

"Are you the one who Alyosha says is like me?"

"Alyosha?" The man frowned, then smiled as if at a private joke. "Ah, that is a—how do you Americans call it?—a *slang* name. His full title is Alexei Nikolaevich Romanov, prince of Russia, heir to the true throne of the Russian Empire."

Tommy frowned, believing the man was joking. "You didn't answer my question."

The priest smiled. A cold chill ran down Tommy's back. "How rude of me. No, I am not like *you*. I am like *Alyosha*."

"Who are you?"

"I am Grigori Yefimovich Rasputin. And we are going to be great friends."

Above the man's head, a flock of gray pigeons wheeled—and in their midst, a snow-white bird danced high, finding a beam of light in this gray day. Tommy's gaze caught upon it, while he remembered the wounded bird back in Masada, the dove with the broken wing. He remembered picking up that injured bird—just before his life fell apart.

Had that act of kindness and mercy doomed him?

He squinted up as the white bird swooped low, passing over the scene. It stared down at Tommy—first with one eye, then the other.

Tommy shuddered and tore his gaze away from the skies.

The bird's eyes had shone green, like slivers of jeweled malachite.

Same as the dove in Masada.

How could that be? How could *any* of this be?

Any moment now, I'll wake in a hospital room with tubes and drugs running into me.

"I want to go back to my old friends," he said, not caring if he sounded like a petulant child.

"You shall make a great many *new* friends over the course of your long, long life," Mr. Rasputin said. "That is your destiny."

Tommy looked back at the birds. He longed to be up there, flying free with them. Why couldn't that be his destiny?

To have wings.

65

October 29, 5:54 A.M., CET
The sanctuary below St. Peter's Basilica, Italy

Rhun touched his cross. They had won the battle. He shuddered to think how close they had come to losing it all. But they had triumphed.

Eleazar paused. He turned the book back to face him and ran his finger under the lines, reading it again, as if he had gotten it wrong the first time. But the words were the same.

"So we won the first battle," Jordan said.

"But what about this 'War of the Heavens' . . . and the 'First Angel'?" Erin asked.

"We found the book," Jordan said with firm conviction. "We can find an angel. I bet the angel is bigger than the book was. How hard can it be, right?"

Erin laughed and leaned against him. "Right."

The soldier was correct. They had accomplished the impossible once already. Rhun looked to Eleazar. "Where shall we begin?"

Eleazar furrowed his brow. "The prophecy. Return to the prophecy."

Rhun waited.

Eleazar recited it. "*The day shall come when the Alpha and the Omega shall pour his wisdom into a Gospel of Precious Blood that the sons of Adam and the daughters of Eve may use it on the day of their need.*

"Until such day, this blessed book shall be hidden in a well of deepest darkness by a Girl of Corrupted Innocence, a Knight of Christ, and a Warrior of Man.

"Likewise shall another trio return the book to the light. Only a Woman of Learning, a Knight of Christ, and a Warrior of Man may open Christ's Gospel and reveal His glory to the world."

"We did that," Jordan said. "What do we need to do *next* to find the angel?"

Eleazar closed the book. "That may never come to pass."

"Why not?" Jordan said with a frown. "We found the book, didn't we?"

Eleazar sighed and hope drained from Rhun with that exhaled breath. "There is a chance that the trio has already been sundered," Eleazar warned.

What was the Risen One saying? Rhun asked himself. *How could the trio have been sundered? They were all here.* He put one hand on Jordan's sleeve, the other on Erin's.

Then Erin closed her eyes. She grew pale.

"What is it, Erin?" Jordan asked.

She cleared her throat. "What if *I* am not part of the trio? What if *I* am not the Woman of Learning?"

"What are you talking about? Of course you are. You solved the mystery of the Gospel. Without you, we never would have found it. You were there when we turned it into a book." The soldier spoke patiently, no worry in his voice.

But fear crept up Rhun's spine.

"Remember the wording of the prophecy," she said. "It says the trio *opens* Christ's Gospel and reveals His glory to the world."

"And?" Jordan asked.

Erin shook her head miserable. "I wasn't there when the book *opened*. I didn't cross the threshold of the basilica before the golden light burst from the book. You did. Rhun did. But I didn't. I was still outside with the guard."

"And you think that's relevant?" Jordan protested. "Like one step across the threshold matters?"

"If I am not the Woman of Learning, *Bathory* was." Erin took another deep breath. "And I killed her."

Rhun strove to find a flaw in her logic, but, as usual, found none. Everyone had assumed that Erin was the Woman of Learning: she had been in Masada, in Germany, in Russia, and in Rome. But Bathory, too, had been in those places. She had been one step ahead of them. She had followed the clues that led to the book, and she had determined how and where it was to be opened. And she had been the one *holding* the book when it transformed.

Rhun closed his eyes, sensing the truth.

Could Cardinal Bernard have been correct all along about Elizabeth Bathory? Is that why the Belial had started collecting a Bathory of each generation and bonding her to their foul purpose, to preserve the Woman of Learning among their own fold?

If this were true, how could they ever hope to find the First Angel?

According to Cardinal Bernard, the woman killed in the necropolis was the last of the Bathory line.

But Rhun knew that wasn't entirely true.

"You guys are nuts," Jordan said, interrupting his thoughts. "Erin did all the heavy lifting on this. And Bathory is dead. If the book is so smart, why would it set an impossible task?"

"The Warrior has wisdom," Eleazar said. "Perhaps he speaks truth. Prophecy is often a two-edged sword that cuts down all who attempt to interpret it."

Erin looked unconvinced.

Eleazar bowed his head, his gaze fixing on Rhun.

Rhun knew that all was not lost.

"I have another matter to discuss with Father Korza," Eleazar said to the others. "If we might have a moment alone."

"Of course," Erin said, and moved off with Jordan.

When the two were no longer in sight, Eleazar spoke again, in a whisper. "Thou must forsake this woman, Rhun. I have seen thy heart, but it cannot be."

Rhun heard truth in those words; it settled in his bones. "I shall."

Eleazar stared long and hard at Rhun, as if peeling away his flesh and baring his bones. The feeling was not entirely fanciful, as Eleazar's next words proved. "Is there *another* of the line of the Woman of Learning?"

Rhun bowed from those penetrating eyes. He knew what was asked. He must own all his sins, unearth all his secrets, or all the world might be lost.

He faced Eleazar with tears in his eyes. "You ask too much."

"It must be done, my son." Eleazar's voice held pity. "We cannot hide from our past forever."

Rhun knew how much Eleazar had also given up for the world—and knew it was time for Eleazar to face that past, too.

Rhun reached into the deep pocket inside his cassock and drew out the doll he had retrieved from the dusty tomb in Masada. It was a tattered thing, sewn from leather, long gone hard, with one eye missing. He placed the bit of the painful past into Eleazar's open palm.

Eleazar had lived for so long that he was more like a statue than any of the Cloistered Ones, resolute, unmoving, more like marble than flesh.

But now those stone fingers shook, barely able to hold aloft the tiny, frail toy. Instead, Eleazar brought it to his chest and cradled it close, as if it were a living child, one he mourned deeply.

"Did she suffer?" he asked.

Rhun thought about the small body hanging on the wall in Masada, pinned by silver bolts that would have burned inside her until she expired.

"She died serving Christ. Her soul is at peace."

Rhun stood and left the Risen One to his grief.

As Rhun turned away, he caught a glimpse of marble breaking.

Eleazar bowed his head.

A tear fell and spattered mournfully upon the doll's stained face.

66

October 29, 6:15 A.M., CET
The sanctuary below St. Peter's Basilica, Italy

Rhun ran through the darkness with unearthly speed, a hammer clenched in his hand. It had been many centuries since his feet had walked these pitch-dark tunnels, but the way opened before him as if his body had always known that it would return here.

He descended deeper than the temple of the Cloistered Ones, deeper than most dared venture. Here he had hidden his greatest secret. He had lied to Bernard; he had broken his vows; he had done penance for it, but never enough.

And now his sin was the only thing that might save them.

He stopped before a featureless wall, ran one hand across it, felt no seam. He had covered it well, four hundred years before.

Rhun raised the hammer above his head and struck the wall. Stone shuddered under the blow. It gave. A mere hairsbreadth, but it gave.

He struck again and again. Bricks crumbled until a small opening appeared. Barely large enough to admit him. That was all he needed.

He climbed through the rough stone, not caring how it scratched his skin. He had to reach the dark room beyond.

Once there, he lit a candle he had brought along with him. The scent of honey and beeswax unfolded in the chamber, driving back the odors of stone, decay, and staleness.

The pale yellow flame reflected off the polished surface of a black marble coffin.

He worked the lid off and lowered it to the rough stone floor of the cell.

The smell of sacramental wine bloomed free. The wet black surface drank the light.

Before he drew out the contents, Rhun cupped his hand and drank of the wine. He would need every ounce of holy fortification for the task ahead. But before the strength, as always, came the penance.

Rhun walked to Rome. Weeks of trekking day and night through cold dark mountain passes had shredded his shoes and then his feet. When he could walk no farther, he sought sanctuary in remote mountain churches, drinking a mouthful of wine before driving himself out into the wild again.

Bernard met him in Rome and took him deep under St. Peter's Basilica, where only the eldest of their kind dared to go. There Rhun did his penance. He fasted. He prayed. He mortified himself. None of his actions lightened the stain of his sin.

A decade later, Bernard sent him out into the world of men again, this time on a new mission to Čachtice Castle, a final penance to rid the world of what his sin created.

Armed men around him kept their swords drawn. Fear shone in their faces, beat through their racing hearts. They were right to be afraid.

The Palatine and Counts *led, casting nervous glances back at their men, as if they feared that their men could not save them. They could not. But Rhun could. He prayed that he would not have to. That the stories were false. That his corrupted love had not caused this.*

But he had also heard other stories . . . of macabre experiments in the dead of night, hinting that there remained some dark purpose to her atrocities, some semblance of her intelligence, of her healing arts, turned to foul intention. That scared him most of all—that some part of her true nature still existed within that monster, degraded now to evil ends.

As they reached the entrance to the castle, men shifted, quick breaths forming clouds in cold air.

The Palatine knocked on a stout oak door built to withstand battering rams. For a moment Rhun prayed that no one would answer, and they would be forced to lay siege to the castle, but Anna opened it. Her birthmark still stained her face, but she was otherwise unrec-

ognizable. Gaunt as a skeleton and covered in scars, she wore only a stained chemise against the biting cold.

The Palatine forced the door open wide. Darkness cloaked the interior, but Rhun smelled what they would find there. Deep underneath that, he also caught the odor of rotten chamomile.

Count Zríni fumbled to light a torch, the burning pitch smell a sharp note in the bouquet of death.

The Palatine took the torch and stepped into the castle. Torchlight fell on a young girl lying stone-cold on the floor. Bruises marred her white flesh. Frozen blood coated her wrists, her neck, the inside of her thighs.

The Palatine crossed himself.

Behind them, a soldier retched into the snow. Rhun took off his cassock and covered the body. But the Church did not have enough cassocks to hide his shame. He had killed this girl as surely as if he had opened her throat himself.

A few steps farther in, two girls huddled under a filthy wooden table. The blond one was barely clinging to life. Her heartbeats fading. He knelt in front of her and administered Last Rites.

"Thank you, Father." The dark-haired girl's voice rasped from a damaged throat.

He lowered his eyes in shame. The deaths here weighed on his conscience, as did all those whom Elisabeta had killed. The love of a Sanguinist brought only death and suffering.

A soldier picked up the still-living girl and carried her to the barren fireplace. He gave her his coat and lit a fire, his eyes focused on his task. Rhun closed her friend's eyes for the last time. Both so young, barely out of girlhood.

A scream cut through the castle. The Palatine cocked his head, as if to locate the sound. Rhun knew where it came from. Elisabeta's private chambers.

He stood and led.

One of the men at arms followed close on his heels. The Palatine seemed to have lost his taste for leadership and trailed near the back. Elisabeta had once called him cousin. The Palatine had chosen the other noblemen because of their ties to her. Each was married to one of her daughters. She would be taken in the presence of nobility, as her stature required.

Rhun pushed open Elisabeta's bedroom door. Inside, a child sobbed in a black corner. Another girl stood in a spiked cage suspended high in the air. Elisabeta stood, naked under it. Two servants swung it from side to side, slamming the girl's soft body against the cage's sharpened spikes. Crimson dripped on Elisabeta's white skin.

Horrified, Rhun fought back tears. He had brought them to this.

The men at arms rushed to apprehend the servants and stop the cage from swinging.

Now the Palatine stepped forward again. "Lady Widow Nádasy, I arrest you in the name of the king."

"You shall pay dearly for this intrusion." Elisabeta made no attempt to cover her nakedness. Dark hair swung across her white back as she turned to face the men.

Her face set when she recognized them. "So." A smile hardened her lips. "You have come to die."

Rhun stepped between her and the men. She could kill them all, but not him. He drew a knife from his sleeve.

"Please," he said. "Don't make me do this."

She stumbled back. "What more would you take from me, Rhun?"

He flinched, then held the knife out where she could see it.

Her lovely silver eyes lingered on the blade. "That is all you have to pierce me with, priest?"

He moved closer. The warm blood smell rising off her skin intoxicated him. He fought his desires.

"Careful, darling," she whispered. "I have seen that look on your face before."

He murmured a prayer, then looped a silk cord around her bare wrists and bound them together.

"There is blessed silver inside," he told her. "If you try to break free, it will burn to the bone."

"Cover her," ordered the Palatine.

The Palatine threw a soiled blanket across her bloodstained shoulders.

She interlaced her fingers as if in prayer. Her eyes found his. He read sorrow there and regret and, still yet, love.

He waited to come back from the past, to inhabit this dank cell.

Once fully returned, he dipped his arms deep into the scalding bath of holy wine. At the bottom, his cold hands found what he sought and drew her forth, back into the world after centuries of slumber.

Wine had stained her fine green cloak burgundy, but her alabaster face shone as white as the day he had immersed her here instead of killing her as Bernard had ordered. He stroked long, dark hair off her still face, caressed her high forehead, her curved cheeks. She was as beautiful as she had been the moment he first saw her, four hundred years ago. Before he destroyed her soul and made her a *strigoi,* she had been a good woman. She had been a healer. She had almost healed him.

Almost.

Rhun whispered a prayer.

Elisabeta's soft storm-gray eyes opened, found him.

Lips moved, no words, only air.

Still Rhun understood what she tried to say, still lost in her dream, her anger still somewhere in the past, leaving only those two words formed by perfect lips.

My love . . .

6:30 A.M.

Erin stumbled up the long dark tunnel. Without the golden light of the book to guide them, Jordan had clicked on his flashlight. Compared with the book, its pale blue light looked cold and feeble. He kept an arm across her shoulder all the long way up.

They came at last to the collapsed baldachin, its base resting on the floor of the tunnel, its canopy extending up into the basilica. The bodies were gone, and the Sanguinists had strewn sand over the blood.

Erin tried to step around the piles, but sand was everywhere. It felt gritty under her shoes, reminding her of the desert around Masada, of her dig site in Caesarea. How would things have played out if she had stayed in the trench with Heinrich, had pulled him out of the way of the horse, had never gotten into the helicopter? He would still be alive, but the Belial would have the book. There would be no hope. They had opened Pandora's box, and the evil had escaped, but hope remained. Not just hope, but a path forward to keep the world safe.

"Halt!" A Sanguinist blocked their path. He was thin, with long spidery fingers. "What is your business here?"

"Sergeant Jordan Stone," Jordan said. "And Dr. Erin Granger."

"Two parts of the trio." The man's voice was reverent. "My apologies."

The Sanguinist gestured to a ladder that had been leaned against the baldachin.

"Ladies first," Jordan said.

Erin climbed, and at the top, needed help to awkwardly step from the ladder back onto the marble floor of the basilica. The immense scale of the building hit her all at once. Everything here was many times larger and grander than life. From the baldachin that now rested on the graves below to the soaring ceilings of Michelangelo that formed a false sky above. She spun in a slow circle, taking in white walls, opulent gilding, graceful statues, and sophisticated art. Men had accomplished great things in this place.

Resolution settled inside her breast at the sights.

They would find the First Angel and make sure that such wonders were protected.

Jordan climbed up next to her and took her hand. Here, too, piles of sand on the polished floor soaked up blood, marking the spots where *strigoi,* Sanguinists, and men had died.

She kept her eyes on the elaborate designs worked into the marble floor and concentrated on putting one foot in front of the other, avoiding the sand. The energy she had received from the book was long gone.

Jordan's legs moved them steadily toward the front door.

He stopped before they reached the portico and veered left.

She raised her eyes from the floor to see what had captured his attention. Michelangelo's *Pietà*. The marble sculpture depicted Mary on the rock of Golgotha, cradling her recently crucified son. Christ lay spread across her lap, head back, arm dangling limply. Mary's head was tilted down, her face marked by sadness. She mourned the loss of her precious son. The death that set these events in motion all those years ago.

Jordan stared at the sculpture.

Erin cleared her throat. "Jordan?"

"Just thinking of the families I'll have to visit when this is over: the Sandersons, the Tysons, the Coopers, and the McKays. The mothers who will look just like that."

She wrapped her arms around his waist.

Eventually, he took her hand again and they stepped out of the basilica into the fresh air of an Italian morning.

He led her to the stairs that rose to the top of the dome.

"It's a long climb." His eyes asked if she wanted to make it.

"I'll go first," she answered, and wended her way up the 320 steps. The sky had lightened to pale gray. Soon the sun would break free of the horizon.

She reached the top, breathing hard. Jordan marched to the east side of the cupola and flung himself down. He patted the floor next to him, and she sat.

The sky paled to almost white.

"You know you're probably wrong, right?" he asked.

She tried to give him a smile. She appreciated the effort. "If I'm not?"

"I want you on my team whether you're part of some prophecy or not. We bumble around like a bunch of knuckleheads when you're not around."

"People sacrificed their lives to save the Woman of Learning," she said. "But all they saved was me."

"You're not so bad." He kissed the top of her head. "It was war, Erin. They were soldiers. Mistakes happen in battle. People die. You forge on—for you as much as for them. The key is to keep fighting."

She tensed in his arms. "But the prophecy—"

"Look." He started a count. "One: who found the medallion in the little girl's hand? You did. Two: who figured out where the bunker was? You again. Three: who figured out the blood and the bone stuff to open the book? You again. It's practically giving me a complex, how good you are at this."

She smiled. He might be onto something. Up until the very end, it had been Bathory who had followed their trail, not the other way around.

She took the scrap of baby quilt out of her pocket and held it in her palm. For the first time, no anger rose in her at the sight of it. The anger had flown when, at death's door, she forgave her father in the tunnels.

"What's that?" Jordan asked.

"A long time ago I made a promise to someone." She stroked the quilt with one fingertip. "I promised that I would never stand by when my heart told me that something was wrong."

"What does your heart say now?"

"That you're right."

He grinned. "I like the sound of that."

Erin let the tiny quilt flutter in the wind, holding it between just her thumb and index finger. Then she let it go. The scrap of fabric floated away into the bustle and life that was Rome.

She turned back to Jordan. "It's about more than spirituality and miracles. It's about logic, too, and having a questioning heart. We will find this First Angel."

Jordan pulled her close. "Of course we will. We found the book, didn't we?"

"We did." She leaned her head against his chest, listened to his steady heartbeat. "And because we did, we have hope."

"Sounds like a good day's work to me." Jordan's voice was husky.

The sun broke over the horizon. Gold rays heated her face.

She tilted her head up toward his. He ran the back of his hand along her cheek, cupped the nape of her neck.

Then she stretched up to kiss him. His lips were warm and soft, different from Rhun's, natural. She slipped her hands under his shirt, sliding her palms along the heat of his skin. He moaned and pulled her in closer, his hands now on her back.

Eventually, she pulled back. Both she and Jordan were breathing hard.

"Too fast?" Jordan asked.

"No." Erin reached for him again. "Too slow."

AND THEN

Late Autumn
Rome, Italy

Brother Leopold threw bills into the front seat for the taxi driver, enough to cover the fare and a small tip. As a humble man of the cloth, he had no room in his life for extravagance.

The man touched his cap in thanks as Leopold shut the door and ducked into a neighboring alley. He scanned the sunlit street. No one had followed him from Vatican City. He had redirected the driver over and over, insisting on abrupt turns, trips down blind alleys, and repeatedly doubled back. Even after all of that, he'd had the driver drop him several blocks away from his real destination.

He had waited so long and worked so hard, he would not fail in the last moment. If he did, then He whom he served would destroy him. Leopold was not so foolish as to think himself irreplaceable.

He walked down the narrow street and approached the glass-and-steel skyscraper with a silver anchor painted on the top panes of glass. It was the logo of the Argentum Corporation. The anchor concealed a cross in its design, the Crux Dissimulata, the symbol used by ancient Christians to show their belief in Christ to other Christians without having to fear reprisals. Today, too, it hid allegiances.

It housed the head of the Belial, He who forged a pact between *strigoi* and humans and wielded both to His own ends. But He was neither man nor beast—instead He was so much more, a figure cursed by Christ's own word to live forever.

All because of a single betrayal.

Leopold trembled at the very thought, knowing he had betrayed the Church many times over, wearing a pious cloth over his traitorous heart as he did His bidding.

But how could he not?

He reached to the logo at the entrance and touched the cross buried in the center of the Argentum symbol, drawing strength in the knowledge that His cause was true and righteous. He was one of the few who walked the right path.

With renewed determination, he entered the building and gave his name at the front desk. The hard-eyed security guard checked him against a list and an online database before ushering him into the VIP elevator. It would stop at only one floor, and only if he had a key.

After the elevator doors slid closed, he lifted his pectoral cross over his head, then pulled off the longer part of the cross to reveal a hidden key. He stuck the key in the elevator lock. A green light told him that it worked. He let out a sigh of relief. He'd never used it before.

The elevator doors opened onto a receptionist in a smart black suit behind an imposing desk. Leopold whispered a quick prayer for protection and stepped out.

"Yes?" Amethyst earrings glittered when she raised her head. She had widely spaced brown eyes and full lips. A face from a Renaissance painting.

"Brother Leopold." He leaned nervously on her tall glass desk. "I was summoned."

She pressed a button with one long purple nail, then spoke into her phone. A one-syllable answer came back.

Yes.

He didn't know whether to be relieved or terrified.

She rose and led him down a long polished hallway to a brushed aluminum door, her hips swaying as she walked.

She opened the door and stepped back.

He must go in alone. The sound of running water filled his ears.

He entered a vast room into which clear Roman sunlight shone through floor-to-ceiling windows.

A large rectangular fountain dominated the center of the room.

Purple water lilies shone against gray slate. Water trickled over a round emerald-green stone. The sound was probably meant to be soothing, but the pattering grated on Leopold's nerves.

Leopold studied the man who had summoned him. He was facing away from the fountain toward the window, probably gazing on the Tiber River far below. His gray hair was cut short, displaying a tanned neck above the collar of an expensive shirt, powerful muscles discernible through the fine linen. Even now, His back remained unbowed by the weight of a millennia-long life.

He turned at Leopold's approach and raised a hand, releasing a small iridescent-winged moth. It fluttered from His palm and landed on a wide glass desk, revealing the insect to be a miniature automaton made of brass, watch gears, and thread-thin wire.

Leopold glanced away from the moth to find quicksilver eyes appraising him.

Intimidated, he dropped to his knees under the weight of that gaze. "It is done," he said, touching his cross, but he found no strength there now. "We have succeeded. The great doom begins."

Footsteps approached him.

Leopold cowered, but he dared not move.

Fingers as strong as stone touched his shoulder, but warmly, gently, lovingly. "You've done well, my son. The book is opened, and the trumpets of war will sound. After millennia of waiting, my destiny has come full circle. I sent the Nazarene from this world—it is now my duty to restore Him to His rightful throne. Even if it means bringing an end to this world."

Leopold let out a quaking sigh, his heart rejoicing. A finger lifted his chin. He stared at the face above, limned against the bright sunshine of a new day, a face Christ had once looked upon with equal love and devotion.

Before cursing him for eternity.

Turning his very name into a word for betrayal.

Leopold's lips silently formed that name now, both in adulation and promise.

Judas.